BICENTENNIAL TRIFECTA

BICENTENNIAL TRIFECTA

PATRIOTS FOR THE AMERICAN EVOLUTION

by
William G. Holst a.k.a. Wm. G. Holst

ISBN Paperback: 978-1-7375940-1-7
ISBN Hardcover: 978-1-7375940-2-4
ISBN Electronic: 978-1-7375940-0-0

Library of Congress Control Number: 2021916085

Printed in the United States of America.

William G. Holst a.k.a. Wm. G. Holst
TRIFECTA PRESS
c/o William G. Holst, Esq.
P.O. Box 469
Smithtown, New York 11787

Bill@BicentennialTrifecta.com
www.BicentennialTrifecta.com

To My Compatriots
who served as members of the United States Armed Forces
during what has been deemed the Cold War
and, in their own way,
nurtured and promoted egalitarianism
at home and abroad.
Bless you, and all who you served!

BICENTENNIAL TRIFECTA

PATRIOTS FOR THE AMERICAN EVOLUTION

Table of Contents

BICENTENNIAL TRIFECTA

Chapter I
LOUISVILLE IN SPRINGTIME

Desi Meets Emily

The first time Desmond Ezra McKoy met Emma Lee Miller was at Churchill Downs in Louisville. It was the afternoon before Derby Day in 1976. Desi had just driven up the Dixie Highway from Fort Knox in his green '73 Super Beetle with expired New York plates. He had registered the car in Kentucky the year before but could not bring himself to change the license plates.

Desi managed to find a spot in the racetrack parking lot with a view of the historic twin steeples. He grabbed a blue blazer and his camera off the back seat and headed for the gated entrance with a sign reading "PRESS" over it. Desi showed the security guard his press pass and was given directions to the media area. As he entered, he heard an announcement for the next Kentucky Oaks Day race that afternoon.

Desi needed to get his credentials for the next day quickly so he could continue up into Louisville to rendezvous with Debi, his ex-fiancée. Inside Churchill Downs, Desi found himself in a long hallway filled with women waiting to use the women's bathroom. He spotted a men's room and decided to make a quick pit stop.

As he stood at a urinal holding the strap of his camera with his left hand and working his zipper with his right, he heard a female voice behind him.

"I'm not looking, not trying to peek. Just need to pee in the stall," a woman said as she walked past him.

"Okay. I'm cool with that," Desi said as he balanced the weight of the camera strapped over his left shoulder so he could use both hands to finish his activity in front of the urinal and zip his jeans back up.

Desi continued to stare straight ahead. He heard the woman whistling several notes of what sounded like a Rolling Stones song from behind the closed stall door. With his pants zipped up, Desi went over to the sink. He took some extra time washing his hands, wondering if the young woman was going to come out. When it seemed she wasn't coming out anytime soon, he pulled a paper towel from the dispenser. "Take care," he said as he tossed the towel into an opening under the dispenser and turned to leave.

"Oh, no. Don't leave me here," the woman pleaded from inside the stall. "I'll be out in just a moment." The whistling resumed, and then Desi heard the sound of a flush. Suddenly, out of the stall came a long-legged brunette with a prom queen smile, who reinforced that image with a small wave of her hand.

Desi stood transfixed by the smile and how her University of Kentucky T-shirt rhythmically moved as she took several long strides towards him. With her left arm, gently yet firmly, she pushed him away from the sink without breaking the smile that seemed to frame perfectly white and aligned teeth.

Desi suddenly found himself thinking of his dentist back on Long Island, Dr. Martin, who would provide his patients with unsolicited advice on how to select a future mate based upon whether they appeared to have good dental care. His dentist would have approved of this young lady. Shrugging away that thought, Desi smiled back.

"It looks like you have something hanging out of your pants," she said, raising an eyebrow.

Desi looked down and saw part of his shirt hanging out of his zipper. "Oh, it's my shirt," he said self-consciously as he bent both knees, adjusted his zipper, and pushed his shirt into his jeans.

She washed and dried her hands and put a manicured finger on the clef of his chin. "You probably already know it, but I have to say, you are really cute," she said, raising both eyebrows. "My name is Emma, but my friends call me Emily."

Desi, regaining his composure and holding out his hand, answered, "It is a pleasure to meet you, Emily. My name is Desi."

Emily took his hand and practically pulled him out of the men's room and into the corridor. "I think it might be better to talk out here," she said, dropping his hand. "Are you here to cover the races today?" she asked, putting her hands on her hips and leaning in toward his face.

Desi leaned in closer, and when he shook his head to indicate no they were just inches away from rubbing noses. "I only stopped by today to get my credentials for tomorrow," Desi explained.

Emily looped her left arm through Desi's right arm and moved him down the hallway. "I'll help you get where you want to go," Emily offered while pressing her hip against Desi's hip. They walked alongside one another down one corridor and then another. "Is this your first time?" she asked with a quizzical grin.

"This is the first time I have been to Churchill Downs," Desi answered flatly. He wasn't sure if she was just being very friendly or was teasing him. Through his blazer, he could feel her left breast rubbing against his right arm. Desi felt distracted by the sensation and struggled to focus on his feet. He did not want to let on that she was making him a bit wobbly.

Emily seemed genuinely interested in him. "Are you a photographer, a photojournalist, or just someone who knows someone who could get them a press pass?" she asked.

"All of the above," Desi replied as he strode arm and arm with Emily with greater confidence, not knowing, or seeming to care, where in the building they were headed.

"Have you studied journalism?" she asked, persisting in her questioning.

"Yeah, that was my major at New York University," Desi replied.

"Did you go to the NYU campus in the Village?" Emily asked, pulling herself even closer as if she were asking Desi to reveal some secret.

"I did." Desi then countered by asking, "Have you been to Washington Square Park?"

"Sure, but my parents didn't want me to go to undergraduate school in Manhattan. I guess they were afraid I would find too many distractions from going to class."

"Do your parents live here in Kentucky?" Desi asked.

"No, they live in Maryland. My father grew up in Kentucky, south of Frankfort. His family had a distillery," she disclosed.

Desi leaned towards her ear. "I have a hip flask in one of my blazer pockets with what, based on what I paid, should be an excellent bourbon. Are you able to judge an outstanding one from one that is just better than average?"

Emily stopped walking. She pulled in even closer. Keeping her lips just inches away from Desi's right ear, she whispered, "I think I can distinguish what is exceptional from what is merely good. I am willing to sample whatever you offer me." She fluttered her eyes and let out a soft laugh as she backed away from him and grabbed his hand. She then tugged him down another hallway, saying, "I think we better wait on drinking the bourbon until we get your credentials for tomorrow."

Desi felt like his mind had been transported to a place where pinball machine lights were flashing. The next words he spoke would either keep the lights flashing or wipe the flashy smile off of Emily's beautiful face and the sparkle from her greenish eyes. So many things he could say might be susceptible to misinterpretation. Desi just smiled back at her and let her lead the way as the heels of her western-style boots clicked along the floor.

He hadn't entirely forgotten about catching up with his ex-fiancée, Debi, and her older sister, Tammy, who was on a modeling assignment in Louisville. It was more like he suddenly realized that he didn't exactly know what Debi and Tammy were planning for that evening, or the next day. Debi hadn't actually committed to going to the Derby, only telling him that she and her sister would be in Louisville.

After Emily brought Desi to the credentialing office, she gave him a soft push on his back and started to walk away.

"Hey, are you leaving me here?" Desi asked.

Emily stopped and walked back. "Look, you probably have someone already lined up to be with on Derby Day. I'm still working on that. Anyway, you were going to leave me alone in that men's room."

"But I didn't," Desi insisted. "And as for tomorrow, I don't know if I have a date or not."

"I guess we all have complications with our relationships," Emily replied.

"Well, is there a chance tomorrow that we might, in an uncomplicated way, have mint juleps together?" Desi asked.

Emily pushed her hands into the front pockets of her tight jeans and swayed back and forth for a few moments while looking up at the ceiling. With a grin, she said, "I know I hope there is a chance of something like that happening." Then, turning, she seemed to glide out of Desi's sight.

Desi Attempts to Keep Debi in Louisville for the Derby

The traffic heading toward downtown Louisville was heavy with the Friday afternoon rush to Indiana, Ohio, and other locations north. Tammy was shooting a commercial for a Japanese Beverage company at a Louisville hotel and Desi was to meet Debi there. Desi didn't get to the hotel until a few minutes after four.

The lobby was crowded. Desi slowly made his way through the people checking in and toward the doors on the north side of the hotel that faced the Ohio River and opened onto a river walk entrance.

On a prior visit to the hotel, Desi had gone through those doors to take a look at the commemorative marker of the fabled spot where Lewis and Clark met up before their famous journey to what would later become Oregon. However, Desi did not journey beyond those doors this evening as he heard Tammy call his name. She was propped against what looked like a six-foot bottle of ginger beer with Japanese and English lettering on it. She was taking a smoke break with a photographer under some umbrella lighting.

Desi walked over to Tammy who looked very imposing in a white and grey fur jacket with a reddish dress underneath. In heels that matched the color of her dress, she stood an inch or two taller than the cardboard cut-out of the ginger beer bottle. Tammy took a deep drag of her cigarette and let out a cloud of smoke towards Desi's face as he came closer.

"I heard you quit smoking and cut your hair," Tammy said. "No more hippie hair and beard. You now look almost as sweet and innocent as you did in high school."

"Actually, I've been hanging out with a tougher crowd since I have been in the Army," Desi said with a smile.

"I thought you were going to law school," Tammy said as she took another long drag on her cigarette.

"I still intend to go to law school," he said confidently.

"You better, if you want to marry my sister someday." She dropped the cigarette and twisted it on the floor with her expensive-looking dark red heels that not only closely matched her dress but also her hair.

"Is Debi still here at the hotel?" Desi asked. "I was trying to get here around three but got delayed, and then there was the traffic."

"Yeah, we heard about the traffic. She's up in room 511. You guys have about half an hour to get reacquainted, and then I think she is flying out with me to Chicago. I have to meet up with the lawyers and sign the papers on this Japanese beverage deal tomorrow morning." Tammy moved her hand as if to shoo him away. "We are only hanging out here a little while longer to get a photo with their head corporate guy in the States. He flew in a few minutes ago and has also hit traffic. I think he wanted us to do the shoot in Louisville so he could be here this weekend for the Derby."

"I was hoping to talk you guys into staying here for the race," Desi said.

Tammy turned to the photographer and jokingly pulled the beret off his head and sized it up as if considering whether to put it on her head. After a moment, she announced, "I don't think I have the hat I would need to be seen at the Derby."

The photographer laughed as she handed him back the beret.

"Alright, I'm going up to see Debi," Desi said, turning and heading for the elevator bank.

The photographer and Tammy watched as Desi walked away. The photographer nodded his head and said to Tammy, "I could see how a guy with a strong jaw and good smile could attract Debi."

Tammy laughed. "You got it all wrong. I was attracted to him in high school. Desi's face is easy on the eyes, but my recollection is that it was his butt that caught my attention." Tammy continued to watch Desi walk away. "He still has a great ass, although it was Debi who ended up getting a chance to take a bite of it."

The photographer looked at her with a very puzzled expression.

"So, Paul. Do you want the abbreviated version of how this younger guy, who I asked to go to my senior prom, ended up taking my sister to his junior prom?" Tammy asked.

"Would it have anything to do with your modeling career?" Paul asked in return.

"Everything to do with it," Tammy said with a sigh.

When the elevator door opened on the fifth floor, Desi heard a door down the hallway open. Debi stepped out into the hallway. She kept one hand on the door to keep it from shutting. It looked like she was only wearing one of his blue short-sleeve work shirts from when he attended the U.S. Merchant Marine Academy right after high school.

Debi gave him a smile that made him want to believe what she had told him the last time they made love - that she still wore that shirt, with his last name stamped above the pocket, every night.

When they embraced, through the back of the USMMA-issued work shirt, Desi could tell she was not wearing a bra. The shirt caught the full curve of her left breast. The stamp of his last name was a bit faded but still visible.

Debi had written to him when he and his classmate Roger were sent out to sea from the academy in early February 1971. She wrote loving letters he received in various ports in Japan and Korea. There was one that even caught up with him when the cargo ship they were on spent five days in Hong Kong Harbor. Those letters reminded him of who he was and who he passionately cared about. It was a time when many men his age were untethered and malleable enough to become ruthless, rootless shells of what they had been before getting out into the larger world.

However, that seemed like a long time ago. Desi hadn't asked Debi to write to him when he joined the Army in late September of 1974. She did send one or two letters while he was in basic training at Fort Dix, but they were not the passionate letters she mailed with ink smudges from teardrops, like when he went out to sea for the first half of 1971, or when she went off to college in the fall of that year. It wasn't clear to Desi if they ever would or could be as important to one another as they were during a couple of their college years. During those years, it seemed that only the voice and touch of the other could serve as the emotional safety net they needed as they ventured through various trials and tribulations.

Desi's Merchant Marine Academy classmate and traveling companion, Roger Sloan, would be arriving for the Derby the next morning. It looked increasingly like Roger would be the person sharing Derby Day with Desi. While Desi may have hoped otherwise, he knew there was little chance Debi would stay in Louisville when her sister wanted her to fly to Chicago. Desi was almost certain that Debi would do everything she could to help make sure Tammy's modeling career stayed on track.

Desi found himself sitting on one of the hotel room beds with Debi, thinking about what Tammy said about the parameters of their being together again. *What would be best,* he wondered, *for the half an hour to get reacquainted?*

"Did Tammy tell you we have about thirty minutes together before she comes back to the room?" Debi asked.

"I'm thinking about that," Desi replied.

"How about taking a shower together?" Debi said with a smile.

"I don't think we had a chance to do that the last time we were together," Desi said as he took off his shoes.

"And it wasn't very good in bed with one another on Christmas Eve either, was it?" Debi said as she pushed him back on the bed and sat on his chest.

"Well, we hadn't seen each other for several months, and I surprised you with a call from LaGuardia. You sounded pretty lonely. I think you had been at a holiday party. You sounded disappointed that you were alone in your apartment on the evening before Christmas and weren't even sure if you were going out to Long Island to be with your parents on Christmas." Desi reached around and put his hands under the back of the faded blue work shirt and confirmed that Debi was wearing panties.

"That was over four months ago, and I am feeling much better now. You seem like you have been doing alright as well," Debi said as she pulled up the front of the blue shirt to reveal her bright, lime green panties. "I hope you still like lime," she added.

Desi, with Debi still pinning him down, picked his head up from the bed and blew a kiss toward the lime panties.

Debi leaned over and kissed his forehead, both of his eyelids, and then his lips. He could not remember the last time she had kissed him with such enthusiasm. She had started to put her tongue inside his mouth when the telephone rang. They both sat up.

"Hello," Debi answered. Desi moved off the bed, stood up, and started taking off his pants.

As Debi listened to what the caller had to say, Desi took off his shirt and stripped down to his briefs. He said quietly, "I'll start the shower."

"Hang on, Dad," Debi said before putting her hand over the mouthpiece. She motioned to Desi to take off the briefs with her other hand. Desi complied with her request and gave her a full viewing of his naked front, back, and front again. Debi smiled and blew him a kiss before he headed off to the shower.

Desi was in the shower for over five minutes before Debi came into the bathroom. She took off the blue USMMA shirt and got in the shower, still wearing the lime green panties.

"Is everything alright at home?" Desi asked.

"When is everything alright with my parents?" Taking a bar of soap, she started to wash Desi's back. "My mom has disappeared again. This time, it has been for more than a couple of days. Dad is calling around to try and find her. He wants me to call my uncle down in Texas to find out if she has been in the Galveston area this week. My dad doesn't talk to Tammy anymore and knows she won't call our uncle. Also, he isn't sure whether my uncle will tell him anything," Debi said as she handed the soap to Desi and leaned against the shower wall so he could wash her back.

"Where could she be? Did your dad call the police?"

Debi arched her back and stretched her neck from side to side as Desi used both hands, first to wash her shoulders, and then her lower back. "That feels really good," she said with a sigh.

Suddenly, the bathroom door opened, and Tammy came into the bathroom wearing nothing but a "Welcome to Louisville" T-shirt. "Hope I'm not interrupting anything," Tammy said.

"Shit, Tammy. Wasn't the door closed? Don't you knock?" Debi yelled.

"Don't worry, I'm just taking a quick piss and I'm out of here," Tammy said. "I can't see anything through the shower curtain, anyway."

Debi got out of the shower and put a towel around her torso. "You aren't hanging out here with us, that's for sure."

"Why the hell are you still wearing your panties?" Tammy asked as she sat on the toilet, with her legs demurely closed together. "I thought the two of you might already be finished humping by now and just getting cleaned up," she added.

"What we have been doing or will be doing is none of your business," Debi answered. "I got stuck on the phone with Dad for ten minutes about Mom running off and disappearing again. This time it has been days."

"Debi, you know what she is doing and who she is with, and who can blame her with that inconsiderate pig of a father we have," Tammy said as she pulled on a toilet paper roll.

"But she is the one running off with a guy who abused her over twenty-five years ago. From what she has told us, he pretty much ruined her modeling career. Is she now looking to go back to Brazil to relive that crap?" Debi responded. "I just wish she could keep her craziness to herself and not always be dragging us into her mood swings."

"Well, I guess you two are in the mood for some good clean fun," Tammy said as she got up from the toilet. She started walking to the door but paused and grabbed the shower curtain. Debi grabbed her wrist.

"I just wanted to say goodbye to Desi. I'm putting on a pair of jeans and taking my suitcase down to the lobby. I think the car service to the airport will be at the front doors in about 15 or 20 minutes," Tammy said.

"Anything else before you leave?" Debi asked. She then removed the towel and placed her hands on the waistband of the lime panties as she thrusted out her full bosom so as to contrast her curves with her taller but more slender sister.

"Yeah," Tammy answered. "I'd recommend that Desi use his teeth to remove those bright panties. That will get us all where we want to go faster." Tammy then gave Debi a very insincere smile and left the bathroom.

"Can you believe that?" Debi said as she got back into the shower with Desi.

Desi put his arms around her and pulled her close. "You mean about the panties?" he said softly. They both laughed before drawing each other closer.

Twenty minutes later, Desi and Debi were waiting at the elevator to go down to the lobby. They quietly got on the elevator when the doors opened and didn't say a word until they got to the lobby.

"You know that I have to stay with Tammy to help her get this agreement done, right?" Debi asked.

"I know she is capable of blowing things up," Desi replied. "I would have preferred to be driving you back to my apartment near Fort Knox, but from what you have told me, this seems to be a make-or-break deal for her career. I do wish her well, and if you can keep her from taking any coke tonight or tomorrow and doing something crazy, it sounds like she could be set for a couple of years."

"Are you going to be staying at Fort Knox for the next year or so, or are you still trying to get stationed in Europe?" Debi asked as she reached to take her suitcase from Desi's hand.

"I'm still trying to get assigned to Armed Forces Television in Germany," Desi responded as he moved the suitcase beyond her reach. "I'll carry your bag outside. I'm not leaving here until I see you safely on your way to the airport."

Debi stopped several feet from the doors. "I feel like I have no idea of where I am going or when I am going to get where I want to be. Let's stop for a moment before I have to spend the rest of this evening with Tammy. I think you know that I was hoping to be spending tonight with you." She gave Desi a quick kiss on the lips, took her suitcase from his hand, and started walking again towards the exit. Right before the doors, she stopped, turned, and tossed something to him. It was her room key.

Desi could see that she had tears streaming down her face. He walked towards her. Debi did a quick sprint out the doors. Tammy was standing alongside a black Lincoln Continental limo talking to a middle-aged man. From his attire, the man appeared to be the limo driver. Debi moved towards Tammy, trying to regain her composure.

"Tammy, you better be nice to me during the ride to the airport, or I am going to leave you at the airport and come back here and spend the weekend with Desi. I gave him the room key."

Tammy stopped her conversation with the limo driver and looked at Debi. She saw Desi approaching. "I don't mind if he keeps the bed warm for you, but I don't know if the Japs paid for two nights or only tonight. I suspect they only paid for one night." Tammy reached out and grabbed the arm of the limo driver. "Pops, what do you think those sneaky Jap bastards did?"

Debi dropped her suitcase and grabbed her sister's shoulder with one hand and put the other hand over her mouth. "Tammy, they have been very nice to you, don't screw things up!"

Tammy shook free from Debi. Tammy looked at the limo driver. "Pops understands what I am saying, don't you?" The limo driver nodded his head in agreement.

"I guess this proves you have to be with her," Desi said to Debi as he picked her suitcase up from the asphalt and handed it to the driver. "Your dad served in the Pacific. Did he tell Tammy something that made her hate the Japanese?" Desi asked Debi.

"I don't think anything my dad says to her has any impact. Tammy's attitude towards Asian people is the problem. Tammy is cool with Afro-Americans and Hispanics, but there is something that sets her off and keeps her from acting civilized around Asian people."

After the driver put Debi's suitcase into the trunk, the driver went around to the rear passenger side door and beckoned Tammy to get inside the vehicle. Tammy went around the front of the limo but stopped at the front passenger door.

"I think I am going to ride up front with Pops. I guess the less I say to Debi right now, the better."

Desi opened the rear driver side door for Debi and gave her a brief kiss. "I'll go up to the room and exercise for a while. Please call me from the airport. Do you have the hotel number with you?"

After pulling the hotel brochure from her purse and waving it, Debi nodded yes. Desi then closed her door, and Debi looked toward the driver and Tammy. The vehicle left the driveway and blended into the traffic of Louisville, joining all the other vehicles jamming the streets on Derby weekend.

Small World in a Big Hotel

After Debi and Tammy left, Desi walked down the block to the parking garage and retrieved his blazer, camera bag, and suit bag from the VW.

As he was heading through the lobby, Desi thought he heard someone call out his name. He paused for a moment, then continued on to the elevator bank. He got in and pressed the button for the fifth floor. As the elevator doors closed, a woman's leg and western boot appeared between the doors, triggering them to reopen. Desi recognized the boot. The woman stepped in, smiling at Desi. Even before she took off her dark glasses and western hat, he knew it was Emily.

"I called out to you, but I guess you wanted me to chase you down," Emily said, sounding a bit out of breath. "What floor are you on?"

"Five. Where is your room?" Desi asked.

"Up on seven. I think we might have a view of the Ohio River," Emily answered.

"You said we?" Desi asked.

"Yeah, I'm in 711 with Linda. She's working with me this weekend on the radio station coverage of the races."

"You work for a radio station here in Louisville?" Desi asked. He added," I thought you went to UK in Lexington."

The elevator doors opened for the fifth floor. Desi moved in between the doors to keep them from closing.

"There is a pool deck. Why don't you meet us there in about half an hour?" Emily asked.

"I've got to settle in, do some exercises, and change. I guess I can be there in about an hour," Desi said as he exited the elevator.

"If we aren't on the pool deck, we'll be in the room," Emily blurted out as the elevator doors closed. Desi nodded his head as he pulled the room key out of his pocket.

Once inside the room, he threw the suit bag on the bed that he and Debi had been sitting on earlier. He dropped into a chair at the desk that held the phone. Desi stared intently at the phone for several minutes as if he could command it to ring. He took off his shoes and hung up his blazer. Then, he sat back in the chair again. Desi knew that he was not going to hear Debi say that she was leaving the airport and coming back to the hotel. He just wanted to hear the sound of her voice again and be connected in some way to her for a few more minutes.

He got out of the chair and went through the two large pockets of the suit bag. Desi found his bathing suit, sat in the chair again, and did a yoga breathing exercise. He stood up from the chair and took off everything but his Jockey briefs. He did a couple dozen pushups and then some yoga stretching exercises. He was doing a shoulder stand when the phone rang.

Desi lifted up the phone to hear Debi's voice on the other end. Tenderly, and almost lyrically, she said something about how she was waiting with Tammy to get the boarding call for the plane to Chicago.

Desi asked if there was any chance she might be able to fly back to Louisville at some point the next day and take off work on Monday.

She said she had to be back to work in Manhattan on Monday and would probably be spending time over the weekend trying to track down her mother, in addition to helping Tammy with whatever assistance she needed. When Debi asked him if he would be back in New York for Memorial Day, Desi said it was more probable that he would be in New York around the Fourth of July.

They settled on agreeing to try to see one another again at some point on the weekend of the Bicentennial. Desi told Debi he was committing to driving to New York for that weekend, and he hoped to take her to the ocean, like they had done during prior summers.

Then there was an announcement for the plane to Chicago, and the connection suddenly ended.

Desi sat with his legs crossed and closed his eyes for several minutes. July seemed like a long way off. He opened his eyes and looked at his watch. He needed to put on his bathing suit, grab his hip flask, and find the pool deck.

Emily, Linda, and a Crowd on the Pool Deck

By the time Desi made it to the pool deck, Emily and Linda had attracted a swarm of men of various ages who surrounded the lounge chairs of the two young women. Guys were standing, sitting, and kneeling about them, offering to buy drinks, dinner, or tickets to the Derby. When Desi joined them, he could hear Emily explaining to one guy how she had a press pass and didn't need tickets to the Derby. Desi smiled at Emily. She stood up and went over to Desi.

She whispered into his ear something about how she needed his help to lose the gaggle of admirers. "Do you remember the number of my room?"

"711, it is pretty easy to remember," Desi whispered back.

"Very good," she responded. "If we get separated, I'll meet you there."

She then introduced the men to Desi and told them that Desi was interested in sharing his bourbon in honor of the Derby.

Desi raised his hip flask and toasted, saying, "Here's to the beautiful horses and women of Kentucky." Everyone took a sip of whatever they were drinking. Desi suggested that they all meet downstairs in one of the restaurants for dinner. The men started to disperse.

"Instead of a restaurant here at the hotel, it's probably better to find a place in the downtown area to have dinner," Desi suggested. "Maybe we can sneak up the staircase to your place and then decide where we want to go." They watched the men walking toward the elevators. Desi then added, "You may have to wear your dark glasses and hat again to get out of the building."

"I don't think it is me so much as they really seem interested in Linda," Emily responded.

Desi took another look at Linda and realized that despite her rather plain face and hair, she was revealing a serious amount of cleavage from the loosely tied hotel robe, with only a very skimpy black bikini top underneath. "She works at a radio station with you?" he asked.

"Kind of. People usually say that they think she is wasting her talents with us, particularly because it is a religious radio network," Emily answered. "But she has had some problems in the past. My father's radio network gave her a job, and my family has tried to give her the support she needs."

"You mean you funded the bikini top?" Desi said with a smirk.

"Very funny," Emily replied. "But it does seem crazy that they took a former Vegas stripper, who allegedly had an affair with a famous evangelical preacher and helped her settle down and have a new life. But that is what my father agreed to do. She lives with me in a house that used to be my father's mother's house near Lexington. She gets a ride with me to campus, takes a few classes, and helps with the fundraising for the radio network."

"What does your mother think of the arrangement?" Desi asked.

"She trusts that my father is not going to be as stupid as the last radio preacher," Emily answered.

"So now Linda is your roommate, and you are responsible for keeping her out of trouble?"

"Does that sound very strange to you?" Emily asked.

"Actually, from my perspective, it is starting to seem almost normal that some women end up trying to keep other women on an even keel, so they don't do themselves in."

"You know other situations like that?"

"My ex-fiancée just left Louisville and flew to Chicago to protect her older sister from herself," Desi said. "But I can tell you more about that at dinner, and you can tell me about your romantic complications."

"I'm pretty sure that Linda, on her own, would be finding herself in trouble again pretty quickly," Emily said as Linda walked towards them. Linda was followed by two men who looked like they were in their fifties.

Emily walked over to Linda and advised her to follow Desi. Emily then turned and intercepted the two men. Desi watched as Emily got the men to stop and talk to her which enabled Linda to reach Desi, who was slowly walking towards a stairwell.

When Desi and Linda made it back to the room, the phone was ringing.

"I think you better be the one who answers it," Desi advised Linda.

Linda picked it up and only got in a few words during the couple of minutes she was on the phone. She hung up and disclosed that it was Emily's mother who had called. Apparently, Emily's parents were not sure if they were going to be able to get to Louisville for the Derby.

Desi realized that this was his opportunity to ask Linda a few things about Emily and her family. He led off by asking, "So, what are Emily's parents like?"

Linda hesitated for a moment before speaking. "They have been wonderful to me. I'm not really sure why they have been so kind. I mean, both of them are well-educated, very spiritual people who live very interesting lives. Emily's father knows Billy Graham and has met almost everyone in politics in Washington. He was originally a medic in World War II but came back and went to seminary school instead of medical school. Emily's mom comes from a very well-to-do family in Philadelphia and became a nurse, like her mother, and has traveled quite a bit, both before and after marrying Emily's dad. Emily's mother has a photograph of herself with Gandhi, as she and her parents were ministering to some of his followers in India after World War II."

"And what about Emily?" Desi asked.

"Emily is a very beautiful person too; she just hasn't found the right 'gentleman' for herself. I say gentleman because her father always wants to know if the guy she is interested in is a gentleman or a scoundrel," Linda said.

"Sounds like he is very protective," Desi said. "It seems to me that Emily is a pretty capable person."

"So, you like her?" Linda asked.

"I find her intriguing," Desi answered. "But she probably has someone who she is interested in being with."

"Have you ever been in a prison?" Linda asked.

"Do you mean metaphorically or literally?"

"You are very clever with your answer. Maybe you are clever enough to convince Emily that she should be interested in you instead of a guy who is currently in jail. Her parents are trying to set her up with other guys. Her mom just called to remind Emily that she has a breakfast date with a young man who is finishing up at the University of Louisville Law School. Emily's parents know the parents of this young man and think he might be the perfect match for Emily."

"So, they want you to remind Emily of her date?" Desi asked.

"I think it was more like me helping them get Emily to call the young man and confirm their meeting. She hasn't done so yet. After that, they want her to contact them at home to confirm she followed through."

"Have you met the law school guy?" Desi asked.

Linda smiled. "So you care if Emily goes to breakfast with this dude?" she said with a soft laugh.

Desi just gave a shrug.

"I don't think you have to worry," Linda said. "Emily makes him sound like a self-centered jerk. I know I just met you, but you seem like you could charm Emily so that she forgets all about having breakfast with the stuffy law student tomorrow." Linda stepped past Desi to get to the hallway door. "What is taking Emily so long to lose those guys?" She opened the door to find Emily standing in the doorway. Desi wasn't sure if Emily had just arrived at the room or had been standing outside the door for some time.

Linda gave Emily a kiss on the cheek, saying, "Thanks for helping me get away from those lost souls. One of those last two put his left hand on my shoulder as he was talking to me and was stupid enough to be moving his hand and his wedding ring closer to my face while telling me some nonsense. He didn't look me in the eye either."

Emily laughed. "They were so blasted they were telling me how much drinking they had done today, as if that would make them more attractive to me."

"Only to themselves," Linda responded.

"Are we ready to sneak out of the hotel to get some dinner? Desi, have you figured out a good place to eat?" Emily asked.

"There is a place only a few blocks away that I would recommend," Desi answered.

"What is the name of the place?" Emily asked.

"That's a good question. I'm not sure it has an actual name," Desi replied. "I call it 'Soul Kitchen' because it has tasty Southern cooking, and there is only a street number on the door."

"That sounds very bohemian. Just like being back in Greenwich Village for you, isn't it, Desi?" Emily inquired.

"A bit like the Village," Desi answered before adding, "but the food is Southern with collard greens, grits, and interesting spices."

"Sounds like it could be tasty," Emily responded. "Let's get going."

"Think I'll just let the two of you go," Linda said. "I don't think the two of you need my help to keep the conversation going."

Emily went over to Linda and kissed her on the cheek. "Don't be silly. We want you to go to dinner with us tonight, don't we, Desi?"

Desi just nodded his head towards Emily. "I have to go downstairs to change out of my bathing suit. Why don't you come down to room 511 after you get changed and maybe we can find a way out of the hotel without going past your fan club that is probably waiting in the main lobby." He looked at Linda. "Unless you want to hang out with the fan club."

Emily gave him a frowning look. "Linda just wants a quiet evening with us, right Linda?" Emily said with a glare.

"Sure," Linda replied.

Escaping to a "Hole in the Wall"

They found their way out of the hotel using the corridor leading towards the river walk. After strolling along the promenade high above the Ohio River, Desi then led them down a staircase to street-level and through a couple of blocks that looked rather desolate.

"Are you sure you know where you are going, Desi?" Emily asked.

"It has only been a few weeks since my former roommate, Charlie, and Stacey, his girlfriend, brought me to this part of town for a farewell dinner, right before Charlie left for Germany. I'm sure we are close."

When they got to the next corner, Desi looked to the right and announced, "I can smell my way to it now."

As they walked down the block, Emily and Linda made sniffing noises.

"See those cars up ahead?" Desi said. "They are parked near the Soul Kitchen."

"I do smell it now," Linda said.

"Me too!" Emily concurred.

When they got to a large metal door with a small half-moon window, Desi stopped and held open the door for them. They were not greeted with the usual noise of a Friday night crowd at a typical restaurant. There were about a couple dozen tables and booths around the large bar, which ran from the center of the room all the way back to the main kitchen. There were a couple of burners with large, covered pots located at the end of the u-shaped bar close to the kitchen. There was jazz music coming from speakers in the ceiling. The music seemed coordinated with the noise from the lids of the pots being lifted then dropped shut by the staff. The staff seemed to be all women with brownish complexions and shortly cut hair. They appeared to be a mix of Afro-American women and women from southern Asia. They displayed different types of silver jewelry on their arms, their ears, and around their necks. Some of the women had Hindu ornamentation on their foreheads. The bar, tables, and booths were all occupied. The staff initially seemed to ignore the presence of Desi, Emily, and Linda.

A table of young people, who appeared to be a mix of Afro-American and white college students, got up from a table and started to leave. After paying at the bar, the young barmaid, who wore a tight yellow "Murrells Inlet SC" T-shirt, motioned Desi, Emily, and Linda to the vacant table. The staff members and customers didn't seem to make any extraneous movements or do much talking either. After Desi, Emily and Linda sat down, an older woman arrived with a plate of cornbread and menus. She was wearing a colorful dashiki and gave them a welcoming smile but didn't say anything.

Linda sat across the table from Desi and Emily. She held the plate up and offered the cornbread to Desi and Emily. They each took a piece and bit into it. Emily looked at Desi with wide eyes. She whispered to Desi, "Would it be totally uncool to tell the waitress how good this cornbread is?"

Desi finished chewing the large piece he had bitten off and said, "Probably."

They each reviewed their menus quietly, and when the woman in the dashiki returned with a notepad they simply gave her their orders. Desi ordered the deep-fried chicken in waffle batter. Emily chose the grilled catfish. Linda wanted the pulled pork with coleslaw and two sauces on a roll. They all wanted sides of the "special southern greens," as well as the "Louisville mac and cheese."

While they waited, Linda pulled out a draft of a fundraising letter for the radio network that she had written earlier in the day. She handed it to Emily to review.

Desi excused himself and headed for the men's room. He headed around the bar and ran into Stacey, his former roommate's girlfriend.

Stacey was sitting by herself at the bar and eating an appetizer. She saw Desi and smiled. Stacey, like Charlie, was a paralegal at the Fort Knox JAG Office. Desi went over to her and gave her a hug. Stacey kissed him on the cheek. "You were the one who turned me on to this place," Desi said. "I brought two people here tonight who are eating here for the first time."

"Desi, I am glad that you enjoy this place. Not too many of the people I know can just sit back and dig, not just the food, but the whole experience," Stacey said.

"It is a unique experience in Louisville," Desi responded. "What is the name of this place?"

"They still have not put a sign outside. According to my cousin, Desdemona, who not only works the bar area and collects the money but is also their bookkeeper, the name is 'Shakta's.' "

"And where are the women from?" Desi asked.

"Most of them are from India. Southern India, I think. Many of them were members of a Hindu sect worshipping a goddess named Shakti, I think the religion is known as Shaktism in the U.S. After emigrating to the USA, they have taken elements of other religions and cultures. They lived in Los Angeles for a few years, but a couple of them toured the country, looking for a place to open their own restaurant. While visiting Louisville, they met Mohammed Ali. After they met Ali, they felt good about moving to Louisville. They bought this place and a farm about 20 miles away. The farm was an old hippie commune that pretty much folded when the Sixties ended, but someone in their group knew the guru who was living there, so most of the staff now lives out in the country with the guru. Before they opened the restaurant, they made the decision to go with the Southern-style cooking, instead of just Indian food, which they eat when they are home at the farm. They grow many of the vegetables they use here in the restaurant. If you want Indian food tonight, they will make it for you."

Desi was amazed by the story of the restaurant's origins. "You didn't tell me any of this the last time we were here."

"Maybe because Charlie had already heard it, and I didn't think the other people we had with us would be interested. Plus, that was one of Charlie's going away parties, so the focus was on him. I think he did a lot of the talking,"

Desdemona came up to the bar and seemed curious as to who Desi was and why Stacey was spending so much time talking to him. "Hi, I'm Desdemona," she said to Desi.

"Desdemona," Desi exclaimed. "That is a very Shakespearean name!"

"I used to live with Desi," Stacey said, putting her arm around him.

Desdemona gave her a puzzled look. "I thought your white boyfriend was in Germany."

"No, I am not Charlie. He is my friend. Stacey lived with Charlie in our two-bedroom apartment," Desi explained.

Desdemona smiled. "So, when Charlie moved out, did Stacey move in with you? I know she has a thing for white guys."

Stacey looked at Desi. "I don't think we even thought about sleeping together. Desi had a woman living in his room at the time. A tall, skinny blonde named Penny, who is in the Army and part of the Fort Knox marching band. Now there is an empty room at Desi's place."

"Sounds like there are two beds that are less than full," Desdemona said. "Does Desi only have a thing for blondes?"

Stacey looked at Desi, and then at Desdemona. "I'll give you Desi's address. I'm sure you can visit him in a Shakespearean bonnet, and I'm sure he'll be happy to run through a few lines from Othello with you."

Desi laughed. "Actually, it's Stacey who likes to read passages from Shakespeare, in her best West Indian accent. Her boyfriend Charlie and I used to find obscure Victorian poetry and update it with more risqué words and phrases."

Stacey shook her head. "They thought they were going to embarrass me, but I found ways to make what I called their 'horny doggerel' more poetic and kinkier," Stacey said to Desdemona with a laugh.

"And a couple of times, I think you embarrassed our dear Charlie," Desi added. "The apartment seems pretty empty without you two. Come to think of it, Stacey, weren't you going to help me locate someone to rent the second bedroom?" Desi asked.

"Desi, I called you at the newspaper office this afternoon to tell you two things. One, the people in Washington told me they are preparing my orders for Germany," Stacey said while holding up one finger.

"That is great news. I am very happy for you and Charlie. And what is the other thing?" Desi asked.

"The other thing is that with one paralegal, Charlie, already gone, and another, namely me, getting orders to leave, the JAG Office is getting a replacement next week. And the guy who is coming in as a replacement has already been speaking to the folks in our office about housing and how to get a place off-post," Stacey revealed while holding up two fingers.

"Oh, well you better get him to see our place first, and I'll get him to sign something before we have a going away party for you. How long did it take for us to clean up after the extended party for Charlie?" Desi asked.

"It was only a couple of days to clean up and then another day or two to return some of the clothing we found," Stacey said.

"I could use a good party," Desdemona said, holding a plate out to Desi with a piece of brownish bread on it.

Desi took a bite out of the bread. He looked at Desdemona. "What do you call this delicious bread?"

"It is Turkish pita bread," Stacey's cousin answered. "Do I get invited if I bring some bread or something," Desdemona asked.

Stacey took out a pen from her purse and wrote on a napkin. "This is Desi's address," she said, handing it to Desdemona. "When we pick a day for my going away party, I'll let you know. I'll let you know if Desi needs a date for the party. I don't think he has been having much luck with finding a date for the Derby."

Desdemona gave Stacey a puzzled look. "I think he came in with the two women in the back booth."

"Oh, really, I was starting to feel sorry for Desi." Stacey got off the barstool and rubbed the back of Desi's head. "I better go over there and talk to them so I can help Desi with his selection for the evening," Stacey started walking to the booth where Emily and Linda were seated.

Desi looked at Desdemona. "I will be having a farewell party for Stacey, regardless of what she tells my dinner companions between the time I visit the men's room and race back over to our booth."

Desdemona reached over the bar and rested her hand on Desi's shoulder. "We like to make it so that people can move slowly and thoughtfully in this place. I'll go over there and keep Stacey from saying too much before you get back to the table."

"Thanks," Desi said as he purposely walked to the men's room.

Adding Some Energy at Shakta's

When Desi came out of the men's room, Emily was right outside the door. "It's all clear in there if you want to use the men's room," Desi said with a smile.

"Who is this Caribbean chick who just came over to our table from the bar? She is talking to us like she knows you really well. Linda saw you talking to her and is telling me that if I don't make a move, you'll find someone else to spend the night with," Emily said.

"I am not looking to have anyone come back to the hotel room I am staying in," Desi said.

"Linda thinks that because you found out I am having breakfast, at my parents' insistence, with some obnoxious law student tomorrow morning, that I have missed my chance with you," Emily said as she pushed Desi back into the men's room. She locked the door once they were both inside.

"I guess you are curious as to what you would be missing?" Desi asked.

Emily brought her lips to meet Desi's lips. She pushed her hips against Desi's.

After a long embrace and deep kiss, Emily took Desi's right hand and put it on her blouse over her left breast. "Now, will you at least consider inviting me to your room this evening?"

Desi slowly pulled his hand away as he whispered into her ear. "It's not really my room."

When they got back to the booth, Stacey, Linda, and Desdemona were laughing so hard their eyes were watering. Emily slid in next to Linda and Desi squeezed in next to Desdemona.

"What's so funny?" Emily asked Linda.

Linda explained that they were talking about how women can intentionally or unintentionally wear T-shirts that spark the sexual imagination of people. She wasn't sure if Desdemona's T-shirt was one that could imply something sexual. When Emily said she wasn't following what Linda was talking about, Linda said, "I used to follow rock and roll bands and buy their T-shirts. One day, I was walking down the street, turning heads with a tight T-shirt, and it seemed more people were looking at me than usual. I then realized that I was wearing my 'Supertramp' T-shirt from a concert."

Emily said, "And you didn't remember what you had emblazoned on that chest of yours until you were out walking around?"

Stacey tried to help Linda explain. "Well, I think she was wondering if by chance Desdemona's name was Murrell, then the 'Murrells Inlet' T-shirt that she's wearing would be rather provocative."

Emily still looked puzzled, so Linda tried to make her point again. "I'll give you an example that hits closer to home. Emily has a breakfast date for tomorrow morning. I asked her what she was going to wear. She said that she has gone out with the guy once or twice before and doesn't really like him. She wasn't going to get dressed up for him and was probably going to just wear a pair of shorts and an old T-shirt. Emily doesn't believe that T-shirts get read by other people or have any significance. So, I asked her to show me what she had in mind to wear. She comes out of the bathroom in short shorts and a 'Morehead State' T-shirt. I didn't think a college would even get approved with a name like that," Linda added.

Stacey laughed along with Linda. Desi remained quiet. Emily shook her head, saying, "The school has been around forever. Linda is from the west coast, but everyone around here has heard of the school before."

Desdemona nodded her head in agreement. "Yeah, and my T-shirt shouldn't be misinterpreted because it says 'South Carolina' right on it."

Stacey, still laughing, managed to say, "Sure, the 'SC' on the T-shirt couldn't stand for anything else." Linda let out another laugh as Desdemona studied the front of her T-shirt.

Desi stood up after Desdemona tapped her leg against his.

Linda said, "I think we are making Desi uncomfortable," and laughed again.

Stacey added, "I think we are overwhelming even Desi."

"They better bring the food soon so that Desi doesn't feel like he's going to be eaten alive," Linda said with a snorting laugh.

Emily objected to Linda and Stacey's laughter. "I think you guys are going too far."

Linda put her hand over her mouth. She took a deep breath and apologized to Emily. "I'm sorry, but you know, I haven't gotten laid in over a month, and I haven't laughed like this in several."

Emily looked at Linda. "Well, Desi has his friend Roger flying in tomorrow morning for the Derby, maybe you can have him help you out."

"Is this the same Roger who explains the sexual revolution by saying that all you have to do is say to a woman, 'Hey, gal. Do you want to shack up?' " Stacey asked Desi.

Desi stepped away from the booth so that Desdemona could get out, and after she left, he slowly sat back down.

"I think you are taking what I told you about Roger out of context."

Linda asked Desi, "What was the context for a guy saying that?"

"Well, we were on a cargo ship off the coast of Siberia. We were drinking in the officers' dining area after dinner with several of the older officers who were second or third mates and who were trying to fill us in regarding the bar girls in Japan and Korea. It was Roger's and my first voyage, and we had gone through four or five significant storms in about the same number of days as we made our way up and through the Aleutian Islands and along Siberia. It was probably the first night that anyone felt like drinking since it was the first night that the 565-foot ship wasn't going up and down like we were on a rollercoaster ride. So, these guys were trying to share their many years of experience with the bar girls. When the discussion went from paying for the bar girls' drinks to paying to go home with them, Roger told them that guys our age don't pay for sex. Roger had spent a year or two in college before he went to Kings Point and told the old guys that women today enjoy sex as much as men and that he wasn't going to be paying for sex," Desi recounted.

Stacey added, "So, when Desi told us this story about Roger, I said that I thought guys had to be more subtle than just coming out with that line about 'shacking up.' "

"So, did you have a suggestion as to how they could be more subtle with their approach?" Linda asked.

"Yeah," Stacey said. "I suggested that a man should first ask another question."

"And what was that question?" Emily asked.

"Do you like ice cream?" Stacey said as she tried to hold back her laughter.

Linda started to laugh, then they all laughed, including Emily.

A couple of staff members arrived with the food for Desi, Emily, and Linda. Desdemona brought over a platter of Turkish pita bread with whipped olive pâté for everyone to share. The group then sat quietly, savoring the flavors on their plates for at least fifteen minutes.

Chapter II

COUNTDOWN TO THE DERBY

Stacey, who was spending the night at Desdemona's apartment a few blocks from the restaurant, accompanied Desi, Emily, and Linda back to their hotel. Stacey explained to them that she didn't want to stay at the restaurant, nor alone at the apartment, until Desdemona got off work. They went back by way of the river walk. The lights along the Ohio River were shining, not so much into the hazy night sky, but seemingly directed to reflect upon and illuminate the river. Before they left the restaurant, Desi, Emily, Linda, and Stacey paused several times along the river walk for Desi to take several shots using the high speed, black and white film he had loaded into his camera.

When they arrived at Emily and Linda's room, Emily turned the radio on and started making mint juleps. After two rounds of drinks, Linda got out a Backgammon set, opened it on her bed, and asked them if they knew how to play.

"I have played before and actually finished a game. Desi claims that women, particularly at NYU, have always gotten him intoxicated before playing and prevented him from learning the actual rules," Stacey answered with a laugh.

Linda looked at Desi. "Sounds like they were getting you to play 'Strip Backgammon,' " she said. "Actually, those rules are very simple. The guy or guys end up naked, and the women end up with just their panties on. Prizes are awarded after that."

Emily closed her eyes and shook her head. "It sounds like playing a game of strip poker with half a deck."

Linda sighed and said, "That can be fun too if it also means getting to the prizes faster!"

Stacey looked at her watch. "I lived in the same place as Desi for several months. It was half of a ranch-style house. The half where we all lived had two bedrooms, but only one bathroom. I've seen Desi totally naked from behind and wouldn't mind seeing his sweet-looking ass again, but I think I should be starting back to Desdemona's apartment in a few minutes." She then paused before apologizing. "Sorry, Desi. I guess I shouldn't be drinking anymore."

"It's alright," Desi said. "I'll walk you to her apartment."

Linda, lifting her third mint julep as if to propose a toast, said, "Why don't we just ask Desi to strip for us? I'll strip along if he would like to see someone who has worked professionally. Just turn the music to something other than what they are playing at the religious radio network."

Emily took a long swig of her drink. "I don't want you guys to think I am just a minister's daughter and that I can't ever have any fun. I'll strip down to my bra and panties. Desi doesn't have to get totally naked if he is willing to strip or have us help strip him down to just his underpants." She turned the radio to an FM rock station playing the Allman Brothers' song "One Way Out."

Emily then went over to Desi and undid his shirt. Linda, who, after arriving back at their room, had gone into the bathroom, and changed into just a Kentucky Derby T-shirt over her panties, came behind him, pulled off his shirt, and rubbed her braless breasts against his back, her nipples protruding through her T-shirt.

Stacey cheered them on. "Who is going to take off Desi's pants?" she shouted out.

Emily, wearing just her bra and panties, worked with Linda to take off Desi's belt and pull his pants down to his ankles. Desi shook his hips, and they sat on their knees to kiss his hips as he moved from side to side.

Stacey took Desi's camera off a night table. "I'll give you each ten bucks if you get in a picture with Desi so I can send it to Charlie, my boyfriend in Germany. That will teach him to miss out on Derby Day in Louisville!"

"I'll do one sitting in bed with Desi, and you won't have to pay me a nickel," Emily replied. "I will need a copy to send to my parents so they will stop feeling obligated to set me up with dates."

Stacey looked at Desi. "Do you think we can get Maurice to print up some copies when he is using the darkroom at the recreation center?"

Desi nodded his head affirmatively. "He'd develop the film and print 20 copies of each shot if you asked him," Desi said. "I'm sure he'd do anything for you," he added.

"Yeah, but he's married, and he gets a little creepy whenever I ask him for a favor," Stacey said as she removed the backgammon set from Linda's bed. "Time for you guys to get under the covers," Stacey said while pointing to the bed. "Emily, I think you should pull your bra straps down and hold the sheet to your chest so that it looks like you are topless," Stacey suggested.

Desi and Emily got into bed. Emily took Stacey's direction as to how to hold the sheet and lean forward to accent her cleavage for the photos.

Linda also made a few posing suggestions but insisted that it would be more natural if Emily simply took off the bra. Emily protested that she could not undo the bra without dropping the sheet.

"Well, maybe Desi could help with the bra," Linda suggested, before adding, "or I can get in the bed on the other side of Desi and reach behind him to help you out of your bra." Desi and Emily sat in the bed together as Linda approached and hopped under the sheets with them. Once she was in bed, she pulled off her T-shirt and held the sheet up to cover her nipples. "I think if you gather the sheet with a couple of fingers of each hand, you can cover each nipple while your hands squeeze your breasts together, so you really don't need the bra," Linda said, as she demonstrated. Desi and Emily were speechless as Linda let go of the sheet, exposing her more than ample breasts and large, hard nipples. She leaned back, resting her bare bosom on Desi's back, as she reached over and undid the three hooks on Emily's bra. "Now it's your turn to try holding the sheet to just cover your nipples," Linda said to Emily.

Stacey had also been quiet while Linda rearranged things. She had been looking through the viewfinder at what had been going on. "Please let me know when you think you are not overexposed," Stacey giggled. Linda then pulled the sheet back up to cover her breasts as Emily settled herself with a deep breath.

Desi also took a deep breath. "I think we have time for one or two more shots, and then I have to walk Stacey to Desdemona's apartment."

Linda laughed. "I was hoping for a shot of Emily and me holding your underwear up over the covers!"

Desi climbed around behind Emily to get out of the bed. "Maybe another time," he said.

Then, just as he had one leg on the outside of Emily's right leg and his left leg on the outside of Emily's left leg, so that Emily was sitting between his legs, Emily grabbed his thighs and pinned down his legs, letting go of the sheet and exposing her breasts. Emily politely asked him, "Desi, would you be so kind as to cover my nipples for the last shot?"

"I can hardly do anything but comply with your request," Desi said as he cupped her breasts and carefully surveyed them to make sure her nipples were not exposed in-between his fingers. After Stacey took that photo, Desi grabbed Emily's light brown hair that was on her back and flipped it so that her long hair substantially covered her breasts. He then put his arms under her breasts and embraced her, resting his face on her left shoulder and giving her shoulder a kiss.

Stacey excitedly took two shots of the kiss on the shoulder before asking, "Desi, can you place the kiss on Emily's neck, and Emily, can you stretch your arms out wide and close your eyes like you are entering dreamland?" Stacey clicked off a couple shots of that pose. With a smile of accomplishment on her face, Stacey said, "Emily, I think we may have one to assure your parents that you're thriving." They all laughed.

Desi got out of the bed and put his pants and shirt back on.

Linda, still sitting in the bed and again holding the sheet in front of her chest, called out to Emily. "Hey, Emma Lee, why don't you make those phone calls and I'll go out and have my evening joint with Desi and Stacey?" Not waiting to get an answer, she hopped out of the bed and, in just her panties, strutted to the bathroom carrying her T-shirt.

"Did she used to be a stripper?" Stacey asked.

"She was, what she terms, an 'exotic dancer' in Las Vegas and in Hong Kong – not necessarily in that order," Emily replied. "The deal we have with her is that she can have one joint a day, which I give her at night, and she has to be back by the time the eleven o'clock news is over to ensure she doesn't get her life back into the shit storm that it was," Emily added.

"And no more exotic dancing?" Desi asked.

"Yeah, she has to stay away from the exotic *and* the erotic," Emily said as Linda came out of the bathroom. She was once again wearing her T-shirt. Linda seemed to know they were talking about her. She gathered up a pair of jeans, a blouse, and her bra. "And I can't have sex with any more with married men," Linda added as she took her clothes into the bathroom.

"Now, how is she going to know who is married or not?" Stacey asked Emily as she handed Desi his camera.

Emily put her hands on her hips and looked at Stacey as if to lecture her. "I think that most women can tell pretty quickly if some guy is married or not. My father used to preach abstinence to young women, but even he seems to accept the fact that women in their twenties are going to be expecting something to happen by the third or fourth date, if not sooner." Emily looked at Desi. "But adultery is still adultery."

Stacey nodded her head. "If there is no spark and something isn't happening by the third date, then why in the hell are you wasting your time?"

Desi, who had his shoes on his feet and camera in hand, opened the door to the hallway. "Are we ready to go?" he asked.

"There is just one more thing I want to ask," Linda said.

"What is that?" Emily asked.

Linda turned to Desi. "Do you, Desi McKoy, solemnly swear that you are not married?" she asked with a chuckle as she walked out into the hallway.

Emily started after Linda, but Desi intercepted Emily in the doorway. Handing Emily his camera, he said, "Let me leave this in your room and I will have Linda back before the end of the eleven o'clock news."

Stacey gave Emily a hug and a kiss on the cheek. "I can vouch for him not being married," she said, before adding, "hope I get a chance to see you again tomorrow at the Derby." Emily simply nodded.

Things Aren't Always What They Seem Rolled Up to Be

When they got to Desdemona's apartment, Linda asked Stacey if she could light up her nightly allotted joint that she had tucked into her bra before they left the hotel. When Stacey agreed, Linda undid a couple of buttons on her blouse and proceeded to produce a perfectly rolled joint from her cleavage. She did not bother re-buttoning her blouse.

Stacey asked Desi if he would like a margarita. He said he would. She also asked Linda if she wanted something to drink. Linda said she would take a couple of tokes first before deciding what she was interested in drinking.

Desi watched Linda as she lit the joint and took a couple of drags. Desi took a drink of the pre-mixed margarita that Stacey had poured from a pitcher in the refrigerator. Linda then handed the joint to Stacey, who took a hit. Linda and Stacey looked at each other and scrunched up their faces.

"This was supposed to be some good shit from someone Emily knows, but it has less of a pot taste than oregano," Linda complained. "I think Emily's dad must have heard that we wanted some weed for the Derby, so he grabbed this stuff from their backyard. Emily probably didn't explain that we needed weed to smoke, not for feeding the horses."

Desi and Stacey laughed.

Stacey stood up from the chair she was sitting in. "I'm going to pour myself a margarita. Can I get you one, Linda?"

Linda stood up. "Let me flush this thing down the toilet. I'll take two margaritas."

"I can do that. I made a whole pitcher full this afternoon, just like we used to do at Charlie and Desi's apartment, except when I made margaritas at their place, I would always look forward to drinking some and climbing into bed with Charlie. This afternoon, when I was mixing things in the pitcher, I felt like I was missing an ingredient. I guess I didn't really appreciate how great those times were."

Linda took a glass and salted the rim. "Emily's father would say that when great times are over, we still have the opportunity to be thankful and recognize that we are blessed to have such happy memories."

Desi nodded. "Emily's father sounds like a rather deep member of the cloth."

"Don't be teasing us with talk about a 'deep member' unless you are prepared to get into something more than just a cold shower back at your hotel room," Linda said as she sipped her margarita and slowly walked towards Desi, pulling her shoulders back and stretching open the front of her blouse.

Desi got up and walked to where Stacey was standing in the kitchen area of the apartment. "What I meant was that Emily's father sounds very spiritual," Desi said a bit defensively. "Is it fair to assume that he, like many people, has suffered a loss?"

"He lost a son – Emily's older brother," Linda said.

"That is very sad," Stacey said.

"Was it in a car accident?" Desi asked.

"No, it was in Vietnam, about a year before American combat operations ended," Linda said.

"In 1972?" Desi inquired.

"Yeah," Linda replied. "I know because I lost my husband, who was in the same unit, right about the same time."

Desi and Stacey gathered around Linda and gave her a hug. "Sorry…" Stacey spoke sympathetically.

"I guess I took the air out of the party," Linda said.

"Does Emily know that you were married and lost your husband about the time that her family lost her brother?" Desi asked.

"Her parents know, but I never told Emily anything about my husband, Scott," Linda said.

"Can you tell us about him?" Desi said. "Was he also from Oregon?"

Linda paused for a moment. "No, he was from a military family and had traveled all around the world as a kid. He was living in California at the time I met him. We met at the Monterey Pop Festival in '68. For my seventeenth birthday, my parents let me drive down with a couple of friends from McMinnville, Oregon, which is about 50 miles south of Portland. I was standing by my mom's station wagon when Scott came walking along and started asking me about what kind of music I liked. Then, we got stoned and danced together. We stayed in touch by writing dozens of letters to one another. In the summer of '69, we drove cross-country to upstate New York to be able to experience Woodstock. While tripping and dancing in the mud there, I told him that I loved him more than anyone in the world. He suggested that we get married if I felt the same way after we came down from the LSD."

"So, you were a real hippie chick," Stacey said. "Did you decide right after that to get married?"

"After we got back to the West Coast, I told him I felt like we should be together as much as we could. We got married in July of 1970, right after I finished my first year of community college. My father was only going to give us money for the wedding if I was earning college credits in addition to working part-time."

Stacey asked, "Were you working part-time as an exotic dancer?"

"No, that came later, after Scott died," Linda said as tears started to fill her eyes.

"We aren't going to ask you anything more," Stacey said as she walked over to Linda and gave her another hug.

"Sometimes I can talk about it – what happened after I lost Scott," Linda said, struggling to regain her normal voice. "But right now, it is better to take Reverend Miller's advice and think about how lucky I am to have such happy memories of being with him, like when I joined him in Hawaii for his week of R&R," she added.

"Wow, that must have been some intense, passionate lovemaking," Stacey commented in a way that revealed her momentary creation in her head of what a few days of being reunited with Charlie would be like. She seemed to struggle with shaking off the image of bodies engaged in raw, uninhibited sex in a steamy hotel. "I'm sorry, I guess I can only hope that Charlie will be as thrilled to get back together with me as I am excited about being with him. Really, I won't know until I get to Germany whether he is still crazy about me or just content making love to whoever he is with."

Linda looked at Stacey before speaking. "I only met you this evening, but I feel like I know you. I believe that you are a woman who, once she gets in a man's heart, leaves a lasting impression."

Stacey smiled, walked over to Linda, and gave her a kiss on each cheek. Desi went over to them to join them in a group hug. They were still hugging when Desdemona opened the door to the apartment.

"I don't know what I just came in on, but when I see my girl Stacey crying those soulful tears, it must have been something very touching," she said while taking off her sweater and once again proudly displaying her "Murrells Inlet" T-shirt, now with some food stains on it. Desdemona put a hand on Desi's shoulder. She smiled at him. "Tell me the truth. Did you have an orgy in my apartment while I was at work?"

Stacey laughed. "No, we absolutely did not." She took a pause, and then, pointing at Linda, added, "She was in bed with Desi and another woman at their hotel and we just came back here to unwind with a couple of drinks."

Desdemona extended her arm around Desi and put her hip up against Desi's. "It seems like you had a busy night. Is all of that true?" Desi, with a feigned sheepish look, nodded his head.

"And what was my cousin Stacey doing while you were in bed with two chicks?"

Linda pointed at Stacey. "She was taking pictures of us."

"Holy shit, girl," Desdemona exclaimed. "You have to share those nasty photos with me." She then added, "And this dude here. Someone at the restaurant claims they saw him pull one of the other chicks you were with tonight into the men's room to do something noisy, if not also nasty. I don't think you are going to have anything left for Derby Day." Desdemona ran her fingers up the back of Desi's neck and through the hair on the back of his head.

Stacey laughed. "I think I have a pretty good idea of Desi's ability to bounce back the day after partying."

Desdemona looked at Linda with her open blouse. "And the people at the restaurant were talking about that chest of yours too. It is usually a quiet place, but the three of you livened it up tonight. They want you all to come back. Maybe even visit their farm."

Linda looked skeptical of Desdemona's sincerity, but simply said, "I enjoyed their food."

Desi stepped away from Desdemona and hugged Stacey again. "We may have an extra ticket or two for the Derby tomorrow. Give me a call at the hotel early tomorrow morning. I am in room 511." Desi looked at his watch. "I told Emily that we were planning to be back by the time the eleven o'clock news was over."

"Is Emily the chick you did in the men's room?" Desdemona asked.

"I am not going to describe what happened in the men's room other than to say that Emily knew I had a hip flask with bourbon in it, which I had promised to share with her," Desi said.

Desdemona studied him for a moment before responding. "I'm sure that isn't all you shared with her in the men's room. But maybe, since the restaurant doesn't have their liquor license yet and people do go into the bathrooms to drink, I will give you the benefit of the doubt. And I have been known to go into the men's room and, after locking the door, indulging in a drink or smoking a joint on a slow night."

Stacey looked at Desdemona. "Well, you are also their bookkeeper, so they will probably let you get away with anything, right?"

"I haven't tested it by having a guy in there with me," Desdemona admitted.

"Well, since we haven't been having Desi perform without his clothes in your apartment, are we cool?" Stacey asked.

"Yeah, I just came home to smoke a joint with you and hang out. When I walked in, I felt like I'd missed some kind of a party," Desdemona answered.

Stacey said to Desdemona, "I am up for smoking that joint with you."

Linda looked at them. "Mind if I join you guys?"

Desdemona reached into her fringed leather handbag and took out a cigarette lighter and a tin bandage box that she opened and held in front of Linda's nose. "You want to roll this shit for us?"

Linda inhaled the aroma of the green contents. "I would love to," she said as she pulled a package of rolling papers out of her shoulder bag.

Desi looked at his watch again, and then at Stacey. "I think I'm going to need a phone to call Emily and tell her we may be running late."

Desdemona said, "Feel free to use my phone and stay as long as you like. *Mi casa es su casa."*

Desi smiled at Desdemona. "I need to be back at my hotel room by midnight to make sure I am going to have extra tickets for Derby Day. I know Stacey bought 'infield' tickets for you, but I am expecting a call to confirm that two of the grandstand tickets I purchased are not going to be used. If those people are not going to be back in Louisville tomorrow, you and Stacey can sit in the grandstands with my friend, Roger."

"The phone is in my bedroom," Desdemona said as she pointed to a door on one side of the living room where they were standing.

Desi went into the bedroom and reached around for a light switch. He flipped on a fluorescent fixture that had been refitted with black light bulbs. The black lights highlighted Desdemona's white bed and bedding. The walls had been painted black, but Desi could make out two posters on the walls: one a portrait of Bob Marley, and the other a head shot of Jimi Hendrix with a large Afro. A red lava lamp on a nightstand sat next to a pink princess phone. He searched his pockets for the number to the hotel and, after finding the right slip of paper in his money clip, he used the light from the lava lamp to dial the hotel. He asked to be connected to room 711.

"Sorry, the guest does not want to be disturbed," a woman at the desk said. "Strangers have been calling her and bothering her for the last hour or so."

"May I leave my name and number and perhaps you can have her call me back?" Desi replied. "Please tell her that Desi and Linda are running late and that she can reach us at…" Desi looked inside the handset and didn't see any number and, while fumbling with the phone, disconnected the call. "Desdemona, I need some help!" he called out.

Desdemona sauntered into the room, inhaling deeply on a lit joint as she walked towards him. She exhaled into his face. "I thought you were just going to call me 'Murrell.' "

"I didn't actually say that" he said a bit defensively. Then, he noticed she was smiling.

"It's okay," she said before taking another long hit on the joint. She pointed to the "SC" on her tight T-shirt. Desi just gave her a puzzled look as she blew more smoke into his face. Stacey and Linda appeared in the doorway.

Desdemona raised her eyebrows and, speaking loudly enough for Linda and Stacey to hear, she said, "If I told you that the 'S' is for 'seeking,' can you guess what the 'C' stands for?"

Desi continued to stand in front of her trying to decipher her expressions as she put the joint in his mouth, put her lips up against his, and gave a forceful exhale that filled his lungs with the tingly smoke.

Stacey gave Linda a high five. "It's time for 'shotguns' all around," Stacey said.

Desdemona pointed to Linda and Stacey. "The ladies want to get the shotgun effect but don't like getting it from another chick. We need you to help us out. So, if you need help from me with something, like finding my telephone number on the phone, then I am asking you to kindly use your manly lips to help us out."

"Very well said," Linda commented. "And I really like this bedroom, Desdemona," she added.

"It's pretty cool, but sadly, underutilized. Oh, you can call me 'Murrell' also," Desdemona said as she walked over and flipped another light switch that set off a strobe light. "I have to wash this T-shirt," she said as she pulled it up and over her head. Her white bra became fluorescent white in the black light.

Desi continued to stand still as the white bra got closer and closer, as if moving frame by frame.

Desdemona put the closed end of the joint in Desi's mouth and then brought her lips over the burning end. Desi then blew through the joint, giving her a blast of the smoke. Desdemona moved away from him, giving Desi a smiling nod of her head. Another white bra appeared in the blacklights and started moving closer to him. Stacey appeared in front of him, and while they were nose-to-nose and lip-to-lip, Desi, with two smoke-filled lungs, exhaled for Stacey.

Linda, with her large white bra, came forward and moved Stacey out of her way. She took her turn getting an exhale from Desi, then took what remained of the joint from his lips. She took out a roach clip, clipped the joint, and took a deep inhale. Then Linda pressed her lips against Desi's and gave him a deep kiss of smoke. She rubbed her chest up against Desi. After he exhaled, she brought the roach to Desi's lips. Linda held it to Desi's lips with one hand, and with the other, she reached around and pulled Desi's hips up against her while rubbing her whole body against him. When she moved the roach clip away from his mouth, her lips fell immediately upon his, waiting for them to part and exchange the potent smoke.

Desi was locked into the kiss that seemed to go on for a minute or more. As it ended, Linda used two hands to pull his head down so his face ended up in her cleavage, and before he realized what he was doing, he kissed both of her breasts. When he picked his head up, Linda was just looking at him – no smile, no frown, just one raised eyebrow, as if to ask, "Where to now?"

With both hands, she again pulled down his head, but only brought it down to give him a kiss on his forehead.

Desdemona came by with a new joint in her mouth and a lighter. She looked at Desi and Linda, who were still standing face to face. "Are you guys ready for the next one?" Desdemona asked. She took the reefer stick out of her mouth and twirled it with the fingers of one hand.

Linda jabbed Desi in the chest with her index finger. "You promised Emily that you would have me back to the hotel before 11:30."

Desi looked at Desdemona and at Stacey before responding to Linda. "Did I really say, 'I promise'?" Desi said jokingly.

"It sounded to me like you did," Linda answered back.

Desdemona shook her head. She said to Stacey, "I think she is trying to get Desi all to herself."

Stacey shrugged. "She can try, but I don't think she will succeed. Tomorrow, Desi will be his young American self, out scouting for a more perfect union. He'll be out there doing what he can to make the world more interesting and fulfilling for someone, but not necessarily Linda."

"Are you just making that stuff up?" Linda asked.

"No. Somebody at Fort Knox asked Desi if he had his own mission statement, and he answered pretty much along those lines," Stacey said.

Linda put her shirt back on and took Desi by the hand. While leading him out of the apartment, she said over her shoulder, "One night that's interesting and fulfilling might be just what I need." Desi just waved goodnight to Stacey and Desdemona, who were still having the strobe and black lights illuminate them like disco goddesses.

They were out of the building and halfway up the block when they heard someone running up behind them. Linda and Desi turned to see Stacey, fully clothed and with something in her hand. Stacey pushed a piece of paper into Desi's hand. "Here's Desdemona's number if you find out that you have a couple of extra tickets for the grandstand. We'll be happy to entertain your friend, Roger, while you are getting photos of the Derby activities tomorrow," Stacey said.

Desi gave her a kiss on the cheek and said, "I'll give you a call in the morning."

The Morning After

When Desi awakened the next morning, he knew he was not in the bed alone, but needed a moment or two after the phone started ringing to recall with whom he was sharing the space. During the night, Emily and Linda, who started the night together in the other bed, both climbed into the bed with him. After the second ring, he climbed as gently as he could over Emily, and, with three hopping steps, grabbed the phone. "Desi?" a female voice asked.

"Debi?" he asked, still somewhat groggy.

"No, try again," Stacey responded.

"Stacey?" he asked on his second try.

"That's better. Do you remember how you said you were going to call us about whether you have grandstand tickets for us after you spoke to someone, who I guessed was Debi, around midnight?"

"Oh, I didn't know you were expecting a call last night. I thought you would just call me this morning," Desi said.

"Well, it is almost eight o'clock now, and Desdemona has been bugging me as to whether we have the tickets for the grandstand, or if she has to dress for the infield."

"I'm sorry," Desi said. "Things got so crazy after getting back to the hotel last night. Emily was upset with guys calling her room and then knocking on her door and having to meet some guy for breakfast this morning. I didn't realize that you were expecting me to call you back last night."

"I tried not to bother you, but I couldn't reach Emily or Linda last night or this morning at their room. Desdemona wants to know whether they are wearing dresses and big hats."

"Didn't I tell you last night that I was staying in room 511 and to call me in the morning?" Desi asked, still trying to clear his head.

"Well," Stacey replied, pausing for a moment, "it's like I said, it's Derby morning."

"You are right. The tickets are yours, and as soon as I pick up Roger at the airport around nine o'clock and get back to the hotel to find out what Emily is doing today, I can get you the tickets."

"And when is that?"

"About 10:30," Desi answered.

"Is there a way I can reach Emily or Linda to find out what they are wearing today?"

"They are here in the room with me, still waking up. They don't seem to be feeling very well. How about if I have them call you back at Desdemona's place?"

"You all slept together last night in the same bed?" Stacey asked.

"Something like that. We all ended up in the same bed together, but there wasn't any sex," Desi added.

"No wonder they aren't feeling well. Help them out for God's sake, and have them call me," Stacey said.

Desi hung up the phone and went over to the bed alongside Emily. He lifted up the bedspread and sheets that Emily had over her head and gave her a kiss on her forehead. "Stacey would like you to call her at Desdemona's," he said softly.

"Did you tell her I was having my period and feeling like crap?" Emily asked.

"No, I just said that you weren't feeling too well. Stacey and Desdemona want to know what you're wearing to the Derby."

"So, you're giving them the grandstand tickets you bought for your ex-fiancée and her sister?" Emily asked.

"Sure, why not?"

"Maybe Linda was planning to hang out with your friend, Roger, rather than having him sitting with two other women," Emily said.

"Linda can hang out with me today if you are going to the Derby with the law school dude," Desi answered.

"So, you want to hang out with Linda today?" Emily said, pulling the sheets and bedspread off of her head and sitting up to look at Desi.

A voice from the other side of the bed chimed in. "What is so bad about me hanging out with Desi? Just because we partied over at Desdemona's place and got back to the hotel a little bit late, that doesn't mean that we are going to be getting it on today," Linda said.

Emily pulled her feet out of bed and slowly stood up on the floor. "I better go back to my room and let the two of you go at it, if that is what you want to do. I have to go and get ready to have breakfast with someone who is probably going to make me feel even sicker than I feel now." Emily found her bathrobe that was hanging over a chair and her slippers under the chair. She put the robe on over her pink pajamas before throwing one slipper at Desi and the other at Linda, who was still in bed.

"Ok, I was feeling like getting it on with Desi last night, but we went to your room, not Desi's. I'm starting my period too, so I just want to hit the bathroom here for a minute, and then I will go upstairs with you," Linda said as she slowly got out of bed and made her way to the bathroom wearing only the blouse she had on from the night before and a pair of gym shorts.

Emily and Desi sat in two chairs facing one another as Linda used the bathroom. Referring to the scrap of paper Stacey handed him the night before, Desi scribbled Desdemona's name and telephone number on the pad of hotel stationery and handed it to Emily. As they sat silently facing one another, someone knocked on the door before pushing an envelope underneath it.

"Oh, no," Emily said. "Now those guys have tracked me down to your room." She got up from the chair and picked up the envelope.

"Well, it isn't exactly my room," Desi said.

As Emily carried the envelope towards Desi, she read the name on it: "Tammy Thompkins."

She handed the envelope to Desi, which had "Tammy Thompkins c/o Sakura Productions" typed on it.

When Linda came out of the bathroom, she saw Emily standing in front of Desi with her hands on her hips, glaring at him. "Who the hell is Tammy Thompkins?" Emily asked.

"She's a model who was here at the hotel yesterday," Linda said. "I know her from Hong Kong and a USO show we did in Seoul Korea. I said hello to her in the lobby and met her sister," she added.

Emily kept glaring at Desi. "A model you were in this room with yesterday?" She turned and stormed out of the room.

Desi looked at Linda. "What can I say? I have known Tammy since high school. I didn't know that she had been to Hong Kong or Korea, but her sister is my ex-fiancée. I told Emily that I had an ex-fiancée in town yesterday."

Linda shrugged and grabbed her shoes she had tossed on the floor the night before. "I'll go tell Emily that the sister was your lover. She is very beautiful, I might add."

Desi shook his head. "Please don't mention how beautiful Debi is to Emily," he said with a pause. "And don't remind me."

Linda walked out of the room and into the hallway. "I guess I shouldn't refer to her as having been your 'lover' either," she said with a bit of a laugh. She then stopped and turned to Desi. "I am sorry. I shouldn't assume that things are over between the two of you."

Desi stood up and watched Linda walk down the hallway towards the elevator carrying her shoes. He closed the door, locked it, and headed for the bathroom. As he turned on the shower, he remembered that he had shared that very shower with Debi only a matter of hours earlier. It took several minutes of the water splashing his face before he cared to open his eyes again.

Roger's Arrival

Desi was standing in the baggage claim area at Louisville International Airport for only a few minutes when he spotted Roger walking towards him with an attractive woman in a business suit. She stopped as the two of them passed a line of payphones. Desi watched as they gave a wave of goodbye to one another.

Desi remembered another reunion he had with Roger back in the summer of '72 at the Zurich train station. Prompted by such a memory, he yelled out Roger's name and walked quickly towards him to give Roger a bear hug. As Roger was a couple of inches taller than Desi and about 30 pounds heavier, Desi seemed to get the bigger hug, and Roger's wire-rimmed eyeglasses clipped Desi in the temple before they ended their embrace.

The woman on the payphone dropped the receiver and walked over to them. Smiling, she said, "It is so great to see men express their feelings and appreciation for one another."

Desi shrugged. "I'm just his driver trying to get him around Louisville on Derby Day."

The woman laughed. "I'm sure you are the gentleman that Roger talked about on the plane." She held out her right hand in a manner that caused Desi to be unsure as to whether he should kiss it or shake it. Puzzled, she said, "You are Desi, right?" Desi nodded and shook her hand.

"My actual name is Daphne, but my friends call me Daisy. I'm Daisy from Louisville," she said as she linked one arm with Desi and her other arm with Roger. They walked arm in arm to the baggage carousel with her pocketbook banging against Desi's thigh.

"I trust Roger can find his own bag, so Desi, would you be a dear and help me find my pink leather suitcase?" she asked. Desi unhooked his arm and walked over to the carousel. Roger followed him while Daisy walked back to the payphone area.

Roger put his right hand on Desi's left shoulder. "She's an unusual woman, isn't she?" Roger said quietly.

Desi stopped and looked directly at Roger, "My guess is that your new friend, Daisy, is almost 30 years old and is calling some guy who will be pissed off that we are even talking to her."

"She told me that she's staying with an aunt who lives here in Louisville. She lived with the aunt from the time she was a kid to the time she finished college. For some reason, she has never been to the Derby. She decided that this was the year she was going to go. I think that she was just planning on changing into her jeans and buying an infield ticket," Roger said.

"I don't think she is your average infield attendee," Desi said as he grabbed a pink leather suitcase off the carousel.

"Well, she doesn't have to watch from the infield. You bought two tickets for me and my date. Since my gal isn't coming, like I told you during our telephone call the other night, then Daisy can be my date for the Derby." Roger took out his wallet and started handing twenty-dollar bills to Desi.

"I guess that since Debi isn't going to be my date for the Derby, and I don't have anyone else lined up, there are plenty of tickets for Daisy. It's just that there are two or three other women who want grandstand seats, and I thought you could hang out with them," Desi replied. "I ended up getting a press area ticket at the last minute, so I think I'll be alright, date or no date," he added.

"Desi, I'm sure you will find someone interesting to be with this afternoon. Daisy seems fascinating to me, perhaps because she is a couple of years older than me. She certainly is more mature than you," Roger said with a laugh.

"If you are sure that some guy with a gun isn't going to show up later to fight for Daisy, then you can have the two tickets as originally planned," Desi said as he reached inside one of his blazer pockets and presented Roger with two tickets. "I hope the two of you have a few laughs together today."

Roger smiled as he took the tickets from Desi. "Daisy has already made me laugh today. Do you know the title of the book she was reading on the plane when I sat down next to her?"

Desi paused for a moment, examining the expression on Roger's face. "Maybe, *Fear of Flying,*" Desi offered.

Roger laughed, saying, "You guessed it! Have you read it? Not on a plane, right?"

Desi nodded. "Certainly, but not on a plane."

Daisy came walking back. Desi held up the pink leather suitcase looking for her approval. Daisy gave him a thumbs-up.

"If you guys can drop me off in Louisville, my aunt has some tea brewing."

"Desi loves a good cup of tea," Roger said.

Managing to Get Through Breakfast

Emily and Linda were sitting at a table in one of the hotel restaurants when Desdemona and Stacey arrived a little out of breath. Stacey volunteered that they had run over from Desdemona's apartment after speaking to Linda on the phone.

Linda motioned for them to sit down at their table and opened her pocketbook. "Desi said he was going to be back from the airport by ten. He seems to be running late. But it doesn't really matter because he dropped off your tickets with me before he went to the airport," she said as she handed Stacey an envelope.

Stacey laughed. "Desi seemed to know we were anxious to get the tickets. Now we can start planning what we are going to wear to the Derby." Stacey took two tickets out of the envelope. "Are you guys going to be wearing big hats and fancy dresses?" she asked.

Emily shook her head. "No, we are going to be covering the afternoon festivities on behalf of the radio station we work for." Emily opened her pocketbook and took out an envelope. "My mom and dad were going to be here today with my car. My father took it back to Maryland last weekend to get it tuned up, but now they have to go to Philadelphia to check on my grandmother instead. I have their two grandstand seats – in a very good section. They may be better than what Desi gave you." Emily handed the envelope to Stacey. "I think there are also a couple of tickets to get you into a couple of the private party areas," she said with a smile.

Desdemona looked at Stacey. "A choice of grandstand seats? That really beats standing in the infield!"

Stacey opened the second envelope and pulled out all the tickets inside. "Sons of the American Revolution tickets?"

Linda pointed at Emily. "Her father's mother's maiden name was Boone, as in Daniel Boone."

"Well, I have already consumed and absorbed a couple of bottles of Boone's Farm beverages, so that might qualify me to go to the party," Stacey said. They all laughed.

A man with long sideburns and a goatee, who appeared to be in his late twenties, came near the table. He waived his attaché case towards Emily.

Emily stood up. "I have to have breakfast with someone, but I will probably see you all at some point this afternoon at Churchill Downs." Stacey and Desdemona simply nodded as Emily walked away from the table. "See you back in the room," Linda said.

Stacey and Desdemona proceeded to tell Linda about a consignment store they had heard of. It was only a few blocks away and sold dresses and Derby hats that women had 'gently worn' for the Derby festivities in prior years.

Emily was seated at a table with the U of L law school guy when Linda, Stacey, and Desdemona got up to leave the restaurant and head to the consignment shop. They talked about getting outfits that would get them into the parties at the Derby, and how they were not looking to gently wear their Derby dresses.

Meanwhile, Desi and Roger did get to enjoy the hospitality of Daisy's Aunt Arbie. They sat with her as Daisy went upstairs to change. To Desi, the home looked like a Louisville version of a Manhattan brownstone. Aunt Arbie had lived there pretty much all of her life and worked at the nearby telephone company office from the time when World War II "altered her life" to the spring of the prior year, 1975. "Over thirty years," she said wistfully.

Aunt Arbie asked Desi and Roger about where they were from. Pointing at Desi, she said, "Well, he says he's from New York, and you say you are from Virginia, but where did you guys meet up?" Desi was preoccupied with eating a scone and sipping some tea, so he left it to Roger to respond.

"It was in New York, on Long Island, at the United States Merchant Marine Academy," Roger answered. Desi nodded his head.

"You mean Kings Point?" Aunt Arbie asked as she held out a silver tray and offered Desi another scone. "Daisy's older brother, George, went there. He sailed for a few years and then went to Georgetown Law School. I went up to Kings Point for his graduation. It's in a lovely area, right on the water. George and his wife live in the city now. He's at an Admiralty Law firm. I think they are looking for a house on Long Island." She offered Desi another scone, which he accepted with a smile. "When did you gentlemen graduate?"

Desi paused, looked at Roger, and then said, "Well, Kings Point sent us out to sea together, and we went all around the Far

East, but each of us, for our own reasons, at some point decided we were not going back to the Academy."

Roger added, "I knew I wanted to go back to a regular college. I did get my undergraduate degree somewhere else, and Desi did too, but when he told me that he wasn't going back to Kings Point, I realized I didn't know why I would want to go back either."

Desi added his perspective. "I went to Kings Point right after high school, and just a couple months after Kent State. It was a very turbulent time. Despite my parents wanting me to go back to the Academy, I knew I just couldn't. After being at sea for about five months, I felt I was ready to live my life on my own terms, with my own goals."

"Your parents were probably afraid that you would get drafted and end up in Vietnam," Aunt Arbie offered.

"That might have been part of it, but not all of it," Desi answered.

"Yes, life is always more complex than one easy answer," Aunt Arbie said wisely. "I was engaged on Derby Day in 1941 and was supposed to be married in June of 1942. I thought I had my whole life figured out at age 20."

With a clicking of high heels on the staircase, Daisy came down in a light blue dress with a large matching bow in her pulled-up light-brown hair. She took a lap around the room where Desi and Roger were sitting and stopped behind the chair where Aunt Arbie was sitting. Daisy leaned over and kissed her aunt on the forehead. "I figured I'd come downstairs and see if any scones were left," she said while continuing to stand behind her aunt. Desi opened his mouth as if to frame a question for Aunt Arbie. Daisy, out of view of her aunt, shook her head to clearly indicate that he should not ask a follow-up question.

Roger looked at Daisy. "You look perfectly lovely."

"Then, may I suggest we head to Churchill Downs?" Daisy said. "I think it promises to be an extraordinary day at the Derby."

Desi and Roger stood up and thanked Aunt Arbie.

"Yes, an extraordinary day. That's the way one should feel before heading off to the Derby," Aunt Arbie said with tears in her eyes as she hurriedly left the room.

"Leave it to me to get caught up in my moment and say the wrong thing," Daisy said as she headed for the front door.

Chapter III

SHOWING UP AND SHOWING OFF ON DERBY AFTERNOON

After arriving at Churchill Downs, Desi walked Roger and Daisy to their seats while telling them about Stacey and Desdemona. As he thought they would be sitting together most of the afternoon, Desi wanted Roger and Daisy to have some background and to clarify that he was "just friends" with the two of them. "Stacey lived in my apartment, but she didn't live with me; she lived with my housemate, Charlie, who is now stationed in Germany," he explained.

"So, when Charlie left for Germany, she moved right out?" Daisy questioned.

"Well, not exactly," Desi answered slowly. "Charlie had paid through the end of the month, and Stacey hung around a bit until she decided that she was going back to live in the barracks."

"You guys weren't shacking up together after he left, right?" Roger asked.

"No, Charlie is a good friend, and now Stacey has orders to go to Germany, and there is a chance that they will be back, as you say, 'shacking up together,' " Desi added.

"So, you didn't start sleeping with your friend's lady after he left for Germany," Daisy said as if to confirm what she was hearing. "But she continued to sleep at your place for a while?"

"Right. She would be in Charlie's bedroom, and I would be in mine," Desi responded.

"And you never had to snuggle up with one another to stay warm?" Daisy persisted.

"No. There was another woman by the name of Penny, a member of the Army Band at Ft. Knox, who would help me keep the bed warm," Desi said.

Roger asked, "What instrument does Penny play?"

Daisy put her hand on Roger's shoulder. With a laugh, she said, "Now I think you are getting too personal!"

They were still laughing when they found the seats in the grandstands for Roger and Daisy. Desi explained he had to get a few photos of the Derby activities for the post newspaper, including a few shots of the Army Band when they were performing.

"I'll stop by throughout the afternoon, but is there anything else that you need to ask before I start earning my press pass?" Desi asked.

Daisy thought for a moment. "Oh, and what does Stacey do in the Army?"

"She is a paralegal in the JAG Office," Desi replied.

Daisy looked surprised. "I'm a paralegal too; at least I was before I moved with several of the attorneys from the old firm to a new firm that does a lot of lobbying and political stuff. Now I am supervising a group of paralegals and research people."

"That sounds like it could be very interesting," Desi said before he headed off to the press area.

After Desi was out of earshot, Daisy asked Roger about his travels with Desi in the Far East.

Roger advised her that they had been on cargo ships originating in the Seattle area and would cross the Pacific. About a week after their ships left the West Coast, they would arrive in Yokohama. They would have a few days in Yokohama to explore Yokohama and the Tokyo area. "My father, a former Naval Officer, still had friends in Japan and Korea, and sometimes I would take Desi to meet them. One time, when we were in Yokohama, we took the train down to Kamakura to visit a family my father knew. We had a nice lunch at their house, and then they took us to see Daibutsu, the Great Buddha statue. One of the times we were in Inchon, we went up to Seoul, where one of my father's friends had his wife take us out on the town to a big dinner and stage show. They even put us up in a hotel so we could see more of the city before we had to go back to Inchon to catch the ship," Roger recounted.

"You know, I could hear you and Desi talking to my aunt when I was upstairs, right?" Daisy said.

"Yeah, I figured you could hear us," Roger responded.

"I know she told you a little bit about my older brother George, who was a deck officer. Were you studying to be on the deck or in the engine room?" Daisy asked.

"Actually, we did both. Desi was up on the bridge for the first ship, and I was in the engine room. On the next voyage, on another cargo ship, I was on deck, and Desi was in the engine room with a chief engineer who was a fairly recent graduate of Kings Point. We used to hang out with him when we got to ports like Kobe and Hong Kong," Roger added.

"Sounds like you had some good adventures together. Do you know what days you were in Hong Kong in early 1971?" Daisy asked.

"Desi would know what days. He kept a journal. Guess he was getting ready to be a journalist, although the only career he talked about back then was being a lawyer. I think we were there in May, but I don't remember what days. Why do you ask?"

"Back then, I was interviewing with several law firms in Washington D.C. for a paralegal job. I complained to my brother that I had nothing to wear to the interviews. He sent me a plane ticket to Hong Kong to meet him and have some clothes made. I was in Hong Kong for a few days in May of '71. I spent two days shopping and getting fitted at the tailor shops. There was one day of just sightseeing in Hong Kong with George. I was able to fly home with one of the outfits my brother bought for me."

"And you recall your job search in DC, but you don't remember seeing me while you were sightseeing in Hong Kong?" Roger said with a chuckle.

Daisy put her hand on Roger's shoulder once again. "I don't remember if it was the job I really wanted, but I think I would remember seeing you in Hong Kong if we had bumped into one another."

"And I would certainly remember you if we had met in Hong Kong," Roger replied.

When Desi got to the press area, he spent a few minutes looking around for Emily. Not seeing her, he headed off to a mint julep stand and ordered his first drink of the day. He spotted a local DJ with a few people crowded around him. The DJ was pontificating about which horse was going to win the "Run for the Roses." When he got his drink, Desi walked over to join the crowd.

Desi had occasionally listened to the DJ's morning show at a Louisville radio station, which included skits involving a stable of characters. When the DJ started posing with some of his gathered fans, a guy with a University of Louisville baseball cap pointed to Desi's camera.

"I see you brought your camera," he said before asking Desi to take a picture of him with the DJ and to send it to him at an address he wrote on a scrap of paper.

Desi agreed. "I'll try to get you in a shot, but you need to get right next to him."

Desi moved in closer to take a photograph of the guy with the U of L baseball cap next to the DJ. As Desi was moving, the

DJ noticed the press credentials hanging around Desi's neck. The DJ asked him, "Are you from one of the local news outlets?" Desi nodded his head in the affirmative.

Right about then, Linda walked by in a yellow chiffon outfit that was cut very low in the front. She wore a large yellow bow in her now curly hair. The DJ pushed the guy in the baseball cap away and held out his hand to Linda. He seemed to use her press pass as an excuse to stare at her chest. "You must be with the network news, my dear," he said with a Cheshire cat smile.

As Linda moved in next to the DJ, Desi took a photo. She then stepped away from the DJ and gave Desi a one-armed embrace and a kiss on the cheek.

The DJ stared at Desi. "You aren't going to charge her for that photo, are you?"

"No, but I'll let her decide if we should send you a copy," Desi answered.

"Well, I'm not going to give you a kiss to get one," he said. "You know who I am, right?"

"Yes, sir, I do, but that doesn't make me a fan," Desi said before turning and walking away with Linda on his arm. Linda seemed to have a prance in her step that Desi had not seen her demonstrate before.

"So, Desi. What do you think of my Derby Day look?" she asked.

"I think you might cause the men here to stampede," Desi said with a smile.

"How about your friend, Roger? Is this going to distract him from reviewing the racing form?" Linda said, folding her hands and arms together for a bosomy pose.

"Hummm," Desi said. He paused for a moment. "Roger may already be distracted."

Linda's prancing and posing came to a halt. In her high heels, she was almost staring directly into Desi's eyes. "Did his girlfriend end up flying in with him?"

"No. What happened was that he met a woman, a very nice woman, on the plane," Desi explained.

"Had you told him anything about me? Couldn't he have at least waited until after he met me?" Linda said with a sigh of exasperation.

"What was there to tell him?" Desi responded. "That you might or might not be interested in meeting him on Derby Day?" Desi said with a shrug. "The woman on Roger's plane is sitting with him now. I could introduce you to the two of them," Desi volunteered.

"I would appreciate that, though I feel like it's the least you should do, given the circumstances."

"Well, let's go find Roger and Daisy," Desi said, again extending his arm to Linda. She linked her arm with his and snuggled in closely.

Roger and Daisy were enjoying mint juleps and were yelling along with the crowd during an early race as the horses crossed the finish line.

Desi waited for the crowd noise to die down before he called out to Roger. "Have you won back the cost of your airfare yet?" Desi exclaimed from the aisle.

Roger smiled and put his arm around Daisy. "You might say that."

Desi made his way through several empty seats to get to where Roger and Daisy were sitting. "I'd like to introduce you to my friend, Linda, who is working up in the press area for a radio station that is syndicated throughout the United States," he said as he sat down next to Roger. Linda bent over to wave hello, which seemed to magnify her ample breasts.

"Nice to see you," Roger said, seeming to pause an extra moment between saying "see" and "you."

Desi motioned for Linda to sit down next to him. After sitting down, she reached across Desi to shake Roger's hand. "Desi mentioned you last night at dinner, but he didn't tell us how ruggedly handsome you are," Linda said, getting a grin from Roger and a frown from Daisy.

"I may be a bit rugged, but Desi is the handsome one who seems to know how to attract the ladies," Roger responded.

Linda shook her head and rolled her eyes. "Don't I know? He must have had three or four women pursuing him yesterday, kissing on him, and who knows what else."

Desi wasn't sure what Linda was trying to do. "I think Linda has a very vivid imagination. Maybe she is still getting over the effects of having gone to Woodstock."

Linda seemed a little taken back at first, but then gave a broad smile. "To his credit, Desi is a gentleman, so he doesn't kiss and tell," Linda added, "But, Desi, I know you have to remember at least a portion of last night." Linda gave Desi a kiss on the cheek before she got up to walk back towards the concourse.

"Nice meeting you," Daisy called out to Linda. "I was at Woodstock too. We'll have to talk again sometime." Linda turned to wave to Daisy and then continued to carefully climb the remaining steps up the aisle.

Desi jumped up. "Got to go, but I will stop back," he said as he hurried to catch up with Linda.

Daisy brought her nose within a few inches of Roger's nose. "So, Desi doesn't generally kiss and tell, but if he spent the night in the sack with Linda, wouldn't he brag about it to you?"

Roger reached over and picked up the racing schedule booklet on the seat that Desi had been sitting on. "I don't think that Desi feels he has to tell me about how many women want to kiss on him." He said while checking out the information on the next race.

Daisy leaned over and gave Roger a quick kiss on the cheek.

When Desi and Linda returned to the hallway outside the press area, the Louisville DJ was back taking photos with fans. He had acquired a cowboy hat, and, when an attractive woman walked by, he would tip his hat and make a comment. Linda did not want to walk past him, so she and Desi just waited in the hallway for the DJ to move on. After about ten or fifteen minutes, the DJ started tipping his hat repeatedly while saying "Howdy" to Linda and Desi. He signaled them to walk over to him. Linda shook her head in refusal. With that, he started walking towards them.

"Let me handle this," Desi said to Linda.

"You better, because I just want to punch him in his little face," Linda said.

Before the DJ could walk up to Linda, Desi stepped in between them.

The DJ took off the cowboy hat and put it over his heart. "Usually, when I say 'Howdy' to someone, they say 'Howdy' right back," the DJ said.

"Isn't that one of your derivative lines that you use on your radio program?" Desi said.

"What are you saying? You don't believe my material is original?" the DJ said, putting the hat on his head and pretending to start rolling up his sleeves.

"I know that there is a DJ in New York who uses almost the exact same expressions and characters that I hear you use here in Louisville," Desi said, shifting the weight in his legs, on the off chance the diminutive DJ actually took a swing at him. Desi then took a step in closer to the DJ, so the tip of his nose was almost on the DJ's forehead.

The DJ backed up. "Well, maybe I worked with that now big-time DJ in New York back in the day at a radio station in the Midwest, and even today, we both poke fun at some of the same types of people."

Suddenly, Emily, in work attire, appeared at Desi's side. She glared at the DJ and, almost snarling at him, said, "And sometimes you name the people who you say you are 'poking fun at,' and keep it going until you ruin their lives."

"So, we have the Reverend Miller's daughter here again this year," the DJ said, stepping away from Desi. "I remember you from when your daddy was cussing me out for picking on one of his phony preacher friends. I can't help the fact that his friend went out of business. That is what it was, wasn't it? He took money from hardworking folk, claiming he was trying to build some monstrous temple of babble. However, despite all the talk and a fancy groundbreaking, he only raised twelve shovels of dirt before he shot himself with a shotgun. Like I said last year, I take no comfort in such an unfortunate end to a troubled soul. And I certainly take no responsibility for the path that con man took."

"I am not here to judge you," Emily said to the DJ while taking Desi and Linda by the arms. "But you will be judged," she added, practically dragging Desi and Linda to the press area.

"Thanks for standing up to that egomaniac," Linda said.

"Yeah, thanks!" Emily added. She ran her hand up the back of Desi's neck and through his hair. "I'll have to tell my father about that encounter. He may want to meet you."

"Desi meeting your father… I'd like to be around for that!" Linda said.

Emily put one arm around Desi's waist. "You think he'd like to hear the story about how I met Desi in a men's room?" Emily said with a laugh.

"He might ask 'how long did it take for Desi to grab your boobs?' " Linda countered.

"You should talk," Emily said, shaking her finger at Linda. "You showed him yours before I did."

"I think you were ready to do it with Desi yesterday, the very day you met him," Linda said. "What would your father think about that?"

"But, even as horny as I have been the past few months, I didn't!" Emily protested.

"Only because you started your period, and you don't think any guy would want you when you are having your period. But you could have asked Desi if he minded doing it while you were menstruating."

"Well, you started your period last night, only a few hours later. Did you ask Desi if he would mind if things got messy?"

"Desi knows that sex is usually a bit messy," Linda said while winking at Desi.

"What are you telling me?" Emily said.

Desi shook his head. "You know that I'm standing right here and listening to all of this. The facts are that I haven't had intercourse with either of you." They both looked at him with a glare. "But that doesn't mean, under the right circumstances, I wouldn't, just that I want to be honest with both of you. I wasn't going to get too crazy with either of you yesterday afternoon or night if my fiancée, or rather my ex-fiancée, was going to be returning to Louisville today."

Linda looked at Emily. "I was walking back with Desi after partying with Desdemona and Stacey last night and wondered if he wanted to spend the night with you or with me. I guess I was pretty high and would have been willing to go to Desi's room with him for a quicky."

"Holy shit, Linda. So you told him that you knew I was having my period and I wouldn't have sex with him?"

"I may have told him something along those lines," Linda admitted, hanging her head. "I didn't want to feel like I would be Desi's second choice."

"No. You used things I told you to be his only choice if he wanted to get laid last night," Emily said frankly.

"Well, I don't know about the 'only choice' part. I did get him out of that apartment, where it was likely that he might have had multiple choices. So, I may have felt somewhat deserving of his affections," Linda confessed.

Desi turned his back to the two of them and walked away, saying, "I have to go get a picture of the Army Band."

As he made his way through the concourse, he stuck his head into several VIP meeting rooms. The security people were polite but told him at the first two meeting rooms that even members of the press would have to be a member or accompanied by a member of their organization. At the third meeting room, Desi asked the name of the organization hosting the "Private Party" as noted on the door. The burly security guard, who wore a photo ID tag identifying him simply as "Phil," looked him over a bit before saying, "Sons of the American Revolution." Desi then took out his Army photo ID and showed it to him.

"I guess that may be good enough. I'll have to check with my supervisor. The party hasn't started yet, so why don't you come back in about an hour?" he added.

Desi put his Army ID back into his money clip. "I think that anyone currently serving in the military of the United States would be welcomed by the descendants of the original patriots," Desi said in a plaintive tone. Phil nodded his head in agreement. "I'll see you later," Desi said with a smile.

Desi continued his walk down the corridor and started to open the next door, marked "Private Party," when, bursting out of the door, was a guy he knew from the dinner theater at Fort Knox. His friend, Randolph 'Randy' Beaujolais, seemed to be in very good spirits. Randy was a talented guy who could act, sing, and dance, but after getting tired of serving as an extra in Broadway and off-Broadway productions, he joined the Army to direct recreational activities.

Desi had volunteered to write the post newspaper's reviews of the dinner theater performances. Randy managed to get Desi complimentary tickets to the shows, including the dinners. He had also drafted Desi to appear in a minor acting role in one of the productions to give Desi the experience of performing at a dinner theater. Desi had found it to be a good lesson. Desi realized there was an art to making planned movements seem natural and spontaneous. Desi had appeared on stage in elementary school but did not remember how difficult it was to project one's voice, but, at the same time, not to overdo it.

After the dinner theater stage experience, Desi found it easier to write a clever and insightful review. While no one ever complimented him for his efforts under the spotlights, he did get calls at the newspaper office from people who wanted to express their appreciation for his capturing the highlights of the performances.

Randy, who was probably too short to portray a leading man, had to put his arms up to exchange hugs with Desi. "Good to see you, brother," Randy said to Desi. "Are you ready to hear me do some genuine East Coast Hip Hop at one of these private parties this afternoon?"

"Yeah, I haven't seen anyone performing Hip Hop here in Kentucky. We had a guy in Basic at Fort Dix who had been a DJ.

He would provide some Hip Hop to entertain us from time to time. He seemed really good. I'm not sure why he volunteered for the Army," Desi said.

"He's probably like a lot of people who have volunteered for the military since Vietnam ended, just trying to make the best of riding out the recession. Maybe he is out entertaining the troops somewhere, perhaps taking Hip Hop to Europe," Randy speculated.

"Enough about that dude," Desi responded. "At which party will you be taking the mic?"

"Well, I haven't found the room yet," Randy said. "It's a group called the Sons of the American Revolution. It sounds like a late Sixties band, doesn't it?"

Desi pointed over his shoulder towards the last private party room he had been in. "There's a guy named Phil who does the security for that room. I'll introduce you, but I think you are going to have to give him the name of whoever hired you."

"It was some guy with one of the American Legion Posts here in Louisville."

"That should be enough," Desi said. "Let's go talk to Phil!"

Randy held his hand up for a 'high five.' Desi slapped his hand, and the two young men, though in civilian clothes and with only semi regulation haircuts, sort of marched together down the hall to talk to the security guard.

Meanwhile, Emily had ditched Linda to check if there were any messages for her in the press area. After making a few phone calls, she decided she had better go look for the Army Band to catch up with Desi. She realized that without her parents driving her car from Maryland to Louisville, she was not going to have a vehicle to get back to the Lexington area. Emily found the band but did not see Desi. There was a tuba player who sat in his seat, apparently resigned to being closely bonded to his instrument for the day. Emily went over to him and tapped him on the shoulder. He turned his head with a laconic roll, as if he was expecting an annoying fellow band member to be pestering him. Instead, he encountered Emily's stunning smile.

"Well, hello there," he said, shifting the weight of the tuba so that he was no longer slouching in the seat. "Do you have any tuba requests?"

"No, I am just here trying to catch up with an Army photographer who said he was going to take some photos of your band. You haven't seen Desi McKoy today, have you?"

"No, I haven't seen Desi today, but if you go over to that tall blonde woman with the saxophone, she might have seen him today," he said, pointing to the spiffy-looking PFC Penny Bright. PFC Bright caught the tuba player pointing her out to Emily and made her way over, saxophone in hand.

"Is someone asking about me?" Penny asked as she came closer to them.

"She is asking about Desi. Wants to know if he has been around taking pictures of us today," the tuba player explained.

Penny shook her head and, at first, turned away. She then went over to Emily and, switching the saxophone over to her left hand, reached out with her right to shake hands with Emily. They then started what became a rather lengthy conversation, even though they each quickly acknowledged they had no real knowledge of Desi's current location.

At first, Penny seemed to assume that Emily was Debi, Desi's high school and college sweetheart from back in New York, who Desi had told Penny about. Emily, although not giving many details, shared that she had only met Desi the day before, but she already "felt some sort of affiliation with him, perhaps as fellow journalists." Emily also revealed that she hoped Desi could do her a favor and give her and her friend Linda a ride back to the Lexington area. Penny volunteered that she hoped to run into Desi that afternoon because she also needed a favor from him, though she did not disclose what the favor was. She also skipped over the fact that she had lived with Desi at his apartment from around Valentine's Day until mid-April. She did tell Emily that she and her twin sister grew up in Michigan, mentioning that her parents were in the process of moving to Tennessee, where her mother grew up, and her father was about to accept a teaching position at the University of the South in Sewanee, outside of Chattanooga. Penny also shared that her twin sister, a violin player, was studying music at Julliard in New York City, but that she had not had the opportunity to visit New York.

After Emily finished her conversation with Penny and left the area where the Fort Knox Army Band was assembled, she wandered down a hallway that led to her running into Desi. "Where have you been keeping yourself?" she asked.

Desi gave her a hug and a kiss on the cheek. "Checking out the places around here that might be serving free bourbon," Desi answered with a twinkle in his eyes.

"I thought you said yesterday that we might have a chance to have some bourbon together today," she said, feigning hurt feelings.

"I found the perfect spot for us to have that drink or two of bourbon, and you can meet Randy, a good friend of mine," Desi said.

"Randy, is she a stripper?"

"No, no," Desi said. "Randy is a guy!"

Emily put her arm around Desi. "I thought most of your friends were women. I just had a talk with one of them – Penny, her name was."

Desi moved so that he could look at her face to face. "You met Penny?"

Emily nodded her head. "She said that she has known you since around the beginning of this year and that she was hoping to see you today because she needs a favor."

"What kind of favor; did she say?" Desi again studied Emily's expressions to see if they revealed something about her conversation with Penny that her words did not.

"No, but before you go running off to find out what she needs you to do, I want to have that drink, and I need to ask you to do a favor for me," she said while maintaining her amazing smile.

Desi decided that he would return her good humor, whether it was sincere or not. "You know that I would practically do anything for you, as we have known each other for how long now?"

"Well, we did sleep in the same bed together last night, however, with all the creeps calling me in my room and knocking on my door, that was perhaps forced upon us," Emily replied somewhat defensively.

"And it wasn't like the two of us were alone in the bed as you brought along your roommate," Desi added.

Emily paused when reminded of Linda. "She seems to feel like she decided to bring me along to the sleepover party in your room."

Desi realized that he was reminding Emily of the uncomfortable exchange she had with Linda earlier. He put his arm around Emily, saying, "Let's go hang out with the Sons of the American Revolution, and you can see that Randy has a mustache and is not one of my female friends."

"And I can ask you about giving me and my roommate a lift this evening back to my grandmother's house near Lexington." Emily squeezed against him as they walked. "I will make breakfast for you tomorrow morning, and then we can all go out to the distilleries in the area."

"You expect me to sleep with you and have a chaperone around again tonight? You aren't planning to have your grandmother in the room with us this evening?"

"My grandmother died about a year ago. And I am not asking you to go to bed with me tonight, just to give us a ride."

"I'm sorry about the grandmother joke, but I guess I am just trying to picture this. Am I spending the night on a couch?"

"We have three bedrooms in the house. You can sleep in the bedroom my parents sleep in when they visit."

Desi offered, "Or I could bring you and Linda to my place? The three of us can have another sleepover in my bed, and we could have Roger and Daisy chaperone from the next room, if they don't get too distracted. I'll fix breakfast and we can still all go to the distilleries in the Bardstown area."

"Where would Roger and Daisy sleep?" Emily asked.

"In the empty bedroom where Stacey and Charlie used to sleep."

"I really don't care if you, me, and Linda have to all sleep together again, or who cooks breakfast, as long as I get a good Sunday breakfast or brunch," Emily conceded. "I guess you told Roger that he could spend the night in your spare bedroom?"

"That was the idea from the start, but then his girlfriend bailed on him. However, I am getting the sense that Daisy is willing to fill in for his girlfriend, or ex-girlfriend," Desi explained.

"And Linda and I can fill in for, according to Linda, your very beautiful ex-fiancée, the sister of a fashion model?" Emily asked.

"Well, all this wasn't part of the original plan, but please think it over," Desi said as they went into the private party room reserved for the Sons of the American Revolution. Inside the room, there were already a few men with American Legion patches on their shirts and a couple of women in full Derby attire. A bar area was now open, and a bartender was serving Randy a mint julep. Phil was standing near the bar and talking to Randy.

Desi walked over to them, temporarily leaving Emily standing alone in the middle of the room. Two middle-aged women with large Derby bonnets walked over to her and introduced themselves. Out of the corner of his eye, Desi could see Emily being practically encircled by the two rather large women and almost having her head disappear behind their hats. Desi then asked Phil if he was approved to join the private party. Phil nodded in confirmation before asking who Emily was. Desi remembered Linda telling him that Emily was related on her father's side to the Boone family and, possibly, the legendary Daniel Boone himself. He told Phil he thought Emily was a direct descendent of Daniel Boone as he took a mint julep off the counter of the bar. He put a crisp dollar bill in the bartender's tip jar.

After what was a kind, yet thorough, cross-examination by the women, Emily emerged from the pair of Derby dames holding a piece of paper and smiling. She then held out the paper to Desi. "They want me to join the DAR. What do you think?"

Desi just shrugged. "Isn't it like being Jewish; doesn't your mother have to be a member?"

"My mother never joined, but her mother, whose maiden name was Lee, as in the Lee family of Virginia, was a member in the early 1920s, before the Depression and before she became an FDR Democrat."

"So, that explains why 'Lee' is your middle name and reveals your south of the Mason-Dixon Line origins," Desi said. He pressed further, "So, I know Kentucky was a border state, which attempted to be neutral but eventually sided with the Union. I think that a very clear majority of Kentucky men fought on the Union side. What side did your father's family line up with?"

"Well, I'm sure you know that before the Revolutionary War, Kentucky was regarded by many Virginians, such as George Washington, as a western extension of Virginia. There's quite a lot more than just a physical connection between the two states. However, by the time of the Civil War, people from many areas had settled in the State of Kentucky. My father's great grandfather, who had spent most of his young life living in Baltimore, fought for the North, and one of his first cousins fought for the South. After the war, they got together and opened a bourbon distillery in Owensboro, Kentucky."

"Does your family still own a distillery?" Desi asked.

"Would you, as you say, 'do almost anything' for me if they did?" Emily asked.

Desi started to frown. "I'm getting the feeling that they don't."

"No, they don't. When prohibition came along, one of my father's uncles used some connections he had to get a license to produce bourbon for medicinal purposes and didn't cut the others in," Emily recounted.

"Well, you have a rich family, maybe not in the bourbon business, but in history," Desi said.

"What about you, Desi? Do you have anyone that would qualify you to be in the Sons of the American Revolution?"

"One of my grandmothers came over from Ireland through Ellis Island around the turn of the century, so that wouldn't do it, but the rest of my grandparents go back a bit further, and some very far back. I know my mother's father's family can trace their ancestry back to before the Revolutionary War. A great uncle, several generations before my grandfather, was a member of the Continental Congress. My grandfather's family tree started with a French Huguenot who, in the last decade of the seventeenth century, escaped persecution and married into a prominent English family on Long Island. Their children and grandchildren married into other prominent English families. The ancestor who was a member of the Continental Congress didn't get any medals for fighting, but he did help raise relief funds for the people of Boston during the British occupation of that city. His brother-in-law got to sign the Declaration of Independence."

"So, no medals, and not given the chance to sign the Declaration of Independence. That might just get chalked up to politics," Emily said. "However, I think that would get you considered as a Son of the American Revolution."

"The security guard just confirmed to me that I am welcomed here, not because of one of my ancestors, but because I am active-duty military. That's fine since I don't see myself joining any sort of fraternity-type organization."

"They didn't have fraternities at NYU?" Emily asked.

"Not that I was aware of," Desi said with a pause, before adding, "other than an honorary journalism association, Kappa Tau Alpha, which was based on academic achievement."

"Sounds like a fraternity to me," Emily mused.

"Well, it was open to both women and men, so I don't think it's like most other fraternities."

"I guess you're right about that difference."

Desi looked at Emily. "What about you? Do you belong to any sort of sorority at UK?"

She put an arm around him. "Don't be concerned, I'm not a southern belle. I don't belong to a sorority, and I am not going to join the DAR. They would have to allow 'Women of Color' to join their organization before I would consider filling out the form. Look, I am just wearing a khaki skirt and a polo shirt, not some frilly costume. Actually, I probably look out of place here."

Desi stepped back and looked her up and down. He took another sip of his mint julep and smiled. "You look just perfect for a night at my place. So, what have you decided? Is it going to be a night to remember in Radcliff, Kentucky? I should tell you that the apartment is just a few blocks from a Kroger, which is able to supply us with all the ingredients necessary for an excellent Sunday brunch."

Emily put a hand on Desi's shoulder. "As long as there is a good Sunday brunch, I am willing to give another night in bed with you a try."

"I like your practical approach and your enthusiasm for a hearty breakfast," Desi said. "I'll be sure to make some breakfast sausage available to you."

"Is that hot sausage or sweet sausage?"

"Which do you prefer?"

"How about if I start with the sweet and see if I am ready to switch to the hot. Does that sound okay?"

"You have me perspiring already," Desi said. "Are you ready for that mint julep? I know I am ready for another."

Emily put her hand against his chest. "Whoa, I thought you still had to take a photo of the Army Band. And don't forget to talk to Penny. I promised her that I would give you the message. Right now, I have to get back to the press room. We can come back here later. I think they will still have some bourbon left," she said as she turned to leave, leaving him standing in the middle of the room this time.

Randy walked over to Desi. "Is everything alright with you and your friend?" Randy asked.

"Yeah," Desi said. "She has to get back to work in the press room, and I have to stop talking about photographing the Army Band and actually go and get a good shot of them rehearsing. I'll check back with you later on."

"Okay, we are going to do a Hip Hop set right before the big race, and another right after."

"I'll try to catch some of both," Desi said as he adjusted his camera strap and headed out.

Linda Isn't Lonesome Very Long

After parting with Emily near the press area, Linda decided to catch up with Stacey and Desdemona, who decided to use the tickets Emily had given them to sit in the seats that Emily's parents would have been sitting in had they been able to attend the Derby. Linda had taken a taxi with Stacey and Desdemona to Churchill Downs after purchasing their Derby outfits in downtown Louisville. She had helped them decide which grandstand tickets to use.

Stacey and Desdemona left their seats to find a ladies' room as Linda went into the grandstand section where their seats were located. Stacey saw Linda and waved. Linda waved back and waited as they made their way towards her.

"Are you guys going to get more drinks?" Linda asked as they approached her.

"No," Desdemona responded. "We have to get to the ladies' room before I have anything more to drink. I've already had three drinks, and it's a few hours until the big race."

"I was hoping that you brought your bandage box from last night so we can get a real buzz going," Linda said to Desdemona as they made their way out into the corridor.

Stacey smiled at Linda. "We have been talking about finding a place around here where we could light one up. I was thinking that the people in the infield have an easy time smoking weed without any hassles. "

"Well, I wanted to get dressed up and sit in the grandstands, so I am not complaining," Desdemona replied. "We are just going to have to use some Geechie-Gullah ingenuity."

"Some what?" Linda asked.

"Desdemona and I have relatives in South Carolina who are known as the Geechie people. They can always find a way to make something from what looks, at first, like nothing," Stacey explained.

Linda pointed at the nearby line for the ladies' room. "That line looks like something I wish I could transform into nothing." They all let out a sigh.

The three of them stood in the line for several minutes, with no sign of much movement forward. Stacey reached into her handbag and took out the package with the tickets from Desi. "Do you think the seats over in the other part of the grandstands would have more bathrooms?" she asked.

"I thought this would be better for you guys as far as being closer to the track," Linda said. "I'm sorry, I didn't pay much attention to the bathroom situation."

Desdemona asked Stacey for the envelope for the tickets they received from Emily. She took out the passes for the Sons of American Revolution private party. "I think we have some options," Desdemona said as she held the passes up in the air.

"There are only two passes," Linda said while giving them a forlorn look.

Desdemona smiled at her before commenting, "The way you look in that yellow dress is your pass to just about anywhere. You have nothing to worry about."

Stacey laughed. "Yeah, in the islands, we say, 'No Problem.' "

The three of them went looking for the Sons of the Revolution private party and ran into Desi coming out of the party room. They surrounded Desi, almost screaming, "Desi, Desi, Desi," as people turned around in the hallway to look for a celebrity among them. Desi just did his typical shrug.

"Do you know where we can find the Sons of the American Revolution party room?" Stacey asked Desi.

He pointed to the door he had just exited. "I just came out of there. Randy from the dinner theater is inside and will be performing there later on. I think he can put you all on his guest list."

Desdemona held up the two guest passes. "We also have a couple of tickets."

Stacey came alongside him and whispered in his ear. "Do they have bathrooms inside?"

"Yeah, and you get free drinks too," Desi added.

Linda grabbed a hold of his blazer. "Where are you going? Desdemona brought along some of that special weed from last night. Don't you want to get high with the three of us again?"

Desi looked at Stacey. "You better talk to Randy before anyone lights up a joint in the place. Maybe he has a dressing room where you can party."

Desdemona looked around, checking to see if anyone was watching them. Not seeing anyone close by, she took out a joint and pointed it at Desi. "We will keep this one for you to share with us later."

Linda took it from Desdemona's hand and tucked the joint down the front of her dress.

Desdemona looked at Linda, and then at Desi. "Remember, we are all going to share the joint with Desi later on."

"I will remember," Desi said. "I am getting a few photos of the Army band and then going back to the press room. I'll let Emily know we are going to be hanging out here." Desi said, before asking Desdemona, "May I have one of those passes for Roger? I don't think Daisy will need a pass."

Desdemona handed him both of them. "Sure, if Stacey is going to get us on the guest list, or if our outfits will be our tickets, I guess we don't need them."

Desi headed down the hallway.

Stacey, Desdemona, and Linda made their way from the hallway to inside the party room. Once inside, Stacey spotted Randy, who introduced them to Phil. Randy got Phil to put them on his guest list. Randy then took them back to a dressing room, which had a private bathroom. The three women took turns using the bathroom for the regular purposes, and then they used the dingy yet clean bathroom together to take hits on a joint. The bathroom had a noisy but effective fan.

Some reggae music was turned on in the large party room shortly before Stacey, Desdemona, and Linda exited the dressing room. They were more than ready to join the people who were dancing. While Linda was dancing with Stacey and Desdemona, she happened to be facing the door. Suddenly, the door from the hallway opened, and into the room stepped Tammy Tompkins. She wore a Derby outfit, including a hat that matched her dark red hair. She was with two corporate executive types who wore well-tailored suits, sans neckties. Linda waved both of her hands to get Tammy's attention as Phil approached Tammy. The security guard directed her and her companions to another room down the hallway. Tammy gave a little wave back to Linda before she left the room.

When the reggae music stopped, and before Randy performed, the two commanders of the American Legion Posts hosting the party welcomed everyone. Stacey asked Linda who she waved to. "I might be too high right now to be sure, but I think it was a fashion model I knew when I lived in Hong Kong named Tammy Tompkins," Linda replied.

Randy then walked over and introduced himself to Linda. The two post commanders came over and, sharing the microphone, pointed out key members of their American Legion posts, who also had the distinction of being members of the Sons of the American Revolution. They also pointed out Randy and Stacey as two active-duty military members.

Randy put his arm around Stacey as if she was his date, and he then proceeded to say a few kind words about the two post commanders and their wives. The first post commander was a tall, slender guy who looked like he could portray a frontiersman character on television, and whose wife was one of the women who had cross-examined Emily earlier. The other post commander was a heavyset Afro-American, who had a very petite Asian wife. Randy noted to the audience that both post commanders had served in the same Army unit during the Korean War. Stacey just stood, almost at attention, still looking uneasy about Randy's arm around her.

She would later ask Desi a few questions about Randy, including whether he was married or not.

When Randy let go of her waist and the reggae music started back up, Stacey walked over to Desdemona and Linda. She took Desdemona by the hand and led her off to the dressing room to talk. "After drinking those mint juleps and smoking that joint, I feel like I'm starting to hit that level of being high when the people in the room seem to be like characters in a movie," Stacey said.

"I dig what you are feeling," Desdemona replied. "If you are starting to feel freaked out, then we can chill out, or…," Desdemona paused, pulled out another joint from her bandage box, and held it out in front of Stacey. Just then, Linda joined them in the dressing room.

"That weed you have is the best I've had since I was in the Far East," Linda said. "I think it is the treated stuff the Hawaiian surfers call 'Buddha.' "

"You hung out in Hawaii?" Stacey asked. "I wanted to get assigned to Hawaii with Charlie, but he got orders for Germany. Pretty soon I'll also head off to Germany instead of those islands in the Pacific."

"You ever get high and do it with one of those Hawaiian surfers?" Desdemona asked Linda.

"If we can share that joint you are holding," Linda said, "I think it might help me remember back to the months after I found out that my husband had been killed in 'Nam. I danced at the clubs in Honolulu and made more than enough money to do some serious partying on the beaches of Maui and Kauai." She closed her eyes for a few moments. "There was this dude who surfed and played guitar. He claimed he smoked hash with George Harrison whenever Harrison was in Hawaii."

Stacey looked at Linda. "Alright, I'm in for another joint if Linda is going to tell us more about partying in Hawaii."

Desdemona stepped into the dressing room's private bathroom and turned on the fan, lighting the joint as soon as the fan started making noise.

"I want to hear more about the Hawaiian surfer and how long he could keep his balance with our girl Linda?" Desdemona said after she took a hit from the joint and passed it to Linda. Linda, in turn, took a toke and passed it on to Stacey.

Linda exhaled and responded to Desdemona's question. "It was long. Now that I am starting to remember, it was wonderfully long."

They all started laughing, coughing, then laughing some more.

Then there was a knock on the bathroom door.

"Who is it?" Stacey asked.

"It's Randy! Do you have Linda in there with you?"

Stacey opened the door a crack. "Yeah, she's in here with us. Is someone looking for her?"

"Does she know someone named Tammy?"

Linda nodded. Stacey opened the door a bit wider, and they could see that behind Randy stood the one and only Tammy Tompkins.

"She says she wants to join your party," Randy said. "I told her that I didn't think it would be a problem."

"It is a bit dingy in here, and the only light that is working in here seems to be a sort of night light plugged into the mirror over the sink," Stacey said as she opened the door wider. "If she doesn't mind partying in here, I think there is room."

Tammy brushed past Randy and extended her perfectly manicured right hand to Stacey. "Hello, I'm Tammy Tompkins."

"I know. We all know, and maybe everyone here at Churchill Downs knows. Very nice to meet you," Stacey said.

Desdemona reached out to Tammy. "I'm Desdemona." Tammy shook her hand.

Tammy then gave Linda a hug, saying, "I hadn't seen you in years, and now we are meeting up two days in a row. You were well-dressed yesterday, but you are simply stunning in that outfit now."

Stacey offered Tammy the joint, which she accepted with a smile. Tammy took a deep inhale and handed the joint to Linda.

Linda noticed that Randy was still standing in the bathroom doorway. She held the tightly wrapped reefer out towards Randy, who shook his head, saying, "I need to go out and get on the stage they are setting up."

Desdemona accepted the joint from Linda after Randy left, and Linda took another hit.

Tammy stepped closer to Desdemona to get ready for another hit. After Desdemona gave her the joint, Desdemona studied Tammy from her shoes to the tastefully ornate pillbox hat on her head.

"If you don't mind, could you give us an idea of how much you spent on those beautiful shoes, dress, and hat?" Desdemona asked.

"I spent a bit of time at a store in Chicago this morning, trying them on and being photographed, so at the end of the shoot, they just gave them to me," Tammy answered.

"Wow, and I thought I got a good deal on this outfit at the consignment store!" Desdemona said.

"That was very smart of you to get something for Derby Day without paying an arm and a leg, like some of the women down the hallway in another party room were talking about," Tammy said.

"They might just be bragging about how much money they have to spend," Linda said, "or about how much they got someone else to spend on them."

"Well, I think we all look great, even though we didn't have to go into debt to be able to strut our stuff a bit," Stacey said before taking another hit on what was quickly becoming a roach. "I was planning on just doing the infield thing this year in a pair of jeans and a T-shirt, but then we got grandstand tickets from Desi and Emily."

Desdemona pulled out a roach clip and put it on what was left of the joint. She took a shallow drag and handed the roach clip to Tammy, saying, "I think there is one good long toke on this baby."

Tammy accepted the roach clip. "Well, I am already feeling pretty good, but I will suck this baby hard like, well, I'll leave it to your imagination." She closed her eyes, puckered her lips and cheeks, and pulled on the roach until there was nothing left.

Stacey looked at Linda, saying, "Like your best baby on a beautiful, deserted sandy beach."

"Amen," Linda said.

A Penny to Disrupt Desi's Thoughts

By the time that Desi arrived in the area where the Army Band from Ft. Knox was seated, the band was starting to rehearse Stephen Foster's "My Old Kentucky Home," the anthem played before the Run for the Roses, the main event on Derby Day. In the past, Desi found the song somewhat ironic, considering that many of the people Desi met in Kentucky seemed to believe the creator of the song was from Kentucky, when, in fact, Stephen Foster was from the Pittsburgh area. Foster only occasionally visited his Kentucky cousins. Desi stood listening to the Army band rehearse the song, while looking out over the track at the cluster of humanity in the infield. He felt himself more accepting of the possibility that the song was designed to convey, for people of all backgrounds, a sense of appreciation for peaceful times spent in the Bluegrass State. Desi knew, from the literature he studied in a music class, that Stephen Foster went on to be deemed the "Father of American Music" and was a master of various types of music, including the "plantation songs," which, reportedly, gave many people of faith in the 1850s a challenging perspective on the horrors of slavery.

The band leader was not satisfied with the initial effort of the soldiers as Desi heard him say, "Let's try this again." He then saw Penny wave to him and mouth the words, "Wait for me." He found himself nodding his head in agreement.

The band started again. Desi pushed himself to focus on the band and get a good group shot for the weekly post newspaper, *Inside the Turret.* After a couple of shots, he switched lenses, and before the song ended, he was able to get a few closeups of Penny playing her saxophone. He thought he might get a photo for her to send to her folks, who he had met in April before she stopped spending nights at his apartment.

Desi heard the band leader give the members a half-hour break.

Penny put her saxophone in a case and came over to Desi. "Did you get the message?" she asked.

"Was it something about needing a favor?" Desi responded.

Penny looked around and saw a couple of band members still sitting close by. "Can we go somewhere to talk?"

"There is a party room down the main corridor that might not be too noisy yet. I don't think anyone from the band will be there to see us talking," Desi said.

"I don't care about that anymore. That whole thing was stupid. Everyone seems to know everything about us anyway," Penny said as they walked into the concourse and then down the hallway.

"I never said anything to anyone about going out with you or whatever happened after Easter," Desi said.

Penny put her hand on his shoulder and gently pulled so as to turn to Desi. They both then stopped and faced each other. "I am not accusing you of anything. I was an idiot to think that people were not going to see us together in Radcliff and around Fort Knox."

"So, you aren't looking forward to swinging at me with your saxophone case?" Desi said with a smile.

"No," Penny said with a muffled laugh. "But you are giving me a good idea as to what I might do to whoever started telling people that I was staying at your place. I hope it wasn't your friend, Stacey."

"She swears it wasn't her," Desi said. "Stacey thinks it was someone who might have seen us shopping together at Kroger. I guess we shouldn't have done that, but I don't think we even did that together very many times," Desi said.

"Now I wish we had done it more," Stacey said a bit loudly, just as a group of people walked by. She paused, dropping her head, and taking a couple of deep breaths. "I think we better go to that party room to talk before I say something or do anything else to publicly embarrass myself anymore."

When Desi entered the Sons of the American Revolution party room, Phil greeted them at the door. He smiled at Desi, looked at Penny in her uniform, and waved her in. Desi walked Penny over to the bar.

"Can I get you a mint julep?" Desi asked.

"Can I just have a sip of yours?" Penny responded.

"Sure," Desi said as he put one of the dollar bills he had in his hand in the tip jar and the other back in his pocket. He handed the drink to Penny and turned back to Phil to ask if Randy was going to be on soon.

There was a tap on his shoulder; it was Linda with her hand on his back. Tammy, with her nose and eyebrows up, was standing a couple of feet behind Linda.

Penny finished her sip of the mint julep and handed the glass back to Desi, who just stared at Linda and Tammy.

"Did I catch you at a bad time?" Linda asked. "I just wanted you to know that I am going with Tammy to a party down the hallway, in case you or Emily might be looking for me."

"Okay," Desi said, as he focused his gaze at Tammy, who then started looking off to the back wall, shaking her head.

"Who is your Army companion, Desi?" Linda asked.

"Oh, I'm sorry. This is Penny. She is a saxophone player in the Army Band." Desi turned to Penny. "And Penny, this is Linda; she is a University of Kentucky student. Today she's covering the Derby for a Christian radio station."

"Nice to meet you," Penny said.

Tammy stepped forward. "Desmond McKoy, aren't you going to introduce me?"

"I guess I am just very surprised to see you back here in Louisville today," Desi said.

"Somebody offered me a seat on a private plane late this morning, and I couldn't resist attending a nice but boring party sponsored by a certain Japanese beverage company. Fortunately, I ran into Linda, who got my attitude adjusted so I can go back there." Tammy held out her hand to Penny. "Do we just shake, or do I have to salute you?"

"We can just shake," Penny responded as she held out her right hand and steadied the top of the saxophone case with her left hand.

"Well, Desi, I always heard that you were one for plenty of good sax," Tammy said as she turned and walked for the door.

Linda, with a puzzled look on her face, followed Tammy.

"Holy shit, Desi," Penny said. "You really do know Tammy Tomkins, and she knows you!" Penny folded both hands on top of the saxophone case. Penny asked Desi, "But where is her sister?"

"Don't tell me you are looking to meet her too?" Desi blurted out.

"I hope I didn't disrupt things for you," Penny added. She paused, "But I do need to ask you a favor that might complicate things even more for you."

"Might as well spell it out," Desi said. Penny took his left hand, brought it near her face, and turned his hand so she would be able to read his watch.

"So, in five minutes or less, I'll fill you in on my problem, and you can think about it and get back to me. Hopefully in the next couple of days."

"Alright, I'll listen," Desi replied.

"My parents have found a house in Tennessee, just outside of Chattanooga. My father is going to accept a professorship, or maybe he has already accepted a position at the University of the South teaching English. My mother, as you know, has been a high school music teacher in Michigan. She's been able to land a music teacher position in Tennessee, and they want us to come down to Chattanooga and celebrate the new house and their move. They want us to have dinner together, like we did in Nashville in early April."

Desi looked at her for a few moments before taking a gulp of the mint julep. "You're right. I am going to need a few days to think about this. I guess you want me to just play along as if nothing has changed since last month."

Penny nodded her head. She then took the glass from his hand and finished off what was left of the mint julep. "I got to get back," Penny said, grabbing the handle of the saxophone case. "Hope you find out what happened to your high school sweetheart."

Randy walked over to him. "Hey, man. You seem to have quite a lot going on today. Are you okay?"

"Yeah, I just better hold back on making any bets this afternoon. The day is not going anything like I would have predicted." Desi paused, and, in an attempt to change the subject, asked Randy, "What horse are you picking to win the Derby?"

Randy smiled. "Mind you, I don't have any sort of clairvoyance, but I'm simply making a ten-dollar bet on "Bold Forbes. In fact, while I still have a few minutes, I am going to head over to one of the betting counters to place that bet."

Desi dug into his pocket and pulled out his money clip. He located a ten-dollar bill. Desi looked at Randy. "Mind if I tag along?" he asked.

They walked together down the corridor to where people were standing in line to place bets. Desi asked Randy about whether his wife would be attending the Derby. He found out that Randy's wife was visiting family in New Orleans and had taken their two young children along with her.

While they were standing in line, Randy shared his insights regarding the different horses. Desi got a sense that his friend's choice of a winner was very likely to place or show, if not win. "Bold Forbes to Place," Desi said when he got to the window. He could hear Randy chuckle behind him.

"Guess I decided to hedge," Desi said.

"Maybe next time you'll decide to go all in," Randy said with another chuckle.

Emma Lee Miller Decides to Broadcast Her Derby Day Crush on Someone

When Emily got back to the press area, a small studio had been set up in a conference room that only seated two or three people. A technician was finishing up his work by arranging a microphone and connecting it to a dedicated phone line. He also connected a tape cartridge machine that could play pre-recorded music and announcements, including a station ID. Emily's job was to provide some local coverage for the race, which would be called by someone watching a TV screen at the main station for the United Christian Broadcasting Network in Charleston, West Virginia.

Their studio, near the University of Kentucky, wasn't much larger, but it had a couple of turntables and a small record library. At that studio, Emily would sometimes do a live newscast, and sometimes she would host a music program, often cueing up the records herself on the turntables. Occasionally, Linda would engineer the music programs and help out by cueing up the records, which gave Emily more time to select them and prepare something to say about the selections. In addition to playing religious music, they would curate classical, big band, and gospel programs.

Emily was thinking about what she was going to say to start the Kentucky Derby coverage. The previous year, her father had hosted the Derby radio program. Emily had basically sat in the other chair and just watched. Now she would need to make some brief remarks.

Emily had just started to write down some notes when one of the two phones in the studio rang.

Emily's mother was on the phone, reporting that they had made it to Philadelphia and had helped Emily's Grandma Litchfield get discharged from the hospital to her home in the Chestnut Hill Section of Philadelphia. Desi would come to learn that Emily's Grandma Litchfield had lived for many years in the Philadelphia area, and it was where Emily's mother grew up. Emily would also tell him about how her Grandma Litchfield, whose maiden name was Lee, had been a nurse in France after World War I and was part of a renowned group of nurses. They assisted the young women of France, who had lost loved ones in the Great War and who struggled to provide for their children in that war-torn nation. Emily's grandfather, on her mother's side, had been a U.S. Army field surgeon in World War I and had stayed on in France for a couple of years to assist with the wounded Americans, as well as help reestablish hospitals in France, including the American Hospital in Paris.

"Emma Lee, are you alright doing the broadcast this afternoon?" Emily's mother asked.

Emily assured her mother she would be "able to come up with a few things to say to fill the five or ten minutes" for which she was responsible.

"Don't forget to mention how much your father regrets not being part of the Derby festivities," Emily's mother said before she handed the phone over to Emily's father.

"Hello, sweetheart," her father said when he came on the line. "Meet any nice young men at the Derby today?" he said with a laugh. "Your mom and your mother's mother are all worrying about you."

Emily could hear her mother arguing with her father to get the phone back. When Emily's mother came on the phone again, she said, "I forgot to ask you how your breakfast date went with the young lawyer. Is he at the Derby with you?"

"No, I can't say I wanted to spend any more time with him. Anyway, he sounded like he was too busy to go to the Derby, either with me or with anyone else."

"I'm sorry, honey," Emily's mother said. "But don't worry. Your grandmother knows a family whose grandson is a young doctor, and who just started working at the hospital where your grandfather spent most of his career. If he's anything like the rest of his family, you should really make an effort to meet him. I think your Grandma Litchfield is already trying to set something up."

"Oh, great," Emily said in a rather flat tone.

"Let us know if you are going to be home one weekend next month."

Emily reminded her mother that she was sitting in the radio studio at the Derby. "I have to start the radio program in a few minutes, and I need to prepare for it. Got to go!"

Emily hung up the phone. She reviewed the notes she had scribbled and then took a quick look at the clock on the wall. Ten minutes to broadcast. She knew they would be calling her from the main studio in West Virginia in about five minutes. Emily expected that they would walk her through the final two minutes before going live, on-air, to radio listeners across the country. She couldn't ask them for more time.

Suddenly, there was a tapping on the glass conference room door. Desi was peering through the glass.

Emily waved him into the small studio.

"Just wanted to wish you a good broadcast," Desi said as he bent over so that only the top half of his body was actually inside the room.

"Sit down with me for a minute or two. Let me try something out on you."

Desi stepped all the way inside the studio and sat in the chair directly opposite Emily, who had her notes spread out on her desk. She moved the microphone away from her face.

"I am thinking about how Derby Day can be something special to people all over this country, like how St. Patrick's Day makes all Americans Irish for a day. There is something magical in that moment that binds everyone together. And I want to wish everyone a bit of that magic and hope that everybody listening has a special someone they can share that magic with for a moment or two," Emily said while looking directly at Desi as if she was looking for a reaction.

Desi stood up and stepped to the doorway of the studio. "I think you have hit on something. I have spent a few minutes today trying to picture Stephen Foster traveling to Kentucky before the Civil War and visiting his cousins to get inspired in some way. I think that in addition to taking a few photos today, I should also try to write something about my time in Kentucky and the people I have met here."

"Can we share some magic this evening, Desi?"

Desi turned, saying, "I certainly hope so," as he exited the studio.

Shortly after he left, Emily received the call from the main studio in West Virginia, and they explained how they would call her with about a minute to go and give her a countdown for going "live."

Desi was still carrying his camera bag with one of the Army's Nikon cameras from the newspaper office, as well as his personal camera, a Canon he had purchased in Japan when he was a U.S. Merchant Marine cadet. He had been shooting black and white film in both cameras for a couple of days. He paused before he entered the grandstands where Roger and Daisy were sitting. He took a few more shots with the Canon to finish the roll. Desi took out the roll and stored it in a plastic container with a cap and put it into a pocket of the camera bag that had a secure zipper. He pulled out a new roll of color film, still in its cardboard box, and loaded it into his personal camera. With the strap of the camera bag over his left shoulder and the Canon camera firmly in his right hand, he made his way to a still-empty seat next to Roger.

Daisy smiled at him as he got closer.

"Mind if I take a picture or two?" Desi asked.

"I don't have a problem with you taking a picture of me," Daisy answered. Roger only muttered.

Desi took a couple of pictures of Daisy, who then put an arm around Roger. Desi took a photo of the two of them together.

Desi stood with them as the Army Band began to play the Derby anthem. Desi was amazed to see how many people, even Roger, had to dry their eyes after the band finished.

The race was, as promised, a very exciting couple of minutes, but Desi was a bit distracted by wondering if there was any way he could listen in on what Emily was saying on-air before and after the Run for the Roses. He hoped that it went well for her and that someone, somewhere, made a tape of her broadcast.

He told himself that he would have to ask Linda if she could get a tape of Emily's on-air performance.

Getting Everyone Together with the Sons of the American Revolution

After the big race, Desi suggested that Roger and Daisy accompany him to see his friend Randy perform at a private party. They followed Desi down the crowded corridor, trying to talk as they pushed through clusters of boisterous people. Daisy said something about being curious as to their plans for the evening. Roger told Daisy that he only had a vague recollection of a conversation he had months earlier with Desi about things they might want to do in the evening and day after the Derby. As they walked, Roger admitted to Daisy that, "All I really remember is that Desi's ideas sounded good to me, but they were probably not going to be acceptable to the woman I was planning on bringing to the Derby."

As Roger pushed through the crowd, with Daisy following in his wake, he called out to Desi, who was half a step ahead and to Roger's left. "What's up for later?"

Desi said something about "a revised plan."

As noisy as the hallway was, they were not ready for the sound inside the party room. Randy was leading the revelers from behind a table that had an electric keyboard and two turntables. A band with electric guitars, drums, and a horn section were on a riser behind him. Randy called out, "Let's get on with the Derby Dancing!"

When the music started and only a few people began to dance, Randy led a chant of "Get off your ass and jam!" which got the dance floor more active. The music got louder, the dance floor filled up, and the dancing became wilder as the chant got louder.

The white American Legion members seemed to be moving along with the rhythms that Randy was blending together as much as the Afro-American American Legion members.

Desi noticed that there were no signs of Phil or any other security people. The two post commanders seemed to be watching the door, standing next to each other with their arms folded. It looked to Desi like they were the only ones in the room who were not dancing. Their wives were dancing together and with anyone else who wanted to join them.

Desi, Roger, and Daisy made their way to the bar at the end of the room. There was no bartender, just two pitchers partly filled with what looked to be some sort of bourbon mixed drink. Desi took a stack of plastic cups off the bar and poured some of the mixture into three cups. He then took a taste from one of the cups and handed Roger and Daisy the other cups. Then, after waiting for each of them to take a taste, he lifted up one of the pitchers. He gave an extra pour to Roger's and Daisy's cups, and the three of them drank their bourbon drinks until there was a break in the music.

Daisy was the first to speak. "Roger says you have invited us to your house for dinner. Are you able to give us a ride to your place, or should I rent a car at the airport?"

"I think the airport is going to be crazy this evening," Desi said.

Roger nodded his head.

"I think everyone can fit in my VW," Desi said confidently.

As Desi was pouring refills into their cups, Linda walked in from the hallway. She came over and gave a hug to Roger and Daisy. Linda gave a kiss on the cheek to Desi, and then a hug, as he tried not to spill what was in the pitcher he was holding in his right hand or have the strap of his camera bag fall off his left shoulder.

"How are you feeling, Linda?" Daisy asked.

"I'm feeling great, Daphne. How are you?" Linda replied.

"Well, a little while ago I was telling Desi that I was thinking of renting a car. Now, I am not sure I can drive." Daisy said as she took another sip from her cup. "And please call me Daisy."

"All the more reason to let Desi drive us to dinner at his house," Roger said.

"Am I invited too?" Linda asked.

"You and Emily are invited. Hope you like spaghetti," Desi said. "But I'm not sure if Emily knows whether to join us here or if we have to go find her."

Linda volunteered to find Emily. "How about if I go back to the press area and look for her. I have to get the suitcase I stashed in the studio anyway."

"Do you think it will fit behind the back seat of a VW?" Desi asked.

"I know it will because a guy in a VW gave us a lift up to Louisville yesterday, and he had the front hatch full, so there was no other place for my suitcase," Linda answered. "I think he had three bags of laundry stuffed in the front hatch to take to his mother's house in Ohio."

"Was he taking it home to have his mommy wash it?" Daisy asked.

"Most likely," Linda said. "I saw a posting on a university bulletin board and gave the guy a call last week. He said he would take $20 for gas money, but as we got near Louisville, he wanted more for dropping us off at Churchill Downs. Emily must have known he was going to be a jerk when he first wanted us to meet him at his frat house. Luckily, we had him pick us up Friday morning at the radio station near the university rather than at Emily's grandma's house. And we never gave him the phone number for Mama Boone's house."

"You and Emily seem to be able to discern the good guys from the jerks," Daisy said as she held her cup out for Desi to refill.

"Sometimes, but not always," Linda said. "Which reminds me, I better go locate Emily."

As she headed towards the door, Phil and Stacey walked in with Desdemona and the bartender. They were laughing as Phil and the bartender waved some cash in their hands.

Phil and the bartender walked over to Randy, who was spending his break time talking to a couple of members of the band. Phil peeled off some of the cash and held it out to Randy. Randy waved off the cash.

Stacey walked over to Desi. "Got to ask you something, dude."

"Feel free," Desi said.

"Actually, there might be a couple of issues."

"Such as…"

"Well, Phil and his buddy, Patrick, just picked the winning horse, and they have invited Desdemona and me out to dinner. They are probably going to ask Randy to come along also, considering Randy gave them the tip on 'Bold Forbes.' "

"So, what's wrong with that?" Desi asked.

"I'm a bit uncomfortable being around Randy. Desdemona thinks he is gay because he hasn't hit on her. I don't know if he is or isn't, but I think he may have said a few things in the past about me and Charlie, so I wasn't sure if he, through other people, was trying to get something going with me. Is he married?"

Desi nodded his head to indicate, "Yes."

"I would appreciate it if you would come along to the restaurant with us, even though you have already been there this weekend. Desdemona wants to go out with them but doesn't want them to pay for us. She eats there for free, and she has to stop by there to check on whether the staff of the restaurant is able to handle all of the visitors to Louisville who might somehow find the place tonight."

You mean she might have to work at the restaurant tonight after partying all day?" Desi asked.

"Yeah, but if she decides she isn't interested in Phil or his sidekick, she can claim she is needed at the restaurant. That way, hanging with these guys will not turn into an all-night thing for her. I don't want to get stuck being alone with them, particularly not with Randy, so maybe you guys can come along to the restaurant, or maybe I should just drive back to Fort Knox."

"Well, I have already invited Roger and his new friend, Daisy, along with Emmy and Linda to my place in Radcliff for dinner," Desi said.

"And you are cooking your one and only specialty – spaghetti?" Stacey asked.

"I might break things up and try making linguine tonight," Desi said with a laugh. "Please don't let on about how limited my culinary skills are."

"At least you aren't still just heating up pre-made dinners in your toaster oven."

They both laughed.

"So how much did Phil and the bartender win?" Desi asked.

"Not sure," Stacey answered. "We walked them down to the cashiers, but we didn't get the specifics on how much they won. They both made some good money working parties here yesterday. I think they bet at least a hundred each."

"I bet only ten dollars for Bold Forbes to Place. Maybe I'll just keep my winning ticket as a souvenir."

Stacey moved closer to Desi and, in a whisper, said, "Maybe I should just go back to Fort Knox."

"And you're sure you won't be leaving Desdemona in the lurch?"

"Why such a sudden concern about Desdemona?"

"I'm just impressed that she has been partying all afternoon and is not too exhausted to consider working at the restaurant tonight," Desi said.

"She is someone with a good deal of stamina, like you, Desi. She always seems to have a second wind. If you didn't already have several women interested in you, I would suggest that you take some time to find out more about my cousin. I don't think she has ever had a white boyfriend."

Desi shook his head. "I don't want to be regarded as someone's white boyfriend. I'm not going to be a Japanese girl's *Gaijin* dude, a Jewish chick's Christian fling, or a black woman's novelty pet."

"Desi, I didn't mean it that way," Stacey said with her head down. "I just don't think that Desdemona quite yet knows what type of man she is seeking."

"Well, if she is searching for her Othello, then maybe she will find some guy who looks like Moses Gunn and find happiness and intimacy rather than just wasting time sampling the ethnic and cultural novelty shops. I know I am past the point of going out with Italian women who want to try being with someone who doesn't remind them of their fathers, or Jewish women who just want to rebel against their parents. I don't want to be treated as if I am representing some sort of two-dimensional stereotype."

"Desi, you know that when you start talking about wanting genuine intimacy, you get me hotter than hell," Stacey said with a giggle.

"And Stacey, you know that whenever you say something that sounds like you want to hook up with me, it sounds like you are setting me up to be your fallback guy, who will be there if things don't work out with Charlie."

"Well, there is something special about you – for the right woman who can see past your big ego. But that's what all the guys I've ever gone out with seem to have." She walked around behind him and whispered, "Would it really hurt if you invited me over some night and let me provide my special recipe to go with that pasta?" Stacey said as she gave him a pinch on his butt. "I know I want to be more than some guy's cartoon fantasy of a Caribbean chick. I think I had that with Charlie. I just don't know what I'll find when I get to Germany. "

Randy then came over to the two of them. "Are we all going out to dinner together?"

Stacey walked around from behind Desi, and with both hands, embraced Randy's hands. "I will meet you at the restaurant. Desdemona will give you a card with the address. Desi already has plans to entertain a few people from out of town at his place."

"Maybe some other time," Desi suggested.

"Looking forward to it," Randy said.

Chapter IV

PARTYING AFTER THE DERBY

Somehow, Desi managed to get Roger to fit into the front passenger seat, with Roger's backpack on the floor between his feet and Desi's camera bag on Roger's lap. Roger's seat was not pushed all the way back, but Emily's knees were still up against the passenger seat in front of her. Linda sat in the middle of the back seat of Desi's green Super Beetle, between Emily and Daisy. They rode down Dixie Highway from Churchill Downs accompanied by an audio cassette of Al Kooper's music that Desi kept in his car. Whenever they stopped at one of the numerous stop lights on Dixie Highway, Desi would point out a business or restaurant he had patronized. Whoever was still awake would simply nod their head. When they got to the first gate of Fort Knox, Desi announced that they would soon be passing the Gold Vault; only Roger opened his eyes to get a look.

Where the commercial properties and stop lights resumed on the highway, and at the south gate of Fort Knox, was the town of Radcliff. When they got to Radcliff, about 45 minutes after leaving the parking lot at Churchill Downs, Desi looked around to see Emily and Linda taking a nap.

"Roger, I forgot to buy coffee at the grocery store," Desi said. I'm going to make a quick stop up here at Kroger. Remind me of the kind of coffee you like."

Roger roused himself. "Maybe I will come in with you," he said.

"Me too!" announced a voice from the back seat.

Desi got out and pulled the back of his driver's seat forward so Daisy could emerge from the vehicle.

"I think I have been to this grocery store before," Daisy said.

"Is this where your Aunt Arbie shops, this far away from Louisville?" Roger asked.

"Unlikely, as she doesn't own a car, and I don't think she ever learned how to drive. She could walk to her job at the telephone company from her home, and there was a grocery store she could walk to on her way home," Daisy said.

"Things don't usually get so convenient, even for most people living in Manhattan," Desi said. "So, how familiar are you with Radcliff?"

"A few years ago, a good friend of mine married an armor officer at a church near Radcliff, and they had their reception at the Officers' Club on Fort Knox. I think I got to this area a bit late for the ceremony and too early for the reception. I was hungry. I didn't see any convenience stores or delis, so I stopped here and bought some fresh fruit," Daisy explained.

"Okay," Desi said. "I think we need coffee, bananas, oranges, and some apples. Anything else?"

"Are we going to have a salad with dinner?" Daisy asked.

"I have plenty of lettuce, but perhaps I could use a tomato," Desi answered.

"Tell you what," Daisy said. "You buy some fruit for the morning, and I will buy the ingredients for my specialty salad, which I will make."

"Sounds like we have a plan," Roger said. "I'll buy a dessert that I think everyone will like." He looked at Daisy. "You do like ice cream, don't you, Daisy?"

Daisy nodded her head.

Desi chuckled.

By the time Desi, Roger, and Daisy came out of the grocery store, Emily had awakened.

Desi pulled his driver's seat forward and held the door open to let Daisy, carrying her pocketbook and a bag full of salad ingredients, back into the rear seat of his car. Desi turned to Emily and, with the bag of fruit in his right hand, offered it to Emily.

"What do you want me to do with that?" she asked.

"Can you hold onto this for a couple of minutes?" Desi asked.

"Well, not really," she replied. "I desperately have to take a pee, so I don't want to put anything on my lap. I've already put my handbag on the floor."

"I'll hold it if Emily can't," Linda said with a short laugh.

"If everyone can hold it for a few blocks, I'll have you at the house in about two or three minutes," Desi said as he started his car.

Emily crossed her legs, making her khaki skirt ride up her thighs. "I have to ask all of you to please not make me laugh," she warned. Roger got back into the VW very carefully to avoid pushing the passenger seat back against Emily's knees.

Slicing and Dicing

Desi let Daisy have a free hand with her salad. He asked Emily and Linda to cut up mushrooms and an onion before he started heating up the water for the linguine.

Desi handed Roger a bottle of red wine to open. "If anyone would prefer white wine, I have a bottle of Sauvignon Blanc."

"Roger, please open that one also," Daisy responded.

Desi, while putting on a black apron with "Shakta's" written in red script, opened a cabinet over the sink. Desi took out a bottle of white wine and placed it on the counter near where Roger was opening the red wine.

"I have some cheese in the fridge, if anyone would like some cheese and crackers as an appetizer," Desi said.

Linda finished slicing the mushrooms and went over to the refrigerator to check out Desi's cheese selection. She opened a drawer with several types of cheese, pulling out several to put on the kitchen table.

Desi handed her a cheese board and a cheese knife. She took them both and started slicing.

"Do you need anything else?" Desi asked.

Linda responded with a smile. "How about some music?"

Desi checked on whether the water in the pasta pot had started boiling. "Sure," he said before turning the heat up.

He then walked into the living room, which was right off the kitchen. "I have several Rolling Stones albums, a Traffic album, a couple by Bonnie Raitt, and…" he said with a pause. "Bonnie Raitt!" Emily, Linda, and Daisy all shouted, almost in unison,

"The Stones would be good, too," Roger said belatedly while pulling the cork on the red wine.

"Stones are always good, but Bonnie is the clear choice," Desi replied as he set the phonograph needle on a record.

Emily, Linda, and Daisy all smiled, gently swaying to the music as they continued helping with the preparation of the dinner.

Desi took a package of ground beef out of the refrigerator. "Would you guys prefer to have the linguine with meat sauce or with meatballs?"

Linda looked at Desi with a frown. "What's the matter?" he asked.

"I've been cutting back on the red meat lately," Linda said.

"I've been cutting back also," Daisy added.

Desi put the pasta in the boiling water. He took out a large saucepan and put it on one of the burners. "I have a large jar of marinara sauce. How about if I cook the onions and mushrooms, then add the marina sauce to this large pan before I divide it into another saucepan. I'll brown the meat for the meat sauce in a second pan."

"And then you'll make the meatballs?" Emily asked.

"I'll make a few," Desi said.

"Yeah, Emily wants to get two of Desi's beefy meatballs," Linda said with a laugh. Daisy covered her mouth after she also let out a laugh.

"Sure, I'm the meathead for saying anything about meat in front of Linda," Emily said as she walked out of the kitchen and into the hallway, before turning right to head out of the house through the side door.

"I better go outside and talk to her," Linda said, following right behind Emily.

Daisy, who was putting her finishing touches on the salad for dinner, looked at Desi. "I was thinking, just a moment ago, about how well we were working on dinner together. Maybe, if I dish out my salad, we could all sit down at the table together. Perhaps we could drink some wine, have some salad, and laugh with one another again, rather than having anyone feeling they were being laughed at. I didn't mean to laugh. I know I can say wacky stuff sometimes."

"Don't we all say nutty stuff?" Roger said.

Daisy went into the hallway and out the side door to talk to Emily and Linda.

Roger and Desi were alone together in the kitchen. "So, are you planning to drive anyone home tonight?" Roger asked.

Desi started heating the onions and mushrooms in a large saucepan. "Not if you can get Daisy to stay with you in the second bedroom. I think Emily and Linda can share my bed. I'll sleep on the floor in my bedroom or on the couch, unless they need me in the bed for warmth," Desi said with a smile. He added, "But I will drive Daisy back to Louisville if she needs to get back to her aunt."

Roger opened the bottle of Sauvignon Blanc. "Let's hope this is a white wine that she really likes!"

Desi stirred the mushrooms and onion pieces a few times. Roger poured himself a taste of the Sauvignon Blanc. I think I remember what they taught us in etiquette class at Kings Point. He swirled the glass, took a sniff, and then took a small sip. "I think this one's a dandy," Roger pronounced.

"Not sure that you have all the terminology right, but you did take the time to smell the 'bouquet' and not just gulp it down," Desi said.

"Maybe I should just say that it tastes like an expensive bottle of wine." Roger said before taking another sip. "Where'd you get it?"

"I received it as a gift from the parents of a young lady I know. I believe her parents are a couple of wine snobs, so it's very likely a much better wine than I would normally buy, even though I do like white wine."

"Like the kind we drank in Germany along the Mosel River?" Roger asked.

"I think that bottle is from France, but from a region not very far from the place in Germany on the Mosel where we stayed."

"What was the name of that town on the Mosel?" Roger asked.

"You mean Bernkastle-Kues?" Desi suggested.

"Yeah, that's it!" Roger said. "I want to go back there some time."

"Me too," Desi said. "If I get orders to be stationed somewhere in Germany, I will definitely go back there."

"I'll fly over on Icelandic Airlines again to meet you there," Roger said.

Desi and Roger heard the front door of the apartment open. They turned to see Emily, Linda, and Daisy step into the living room from the front lawn.

"Where are you guys meeting?" Emily asked.

"At a place in Germany, Bernkastle-Kues. It's a very quaint town on the Mosel River that produces wonderful white wine. We spent a night there during the summer of '72. If I get orders for Germany this year, Roger was saying he would visit me in Europe. Maybe we will hit Copenhagen again too," Desi said.

"You guys traveled to Europe together, as well as spent time on cargo ships going around the Far East?" Daisy asked.

"Desi, you think you might be off to Europe this year?" Emily asked.

"Where else did you guys go in Europe?" Linda asked.

Desi beckoned the women into the kitchen. "Why don't you all sit down and start in on the salad Daisy made. We can tell you more about our travels over dinner. Roger can pour the wine, and I will finish preparing the vegetarian-style pasta. We will also have available the optional, carnivore-style pasta. I am going to put some garlic bread in the toaster oven if anyone wants some bread."

"Is anyone going to say grace?" Emily asked.

"Would you like to lead us?" Desi said.

Emily looked at him. "I don't have anything prepared."

"Just pretend that you are the evening DJ for your religious radio station, and be spontaneous," Desi said.

"Ok," Emily said, sounding a bit hesitant. "Dear Lord, we thank you for providing many blessings, including the food and the company we are sharing. May we enjoy good food and each other this evening and on future occasions. Amen."

"Amen," the others repeated as Daisy blessed herself with the sign of the cross.

Roger poured and distributed the wine. Desi took a bite of the salad and got up to finish working on the pasta. He then added the marinara sauce to the pan with the onions and mushrooms. Desi turned some meatballs he was cooking in another pan. He tested a piece of the pasta and determined it was time to drain the pot of pasta.

Daisy tasted the white wine and asked for a full glass. "Desi, I really like the Sauvignon Blanc. May I see the bottle?"

Roger handed her the bottle.

"May I keep that bottle near me?" Daisy asked.

Roger quickly answered, "Sure!" He then added, "As long as it's alright with Desi."

"It's alright with me," Desi said. "As long as you leave me half a glass of it."

"That might be all you get," Daisy said with a laugh as she poured herself more of the white wine.

When Desi heard the toaster oven ring, he stood up and retrieved the garlic bread. Desi put it on a plate and offered it around.

"Wow," Emily said. "You got the bread perfect, just using a toaster oven."

"I am still learning about the stove, but I am pretty skilled when it comes to using a toaster oven."

They all laughed and had some more wine as they took bites of the garlic bread.

When the meatballs were ready, Desi put them in a bowl with a serving spoon. He distributed the pasta with the marinara sauce and invited anyone who wanted meatballs to serve themselves. He also brought over a gravy server with extra sauce for anyone who wanted it.

Daisy took a serving spoon and loaded it with a couple of meatballs. "I think I've changed my mind about the meatballs. I'm going to try a couple."

Linda took the serving spoon and also scooped up meatballs from the bowl. "I also changed my mind." She picked up the handle of the gravy server and poured the marinara sauce with the mushrooms and onion over the meatballs. She realized that everyone at the table was watching her.

"I guess I like my meatballs like I enjoy my men."

"How's that?" Daisy asked.

"Really saucy," Linda said.

"We will have to ask Desi and Roger to share some of their Merchant Marine stories," Daisy said.

They all laughed.

The phone on the wall in the kitchen rang and Desi answered it. He stretched the long cord on the handset along part of the wall in the kitchen, around the kitchen doorway, and into the hallway.

"Hello," Desi said.

"Hey, it's Stacey. What are you guys doing?"

"Hanging out in the kitchen, drinking some wine, and eating pasta. Where are you?"

"I'm at the restaurant, but I think I'll head back to Fort Knox. Randy, Phil, and the bartender guy showed up here totally drunk after stopping at a topless bar. Desdemona, who has to work, is totally turned off by the three of them. Randy keeps putting his arm around me like I am his favorite girlfriend. I keep reminding him that he has a wife, even though she is out of town for the weekend, the week, or whatever. He doesn't seem sure about when or if she is coming back. I made up some excuse about having to stop by your place tonight."

"Why an excuse? It's not like you need one to stop by."

"Well, if he calls you to ask about me, please just tell him that I sometimes stay at your place, okay?"

"I don't think he even has my telephone number," Desi said.

"Well, I think I gave him the impression that we have more than a platonic friendship. He may call you, or you'll see him sometime."

"Alright but give me a call from the barracks when you get to Fort Knox just to let me know that you are alright and that you made it there," Desi said.

"Thanks," Stacey said before hanging up.

Desi brought the handset back into the kitchen and placed it on its wall phone base.

"Everything okay?" Emily asked.

"It was Stacey. I'm not really sure, but she says she is driving back to Fort Knox and will give me a call when she gets there."

"She's the paralegal, right?" Daisy asked.

"Yeah, she and my friend Charlie lived down this hallway, in the bedroom closest to the bathroom."

"And Penny lived with you in the other bedroom, right?" Linda added.

"The blonde in the Army Band also lived with you?" Emily asked. "Somehow, I missed that. She didn't elaborate on that aspect of knowing Desi when I spoke to her."

"It isn't something she would mention because it's in the past," Desi said gruffly.

"Months ago, or weeks ago?" Emily inquired.

"Closer to a month, not just weeks ago," Desi said.

"That's a pretty poor attempt at parsing the truth," Emily admonished. She then turned to Linda. "You know what my father says about parsing the truth, right?" Linda nodded. "If you are clever enough to attempt parsing the truth, then you should be clever enough to simply keep your mouth shut. Don't insult the intelligence of others," Emily added.

"I don't think it was me parsing the truth with you," Desi responded. "You spoke to her directly, and apparently she withheld information about living with me that you believe she should have shared."

Emily looked at Linda. "What do you think?"

"I heard that Penny and Desi lived together," Linda answered. "I also suspect that Penny still cares about Desi."

"Well, she must feel very foolish to be caring about Desi after he dumped her," Emily said.

"I didn't dump her; she just left. She packed up all of her stuff one day. Everything but an old, extra flute that she said she has carried around since getting it as a present on her sixteenth birthday," Desi recounted.

"Did she take anything of yours?" Daisy asked Desi.

Desi sat thoughtfully for a couple of moments. "Maybe she took a couple of my college T-shirts. I went to Kings Point, Suffolk Community College, and Stony Brook University before earning my undergraduate degree from NYU. She used to wear some of them as nightshirts. I don't know how many she kept. How does that matter?"

Daisy said, "It would seem likely that she took those T-shirts to keep as souvenirs."

Desi shook his head. "She may have taken them, but she has probably thrown them out by now."

Emily looked at him. "Or, after only a couple of weeks, maybe she hasn't!"

Desi put his head in his hands on the kitchen table.

Roger stood up and announced, "I need an ice cream break. Anyone want to join me?"

"Yeah," Desi, Daisy, and Linda all said in unison.

Emily waited until Roger started dishing the ice cream out before she said, "Please."

As they started to eat their ice cream, Linda pulled out the joint she had tucked into her bra that afternoon. "I almost forgot!" she exclaimed before getting up and heading into the living room, where she retrieved her pocketbook off the large couch. The legs of the couch seemed to anchor the long, heavy curtains covering the front windows so they could not be easily opened. Linda took out a lighter from her pocketbook, and, after lighting up, took a toke. She carried the joint back into the kitchen and offered it to Daisy.

"I can't remember the last time anyone offered me some weed," Daisy said, taking the joint.

She took a long drag and handed it to Desi. He took it, inhaled, and passed it to Emily. Emily shook her head to indicate she was not interested. Linda, who was standing behind Emily, took the smoldering reefer from Desi, bent over, and gave Emily a shotgun blast from her lips. Linda then gave Roger a shotgun-style shot of the weed and took it over to Daisy. With their lips softly touching, Linda gave a shotgun blast to Daisy. Linda then went over to Desi and turned to Emily. "The joint is burned down pretty far. Do you want to give Desi a shotgun or can I?" she asked.

"Let me give him one that earns me a T-shirt," Emily said. She motioned for Desi to push his chair back from the table. With her khaki skirt riding up her long legs, Emily straddled Desi's chair and sat on his lap. She reached out and took the joint from Linda's hand. Emily then took a long drag on the joint and wrapped her lips against Desi's. Emily then filled his lungs with the smoke she had inhaled. Their lips seemed to be joined together for a couple of minutes.

When they finally separated their lips and opened their eyes, they continued to stare at each other until Emily broke the silence. "Well?"

"Well, what?" Desi replied.

"Well, do I get to pick out one of your T-shirts?" Emily asked as she moved slowly up from Desi's lap, pulling the skirt back down as she straightened her legs.

"You certainly do," Desi said as he led her to his bedroom and closed the bedroom door.

Daisy poured the remainder of the bottle of Sauvignon Blanc into her glass and took a long sip. "That certainly made me thirsty. She stood up and gave Linda a kiss on the cheek. "Thank you, Linda. You really know how to get a party going."

Linda looked at Daisy. "Thanks for joining in on the party."

Daisy laughed with almost a girlish giggle. "I don't know when I last partied like this. But I may not remember this party tomorrow."

Linda took a pitcher of ice water on the counter and poured a tall glass for Daisy. "Drink some of this so you don't get a headache."

Daisy took a long drink of the water. She looked at Roger. "Roger, I need to get something out of my pocketbook. In what room did you put my pocketbook?"

"It's in the second bedroom, the door right before the bathroom," Roger answered.

"Come on and show me where in the room you put it," Daisy said, practically pulling Roger out of his chair.

Roger smiled at Linda, saying, "Excuse me," before following Daisy.

Linda served herself another scoop of ice cream. She was pulling out plastic food containers from under the sink, to put the extra food away, when the phone in the kitchen rang again.

On the fourth or fifth ring, Desi came out of his bedroom wearing just a pair of blue gym shorts. He smiled at Linda and grabbed the phone.

"Yeah," Linda heard Desi say before he paused for a moment. "Yeah," he said again, then another pause, and another "Yeah."

"I didn't know if you wanted me to answer the phone, so I didn't," Linda said after Desi hung up the phone.

"I appreciate your discretion, but it was only Stacey calling back," Desi said.

"After talking with Tammy this afternoon, I thought it might be Debi calling you from Texas," Linda said.

"Texas?" Desi asked.

"I guess Tammy didn't tell you that Debi flew from Chicago to Texas to meet with their uncle, their father, and the authorities in Texas to file a missing persons report on the mother. They think the mother is flying around with some South American cattle rancher," Linda said.

"Oh, the guy who used to be the modeling manager for their mother in Brazil? I heard about him, but I don't think there is much that Debi can do to help locate her mother. She only might serve to get her father and her uncle to talk with one another." Desi looked at Linda, trying to gauge how much she knew, before adding, "Their mother seems to be going through some midlife crisis. She is being very inconsiderate about the impact she is having on other people."

"Desi, some people might say you are inconsiderate if you don't decide whether or not you love Tammy's sister, Debi. It's like you don't want to stop making other women think that your heart is up for grabs," Linda said with her hands on her hips.

"But I'm not going through a midlife crisis," Desi said with a smile.

"I was trying to be serious with you for a minute," Linda said as she threw up her hands and walked away from Desi.

"Alright, I don't feel that Debi loves me anymore, or at least not like she did in the past. Anything less than what it was a couple of years ago won't keep me from looking for somebody else," Desi admitted.

"I just hope you don't get Emily falling for you and then lose interest in her if you think it's really Debi you still want in your life," she said, moving in closer to him.

"Emily is still hoping to get her old boyfriend out of jail, and if she doesn't get back together with him, then she is probably going to be with that lawyer, the family friend, the guy she had breakfast with this morning. Emily is not seeing any long-term thing with me," Desi said while shaking his head.

Linda reached out and held his head between her hands. "She's not? Right now, she is in your bed, in some stage of undress. She is afraid of making a fool of herself by falling for you, but I don't know if she can help it. Emily, for better or worse, needs to be around someone like you at this point in her life," Linda said while stabbing Desi with one of her index fingers into his bare chest, just above his heart.

"She may like the way I look, or talk, but I think I have pissed her off a couple of times since we have been here in Radcliff."

"Do you know what she just confided in me outside in your yard?" Linda said as she moved in closer to Desi, as if sharing her deepest secret. "When you came to the studio at Churchill Downs this afternoon, she said you both seemed to be 'on the same wavelength.' " Linda started to gently run her hands through Desi's chest hair with both hands. "Emily told me that after you had a discussion with her for just a few minutes, you had her gushing over the radio that she had 'experienced some real magic at the Derby and found someone to share it with.'" Linda took his hands and put them on her ample cleavage, which seemed to be on the verge of bursting out of the top of her yellow Derby dress.

Without looking at her chest or succumbing to the temptation to massage her breasts, he examined the expression on Linda's face for some hint of what she needed before he asked Linda for what he wanted. "Can you get me a transcript or tape of what Emily said in that vulnerable moment? I want to know if it was said with real passion, or if it was merely for consumption by her parents."

"Desi, she already suspects that you want to get a tape or a transcript of what she said, but I don't think I can get it for you. She feels that if you find out what she said on air, it might make her seem pathetic, and that you will walk or run away. And now she hears that you might be getting orders to go to Germany for a year or so. It won't help her if all you want her for is sex." Linda lowered a hand down to Desi's crotch. "You aren't intending to spear me with that thing, are you?"

Desi removed his hands from Linda's breasts. "I think Stacey is going to be arriving here any minute," Desi said. "I should go check on Emily. If she is awake, she may be wondering where I went. Thanks for not answering the phone. But the fact that it wasn't Debi and that I don't know where she is right now should support what I've said about how limited my contact with her is at this point. And I am not looking to hurt Emily. I honestly feel that she could become an important person in my life, and that, maybe, I could be a positive influence in her life."

"Well, according to Tammy, you had sex with Debi in the hotel room where Emily, you, and I slept last night. Tammy thinks the only reason you didn't get it on with Emily or me, or both of us, was because Debi took care of your business earlier in the day," Linda said.

"That sounds like some sort of resentment from Tammy," Desi answered. "I'll remember not to use her as a character reference."

"Tammy claims she has never had sex with you, nor did she ever really want to have sex with you. She delighted in telling me what she says is the 'true full story' about how she spotted you and used you for her own purposes."

Desi raised his eyebrows. "She's correct about the 'never had sex' part, but Debi and I spotted one another weeks before when Tammy claims she first introduced us. And nothing Tammy has ever done, including telling me to go out and say hello to her sister, who was sitting by their parents' pool, was ever done out of the goodness of Tammy's heart. When there is time, I will be happy to debunk that fanciful story Tammy tells people. Right now, before Stacey gets here, I better get some more clothes on."

"Yeah, that bulge could also complicate your relationship with Stacey," Linda said.

Desi opened the door of his bedroom and went inside without turning on the overhead light. He had previously left the room with Emily on the bed wearing just her panties. Desi turned on a small night light to see Emily asleep, wearing one of his NYU T-shirts over her panties.

Desi found a pair of blue jeans and a collared short-sleeved shirt. After pulling his jeans over his gym shorts, Desi reached for some footwear inside a closet near the bedroom door. A flute case spilled out of the closet when he pulled on some flip-flops at the bottom of the closet. He pushed the container with the musical instrument back in with one hand while grabbing an assortment of flip-flops. Even with limited lighting, Desi managed to get one for his left foot and one for the right that seemed to be close to the same color.

As Desi left the bedroom, there was a knock on the side door. After making sure his bedroom door was fully closed, he then took a couple steps to the side door. Desi flipped the switch for the outside light and saw Stacey. He unlocked the door and let her in.

"You locked the door?" Stacey said with some amazement.

"I didn't want any of the nosey neighbors trying to break in on our dinner party. I already caught that woman next door looking in the windows this week," Desi said.

"Her husband invited Charlie to come over and go skinny dipping in their hot tub with them last summer, before you lived here. Maybe they will invite you this summer," Stacey said as she stepped into the kitchen.

Linda was standing by the sink, drying plates. Her Derby attire was a bit askew, with much of her bra and a good deal of her cleavage showing, but she had her back to Stacey.

Stacey looked around. "Doesn't look or sound much like a party here."

"I could get back into the partying spirit if you've brought anything to party with," Linda said, turning around to face Stacey.

"Yes, it looks like you could," Stacey said. She took a glance at Desi. "I think you said something about drinking some wine when I called from Louisville. My throat feels parched right now."

"I can fix you up with something to take care of that. I have red and white wine, tequila, bourbon, and some Irish whiskey," Desi said.

"How about Irish whiskey with some ice cubes?" Stacey said.

"Make that two," Linda said as she adjusted the top of her dress.

"I'll get out three glasses," Desi said as he lifted a bottle of Jameson out of a cabinet.

While Stacey, Linda, and Desi sat at the kitchen table drinking the Irish whiskey, all of a sudden, they heard a moaning and groaning sound coming from down the hallway.

Stacey's face lit up. "Now it sounds like a party," she said as she held up her glass. "Noise from the noisy girl's room."

Linda looked at Stacey as she asked, "The noisy girl's room?"

"That's what we call it," Desi replied in brief.

Stacey nodded her head. "I have an admission as to how that started. I was the 'noisy girl.' There could be music and partying in the living room, but the people in the kitchen always seemed to know when Charlie and I disappeared to his bedroom."

"So Desi started calling you the noisy girl?"

"No," Stacey said. "I think it started with one of the Twins."

"The who?" Linda asked.

"Two beautiful brunettes, Kathy and Brenda, who are helicopter repair mechanics at Godman Field," Stacey said.

"Where is that?" Linda asked as she finished her drink.

"At Fort Knox," Stacey said.

Linda thought for a moment before pouring herself some more Irish whiskey. "I have been to the Patton Museum at Fort Knox, but I don't think I ever saw an airfield."

Stacey looked over to Desi. "Isn't Godman Field in one of the last scenes in the movie *Goldfinger*?"

"Yeah, there is a Presidential jet outside a hangar at Godman, or what was made to look like Godman," Desi said. "James

Bond gets on the jet thinking that he's going to Washington to get some award or reward, but the jet has been hijacked by Auric Goldfinger. Fortunately for 007, he ends up getting 'rewarded' by Honor Blackman's character."

Linda nodded her head. "Well, rewarded, as I recall. At the Patton Museum, I think I saw the model of the gold vault used in the movie."

Stacey poured herself some more Irish whiskey. "Desi took one of the Twins, Kathy, to the Patton Museum one afternoon, which led to an adventure with an Army helicopter pilot buzzing Desi's car between Radcliff and Elizabethtown."

Desi held his hand up in an effort to stop Stacey. "It was somebody we knew. He wasn't going to hit my car with the helicopter, certainly not with Kathy inside," Desi said.

"Now I want to hear the whole story," Linda said.

Stacey took out a joint from her pocketbook and lit it up. After taking a toke, she handed it to Linda. Linda took a long drag and offered it to Desi.

Desi shook his head. "I still have to get a few things out of my car, including Linda's suitcase." Desi then got up from the table and walked out of the kitchen, through the living room, and out the front door.

"So, where were we?" Linda asked, handing the joint to Stacey.

"Desi is in his car with Kathy. They are heading south from Fort Knox towards Elizabethtown," Stacey said before stopping to take a hit. "But maybe I have to back up. Kathy had been going out with the helicopter pilot, a warrant officer, for a while, and we all knew them both. Around the time of the previous Thanksgiving, Brenda was asked by Jeff, the helicopter pilot, who he should talk to in their family about proposing to Kathy around Christmas. Well, the twins' parents have been divorced for some time. They didn't have much contact with their mother, who had recently gotten remarried and moved from their hometown in Ohio. They haven't been in contact with their biological dad for years. The facts are that the two of them are in their early twenties, they have good jobs that should get them good salaries in the civilian world after the Army, and their 'family' really is just each other. Brenda tells Jeff that she is happy for them. She consents on behalf of the family and says she will give away her sister at the wedding."

"Sounds good so far. So, what happens next?" Linda asked while taking another toke and handing the joint to Stacey.

"Well, shit usually happens, right?" Stacey said while taking a hit. "Brenda tells us that Jeff and Kathy are getting engaged. Everyone wants to have a party. Christmas comes and goes, and Kathy still doesn't have a ring. A paralegal friend moves out of the house in mid-December and Desi moves in. New Year's Eve comes along, and we are having one of the biggest parties we ever had here to celebrate. As midnight approaches, we have a few of the helicopter pilots who flew in Vietnam celebrating with us at the house, including one who goes out the front door, takes off all of his clothes, and then comes back and walks through the party naked. But there's no Jeff. He doesn't show. Kathy is crying by 11:30. She is drinking and getting really blasted. Brenda is by her side, trying to convince her that everything is alright – that everything will work out for the best. Midnight comes and everyone is hugging and kissing, except Kathy. Desi is sort of going out with Penny, but Penny doesn't want anyone to know they are dating. I think they went up to Louisville for a couple of dates they had in December. Anyway, they give each other friendly-type kisses. Desi kisses Brenda, and when he turns to Kathy, she grabs him and gives him a real lip lock. Desi doesn't really say much, but a couple of days later, he hears from Brenda that Kathy needs to go out. Brenda wants to know if Desi will take Kathy to a movie on post. They go out, and Kathy has a few laughs with Desi. She seems like she is feeling better. She tells everyone that Jeff has a new assignment down at Fort Campbell, doing something with a helicopter flight simulator project, and that they are moving on with their lives. Desi goes out with Kathy a few more times, sometimes with Brenda riding along."

Stacey poured herself more of the Irish whiskey and drank it down in one shot. "Then, Jeff starts telling people that it was Brenda who screwed everything up. Something about Brenda wanting to take control of planning the wedding, not wanting Kathy to have a church wedding, and not getting along with his mother and father, who are very traditional and wanted a church wedding."

Linda took multiple hits on the joint as Stacey kept talking.

"Desi may have been meeting up with Penny in Louisville, but around Fort Knox, he was either with Kathy alone or with Kathy and her sister. So, Valentine's Day is coming up, and on an almost spring-like day, the weekend before Valentine's Day, Desi and Kathy are spotted together at the Patton Museum. Somebody gets word to Jeff as he is flying up from Fort Campbell. Jeff has decided that he is going to propose to Kathy and that the two of them will plan their own wedding, for as soon as they can make the arrangements. Jeff hears that Kathy might be heading towards Desi's apartment in Radcliff. Then, another pilot tells him they are parked in Radcliff near one of the motels. I am not sure if the other helicopter pilots were just trying to make him crazy, but they ended up getting him to follow Desi's car south towards Elizabethtown. Supposedly, he lowers the helicopter down to where he is practically alongside Desi's car, and signals Desi to pull over. Desi pulls off the highway and into a big empty parking lot. Jeff lands and hops out of the helicopter. He comes over to Desi's car and politely asks Kathy if he can speak with her. They talk along the roadside. Jeff gets down on a knee and proposes to her. Kathy accepts his proposal, and they go back to Desi's car. Jeff then politely asks Desi if he would drive Kathy up to Godman, where he wants Desi to take a picture of him down on one knee proposing to Kathy again."

Stacey grabbed what was left of the joint from Linda and took a hit.

"Does Desi take the picture?" Linda asked.

"Desi says he was happy to take that picture. I think there is a copy of it somewhere around here," Stacey said. "Desi never brought Kathy here to spend the night or did anything but help her get through a very tough few weeks."

"I'm sorry if I was bogarting your pot while you were telling that tale," Linda said. "I'm trying to figure out if and how Desi got rewarded for his good deed."

"I don't know the answer. Maybe, sometime, you can get him to tell you his perspective on what happened and ask him if he got rewarded in some way," Stacey said.

Desi then entered through the side door carrying Linda's suitcase and a couple of bags she had also put behind his seat.

"What took you so long?" Stacey asked. "You missed my retelling of the story of Kathy and Jeff."

"Something fell out of one of the bags and rolled under my car. It looks like something that Tammy may have given to Linda." Desi held up a prescription bottle with Tammy's name on it. "It is labeled to look like it was something prescribed by a doctor, but I've looked inside, and it looks like coke."

Linda looked at Desi with a pained expression. "You aren't going to tell Emily, are you? Tammy warned me about you hating people who do coke. I haven't done it with a guy in over a year and I thought there might be a chance I could change your mind this weekend."

Desi held up the bottle. "Do you know how many chemicals this crap gets mixed with before it even gets into the United States? I heard you agreed on two rules when living with Emily: no sex with married guys, and no cocaine."

"Well, Stacey says you aren't married," Linda said while forcing a smile. "That's something, right?"

Stacey took the prescription bottle out of Desi's hand. She opened it and dipped in her pinky before pulling it out again. "I think Desi's right. It seems like you have cocaine. I think Desi should warn Emily that you are carrying it around with you." She handed the container back to Desi.

"Tammy was searching for someone at Churchill Down who would get her some. I know this because she asked Desdemona, who was a bit pissed off with having some white chick asking her about coke within a few minutes of meeting her. We thought Tammy would be cool partying with us and just enjoying our pot. Guess we were wrong about her. We may be wrong about you, Linda," Stacey said.

"Hey, I didn't do any blow with Tammy. She did some with the guy who got it for her. She gave this to me because she didn't want to get on a plane with it," Linda said.

"Great," Desi said. "This is one of the reasons I hate the whole coke scene. Some innocent person gets stuck having it in their car or in their house. You were planning to take this back to Emily's house?"

"No. I was hoping to do it with some dude before I even got back to Emily's," Linda said.

"Well, it is not going to be me," Desi said.

Suddenly, more moaning and groaning came from the noisy girl's room. As they stood looking at one another, Desi was still holding the prescription bottle.

Then, Desi's bedroom door burst open, and out stumbled Emily, with her hair all tousled, still wearing just the NYU T-shirt and panties. "What's with all the noise?" Emily asked.

Desi put the prescription bottle in his pocket. "I'll put some music on," he said as he walked into the living room to put on an Allman Brothers album. When he returned to the kitchen, he put the tea kettle on the stove. Stacey was sitting at the table with an envelope in front of her. Desi sat down next to her. Emily came over and sat down on the other side of Desi.

"Have you opened it?" Desi asked Stacey.

"No. I haven't checked my mailbox at the barracks for the past couple of days. I guess I have been afraid that it may be too late to get Charlie back in my corner. Afraid that even if I got my orders and made it to Germany, he might make excuses about why we are not going to be able to see each other every weekend."

"At least you now know that you have orders for Germany. That's a plus," Desi said.

Stacey continued. "Well, I got back to the barracks tonight, feeling a bit ticked off about not having received a letter for about two weeks and wondering if I was ever going to be able to speak to him again. I avoided the mailboxes on the way upstairs to my room. My roommate was there with several of her friends, mostly women who I had met before. My roommate doesn't really say hello. Just says something about not expecting to see me back tonight. I go back to the staircase and start walking down. A young guy, who I haven't ever seen before, started up the staircase for the women's side of the barracks. I asked him who he was looking for. He says that he was looking for me and raps on with a bunch of nonsense. I continued to walk down the stairs and into the day room and started talking to a couple of people by the pool tables. The guy on the staircase follows me. I pretend to watch TV in the dayroom. He stays by one of the pool tables watching me look at the TV. It's then, and only then, that I make the decision to face whatever is in my mailbox. I am not sure what is worse: getting no letter, or a letter that doesn't have anything I want to read. I couldn't bring myself to read this in the dayroom. I didn't want to take it back to my room with my roommate and her assembled female friends."

"So, now you have a letter from Charlie," Desi said as he put a hand on her arm. "I'll fix you some tea and bring you a cup in the living room. When you're ready to read it, we'll be here if there is anything you want to share."

Stacey stood up and, with a sweep of her hand over the kitchen table, she secured the envelope between two fingers and fiddled with it while slowly walking into the living room. She then let it drop on the coffee table. Stacey sat on the couch, staring at the envelope in front of her.

Desi pulled from a cabinet a fancy Japanese tea set that one of the prior tenants had left behind. He poured enough hot water from the tea kettle into the teapot to make tea for everyone, and then put three bags of green tea in the teapot.

When he brought a cup of the tea into the living room, he saw Stacey reading the letter. She had tears streaming down her face. Stacey had two pages of the letter face down on the coffee table and held two more pages in her hand. Desi put Stacey's teacup on the table and turned to go back into the kitchen.

"Please sit down with me, Desi. I'm almost on the last page," Stacey said, while not revealing anything with the tone of her voice.

Desi sat down on the couch about two feet away from Stacey.

When Stacey turned to the final page, Desi noticed her face brighten. Stacey seemed to bounce from where she had been sitting to the cushion where Desi was sitting, knocking him onto an armrest. Desi exaggerated the impact by collapsing onto the floor. Stacey jumped on top of him to pin down Desi's outstretched arms with her knees. Desi remained lifeless while Stacey kissed him on one cheek, then the other cheek, and then on his forehead.

Emily and Linda got up from the kitchen table and watched from where the carpet of the living room met the linoleum of the kitchen. Stacey sat on Desi's chest, shouting, "Charlie still loves me," for over a minute. Desi managed to roll over onto his stomach and get to his knees and elbows, only to have Stacey sit on his back. He then lifted himself and Stacey up so that she rode him, piggyback style, for one or two loops around the coffee table. Then, Desi leaned over the couch so that Stacey would fall back onto the couch. While lying there, Stacey reached over to the coffee table and grabbed the four pages of the letter.

Linda looked over to Emily. "It's a multi-page letter. That's usually a good sign."

"Not always for me," Emily said, looking at Linda. "Why are you still wearing your Derby costume?"

"Desi only brought my suitcase out of his car a few minutes ago," Linda said.

"What have you guys been doing? Your dress looks rumbled. Has Desi been giving you both piggyback rides?" Emily asked.

"Stacey was sharing a joint with me and telling a very interesting story about Desi, who went out with a woman a few times and ended up helping her get a marriage proposal from a helicopter pilot," Linda said.

"Did she have more stories about Desi having a similar effect on women? Getting them to want to marry someone else?" Emily asked.

"I don't know if that was the point of the story," Linda said.

"Maybe you can share it with me some time," Emily added as she watched Desi and Stacey once again sit on the couch together. "It looks like Desi has again succeeded in driving a woman to seriously think about getting married, only to someone else."

"Emily, what is that saying?" Linda asked. "Always the groomsman but never the groom?"

"That may be Desi," Emily mused. "Never the groom, needing more room, fearing some bliss-less doom."

Linda laughed. "Desi, Emma Lee has a poem for you."

"Well then, I have a whole book of Victorian poetry that may inspire her further," Desi said as he looked through the books and assorted magazines kept in storage boxes within the coffee table.

Stacey folded up her letter and put it back into the envelope. "Are you sure that Charlie didn't take it with him to Germany?"

"I bought the book in Louisville and let him borrow it to give him ideas of what to write to you from Germany, like that poem about love and sleep," Desi said as he continued his search.

After finding the book, he flopped himself back onto the couch and thumbed through its pages. Emily walked over and sat next to him. "Sometimes we would use an English Victorian poem in the book that was very prim and proper as a base to launch into something that was a bit raunchy," Desi explained to Emily. "And sometimes we would use a poem as if it was in Mad Lib format and replace key nouns and verbs. We had a woman here at one of our parties, who we never heard use a four-letter word, so we got her to agree to read aloud a poem that was laced with nasty words and sexual innuendo."

Stacey, standing on the other side of the coffee table from where Desi and Emily were sitting, motioned to Desi to give her the book, which Desi did. "Desi was our go-to guy when we needed some good sexual innuendo," Stacey said.

"I can believe that," Emily said as she put an arm around Desi. As she moved in closer to Desi, her NYU T-shirt hiked up even higher so that it barely covered her panties. Desi put a hand on her bare left thigh.

Stacey let out a shriek. "I found it!" she said. "And yes, Charlie put a modified version in his letter."

Stacey began to read:

"A Love so wonderful and so right,
While lying asleep between strokings in the night,
I saw my Lover lean over to be sure I was not dead.
Her dusky hand like a lily's leaf swept my head,
Smooth-skinned and darkish, with a bare throat made to bite.
Too late for any blushing – we would wrestle but not fight,
She is perfect-colored without red or white,
And her lips open amorously, bringing my whole being Delight.
All of her body is, to my mouth, like honey,
Her hot hands warm my skin and make my soul sunny.
The quivering flanks, hair smelling of Islands in the Stream,
Our footprints in the sand, captured in the surge of a shared dream."

"Is that the original Victorian poem that you read, or was it with added sexual content," Emily asked Stacey.

Stacey laughed. "I read it with all the changes that Desi, Charlie, and I made after a tequila party here one night. "I am going to look through this book for any other strokes of genius we came up with," Stacey said as she walked around the coffee table and joined them on the couch.

Desi gave her a look of surprise. "You are going to fall asleep on the couch. Do you want to spend the night here?"

"I pretty much have to spend the night because Charlie is calling me here in the morning. Did I forget to tell you about that part of the letter?" Stacey asked.

Desi got up off the couch. "I guess we should open up the couch, so you have a bed when you are ready to go to sleep. I'll get you some sheets for the sofa bed," Desi said as he walked to his bedroom.

Stacey asked Emily to help her move the coffee table out of the way. The two of them had lifted and moved the table by the time Desi returned.

Emily was taking the cushions off the sofa so they could open the bed. Under one of the cushions, she discovered a copy of *Cosmopolitan*. "Whose copy of *Cosmo* is this?" she said while holding up the magazine. Linda came over to the couch and took it from Emily's hand. Linda started reading the cover, which noted the articles inside.

"Sounds like every article is about sex," Emily said.

"I think it belongs to the twins – Kathy and Brenda. What do you think, Desi?" Stacey asked while starting to lift the frame on one side of the sofa bed.

"Probably," Desi said as he gave an upward tug on the other side of the bed frame. Stacey and Desi then unfolded the bed.

"Who are the twins?" Emily asked.

"One is the woman in the story about the proposal from a helicopter pilot. The other is probably still reading *Cosmo* to get to sleep at night, like me," Stacey said.

"Are we sleeping with Desi again tonight?" Linda asked.

"As far as I know, he's sleeping in his bed tonight and we aren't sleeping on the couch," Emily replied.

"I think Desi is upset with me," Linda revealed. "I'm not sure if he wants to share his bed with me."

"What is that all about?" Emily asked.

Linda took a deep breath. "I'm not sure that it is something I want to give you all the details on. I was thinking about doing something that Desi knew you would not approve of," she added.

Emily put both hands on her hips. "How can you just leave it like that? Of course, I am going to want to know the details."

"I'm going to get changed in Desi's bedroom," Linda said, picking up her suitcase. "Let him tell you what happened, and the two of you can tell me how to resolve the issue."

"It seems like you are intent upon making things mysterious," Emily said. "Will Desi be able to fill me in on everything that happened?"

"I think he can, so my fate is pretty much in his hands," Linda said. "He can tell you everything," Linda said before a slight pause. "Or he can tell you nothing at all if he's chalking it up as nothing more than a misunderstanding."

Emily looked at Linda. "Is this going to get me really upset?"

Linda looked right back at her. "It's all up to what Desi tells you."

"That is a great way to leave it, Linda," Emily said with a sarcastic sneer.

"Emmy, I am not going to incriminate myself. I think Tammy Tompkins may have set me up," Linda said as she left the living room and headed for Desi's bedroom.

Emily looked at Desi. "Is Linda in some legal trouble?"

"Did she tell you she was?" he nonchalantly replied.

"Now you are doing it to me. Can't one of you tell me what happened? She wants to leave it to you to tell me," Emily said as she grabbed the top of her head with both hands and pushed her long fingers through her hair.

Desi sat quietly for a moment. "You, Linda, and I should meet in the bathroom, and I will show you something that Tammy Tompkins gave Linda at Churchill Downs."

"It's not a naked picture of you, is it, Desi?" Emily asked, as she attempted a smile.

"It's more complicated than that," Desi said.

Emily then went into Desi's bedroom, where she found Linda sitting on the end of the bed, crying.

"Desi wants to meet us in the bathroom," Emily announced while standing in the doorway.

"Does he know how sick I feel? I might be ready to throw up," Linda said as she slowly stood up.

"All the better that we are meeting in the bathroom," Emily said coldly. She took a hard look at Linda. "Is that why you are wearing that crappy-looking 'Mammoth Cave' T-shirt?"

"It is a bit faded," Linda said while looking down at the wrinkled dull-green front of her T-shirt.

Emily took Linda by the hand, leading her out of the bedroom and down the hallway towards the bathroom. As they approached, out of the bathroom came Stacey, who immediately read Linda's T-shirt.

"Mammoth Cave. That sounds like a destination for people wanting to do it outside but don't want to risk getting rained on.

"Actually, there are a number of spots in Mammoth Cave where you could do it, but might get dripped on," Linda said absentmindedly.

Desi came into the hallway from the kitchen.

Stacey pointed out the "Mammoth Cave" T–shirt to Desi. "What sexual innuendo is that Desi?"

Desi shook his head, saying, "Be nice."

Desi, Emily, and Linda were in the bathroom for over a minute before anyone said anything.

Linda started things off with, "Are you guys going to be nice to me?"

"I guess it depends," Desi said.

"Depends on what?" Linda asked.

"Depends on what you intend to do with this," Desi said, holding up a medicine bottle with Tammy Tompkins' name on it.

"What is that?" Emily asked.

Desi looked at Linda, saying, "Go ahead and tell Emily what's inside."

"I am not sure," Linda said. "I really don't know."

"So, you won't care if I dump whatever is inside of this bottle into the toilet?" Desi asked.

"Maybe Tammy Tompkins might care, but I don't," Linda said.

Desi unscrewed the top of the bottle. "Ok, then I will just pour it into the toilet," he said as he slowly poured out the white power so that it created a thin white film on the toilet bowl water.

Emily looked at Linda, and then at Desi. "Should we have Linda flush that shit?"

Desi nodded his head and then moved so Linda could reach the handle of the toilet. Linda quickly pushed the handle down.

Linda looked at Desi. "Now, will you give me one of your T-shirts to wear tonight? I don't want to feel any uglier than I feel right now."

"Sure, you have your choice of what's left," Desi said.

"Do you have any 'Grateful Dead' T-shirts?" Linda asked.

"I might have a 'Europe '72' T-shirt buried away in a drawer," Desi replied.

"You and Roger saw the Dead in Europe?" Emily asked.

"No. We were only close enough to see people selling T-shirts in cities where they had played or were scheduled to play. But other friends of mine, true Deadheads, actually followed them around Europe and saw them in a few cities," Desi explained.

"I got to see the Dead a couple times in California," Linda said.

"I don't think I even have one of their albums," Emily mused.

"Well, maybe that's why you never did acid," Linda said. "If you didn't hang with Deadheads and didn't buy any Dead records, it almost certainly limits your access to hallucinogens."

Linda looked at Desi. "How many Dead records and how many hallucinogens did you have?"

Desi held up one finger.

There was a knock on the bathroom door.

"We'll be out in two seconds," Desi said.

Desi opened the door to allow Linda and Emily to file out. He noticed the curious look on Daisy's face as they passed her. "I was just showing them how to work the shower so that the tub doesn't fill up with water."

Daisy looked at him with a smile. "I thought you might be trying to get them to help save on hot water by showering together with you."

Desi called out to Linda and Emily, "Ladies, did you hear Daisy's suggestion about how we can save hot water tomorrow morning?"

Linda turned. "Desi, you are going to be so warm tonight sleeping between the two of us that we are just going to take you outside and hose you down."

"What will the neighbors say?" Daisy said as she shut the bathroom door.

Linda and Emily went into Desi's bedroom. Desi stepped into the bedroom and pointed to the draw containing shorts and T-shirts. He then went into the living room to check on Stacey.

Stacey was on the sofa bed, rereading the letter from Charlie. She looked up at Desi. "I understand what you said about not wanting to be somebody's 'white boyfriend.' This letter makes it very clear that Charlie loves me for reasons beyond what I look like and what other people assume about me. He knows me and is interested in growing with me, so that I can be better than I am today."

"I don't think that people would see too much about you in need of improving," Desi said as he sat at the foot of the sofa bed. "Not only are you physically attractive but you are accomplished enough that even with all the thousands of people in the Army, you got picked for what is probably going to be a choice assignment in Germany."

Stacey looked at Desi. "And what about you? I know you want to go to Europe because Armed Force Radio and Television in Europe now has color TV studios, but do you really think that is going to make you a better writer or just an attractive talking head? I'm afraid they will end up wasting your creative talent."

Desi looked at her before speaking. "Part of the reason I joined the Army was the opportunity to do some more traveling. But there is a serious side to young people like us going overseas. I was covering an AUSA convention in Washington a few months ago, and most of the discussions seemed to focus on Europe. Most of the speakers expressed a sense of there still being a need for a lot of work to be done with our NATO allies. There was even a retired general, who got the George Marshall Award, talking about the role of the United States in strengthening democracy. Once you get to Germany, I am sure you are going to have opportunities to travel all around Europe, sometimes with Charlie. You will be the human face of one of the two superpowers in the world today."

"And you, Desi, may be the human face I recognize when I turn on Armed Forces TV in Europe."

Desi stood up. "Let's make every effort to be good ambassadors of the best things our country is about."

"And you will make sure that I will get weekly copies of *Inside the Turret* so I can stay updated as to the happenings at Fort Knox and what you are writing about?" Stacey asked.

Desi nodded his head. "Sure, at least as long as I am at Fort Knox."

Desi started walking to the kitchen but turned to Stacey before he reached the refrigerator. "Stacey, I forgot to tell you. Roger bought some ice cream."

Stacey smiled. "So, now he has opted for the subtle approach?"

"You were right," Desi said. "That approach seems to be working for him."

Chapter V

OFF TO BARDSTOWN

When Sunday morning arrived, Desi once again woke up in-between Emily and Linda.

As Desi sat up in his bed, Emily began to stir. She opened her eyes and gave him a wonderful smile that seemed to shine across her face so effortlessly. "Did you sleep well?" Emily asked.

"How could I not when dreaming about being with you?" Desi said as he leaned over and gave her a kiss on the cheek.

"That's the best you can do after I spend the night in your bed, waiting for a real kiss?" Emily responded.

When Desi lifted up the sheet, he saw Emily's navel and midsection exposed between the T-shirt and her panties. He put his head underneath the sheet and playfully imparted a series of kisses around her navel.

Emily started to giggle.

Linda began to stir. "What the hell are you guys doing?" she said with a groan.

Desi emerged from under the sheet so that he was face to face with Emily. Desi's body was resting on top of Emily. "I am getting up to go brush my teeth," Desi announced.

Emily threw her arms around his head and pulled him down, so they were nose to nose. "I don't want to wait; I want it right now!" Emily said as she pulled his lips down to her own.

"Just get it over with so I can go back to sleep," Linda pleaded. She looked at her watch. "It's not even seven o'clock," she added. "The phone rang at about five-thirty. It sounded like Stacey who answered it. But I had a hard time getting back to sleep."

Desi slipped himself off the bed and headed for the bathroom. Emily gave chase and practically pushed Desi against the hallway wall to get to the bathroom before him. She went into the bathroom and shut the door in his face. Desi knocked on the door. "You will just have to wait," Emily responded.

Desi waited, but when he heard the sound of water running in the sink, he knocked again. After hearing the toilet flush, the door opened and he saw Emily standing by the sink, toothbrush in hand.

"I thought we could save some water by brushing our teeth together," Emily said with a grin.

Desi pulled his toothbrush out of the toothbrush holder on the sink. Emily took a look at his toothbrush and hers. Her toothbrush was white with a blue stripe, and Desi's was blue with a white stripe. "I was afraid that we might be incompatible in the toothbrush department," Emily said. "But it looks like we're more than okay."

"You mean the type or color?" Desi asked.

"I guess I would be concerned if they were both exactly the same color, then I could never move in with you. We wouldn't be able to distinguish one from the other," Emily said.

"You're thinking of moving in sometime soon?" Desi asked.

"You kept me warm, and I did get a very restful sleep last night," Emily said.

"Would you be moving in with Linda too?" Desi asked.

"She might want to move in also, or just move in without me," Emily replied.

"Well, the water and the heating bills for all the hot showers would then be through the roof," Desi said as he finished brushing his teeth. He then walked over to the tub and turned on the shower. "I guess I need to know what your compatibility is when it comes to saving on hot water."

"In one of our bathrooms in my parents' house, we used to have one of those refrigerator magnets from the '60s, saying something about saving water by showering with a friend," Emily said as she pulled the T-shirt over her head. "I think it was my brother's."

Desi adjusted the temperature of the water and pulled off his gym shorts, so he was naked with his back to Emily. "Well, let's see if we can have a friendly shower and try to save water," he said as he stepped into the tub. The shower water splashed onto his shoulders.

"Is it warm?" Emily asked as she put a foot over the side of the tub to test the water.

"We don't have time to get things really hot because everyone will want to get into the bathroom after they wake up," Desi said.

Emily stepped fully into the tub, still wearing her panties. "Would it speed things up if I washed your back?" she asked.

Desi moved his back away from the direct stream to allow Emily to get in under the water. After handing her the soap, she soaped up his back and guided him back under the stream of water to rinse. She then took off her panties and washed them with the soap. Desi watched as Emily washed her naked body using the panties as a washcloth. She first soaped her breasts and stomach, and then proceeded to rub the soapy panties over her pubic hair. Taking the soapy panties in one hand, with a dainty, yet bold move, she looped them over Desi's male protrusion.

"I need you to be a dear and rinse them off for me," Emily said innocently.

Desi turned into the water to comply with her request. "I guess that is one way to get into a woman's panties," he said as he turned back to Emily, the panties still hanging from his anatomy.

"I'm getting the idea that I have turned you onto something new to do with that thing," Emily said.

Desi looked down, expecting Emily to reach over to retrieve the panties that remained looped around his erection. "I think you are underutilizing one of my best assets," Desi said.

"Oh yeah," Emily said. "Why don't you turn around again and let me get a real feel of your other ass...set." After Desi spun around, Emily crouched down, grabbed his butt with two hands, and put a bite on each of his cheeks.

Desi stood up on his toes in response. "I didn't suspect you were going to bite. Please don't leave any permanent damage."

Emily stood up and wrapped her arms around Desi so that her breasts were tightly pressed against his back. "I'm just trying to leave a lasting impression on you," Emily said as her hands made their way down Desi's chest and over his hip bones, finally converging between his legs. "I wish we had more time this morning," she cooed into his left ear.

"Oh yeah," Desi said. "What would you like to do?"

"Well," Emily said, "I could put my panties over one of your other sex organs, so your manhood won't feel like it is being misused."

"You are going to do what?" Desi asked.

"Didn't you take sex education in high school?" Emily paused for a moment as if to concentrate on her hands and the massage she was giving Desi's erection. She took the panties off his erection, reached up, and put the panties on Desi's head.

"And what is the idea of me wearing your panties on my head?"

"A human being's largest sex organ is the brain; at least that is what they taught me in high school. Besides, my panties will dry faster on the top of your head. "

"You're giving me a whole new appreciation of brainiacs," Desi said. "So, what can I do for your brain or body parts?"

"I liked the kisses around my navel earlier, but I really would appreciate you going a bit lower the next time."

"Anything else for the next time?" Desi asked.

"The next time we take a shower, you might massage me in the area where I massaged you, and maybe you'll get the opportunity to fully explore the Garden of Emily," she suggested. She grabbed Desi's hip bones and pumped her hips against his butt. "Got the idea?" she said softly.

"You are giving me lots of ideas for the next time we find ourselves in close quarters without any clothes on," Desi said a bit breathlessly. "But I can't keep these panties on my head until they dry."

Emily pulled herself away from Desi. "There is just one thing," Emily said. "There is no more kissing on Linda if you want to have a next time in the shower with me."

"I understand, and I think Linda knows, especially after last night, that I am not the guy for her."

"If she didn't get the message last night, then maybe our showering together this morning will clarify things for her," Emily said as she reached for a grey towel. "Keep the panties on till we get back to the bedroom. I think I want Linda to see where your head is right now."

"You know, you just took my towel," Desi said as he turned off the shower.

"Sorry, I didn't see the pink one until just this minute. Is this going to create compatibility issues?"

"Only if you are going to insist that I always use the pink towel."

"I don't have to have my way all the time, but this grey towel is really a lot nicer than the pink one," Emily said.

"I'll have to go to the PX and get some more new towels before you make a decision about moving in."

"I am only half-joking about maybe needing a place after the semester is over. My father is talking to a real estate broker about renting out my grandmother's house for June, July, and

August," Emily said. "I don't think I want to spend the summer at my parents' house after graduating from college. That would be really nerdy."

"Where will Linda stay for the summer? Would she be at your parents' house while you lived somewhere else?"

"Linda is not going to be my problem for the summer," Emily said as she partially dried her hair, then wrapped the fluffy, large, grey towel around her.

Desi tried to wrap the flimsy pink towel around himself, but it came undone whenever he moved. "Think I'm putting my grey gym shorts back on, even though the pink towel does seem to go with the pink panties," he said. Desi put the shorts on over his still erect penis.

Emily looked at the lump in his gym shorts. "Maybe I need to help you out before you leave the bathroom. She sat on the closed toilet and beckoned him over to her. She pulled his shorts down to his ankles and undid the top of the towel she was wearing with a simple arch of her back. Pressing her sternum against Desi's penis, Emily massaged her breasts together, stirring Desi even further than she had in the shower.

There was a knock on the door. From outside the bathroom, Daisy pleaded, "Can I get in there sometime soon?"

"Desi has to cover up, and then we'll be out," Emily coolly replied. She stood up and passed the grey towel to Desi. Emily found the pink towel, and with one hand holding it in place at her waist, opened the bathroom door and left the bathroom.

Desi walked out of the bathroom with the gym shorts around his ankles, the grey towel around his hips, and Emily's panties still on his head. He gave Daisy a quick nod.

"Nice shower cap. Sorry if I broke up your fun," Daisy said as she closed the bathroom door behind her.

Breakfast Made to Order

When Roger wandered into the kitchen, Desi and Emily had some bacon cooking in one pan and some peppers and onions heating up in another. "Am I smelling bacon?" Roger asked.

"We're all out of wild boar, I'm afraid," Desi said sardonically.

"Good morning, Roger," Emily said. "Are you interested in having an omelet or maybe an egg sandwich?"

"Good morning, Miss Miller," Roger said. "Daisy should be along in a couple of minutes. Maybe I'll just fix some coffee until she joins us. I know I ruined Desi on ever fixing coffee again."

"Roger got sick in front of me while we were in a big storm off the coast of Alaska near the Bering Strait. I had just had a cup of coffee and emptied the grinds from the pot in the officers' kitchen," Desi recounted. "But I will spare you any more details as we are getting ready to make breakfast."

Roger went over to the counter where Desi had put out the coffee pot and the coffee. "That was the only instance I can recall of ever getting seasick. Unfortunately, I lost my dinner right in front of Desi," Roger said.

"Thanks for reminding me of that image," Desi said.

"Sorry," Roger said.

"Up until that moment when Roger got sick, I didn't know that seasickness is contagious," Desi added.

"It is?" Daisy asked as she entered the kitchen.

"Is that the end of the story?" Emily asked.

"The end of the story is that Desi got sick a few moments after me. But my guess is he hadn't been able to even think about hitting his rack that night, what with all the rocking and rolling going on, and he probably was a bit queasy before that. When he got sick, he threw up into the sink containing the garbage disposal, where he had dumped coffee grounds. So, while throwing up, he could smell the coffee grinds," Roger surmised.

"Maybe we shouldn't have coffee in Desi's kitchen. I know I can wait to get some coffee later down in Bardstown," Daisy suggested. "I'd be happy with just a cup of hot tea right now."

"Are you familiar with Bardstown?" Emily asked.

"Yes. It is a lovely area; not that Louisville isn't nice. Louisville, particularly the area where my aunt lives, is very nice too," she said a bit defensively. "I went to college in the downtown area."

"What college was that?" Desi asked as he turned away from the stove.

"Oh, I'm sure you've never heard of it," Daisy replied. "It was a small, women-only Catholic College, but now I think it has a few men attending."

"Were nuns teaching there?" Roger asked.

"Yeah, there weren't any wild parties with all of the nuns around," Daisy reported.

"I guess you are Catholic?" Emily asked.

"Yes, are you?" Daisy asked with an expectant smile.

"My father is a Protestant minister, a radio minister," Emily clarified.

"But you go to church on Sundays, right?" Daisy asked.

"Quite often, but 'everything in moderation' is my credo," Emily said with a laugh before adding, "including the moderation, and I needed to go a bit crazy this weekend and I am not likely to make it to where we normally attend church in Lexington today."

There were a few moments when no one spoke before Stacey entered the kitchen from the hallway.

"I heard you guys talking about going to church," Stacey said. "I'm up for going to church today. I want to say a little prayer of thanksgiving for getting orders for Germany, getting a letter from Charlie, and talking to Charlie this morning."

"Well," Daisy said, "I know a great place to go to church in the Bardstown area. It's really a famous monastery. We could go there before we hit one of the distilleries."

"Sounds good to me," Stacey said. "I can take a couple of people to the monastery in my car, and we can all meet at a distillery afterwards. We couldn't fit everyone into one car anyway."

Desi nodded his head. "Ok, I need to know who wants omelets and who wants egg sandwiches, as well as what you want in them. I'm trying to get the day going right with breakfast made to order," Desi said. "Daisy, how about if I start with your order?"

"I would just like one poached egg, with a piece of toast," Daisy requested.

"I don't have a poacher, but I could make you an egg, over easy, inside a piece of toast. We call it 'an egg in a frame,' " Desi said. "And I am working on that cup of tea."

Daisy nodded her approval.

"Emily, what do you feel like having?"

"I'll take two eggs," Emily said a bit absentmindedly as she went through a newspaper.

"And how do you like your eggs?"

Closing the newspaper and looking at Desi, Emily said, "I like them the way I like my man–sunny side up!" She triggered a smile from Desi.

A Drive-By of My Old Kentucky Home

As Desi and Emily drove into Bardstown in Desi's car, Stacey followed with Roger, Daisy, and Linda in her vehicle. Emily rolled down the passenger side window and pointed out the home where Stephen Foster's cousins lived, who Foster visited throughout his lifetime. Desi remembered reading that Foster's visits to Kentucky may have inspired some of his music.

They split up in the center of town, near a sign that read "Bourbon Capital of the World." From that point on, Daisy gave directions to Stacey for getting to the Abbey of Gethsemane.

Desi parked near the Chamber of Commerce Office. Desi and Emily walked hand in hand to the Chamber Office. Once inside the office, they found racks of booklets, flyers, and maps of the local area, as well as for the entire State of Kentucky. A woman in her forties walked out of a door at the back of the room and approached them.

"May I help you?" asked the woman.

"We are trying to find out about any distillery that has a tour today and want to bring along four of our friends who have headed over to the monastery." Desi, after a pause added, "that may have sounded a little strange, talking about the monastery in the same breath as scheduling a distillery tour."

The woman just smiled at Desi and Emily. "No, maybe different types of spirits, but it's spirits that you seek." She reached out to one of the racks and pulled out a map of Bardstown and the surrounding areas, along with an accompanying list of distilleries with phone numbers. "You have to call the distilleries ahead of time to set up the tours. They usually want a group to go through at one time. I don't know if they have tours this Sunday, but I could make a couple of calls to places I think might take a group today. So, there are a total of six people in your group?" she asked.

"Yes, there are six people, and we would like a tour in a couple of hours, say around one," Desi replied. "Oh, and in our group is Emma Lee Miller, a Boone descendant," Desi added, pointing to Emily.

"There used to be a Boone Brothers Distillery where the Willett Distillery went in. I think it may now be part of all the Schenley distilleries. I can make a call to someone I know and, if all you have is half a dozen people, they may give your group a tour today. It's a little early, but they may be already at the distillery. They might be checking on the spirits as we speak," the Chamber of Commerce representative said.

The woman walked back to the door she had come out of and disappeared behind the door.

"I'm not sure it was a good idea to mention my name to her," Emily said.

"I think it helped to get her to make the calls," Desi said. "She sounds like she has some good contacts and really knows about the distilleries."

The woman came back to them about five minutes later. She had a map in her hand with a distillery circled on it. It was in the Bardstown area. She handed the map to Desi. "Are you Reverend Miller's daughter?" she asked Emily.

"Yes, ma'am," Emily replied with a bit of a drawl for effect. Emily held out her hand.

"Nice to meet you," the woman said as she walked them to the door. "They are expecting you between one and one-thirty. I told them you were probably going to the monastery first."

The woman closed the Chamber of Commerce Office door behind them, calling out, "Have fun," through the glass window on the wooden door. Desi and Emily heard her lock the deadbolt on the door.

"Guess she is done for the day," Desi said.

"That, or she is going to follow us," Emily replied.

"Why would she do that?"

"I don't know, but we may find out."

They went back to Desi's car and drove towards the monastery.

"Wasn't Gethsemane the name of the garden where Jesus got arrested?" Emily asked.

"You know your bible," Desi replied.

"At least the New Testament." Emily paused. "I don't understand why they would name a monastery after such an unhappy place."

"We'll have to ask the Trappist monks that question when we get there," Desi said.

"Is that why you want to go to the monastery?"

"No. I want to go to see the place where Thomas Merton, one of the foremost spiritual writers of the twentieth century, lived for much of his life. He wrote my favorite book in the philosophy of religion class that I took at NYU," Desi said. "I also heard an excellent lecture on Merton given by a Jesuit priest up at Fordham."

"Which Merton book did you read?" asked Emily.

"It's a book about people of many, if not all, religions who seek a path leading to metaphysical awareness. The name of the book is *Mystics and Zen Masters*," Desi answered.

Emily nodded, saying, "And this monastery is sort of a Shaolin temple, like on the TV show KUNG FU?"

"I am not sure if they do martial arts training, but from what I have heard, from people I know who have been to the monastery, the place is very interesting," Desi said.

"I think my father may have gone to this monastery as part of a retreat, after we lost my brother," Emily volunteered.

"I can understand someone needing to go on a retreat after suffering such a loss."

"But it's not sounding anything like an amusement park," Emily commented. "My boyfriend took me to an amusement park to try to cheer me up after I got the news about my brother."

"I don't know that even Merton was happy there. He wrote about what constitutes happiness, but I don't think he found happiness in his life there, or anywhere else for that matter."

"Problems with the ladies?" Emily asked. "Being a monk probably didn't help with that."

"His path was one that involved a good deal of personal suffering. In 1968, when he got the chance to do an Asian lecture tour and spend time with Buddhist monks, he met his untimely death in Thailand."

"That part sounds interesting," Emily said.

"He was found to have been electrocuted by a fan after taking a shower, but an autopsy was waived so they could get his body to a U.S. military plane heading back to the States, together with the bodies of members of our Armed Forces killed in Vietnam."

"Wasn't Merton one of the Catholic priests who were outspoken antiwar activists?" Emily asked.

"Yes. In the last few years of his life, Merton developed relationships with Vietnamese Buddhist monks, who, though non-violent, were frequently involved with protests as they did not accept the social order of the French, the Americans, or the communists."

"Is his grave at the Abbey?" Emily asked.

"I understand from people who have been there that it is, but that the grave marker does not have 'Thomas Merton' written on it, only his priest name," Desi said.

"So, notwithstanding all the books, essays, and other things that he wrote, he doesn't get his byline on his own grave," Emily concluded. "His spirit must still be suffering."

Desi nodded in agreement. "We must find the grave and say a prayer for his soul."

Chapel Lined With Monks

When Desi and Emily got to the chapel at the Abbey, they saw that Roger, Daisy, and Linda had already found seats in a pew near the back of the chapel. Desi and Emily sat down in the pew behind them.

The monks were chanting. The acoustics of the chapel made the voices of three or four dozen monks sound like there were hundreds of male voices.

The eleven o'clock service was a mass. Almost all of the monks were sitting in roped-off areas on either side of the chapel so that they faced the main center aisle. The seating for the monks covered three-quarters of the length of the chapel. The public sat in cordoned off pews facing the altar, which was located at the opposite end of the chapel, even beyond the seating for the monks. The monks all wore dark-colored robes. As the service went on, a priest in white vestments and two monks in their dark attire appeared to serve the bread and wine.

Daisy rose to walk up and receive communion. Roger and Linda followed behind. They made their way up to the railing, behind which stood the celebrant and the two assistant monks. Desi and Emily stayed seated.

When the mass was over, they all quietly left the chapel and made their way to the gift shop. Desi bought a couple of postcards depicting the monastery in different seasons. Daisy bought some cheese, which the monks made at the monastery.

"I think this is the same type of cheese I bought the last time I was here, back when I was in college," Daisy said. "We used to have an annual field trip to this Abbey."

"That certainly was a wild and crazy college you went to," Emily said.

"There was another monastery we once went to that had great bread," Daisy said, ignoring the comment.

"Daisy," Desi said, "since you have been here a few times before, can you show us the grounds?"

"Do you know the location of the grave for Thomas Merton?" Emily asked.

"We have to look for a marker that says, 'Brother Louis' or 'Father Louis,' I forget which," Daisy admitted.

"Emily and I were talking about his grave marker on the way here," Desi said.

"Whose grave marker?" Roger said.

"Desi's favorite theology writer of the twentieth century," Emily said.

"I don't think I have a favorite theology writer of any century," Roger admitted.

"I guess you didn't have to take any religion classes at the Merchant Marine Academy," Daisy said.

"I don't remember there being any electives, but Desi and I only attended Kings Point for a year, and about five months of that was spent at sea," Roger said.

"I don't think I've taken any religion classes at UK or when I was going to community college in Oregon," Linda announced. "But I did bible studies with Pastor Rick; not that those studies turned out very well."

"What happened?" Daisy asked.

"Basically, I just got screwed," Linda said. "But I can't take it personally because Pastor Rick screwed everyone, one way or another."

"So, what is Pastor Rick doing now?" Daisy asked.

Linda was silent for a moment. Only after about a minute did she answer. "I don't think he can hurt anyone anymore."

"Did he go to jail, or did he just flee the country?"

"He owed lots of people money, and there were people coming after him. The big church he claimed he was building barely had a hole dug in the ground. But he used his shotgun on himself before anyone got the satisfaction of wringing his neck," Linda said. "If you believe in hell, then Pastor Rick must be there."

"Well," Daisy said, taking a deep breath. "Let me show y'all the grave of Thomas Merton. He was searching for the Spirit and Truth and trying to keep to the path of Jesus as best he could," Daisy said.

"That phrase of worshipping God in 'Spirit and Truth' comes from one of the Gospels, but I can't recall exactly which one," Emily said.

"I didn't take religion classes, but I did take a philosophy of religion class in college," Desi said. "I think that phrase is used in the Gospel about Jesus encountering the Samaritan woman at the well of Jacob."

Emily nodded her head. "And Jesus asks her for a drink. But I am not sure of who Jacob was or what he did."

"Is there a well here too?" Roger asked.

"I think we are free to walk around the grounds, so let's go and look," Daisy said.

They walked through a field to the tree line. They spotted a pathway at the edge of the forest. Just inside the forest sat a monk whittling walking sticks. When Desi, Emily, Roger, Daisy, Stacey, and Linda came close to the monk, he looked up and gave them a nod. They all nodded back.

"I don't think we should try to engage in conversation with any of the monks," Daisy said.

When the monk smiled at her, Daisy smiled back.

The monk made a couple more cuts in the walking stick he was working on and then ran his hand along the stick, checking its smoothness. The monk then offered Daisy the stick, which was about five feet long and over an inch thick.

With a wave of her hand, she declined to take the stick.

The monk looked at Roger, who was standing next to Daisy. He offered it to Roger, who took it into his hands, gave it an admiring look, and then gave the monk a short bow. The group then turned away as they continued their walk into the forest.

The monk followed them walking with another walking stick. After they walked a couple hundred yards on the pathway, they got to a clearing. At the clearing, the monk caught up to Desi. He put his hand on Desi's back. When Desi turned to him, he put the walking stick he was using into one of Desi's hands.

Desi gave him a bow of his head in appreciation, took the walking stick in both hands, and swung it like a baseball bat. The monk shook his head to indicate his displeasure before pointing to Roger.

Desi then held the walking stick as if it were a kendo stick and assumed a pose as if he was going to engage Roger in a duel. The monk smiled and nodded his head in approval.

Roger also accommodated the monk's wishes and assumed a kendo pose. Desi and Roger circled each other in the center of the clearing and then took turns attacking and defending. The sound of the clashing walking sticks echoed off the trees. The monk seemed delighted. Emily, Daisy, and Linda looked puzzled. Stacey did not look surprised.

After about five minutes of battling, Desi and Roger first bowed to each other, and then to the monk. Once again, they admired the walking sticks as if they were approving the walking sticks as effective weapons.

With a smile, the monk waved to them and walked away.

Emily turned to Desi and asked, "Did you guys somehow rehearse all of that with the monk?"

"Yeah, what was that all about?" Linda asked. "You suddenly seemed to know what to do with those sticks. Did that monk know what you were going to do with them?"

Stacey started to laugh. "The sticks are like those used in Kendo martial arts training. I've seen Desi use broomsticks as if he was practicing some martial arts moves, but I thought he was just kidding around. You guys looked like you actually have skills."

Roger took a stance with his stick. "We did get some training in a martial arts club we joined at Kings Point."

"That martial arts class was where I first met Roger," Desi said. "The instructor was a black belt karate and jujitsu instructor who taught members of the Strategic Air Command how to kill the enemy if they were ever shot down and had to fight their way out. Kings Point brought him in to train any of us who were interested in martial arts. Roger was my partner, but what the sensei was teaching us really wasn't safe to practice with physical contact on anyone. So, he added Kendo to the class so that we could do something with physical contact," Desi said.

"So, when we ended up going to sea together, we had an opportunity to practice our Kendo," Roger said.

"In Japan, we bought some good sticks and went to see Kendo matches between some highly trained teams," Desi said.

"And I thought that Desi was a lover, not a fighter," Emily said.

"A man can be both," Linda said.

Desi looked at his watch. "Hey, we better get going if we are going to make it to the distillery by one o'clock."

"Let's say a quick prayer at Merton's grave and head out," Daisy said. Everyone nodded in agreement.

Hank's Rules at the Distillery

When they arrived at the distillery, Roger got out of the back seat of Stacey's car, his new walking stick in hand.

Desi stuck his head out of his driver's window and called out to Roger, "Hey man, the distillery tour isn't so long that you need a walking stick."

Roger hugged his walking stick. "What do the Shaolin say about walking softly but carrying a big stick?"

"Not sure if you even have the attribution right on that one," Desi responded.

There was a barn with a sign over the door saying "Visitors." They headed to that barn instead of the unmarked barns on the property. When they got to the barn door, they were greeted by a burley-looking man with an apron. He led them around the barn explaining the production requirements for making bourbon, including that the bourbon must have a corn content of no less than fifty-one percent.

As he opened a barrel to take a sample, a couple in their twenties came into the barn and greeted the guide with, "Hi, Hank. Are we too late?"

Hank first gave the woman a hug, and then the young man. After the hugs, he gave the couple the first samples from the barrel.

Emily nudged Desi, whispering, "Aren't you going to say anything about them cutting to the head of the line?"

Desi put his hand on her arm. While giving her a kiss on the cheek, he calmly rubbed her arm.

When the bourbon guide asked the couple if they liked what they tasted, they nodded their approval. "Honey," the guide said to the young woman, "I'm glad you like it because we are naming this batch after you, 'Honey Rose.' " The young man clapped his hands.

"Are you going to give us a sample, or do we have to wait until after you name a barrel after us?" Emily asked, unable to contain herself any longer.

"And what is your name?" The guide asked while looking at Emily.

Emily glared back at him with her hands on her hips. "I'm Emma Lee Miller, and my family members have been distillers and owners of distilleries for generations."

"Well, calm down. I'll get you all a sample," said the guide.

"She is also one of my cousins, though I haven't seen her since we were girls," Honey said.

Roger looked at Honey, then at Emily. "There is a resemblance," Roger said as he accepted a sample of the bourbon in a short glass that Hank handed him.

Hank then gave glasses of bourbon to Daisy, Linda, and Stacey. He then walked over to Emily. "What'd you order, a glass or a barrel?"

"You are kidding, aren't you?" Desi asked.

"No, I'm not," Hank answered. "If the young lady is going to buy her own barrel, then I'm not going to charge her by the glass."

"Charge her?" Roger asked. "I thought we were getting a free tour."

"Young man, there ain't nothin' in this world that's free," Hank said.

"What about love?" Roger said wryly. He downed his bourbon and set his empty glass on a barrel top. Roger strode forward to confront Hank. "Show me the sign saying there is a charge for the tour," he demanded.

"I'm going to show you my Louisville Slugger," Hank said as he pointed to a baseball bat leaning against a barn wall.

Roger reached over and grabbed his walking stick, which he had left resting against a barrel. Roger shouted at Hank, "You want to take it outside, or do you want to resolve this here and now?"

Daisy went over to Roger to calm him down. She looked at Hank and opened her pocketbook. "How much do we owe you?"

"It's five dollars a person," Hank said as he poured two more glasses of bourbon. "So, it's forty, after I serve everyone," he said, pointing to Desi and Emily.

Daisy took two twenty-dollar bills out of her pocketbook and held them out. As Hank started to walk over to take the money, Roger grabbed the money out of Daisy's hand and pushed the money back into her pocketbook.

"You want us to pay for their drinks too?" Roger fumed as he pointed to Honey and her boyfriend.

"That's the way it works. It came out of Honey's barrel, so it's free for her," Hank answered.

Roger paused for a moment before speaking. "And what about that guy – he gets to drink for free too?"

"Yeah," Hank said. "Rusty, as her guest, gets to drink for free too."

Rusty glared at Roger for a moment. He went over to the barn wall and grabbed the baseball bat. "Hey, four eyes," he said to Roger. "Let's make this interesting. You get me to drop the bat, and there is no charge to you guys. If I make you drop the stick, you or your girlfriend pays Hank the forty bucks." Rusty looked over to Hank. "Does that sound fair to you?"

"Just take it outside the barn, alright?" Hank responded.

Roger headed for the outdoors. Daisy, Stacey, and Linda followed along.

Emily walked over to Honey. "You knew I was going to be here this afternoon, didn't you?" Emily asked her.

"I had reason to believe that you might be here, but I didn't think this would happen. I just needed to talk to you about something involving your father – what he wants from my mother and his other cousins," Honey said. "Your father is being stubborn and unfair."

"So, what is it that you want me to do?" Emily asked.

"Just give him a warning," Honey said.

"Will you call off your boyfriend?" Emily asked.

"Sure. Just tell your father to stop stalling and settle things with his cousins so we don't have to go to the newspapers about his financial connections with Pastor Rick. Don't think he would want that!" Honey said.

"Ok, but stop your boyfriend before someone gets hurt," Emily said.

"Rusty is not the one who is going to get hurt," Honey said as she walked away from Emily and toward the barn door, where Rusty was waiting for her.

As Emily and Desi approached Honey and Rusty at the barn door, Honey turned to them to make a statement. "Rusty thinks I should get you to make a promise that you will help, and that I should hold your fancy watch until you keep your promise. Otherwise, he wants to demonstrate what he can do to your friend or your daddy."

"I told you what I will do, and that should be enough," Emily screamed as she lunged forward and knocked Honey backwards over a hay bale.

Rusty raised the bat as if preparing to hit Emily. Desi then put one arm around Rusty's throat, and with his other arm, wrestled the baseball bat out of Rusty's hand.

Holding the bat in one hand, Desi released his hold on Rusty's throat and stepped away from Rusty. Honey had picked herself up off the ground. Honey suddenly hopped onto the hay bale and launched herself at Emily, knocking her off her feet, and the two of them wrestled on the ground for a couple of minutes before Linda and Stacey were able to separate them.

Emily and Honey dusted themselves off while swearing at each other.

Rusty glared at Desi. "I got challenged to a fight," Rusty said. "I want the baseball bat as I have the right to meet that challenge. I don't care if it is against you or four eyes, but you guys started this."

"That is quite debatable," Desi said. "However, to end the debate, I will resolve it with you. But I'm only going to give you the bat back once. You drop it, that's the end. That was the original challenge. Do you agree?" Desi asked.

Rusty simply nodded.

Hank came out from inside the barn and stood in the doorway.

"The witnesses to any duel have to clearly hear a 'Yes' or a 'No,' " Desi said.

Rusty held out his hand, saying, "Yes! Now give me the baseball bat."

Desi looked over to Roger, who tossed Desi the walking stick.

Daisy looked at Roger. "You aren't going to try to stop this?"

"I don't think this is going to take Desi very long to finish," Roger answered.

Desi rolled the bat over to Rusty on the ground with his foot. Desi assumed a stance that made it look like he was preparing to defend against a swing of the bat. However, when Rusty took a full swing at Desi, the bat missed, and Desi stepped to the side and poked one end of the walking stick into Rusty's midsection. Rusty bent to one side, exposing one of his hands. Desi brought the other end of the stick up and over his head, and then onto Rusty's exposed hand with the full force of the swing. After Desi's strike, the pain in Rusty's hand caused him to grab the injured hand with the hand holding the bat. The bat fell to the ground. Tears came to Rusty's eyes.

Roger moved right in to stand on the bat.

"Was that a fair fight?" Hank asked as he walked over to Honey.

"Yeah," Honey said. "We don't need to get anyone bleeding."

Emily walked over to Honey. "I will talk with my father, but you should never again threaten him or any of my friends with physical harm."

"Alright, do what you can. I better take Rusty back to my place and get some ice on that hand," Honey said as she walked over to her boyfriend. Rusty was still bent over.

Emily walked back into the barn with Hank walking alongside her. Linda, Stacey, and Daisy followed them.

Desi and Roger watched as Honey helped Rusty get into her car. Roger shook his head as Honey and Rusty drove away. "Honey really does look a lot like Emily," Roger said. "What the hell is she doing with such a loser?"

They walked into the barn to join the others. Emily brought Desi the bourbon sample that Desi hadn't had a chance to taste. Emily had her glass in her hand. "It's time to take Linda and me back to my grandmother's house. Everyone can come along. There is a lot of food in the refrigerator because we thought my parents were coming for the Derby."

"But first a toast," Desi said, holding up his glass. "To battles that end well!"

"I'll drink to that," Emily said while clanking Desi's glass. "But I'm afraid my father may have a war on his hands."

Dinner at Grandma Boone's House

When they arrived at the house where Emily's late grandmother had lived, the caretaker, a gentleman about seventy years old, was vacuuming the in-ground pool on the west side of the house, which overlooked a field of several acres. Emily got out of Desi's car and waved to him. The caretaker smiled and waved back. Desi parked near the north end of the large ranch house in a space between the house and a separate garage. The garage had an old pickup truck in one of the bays. Emily directed everyone to the east entrance, which she called the "front doors" of the house. The house was located about halfway between Bardstown and Lexington in what had been a rural town that was becoming increasingly suburban.

Daisy insisted on a tour, and Emily was happy to oblige. The first room they visited was the good-sized kitchen to the right of the main entrance way. Then, they moved on to a dining area that looked out on farmland that sloped slightly up to a tree line in the distance. To the right of the main hallway, and beyond the kitchen and dining areas, was a sunken living room, which was the full width of the kitchen and dining area. The living room had a large stone fireplace.

"I absolutely love stone fireplaces," Daisy said.

Emily stared at the fireplace. "This one was built to replace the old brick fireplace, and it was rebuilt with rocks selected by my brother and father, mostly by my late brother."

"Sorry to hear about your loss," Daisy said as she stepped closer to Emily and put her hand on Emily's shoulder.

"My father says to focus on the happy memories of the events that we shared," Emily said. "So, when I look at the fireplace, I remember how we gathered to celebrate its completion and how happy my grandmother was to have a unique-looking fireplace."

"And a unique and loving family gathered together, I am sure," Daisy added.

There was a knock on the sliding glass doors in the dining area. They looked over to see the caretaker standing on the patio with a bucket in his hand. Emily and Linda went over to the sliding glass doors, and Emily opened one of them. "Hello, Frank," Emily said to the caretaker.

"I'm getting ready to put the last of the chemicals in the pool," Frank said. "It needs another day or so before you swim in it, but I can hold off on putting in the algaecide if you want to sit on the edge with your feet in the pool this evening."

"That would be great," Emily replied. "I can add it later tonight if you aren't stopping by tomorrow."

"I'll leave this bucket with two containers of algaecide in it on the patio, but I should be driving over here tomorrow with my tractor," Frank said.

"There's no rush on the algaecide, anyway, is there?" Emily asked. She then stepped out onto the patio and took a couple of steps towards the pool. "It looks pretty clear. I guess with your running the filter and vacuuming it, the pool already looks good."

"But the chlorine levels are very high, so it would not be good for your eyes right now," Frank cautioned.

"Thanks," Emily said. "I'll let everyone know – feet can go in, but no eyes!"

Frank put down the bucket with two plastic containers inside on the patio and started walking to the garage.

Desi, Linda, Roger, and Daisy joined Emily on the patio.

Desi began to take off his shoes. "It's okay if I test the chlorine level with my feet, right?" he asked.

"Sure, if you want to be the guinea pig, go ahead," Emily said.

Daisy took a package out of her purse and handed it to Emily, saying, "I brought you something from the distillery as a hostess gift."

"That was very nice of you," Emily said while taking the bag. She didn't have to open the bag to know it contained a bottle of bourbon. "I think I will pour everyone something to drink by the pool."

When Emily went back to the house, she found Stacey lying on one of the couches. "I'm pouring some bourbon. You want to join us by the pool?" Emily asked Stacey.

"This couch is very comfortable, and your house is beautiful," Stacey said. "I hope I get to live like this someday."

"I am sure you will," Emily said as she brought Stacey a glass of bourbon from the kitchen.

Emily sat down in a chair near the couch on which Stacey was half sitting and half lying on. "Are you alright?" Emily asked.

"It's been quite a day. Talking to Charlie this morning was great. It sounds like he is looking forward to me getting to Germany. But when we were at the Abbey, I started to wonder if there was anything for me in Germany other than Charlie. Desi always seems to have multiple interests, and I don't mean just with women. I don't know what interests I am going to be able to share with Charlie other than having a good time in bed."

"Well, there are lots of places for the two of you to travel to. A weekend in Paris is just a train ride away," Emily suggested.

"But you and Desi, if you guys were in Paris, you would both want to go to museums and to the churches. I don't know if I could get Charlie to go to Notre Dame."

"Stacey, I think you're a wonderful person, and you're still young. If things don't work out with Charlie, all you have to do is remain that same loveable person you are, and good things will happen," Emily said as she stood up and motioned Stacey to stand up. "Come on outside and join us in testing the pool water with our feet."

Stacey followed Emily outside to the pool. Desi, Roger, and Daisy were already sitting on the edge of the pool with their feet in the water and sipping their glasses of bourbon. Linda was talking over the pool fence with Frank. Emily sat down next to Desi.

Desi turned to Emily. "We are sitting here talking about what a great place you have for a pool party."

"If I am going to have one, it ought to be pretty soon if my father is going to rent out the place for the summer," Emily responded.

"Oh, no," Daisy said. "It's such a lovely place. I was hoping you were going to invite me back."

"I'll come back if I get to see you wrestle your cousin again," Stacey said. "I'll have to tell my cousin Desdemona about that, and maybe we'll see if we can put on our own performance, either with or without a hay bale."

Emily laughed. "Honey and I used to wrestle in a barn when we were nine or ten, so using hay bales is nothing new for us. Guess we were both tomboys trying to keep up with older brothers. I think Honey had a crush on my brother, who was a few years older than us."

"Did Honey ever wrestle your brother in the barn?" Stacey asked.

"Not when she was nine or ten," Emily said. "But they may have been 'kissing cousins' at some point."

"I think the shallow end of this pool looks perfect for some chicken fights, with a guy on the bottom and a woman on his shoulders," Desi said.

"Like that hotel pool in Ibiza," Roger said. "Those women weren't satisfied with pushing the other women off the shoulders of the guys – they were out to rip off bikini tops too."

"That must have been traumatic for you and Desi to watch," Daisy said.

"As I recall, it was hard getting to sleep that night," Desi confessed.

"I'm not going to ask you how hard," Emily said to Desi. "I'll just suggest that if we have a pool party here this summer, the women are on notice not to wear a bikini top that comes off with one tug on a string."

"I would suggest a double knot for the string bikini tops," Stacey said. "Come to think about it, the same goes for the string bikini bottoms," she added.

"Maybe I can start planning something for late May," Emily said.

Linda came over from where she had been talking to Fred to stand behind Desi. Emily asked Linda, "Could you and Fred hear what we were saying from over there?"

"Some of it," Linda said. "Thinking about a pool party made me hungry. Are we going to put something on the grill anytime soon?"

Emily stood up and tugged on Desi's shirt sleeve, who then also stood up.

"I'm going into the kitchen to pull a few steaks out of the refrigerator," Emily announced to the group. "We can also have some sea scallops as appetizers. If you don't like steak, you can have a larger salad with whatever you find in the fridge. There may be some leftover grilled chicken from a couple of nights ago. I've designated Desi to be the grill master for the festivities this afternoon and evening. Please let Desi know how you like your meat."

"Rare, with a foreign accent for me," Linda said.

"Hot, sweaty, and juicy for me," Stacey said.

Emily looked at Linda and Stacey and shook her head.

After dinner, Roger and Daisy made their apologies for having to leave and offered to get a cab back to Louisville. "I don't think they have any cabs in this town," Daisy said. "I think the nearest place for cabs would be Lexington, but you would be going further away from Louisville if Desi took you there for a cab."

"No, I won't hear of it," Desi said. "I told Roger I'd be able to get him to the airport in Louisville tonight for his flight back to Washington, and that I'd also get Daisy back to her Aunt Arbie's. It's only seven o'clock, so if we leave in the next few minutes, we'll have time to get to Daisy's aunt's house and then to the airport in time."

Daisy and Roger gave hugs to Emily, Linda, and Stacey.

Stacey then hugged Linda, who looked back at Stacey. "Are you leaving too?" she asked.

Stacey nodded affirmatively.

Linda looked disappointed. "I thought we might have another chance to share a joint if you have any weed left."

"Sorry," Stacey said. "It was Desdemona's, and last night we went through all that was left. I don't really buy my own, and I try not to carry any in my car."

"I understand," Linda said. She gave Stacey a kiss on the cheek. "I am going to make sure that Emily puts you on the pool party list," Linda said to Stacey.

"Stacey, you are definitely on the pool party list," Emily said before pointing at Desi. "This guy would be on the list too if he would guarantee not to show up with an old girlfriend on his arm or on his mind."

Desi handed Emily a piece of paper. "I wrote down my phone number, and if you don't call me this week, I might just stop by here next weekend to check on things," he said as he leaned forward to bring his face closer to hers.

"That sounds more than fair," Emily said as she brought her lips to his and put her arms around him.

Chapter VI

TAKING INVENTORY AFTER THE DERBY

There were a number of phone calls between Emily and Desi the week following the Derby. The calls culminated in their agreeing upon Desi stopping by Emily's grandmother's house around noon on Saturday, the second Saturday of May.

Desi also received several short but complicated calls from Penny, who wanted Desi to go to Tennessee with her for the weekend. It started with Penny trying to have Desi reserve the whole weekend for going to the Chattanooga area, staying at her parents' new house, and having several meals with her parents. Penny conceded they would not be able to maintain a pretext of having an ongoing relationship if they were around her parents for that much time. There would also be the awkward issue of sleeping arrangements at her parents' new house. Desi said he was willing to play along, but only for one meal – a brunch or early dinner on Sunday – and it would have to be in Nashville, about two and a half hours south of Fort Knox. As Penny was not interested in spending over ten hours on the road for a brief visit, which is what it would take for a road trip from Fort Knox to Chattanooga and back, just to have brunch with her folks, she accepted Desi's plan. Given that her mother grew up in the Nashville area and still had family there, Penny was able to get her parents to "meet them halfway" and bring pictures of the new house.

Desi also made a couple of calls to Debi to be sure she made it safely back to her apartment in Manhattan. On Desi's third attempt to reach her, Debi answered her phone sounding a bit frazzled. She reported to Desi that, after splitting up from her sister in Chicago, she flew to Texas on Derby Day and could not get back to New York until late Monday evening. Debi told Desi that the authorities in Texas advised her of the legal problems facing the guy her mother was flying around with. He was reportedly wanted on embezzlement charges in three countries in South America and in the state of Arizona. Debi also learned that he had filed a flight plan for several stops along the Pacific coast. Debi said she had heard from Tammy, who told her that Desi seemed to be enjoying the Derby and everything that it had to offer. Desi merely acknowledged he had seen Tammy on Derby Day.

Stacey had called Desi midweek and said she wanted to bring over the "new guy" in her office who was "looking for off post housing." Desi agreed to an early Saturday morning meeting so he could keep his date with Emily.

Can't Sell the Forest Without an Inventory of the Trees

Desi spent a good portion of the week going out to the wooded areas on post around the ranges with the foresters to take some pictures and notes regarding their activities. He made a good start on an article about efforts to "harvest and replenish" the woodlands at Fort Knox. His editor also told him that his story and photos would get a full page in the following week's edition of *Inside the Turret*. Desi also had to write a couple of shorter articles for that week's edition and go to the printing company in Elizabethtown on Wednesday afternoon to lay out that week's edition of the post newspaper. They would be following their regular schedule of laying out the paper on Wednesday afternoon to have it printed by Wednesday evening and distributed on Thursday.

Desi rode down to Elizabethtown with his editor, who had started his journalistic career in Vietnam, right after the My Lai Massacre. When Desi first arrived at Fort Knox, the editor had revealed to Desi that after the massacre the Army brass established a "Glad You Asked Policy" of being more forthright so as to restore some credibility for the U.S. Army with the media. Desi figured the editor was trying to get him and other members of the newspaper staff in on the editor's cautious optimism about the continuation of the new policy. Desi took his editor's remarks as a green light to write a few articles that noted problems with training and retention of soldiers. Some of the articles Desi wrote reflected the concerns within the Army about the transition to an all-volunteer Army, and whether it could be molded into an effective military force.

Most of Desi's efforts seemed to be accepted. However, one of Desi's articles about drill sergeant training and the role of drill sergeants in the volunteer Army got the letters to the editor column buzzing with flying arrows.

A colonel of a training brigade wrote a letter disputing an incident involving an unnamed drill sergeant, which Desi included in his article as an example of what drill sergeants should not do with their vast authority over trainees. The colonel was able to get a couple of friends to also send in letters attacking Desi's article, the post paper, and Desi himself. The full colonel in charge of the Public Affairs Office called Desi into his office, asked Desi a few questions, and later covered Desi's back. The Public Affairs Officer, who reported directly to the Commanding General of Fort Knox, did not ask Desi to reveal the name of the drill sergeant.

Only weeks later did the matter get fully resolved when the Public Affairs Officer, a West Point graduate, advised Desi that the drill sergeant had, of his own accord, gone to the training brigade colonel and, while expressing his regrets for creating the public controversy, admitted he committed the faux pas that Desi reported.

Desi had been impressed with the honesty of the drill sergeant and the respect he had received as a journalist by the chief Public Affairs Officer. The result of the incident was that Desi worked even harder to fill the pages of the post newspaper with his articles and photographs.

During the drive down to Elizabethtown, Desi described to his editor how he had been out with the foresters for a whole morning and spent much of another afternoon at their office. On a third day, he visited a site with excessive amounts of shrapnel in the trees. He also told his editor about how the foresters used metal detectors to determine which trees could be safely cut and utilized for lumber. Desi was certain he got some "great shots" of the foresters using their metal detectors on trees.

When they got to the offices of the civilian enterprise newspaper that printed *Inside the Turret*, along with a weekly newspaper covering Elizabethtown, Desi was not very pleased to hear he was only getting one of the photographs he took of Derby activities into the paper. What seemed to make it worse for Desi was that the image the editor chose was not one of the photos he took on Derby Day, but one he took of the Army Band a couple of days earlier while marching in downtown Louisville as part of the Pegasus parade.

He and the editor laid out the newspaper in a couple of hours, even with what seemed to be an excessive amount of headlines not fitting and articles jumping to extra pages. By the time they walked out of the printer's offices, Desi had cooled down about only getting one of his photos into that week's edition. He was relatively pleased with the placement of two of his bylined articles.

They passed a couple of restaurants on the outskirts of Elizabethtown as they headed back up the highway towards Fort Knox. Desi told his editor about *Shakta's* restaurant in Louisville and suggested that he take his wife there for Mother's Day, even though he doubted his supervisor would pay for a babysitter to watch their two kids.

Can't Agree on Anything Without an Inventory

On the morning of the second Saturday of May, there was a knock on the side door of Desi's apartment a few minutes before nine o'clock. Desi was expecting Stacey and the new paralegal from Stacey's office, but it turned out to be the woman from next door wearing a tube top stretched to its limits and a short skirt that revealed very chubby legs. Through the windowpane in the door, Desi could see that his neighbor, Edna, was holding a cardboard box of what looked like asparagus.

When he opened the door, Desi was greeted with, "Good morning, hope I am not disturbing anything."

"No, it's pretty quiet here today, but I am having someone come by and take a look at the empty bedroom in a few minutes. Why don't you come into the kitchen with whatever you are carrying?" Desi said in a welcoming manner.

"I have some nice fresh asparagus from my garden," Edna said as she put the box on the kitchen table. "I am glad to hear that you may have found someone. We've been meaning to tell you that our real estate partners are getting anxious as the money from Charlie ran out in March. I told them that you were working on it."

Desi nodded his head. "I'll show the guy around, and if he wants to speak with you, I'll send him over."

"I will either be out working in my garden, or my husband and I will be in the house," Edna said. "Do you mind if I take a look at Charlie's old room to make sure he didn't leave a mess. I wouldn't want someone to get turned off by soiled bed sheets or anything, although my husband might get turned on by the smell of hot sex on a used bed sheet," Edna said with a cackling laugh.

"It's been a while since anyone had sex in that room, but go ahead and look," Desi said while motioning toward the bedroom down the hall.

Desi listened from the kitchen as Edna clomped down the hallway to the empty bedroom, took some steps into the tiled bathroom, and then clomped again on the wooden floor in the hallway until she paused by the door to Desi's bedroom before returning to the kitchen.

"You didn't find any lacey thongs to take home to wear for your husband, right?" Desi asked.

"I have my own lacey thongs," she said with a twist of her ample hips.

"I don't doubt it," Desi said as he walked into the living room. "Do you want to check in here?"

Edna followed him into the living room. She looked at the coffee table and the couch, as well as the armchair. "The carpet and the furniture look fine, but I certainly don't like what is on the wall," she said as she pointed to the black velvet picture of dogs playing cards and drinking.

"Yeah, I think that was Charlie's. I haven't had the heart to take it down, but maybe the time has come," Desi said. He went over to the picture and removed it from the wall over the TV. "Can't say I ever liked it either or ever understood why Charlie had it on display. Maybe it was left by the guy who was in my room before me."

"I think taking it down makes the room more inviting," Edna said. "So, you think you found a young man who would like to live here?" she asked.

"I really don't know as I haven't actually spoken to the guy. Stacey, Charlie's girlfriend, met him the other day, and they now work in the same office. She will be driving him over because the guy is awaiting the delivery of his car from California. But if he's not interested, there are two college women from the University of Kentucky, who I will be seeing this afternoon, and they may need a place once school ends."

"And you think they will pay to live here with you?" Edna asked.

"I can ask. They are having a pool party at a house south of Bardstown where they have been living, but the house with the nice pool may get rented out for the summer," Desi explained.

"They tell me they bought new string bikinis for the party we are having."

"Did they buy one for you too?" Edna asked.

"I don't know if they have anything for me to wear in the pool," Desi replied with a shrug.

Edna looked Desi up and down. "My God, what I would give to be a college girl now," she said as she put a hand on her heart.

There was the sound of the side door opening and Stacey appeared with a solid-looking, dark-haired guy, with eyes seemingly set in steel.

Stacey walked into the living room and gave Desi a hug. She then gave Edna a handshake, saying, "Good to see you again."

Edna nodded her head. "I saw your car here last Saturday night and Sunday morning. I was going to come over and say 'hello,' but I didn't want to intrude when people might be sleeping or something. Then, by Sunday afternoon, everyone was gone. But I hear from people I work with on post that you'll soon be leaving for Germany."

Stacey shrugged. "Guess I don't have any news for you."

"I offered to have a going away party for Stacey here this month," Desi said. "I'll give you a heads up once we pick the date. That will give you the option of visiting your relatives in New Jersey that weekend."

Edna shook her head in disagreement. "You guys always have very interesting parties. I met a helicopter pilot on New Year's Eve who was naked on the front lawn, and who told me why he still enjoys life, even after all the tragic things that he has seen and been through."

"Yeah, he's quite a guy. Troubled and beautiful, all at the same time," Stacey said.

"Don't worry about any parties for people who have served. And Desi, if you are ever interested in planting something in my garden, you are welcome to it," Edna said as she walked to the side door to leave the apartment.

"Thanks for the asparagus," Desi called out to Edna as she closed the door.

Stacey looked at Desi with furrowed brows. "She's giving you access to plant something in her garden?" Stacey asked. "Sounds like she's inviting you over to skinny dip in her hot tub. And what about that outfit she was wearing, with the belly roll over the short skirt?"

"Hey, she's my landlord, and she and her family own two or three houses on this street. She hasn't hassled me or even mentioned the lost rent for the empty bedroom, until today," Desi said.

"I think they charge the people in the other half of this house enough so that whatever they make on this side is gravy," Stacey said.

"That was Charlie's theory, and maybe they do overcharge the retired people who sometimes live here when they aren't in Florida or on a cruise. So what if they pay the bulk of the costs? Even if what we are paying is just gravy to them, then there has been less financial gravy for them lately," Desi said. "Maybe they just enjoy the entertainment provided by young soldiers."

"Edna seems to know a lot about us from her civilian job on post, and I think her husband works on post as well," Stacey added.

"I hope this doesn't discourage you from thinking about living here," Desi said to the young man who had been quietly waiting to introduce himself.

The young man, who was wearing a Native American necklace, held out his hand to Desi. "My name is Sam. The apartment is just like Stacey described it. But even though it sounded great, I really needed to check it out for myself."

"Understood," Desi said. "Take a look around while I make a call to someone about a pool party."

"Emily?" Stacey asked.

"Yeah," Desi responded.

"I have something in my emergency kit from Desdemona for Emily and Linda," Stacey said. "You mentioned to me the other day that if the weather was good enough for a pool party, then I would be invited along."

"You and Desdemona are now using emergency kits instead of a bandage box?" Desi asked.

"A tampon box, actually," Stacey said. "But it's the same idea."

"I know that a joint or two would definitely make Linda happy," Desi said. He looked at Sam, who was waiting for Stacey to give him the tour. "Sam, do you have any plans for the afternoon?"

Sam shook his head. "Not really, I've only been on post for a few days, and I am pretty far from my home in California. I'm not like the people who have families in Indiana or Ohio."

"Well, I think you would enjoy having lunch at Mama Boone's house, and it would give you a chance to check out the scenery between here and there," Desi said.

"Is that what Emily called her grandmother – Mama Boone?" Stacey asked.

"Her late grandmother is one of the many topics we discussed during our telephone conversations this week," Desi said.

"Tell me what other things you found out," Stacey said.

Desi motioned for Stacey to go as he picked up the handset of the wall phone in the kitchen to make a call to Emily. "Go and show Sam the apartment. We will have plenty of time in the car to talk about Emily and Linda," Desi said. "And Sam can tell us about his necklace and where his family lives in California."

Inventorying the Bluegrass Parkway

Desi decided they would head down to Elizabethtown to take the Bluegrass Parkway to Grandma Boone's house.

Sam explained to Desi and Stacey that he wore a Navajo necklace in memory of his father, who had served as a Navajo Code Talker during World War II. His father stayed in the Army through the Korean War and was stationed in Hawaii when Sam was born. Sam's mother's background was Korean, but she had gone to high school in Hawaii. Sam's parents moved to southern California right after Hawaii became a state in 1959, when Sam was about seven years old. He started playing the ukulele, and then the guitar, when he was nine or ten. Sam's father died in a construction accident when Sam was seventeen. After his father's death, Sam spent a good deal of time practicing his electric guitar and performing at rock concerts, usually as part of a warm-up band, but sometimes as a solo artist before the featured artist. He claimed that he toured with the band 'Heart' before joining the Army.

"Did you ask to get stationed at Fort Knox for some reason," Stacey inquired from the passenger seat of Desi's car.

"No. I got the orders at the end of AIT and wasn't looking for a particular place to serve as a paralegal. But I do like the idea of being close to Louisville," Sam answered, a little scrunched up in the back seat.

"Desi and I have enjoyed Louisville," Stacey said. "I have a cousin who lives and works there. She is also finishing up her undergraduate degree at U of L. Desi likes Louisville because he can take women up there on secret dates or find women up there."

"Stacey seems to be making it sound like dozens of women when it really has only been two or three," Desi said.

"For this week," Stacey interjected.

"I don't want to distract Desi by asking him to tell me about the women we are going to visit this afternoon," Sam said. "But Stacey, maybe you can fill me in on who they are."

"Emily and Linda are Desi's newest female friends, and they became such fast friends with Desi that they hopped in bed with him the first day they met him," Stacey recounted with a laugh.

"Again, Stacey seems to want to exaggerate what actually transpired," Desi said.

"Well, in my hand," Stacey said, holding up a 10" by 12" manila envelope, "are actual photos of Desi in bed with those two women. Proof of what I said happened last Friday night."

"Stacey, please tell Sam, who took the pictures of such goings on," Desi replied. "And after you admit to taking the photos, tell him whether you observed any sexual intercourse going on in that bed."

"I did not," Stacey said in a deflated tone.

"And the truth is that under the covers, we were all wearing some sort of clothing, weren't we?" Desi pressed.

Stacey turned around to Sam. "Desi is just practicing for when he gets out of the Army and goes to law school."

"Desi, are you getting out of the Army sometime soon?"

"No, I still have some more traveling to do as an Army journalist," Desi answered.

"He's trying to get assigned to Armed Forces Television in Germany. That's how the Army recruiter hooked Desi," Stacey said.

"I might still get that assignment, but it hasn't been as easy as I thought it would be," Desi admitted.

"I hope they don't waste Desi's talents," Stacey said.

"Sounds like Desi has quite a number of talents," Sam said.

Stacey laughed. "Well, since you've decided to be his house mate, I guess you might be able to compile a list over the weeks and months ahead."

When they arrived at Grandma Boone's house, they found Emily trying to start the old pickup truck in the garage. Desi walked over to her to see if he could help.

"I don't understand this," she said while turning the key several times, almost getting the starter motor to engage the engine. "We've been using the truck this week. Fred used it this morning to go pick up some stuff for the pool."

"Well, if you want me to go get something from a store, just give me a list and head me in the right direction," Desi said.

"I have pretty much everything, but instead of using frozen burgers, I was going to run out to the local butcher," Emily explained. "I was hoping to make things extra special for you. I would have already been there and back if I had my Mustang.

My father said he would have it back to me by Derby weekend, but that certainly didn't happen."

"You don't have to go crazy for me. But if you want me to go to the butcher shop, I'll be happy to go," Desi said.

"I'd be happy to go a little crazy today for you," Emily said. "Why don't you drive me to the meat store in your car?"

"Sure," Desi said. "Let me tell Stacey what is going on. I should probably introduce you to Sam, too."

"I think you might want to say hello to Linda. She has a new bikini she wants your opinion on." Emily paused. "She's wearing a cover-up now because she is working on the margaritas, so I'm sure she'll want to save her unveiling for after we get back. She wants to talk to you about taking her to one of the pools at Fort Knox and helping her meet a summer romance."

"She wants me to walk her around like I'm some sort of pimp?" Desi asked. "I can't do that. Lots of people know me and recognize me at Fort Knox."

"I guess she feels like the whole thing with Roger didn't work out and you somehow owe her something," Emily replied.

"She feels like she came away empty-handed last weekend?" Desi asked.

Linda seems to think you teased her with a bit more than simple flirting the night before Derby Day," Emily answered.

"We did do some serious partying, but I don't think it was anything more than that."

"But you do want to have a meaningful relationship with me, right?' Emily asked. She put her head down for a moment. "I have to warn you. I have little or no record of having any relationship that doesn't stall out in some way before things really get going. Just like with this pick-up truck."

"You probably just flooded it," Desi said. "If you hop out, I'll give it a try, but it probably just needs to sit."

Emily, who was wearing some very short cutoffs, swung her long legs from under the steering wheel and out the driver's door. Desi held out a hand to help her, but she brushed his hand aside. "You try, hot shot!" Emily said, as if she was hoping it wouldn't start for Desi.

Desi got in the pickup truck and tried starting it without pressing on the gas pedal. It sounded no better or worse than when Emily tried it with some gas.

"Like I said, we need to leave it for a while," Desi concluded. "I'll run you to the fresh meat market in my car."

Sam came walking up to the garage as Desi was getting out of the pickup truck. "Emily, this is Sam," Desi said. "He's going to be renting the second bedroom of my apartment in Radcliff."

"You mean what Stacey calls the noisy girl's room," Emily teased.

"I think she says that as a sort of confession or apology for the nights I was awakened by her rambunctious activities," Desi said. "Hope that information doesn't give Sam second thoughts."

"Stacey told me what she calls the room and assures me there will not be any haunting reverberations," Sam said.

"Yeah, once Stacey heads off for Germany, we should be fine," Desi said confidently.

"Unless Daisy from Louisville comes repeatedly to Radcliff," Emily said.

Desi frowned at Emily to get her to stop making remarks that might cause problems.

"Sam, if you don't mind, could you try starting this old truck in about fifteen or twenty minutes?" Desi asked. "I think she's just flooded."

"Sure, I am pretty good with my hands and will also take a look under the hood to see if any of the wiring is loose," Sam answered.

Desi and Emily walked to Desi's green Super Beetle. Desi held the door for Emily. Before she got in, she took the bottom of her blouse and tied it in a knot to expose her midriff. She then used her stomach muscles to seductively lower herself into the passenger seat. "Can you adjust the seat for me?" Emily asked.

"How do you like it?" Desi asked.

"All the way back, so I have plenty of legroom," Emily said. "And show me how far back the seat will recline. There's a place along the way with the soothing sounds of a river that I would like to share with you."

"Show me the way," Desi said as he quickly went around the car and jumped into the driver's seat.

About half a mile down the paved road into town, Emily pointed as she said, "turn between those two trees and follow the dirt road to the river."

The dirt road ended in a cul-de-sac, bounded by pine trees at the edge of a small river.

"Are we getting out?" Desi asked as he turned off his car.

"Maybe, but what's your hurry?" Emily said as she reached behind her back and undid the hooks to her bra. Emily then reached inside her blouse and, with a couple of quick maneuvers, managed to take her bra off without taking off the blouse. She threw the blue bra into the back seat. "Desi, I am not sure I am going to be able to control myself around you. You look so good today, even better than you did last weekend."

"And you, with your legs in those shorts, are making my head spin," Desi said.

"What would your head do if I took off the shorts, so you got a better look at my long legs?" Emily cooed. Not waiting for an answer, she took off the shorts to reveal her lacey blue panties.

Rolling his window down, Desi listened for any other vehicles. He could only hear the sound of the river, which was down an embankment about 20 feet beyond the car. Emily took one of his hands and put it inside her blouse, placing his hand on one of her bare breasts. She took his other hand and rested it on her inner left thigh. Desi massaged her breasts with one hand and moved his other hand steadily up her thigh until his fingers reached her panties. Emily's kisses became increasingly stronger as she moved her tongue inside his mouth. Her hands undid Desi's belt buckle. She struggled with the zipper of his pants, which was tightly hugging the part of his anatomy to which Emily was shamelessly seeking access. Rather than pausing to assist Emily in getting his zipper undone, Desi sent his fingers on ahead, first inside the panties along the leg line, and then up, over, and under the waistband, into what she had described the prior weekend as the "Garden of Emily." Emily's body soon started to quiver, so she gave up her struggle with Desi's zipper. As Desi continued his massage, she hungrily kissed him until she collapsed in his arms.

All that Desi could then sense was the sound of the river in the distance. Desi imagined that Emily was also tuned in to the calming sound of the water sliding over the river rocks, and then off to some unseen destination.

A couple of minutes went by before Emily abruptly sat up. "Shit, dude. I'm sorry I came so fast, but it has been a long time since anyone touched me down there. And I don't think anyone ever touched me so I lost it like that."

"I'm glad you didn't hold back and just enjoyed it," Desi said. "It is very peaceful out here. Is this one of the make out spots for the locals?"

"When I visited Mama Boone during my high school summers, I did get invited by boys to do some 'necking' out here. But today was a whole new experience."

"I was wondering if the local sheriff regularly patrols the area."

"I don't think they bother people who park here during the daytime. Maybe I can do something special for you?" Emily offered.

"Maybe you can later, back at the house, when I don't feel like I have to be watching for the sheriff, fishermen, or any other surprises."

"All right, we better go, but thanks for spicing up my afternoon," Emily said. "I'd say let's come back here tonight, but that's probably when the high school kids arrive. Glad you accommodated my needs, and I didn't have to wait until dark."

"Stacey refers to sex around lunchtime as an 'afternoon matinee,' " Desi shared. "I'd stop by the house on a beautiful Saturday or Sunday after covering an event for the paper, and

I'd ask Charlie and Stacey why they weren't out and about. They would tell me they had enjoyed an 'afternoon matinee.' I guess they prefer the indoor movie theater atmosphere of a bedroom with the TV on, rather than woodsy, nature trail sex."

"Well, which do you prefer, Desi?"

"It might depend on the time of day. The first time I got lucky was on the top of a picnic table in a public park, on a quiet weekday, right about this time of day," Desi admitted. "At night, an outdoor movie theater in a station wagon works for me."

"Are you telling me that, if this place had a picnic table, I could convince you to stay here a bit longer?"

"I'm just saying that the next time you steer me off to some secluded spot, it better have a picnic table or a nature walk leading to a leafy, canopied clearing,"

"Wow, I wouldn't have guessed that a guy who went to NYU would be so into the outdoor sex thing," Emily said. "I do know a few places that might put the 'Great' into the Great Outdoors for you. My parents' house in Maryland has a treehouse in the backyard. "

"A tree house might be even better than a picnic table."

"I used to play with my dolls in that sweet old tree house," Emily remembered. "My Ken doll would make-out with Barbie up there in the tree house when I was in sixth grade. I think I was jealous of Barbie."

"Have you ever considered taking your dolls in for some sort of group therapy?" Desi asked with a smile. "I thought the girls in my sixth-grade class were delusional, but you might have outdone them with your fixation on inanimate objects. The girls I knew would spend hours arguing over which one of the Beatles they would pick to make out with, but as improbable as any of that is, at least it would have been humanly possible."

Emily punched Desi in the arm. "And when *you* go to therapy, you should tell them that you're still scarred from girls ignoring you in sixth grade."

They both were laughing as Desi started up his car and headed back along the dirt road to the paved country thoroughfare going into town. By the time they got to the meat store, Emily had put her shorts back on. She fully buttoned her blouse but was braless when she walked into the butcher shop with Desi.

The middle-aged man behind the counter greeted her with a hearty, "Good afternoon, Miss Miller," followed by the question she knew she was going to get." Did your parents enjoy those steaks last weekend?"

"Sorry to say that my parents weren't able to make it to Kentucky for the Derby last weekend, Mr. Mercer," was Emily's answer. "But those wonderful steaks didn't go to waste. My friend here made sure they were individually cooked to everyone's taste and enjoyment."

"Are you a Kentucky grilling master?" the store's proprietor asked Desi as he reached across the counter to shake Desi's hand.

"No sir," Desi replied. "I'm from Long Island, in New York. Emily's family has a very fancy outdoor gas grill that provides the heat the steaks deserve."

"Yes, you are right. If you don't have a grill that gives the steaks that seared flavor, you might as well not bother with buying steaks," the butcher shop owner said. "It's like my daddy used to say, you have to treat your steaks like your women, with all the attention to their needs that you can muster."

"Don't think I ever heard that one before," Desi said.

"Guess they don't say that up in New York," the butcher said. "That's too bad for the steaks and for the women."

Emily laughed out loud. Desi just smiled.

"So, you drove down from New York for the Derby and decided to hang around?"

"I'm stationed at Fort Knox and have been in Kentucky for about a year."

"Well, you managed to find one of the finest women in this state or any state," the butcher said. "The boys around here, like my son, aren't smart enough to appreciate a woman like Emma Lee Miller."

Desi just shrugged.

"How is Jesse?" Emily asked.

"Don't really know. He was supposed to come in and help me with the store today, but he still hasn't shown up," Mercer said. "I'll tell him that he missed you."

"Please say hello for me," Emily requested. "Guess I haven't seen him in years."

Another customer came into the store. The butcher, who had been leaning over the counter and smiling at Emily, suddenly straightened up and spoke in a more serious tone. "I am sure that you did not stop by to say hello to Jesse. What can I get for you?"

Emily sensed that the chit chat was over. "I know you sometimes have some freshly ground hamburger meat," Emily said.

"Well, I did earlier, but we sold the last of it just about ten or fifteen minutes ago."

Emily's smile disappeared from her face.

The butcher said, "We have a special on the frozen burgers. You get two dozen in the package."

"No, I already have a package of them back at the house. Guess we'll just put the ones I already have on the grill. I was just trying to have something special for my guests today."

"Tell you what, I have a half-dozen lamb chops left that would be great for appetizers. Young man, can you muster your grilling skills to fix some delicious lamb chops?"

Desi nodded to confirm his interest in trying.

The butcher wrapped up the lamb chops remaining in his glass case and put them on the counter. "I've got some special homemade mint sauce. Do you think you would use it?"

"I know I will," Desi said.

"Young lady," the butcher said. "I am going to put this on your daddy's tab, but if you don't like these lamb chops, it's on the house. Sorry, we were out of what you wanted." He then handed Desi the package of lamb chops, along with a small glass jar of the mint sauce with the meat store's label on it.

He turned to the next customer saying, "Howdy, Mitch."

When they got back into the car, Emily said, "I can't believe we missed getting the fresh ground beef by just a few minutes."

"I'm looking forward to taking a bite out of a lamb chop," Desi said as he kissed and then started to bite Emily's neck.

"You had your chance to give me a hickey earlier," Emily said as she pulled away. "We better get back to the house."

While Emily and Desi were away from Emily's grandmother's house, Sam managed to get the pickup truck to start. Stacey rewarded him with a margarita and a few tokes off of one of the joints Desdemona had provided. Sam, Stacey, and Linda had seemingly started playing cards on the patio by the pool, though they kept having to restart after one of them received a hand they didn't like and protested about how the cards were not properly shuffled. When Linda protested, she insisted they change the game they were playing. Even after repeated new shuffles and calls for changing what game they were playing led to no result, it didn't seem to bother any of them.

When Desi and Emily walked into the pool area from the gate leading to the garage and asked who was winning, they were met with numerous allegations of who was cheating or simply not playing by the rules. All the allegations were accompanied with plenty of laughter from Sam, Stacey, and Linda.

"Guess they didn't miss us," Emily said to Desi as she walked over to one of the sliding doors that led inside the house. Desi followed behind her holding the package of lamb chops.

Once inside the house, Emily turned to Desi and asked, "What would you like to nibble on first, me or those lamb chops?"

Desi looked down at the lamb chops. "It's only going to take a few minutes to get the lamb chops cooked on the grill and a matter of seconds for us to eat them. I will happily do anything for you after that."

Emily shook her head. "We had what I thought was good phone sex this week, but after what you did for me today down by the river, you have me crazy for more." She took in a deep breath and then let out a long exhale. "Alright, go play with the grill. But after that, I am going to hold you to your promise to do anything I want."

"I'm sure that your pleasure will be my pleasure," Desi said as he walked back out to the patio.

As Desi started up the propane grill, Sam got up out of his chair and walked over to see if he could help Desi. "What's ya got to put on the grill?" Sam asked. "I am starting to get a bad case of the munchies."

"I figured you might be in the mood to share some lamb chops," Desi said. "I am getting pretty hungry too." Desi opened the package and let Sam take a look at the chops.

"Those look great!" Sam exclaimed. "Is that Colorado lamb?"

"I don't know, the butcher said it was really fresh. Not sure if it came from Colorado or whether it is Kentucky lamb. Ever had Colorado lamb in Colorado?" Desi asked as he got the heat going on the three-burner grill.

"I was doing a tour with a band in Nevada and Arizona," Sam said. "We were playing in a casino town named Laughlin. The casino where we played was right on the Colorado River. The manager of the place told us that they would pay us a hundred dollars each, and with tips, we might each take away another hundred. Not sure why it didn't go as well as we had hoped. Either the gamblers were broke or the people there just weren't into the music we were playing. We covered a lot of songs by The Doors that night because we had a great keyboard player with us, and we were really into hearing how well he could play their music. So, in the end, I think we only made a hundred bucks and enough for a good dinner. The place made us pay for our food and drinks. Anyway, they had great dinners, and the lamb chops were so good, they were…" Sam paused to think more about describing them.

"Unforgettable?" Desi suggested.

Sam smiled, and nodded his head.

Stacey came alongside them at that moment. "Unforgettable?" she asked. "Are you guys talking about me?"

"Sam is sharing a story about eating at a place on the Colorado River that had delicious Colorado lamb chops," Desi explained. "Do you have a best lamb dinner story?"

"Well, I don't think I've had the lamb at that restaurant on the Colorado River," Stacey said. "In fact, I know I haven't because I have never been west of the Mississippi River. But at Shakta's restaurant one night, they were serving Indian food with some American twists. They had the Lamb Saag with not just spinach but also collard greens and various other kinds of greens all mixed in."

"Sounds good," Desi said as he put the lamb chops on the grill. "I may have to try that sometime."

"I think you may be getting your chance sometime soon," Stacey revealed. "I haven't had the chance to tell you yet, but we have a couple of guests for my going away party that may force a change of location from your place to the restaurant or to the farm."

"The farm?" Desi asked. "The place with the guru and the husbands of the women who work at Shakta's? Who are these special guests who are changing the location of your going away event?"

"Try my mother and my aunt, Desdemona's mother," Stacey said.

"Really?" Desi exclaimed, as if he was amazed with Stacey's response. "And you don't want your mother and your aunt seeing where you lived with Charlie?"

Stacey was quiet.

"What are their names?" Desi asked.

"My mother's name is Kadiatu, and Desdemona's mother's name is Isata," Stacey said. "Both of their names are pretty common for women of the Geechi-Gullah culture. They want to see me and give me a gift before I go to Germany. I don't need anything more to take overseas, but I've asked them to bring me an African style straw basket so I can give it to you, Desi."

"Why would you want to give me the gift that they are bringing?" Desi asked.

"I guess I want to leave something with you so you will describe me as unforgettable," Stacey said.

Desi found his eyes tearing up as he gave Stacey a hug. "Maybe we could still do a small dinner with anyone you want at the house," Desi said.

"Probably not with my mom and my aunt," Stacey replied, her eyes also appearing moist.

Sam tapped Desi on the shoulder. "You want me to take over with the lamb chops?" he asked.

Desi wiped his eyes, stepped back from Stacey, and flipped the lamb chops. "I won't be surprised if it is just the three of us eating the six lamb chops."

"I don't think I need more than one," Stacey said.

"Just taste one with the special mint sauce and give us your critique. That's all I ask," Desi said.

Linda walked up to Desi in her new French bikini, which, even when covered with an open knit bathing suit cover-up, revealed all the generous curves of her body. She offered Desi a freshly made margarita. "I got something special for you, Desi," she said with a wink.

Stacey shook her head. "Linda has been asking about you for about an hour. She's been saying she wants to 'unveil' her new bathing suit for you even before she got high and had several drinks."

"Hello, Linda," Desi said as he took one of the lamb chops off the grill and put it on a plate with some of the special mint sauce on the side. "And I have something special for you."

"Something hot to put in my mouth?" Linda asked as she took the plate from Desi. "Oh, there's a nice hard bone to hold," she said as she lifted the lamb chop off the plate and licked at the meat.

Emily came out of the house wearing her new string bikini. She looked at Linda licking the lamb chop. "Was that part of your erotic dancer routine?" she asked.

Linda nodded her head to indicate "yes." She then opened her mouth and took a large bite.

"I bet the bite part made the fellas squirm," Stacey opined.

Desi handed a plate to Stacey with a lamb chop and special mint sauce on it. She lifted the chop up in the air like Linda. "Did two of the dancers ever demonstrate their licking ability at the same time?" Stacey asked as she moved close to Linda.

"You mean like this?" Linda asked as she pushed in close to Stacey and started to lick one side of the lamb chop that Stacey held up. Stacey stuck out her tongue and began licking her side of the same lamb chop.

"I should get a picture of this so the meat store can hang it in their window," Desi said. "The caption could be 'women go crazy over our meat.' "

"Desi, one of your God given talents may be marketing," Sam said without taking his eyes off of Stacey's and Linda's antics.

Stacey stopped licking the lamb chop. "See," she said while looking at Sam but pointing to Desi. "There's another of Desi's talents for the list."

Desi offered a plate to Emily with a lamb chop and the special mint sauce on the side. She waved the plate off.

"I thought Desi would use the appetizers from the butcher's shop to show off his cooking ability, not to feature in some R-rated talent contest," Emily said. "Think I'll take a pass on the lamb chop."

Stacey looked at the lamb chop she was holding. "Not sure what I want to do with this one," she said.

"Have Desi put it back on the grill for a minute or two. Someone will eat it," Linda said as she finished eating her lamb chop. "They are really tasty with that special sauce."

Desi handed Sam a plate with two lamb chops covered with the mint sauce. Sam wolfed them both down. Desi then gave Stacey a replacement lamb chop and took the slightly used one from her. Desi put Stacey's first lamb chop back on the grill and ate the remaining plated lamb chop himself. The reheated lamb chop stayed on the grill. Desi turned the gas off and pulled the hood down.

"When are we going to have that chicken fight in the pool?" Emily asked. "Who is willing to try and knock me off of Desi's shoulders?"

Stacey took the last bite of her replacement lamb chop. "Sam and I will take that challenge," Stacey announced while tossing the remnant in a nearby garbage can.

"We will?" Sam questioned. "I didn't even bring a bathing suit."

"That will really make things interesting," Stacey replied.

"I have a pair of my friend's gym shorts that he left at my house last weekend," Desi said. "I forgot to mail them to him this week. I have them in the front trunk of my car. You look to be about the same size as Roger. What size is your waist?"

"I wear a size 36," Sam said. "I got down to 34 in basic training, but I sort of inched my way back up."

"Sounds like you've used that pun before, "Desi said. "I'll go out to the car and get those gym shorts and my swim stuff from the trunk."

"You keep your swim trunks in a trunk," remarked Emily. "A bit repetitive, but appropriate. Please hurry back before I change my mind about the pool activities and what's appropriate for me to do in a string bikini."

"I'll be guided accordingly," Desi said.

Within ten minutes, they were all suited up and in the pool.

"Desi, I am feeling very vulnerable in a string bikini when Stacey is wearing a one piece," Emily whispered to Desi.

"Don't worry," Desi whispered back. "I have a plan."

"I'm certainly going to lose my bathing suit if it is not a good one," Emily fretted.

After a few preliminary moves by both teams, Desi managed to get to a position behind Sam, and Stacey. By pressing the front of his knee behind one of Sam's knees, Desi forced Sam to take a step closer to the edge where the shallow end of the pool fell off into the deep end. "Wrap your legs tightly around my neck," Desi called out to Emily. He then took his hands off Emily's thighs and helped Emily push Stacey into the deep end. Sam made another step to keep Stacey from falling forward but his foot skidded down into the deep end and both Stacey and Sam went under.

Emily got so excited with their win that she squeezed Desi's neck even tighter with her legs. When he felt he was being choked, Desi started coughing. He tapped on her thighs.

"Sorry, Desi," Emily said when she realized she was taking Desi's breath away.

Linda stood up from her lounge chair. She undid the front bow of her belt and a back button of her beach cover-up, letting the garment fall to the patio deck. "You may have won that round, Emily, but get ready for the main event," Linda said.

"This is going to be a real fight to keep my bikini on," Emily said to Desi.

"You have to grab her top first and hope she gives up," Desi said.

Sam swam to the ladder in the deep end where Linda was waiting for him. She walked down the ladder backwards to get on his shoulders. Once Linda was on Sam's broad shoulders, they inched along the side of the pool with Sam carefully walking along a small ledge about five feet below the surface.

"I think Linda is tiring Sam just by getting her to the shallow end," Desi said. "Maybe we have a chance."

At first, the two couples merely circled each other in the shallow end . Desi then tried a forward lunge and a quick step back to get Linda to reach out and off balanced. He did that several times before Emily was able to grab and pull off Linda's bikini top. Emily held it up, declaring, "We win!"

Linda ran her hands up through her hair, not bothering to cover her large nipples. "Not so fast," she said. "You haven't knocked me off my steed."

When they resumed their aquatic battle, Desi and Sam had their legs in chockablock positions. Linda and Emily had their arms so intertwined they could hardly push each other with their hands. Each team was so intently involved in the skirmish that they had failed to see Emily's father walk out of the house and onto the patio deck. Wearing a blue golf shirt and white trousers with some fashionable footwear, his outfit would have served him well at a golf club cocktail party. His face was fixed in a scowl for several moments before he bellowed, "Emma Lee," loudly enough that there seemed to be an echo off the rise on the other side of the cornfield.

Emily, suddenly distracted, dropped her defenses. Linda, still not realizing who had shouted Emily's name, grabbed the front of Emily's top and pulled it away from Emily's torso.

For a moment, Emily was sitting astride Desi's shoulders, staring at her father with no top on. She then kicked out her legs and fell back into the water.

"We win!" Linda, still topless and holding Emily's bikini top, hollered out. Then she noticed Emily's father out of the corner of her eye. Linda covered her nipples but stayed on Sam's shoulders.

Desi motioned for Sam to head for the deep end as Desi began his swim behind Emily towards the ladder in the deep end, which was on the other side of the pool from where her father was standing. After climbing up the ladder, Emily went over to the lounge chair next to the one where Linda had been sitting earlier. Emily grabbed a folded beach towel off the lounge chair and wrapped herself in it. After walking around the pool to confront her father, the two of them looked at each other for a moment and then went into the house.

Desi went up the ladder and found a lounge chair to sit on while he waited for Emily to return.

Linda and Sam also got out of the pool by way of the ladder. Linda, still topless and with Emily's bikini top in her hand, walked in front of Desi and threw the black bikini top with gold ribbing at Desi. She then returned to her lounge chair and sunned herself on her stomach to dry off. Sam found a lounge chair away from Desi, and even further away from Linda. Stacey walked over and sat on the lounge chair next to Desi. She joined Desi in squinting their eyes to try to read the lips of Emily and her father. They couldn't make out much more than that Emily was crying, and her father was doing most of the talking.

After about fifteen minutes, Emily's father came out from the house and opened the cover of the grill. He had a handful of the photographs that Stacey brought with her in the large envelope.

"Oh shit," Stacey said to Desi. "He's got the photos of you guys in bed."

"How did he get them?" Desi asked.

"After Linda and I got high, I was showing her the pictures while we were sitting by the fireplace. I guess we left them out on the sofa."

Linda wrapped a towel around herself and came over to the lounge chair where Stacey was sitting. She sat down next to Stacey, who was facing Desi. "He doesn't have the photos with Desi's hands on Emily's bare chest," Linda said. "I put those under Emily's pillow, so the next time she has phone sex with Desi she'll have them to look at."

"If there is a next time," Desi said. "She may never want to see or talk to me again."

"Her father probably doesn't want Emily to ever talk to you or see you again," Stacey said. "I wonder if there is anything we can do to calm things down."

Desi looked at Linda. "Do you have any ideas?"

Linda nodded her head before answering. "He should know that the more he tries to restrict Emily from being with Desi, the more determined Emily will be to find ways to be with Desi," She then stood up and started walking around the pool towards Emily's father with the towel draped over her shoulders and her arms folded over her chest.

By the time she got to the grill area, Emily's father had the burners going and was starting to feed the photos into the flames.

"Whose lamb chop is this?" Reverend Miller said abruptly to Linda as she approached him.

"It's your grill and your house, so it must belong to you," Linda said in reply.

Emily's father fed another couple of photos into the flames. "I haven't had anything to eat since I started the drive here early this morning," he said. "I see there is still some of the special mint sauce from the meat shop left too."

"Go ahead," Linda said. "Emily said the butcher put it all on your tab, so enjoy."

Emily's father stopped feeding the photos into the burners. He took the remaining few photos and threw them in the garbage. He focused on the well-cooked lamb chop and getting it on a plate with some of the mint sauce. After taking a bite, he turned to Linda. "So, what do you think?"

"I think I was right," Linda said.

"Right about what?" Reverend Miller asked.

"I told everyone that someone would want a lamb chop that's been around a bit," Linda said.

"No, I don't mean about the lamb chop. What do you think about this guy, Desi?"

Linda unfolded her arms to reveal some of her substantial cleavage. "If Emily left Desi out on a plate, I'd be willing to take a bite of him," she said as she walked into the house.

Reverend Miller chewed on the remaining part of the lamb chop and gazed across the pool at Desi, Sam, and Stacey. When he finished eating, he walked around the pool and introduced himself.

Desi, Sam and Stacey all stood up to greet him. Without Emily making the introductions, the formality of the greetings seemed quite strained.

Desi then noticed Linda, looking agitated, stumbling out of the house in a pair of shorts and an "Oregon" T-shirt. "Desi, Emily is leaving," Linda said. "Maybe you can stop her."

Desi ran around the pool, past Linda, and into the house. He got to the front door just as Emily was driving down the driveway. She turned her blue Mustang onto the road into town. A few moments later, Desi was joined at the front door by Linda and Emily's dad.

"Did she say where she was going?" Desi asked Linda.

Linda shook her head.

"Holy Moses!" Emily's father said. "I was thinking she would drive me to the airport so I can get back to Baltimore this evening."

"She probably is heading to Lexington," Linda surmised.

"And I forgot to give her the letter from the University of Louisville Law School that came to our house," Emily's father said. "I think she has been accepted."

"I knew she would get in," Linda said. "She is graduating in a couple weeks and now has a law school all lined up. Meanwhile, I am going to be a couple credits shy of graduating and nobody seems to want me," Linda said sullenly.

"I think you are putting your situation in the worst possible light. You can easily get a couple of credits during the summer and have your degree before the end of this year," Reverend Miller pointed out.

"I needed one credit to graduate from NYU. One of my journalism professors came up with a project where I was able to do some research and write a paper for the one credit," Desi said. "The independent study regarded the Centennial of the Declaration of Independence. I think he was working on something back in 1974 that was in connection with preparations for the Bicentennial this year. So, I did some research and wrote a paper on the exposition in Philadelphia in 1876, just a few years after the Civil War," Desi explained. "The research and the paper took less than five weeks, and with that one last credit, I then had everything for my undergraduate degree."

"Do you still have a copy of that paper?" Linda asked.

"Desi can't do it for you," Reverend Miller replied sternly.

"I can't do it for you, but you might want to pitch the idea of doing something regarding the Bicentennial to one of your professors," Desi said. "I still have a copy of that paper in the portfolio I keep of my writing. You can take a look at it and maybe get a few ideas."

"That could be interesting for you, Linda," Reverend Miller said. "Maybe you could find out what activities are being planned here in Kentucky and in the cities that have been our Nation's Capitals."

"I think the Bicentennial would be more interesting for me than the Centennial," Linda said.

"Linda, can I leave the U of L Law School letter with you to give to Emma Lee?" Reverend Miller asked. "I have to get it out of the bag I dropped by the fireplace. Guess my jaw also dropped when I saw those photos spread out on the couch."

He walked from the front door into the living room to retrieve his bag. Reverend Miller came back with the letter in one hand and his canvas beach bag in the other. The blue canvas bag had "DELMAR" written in white letters on each side.

He handed the letter to Linda and looked at his watch. "I gotta get going if I want to make my plane."

Emily's father took his bag and headed to the garage. Desi went outside by the pool and listened to hear if Reverend Miller could get the pickup truck to start. After several attempts, Emily's father walked over to the pool patio.

"Young man," he said to Desi. "Would you be so kind as to give an Army veteran a ride to the Lexington Airport."

"I would be happy to drop you at the airport," Desi said, catching himself when he started emphasizing the word "drop." Desi paused. "How about if I carry your bag?" he asked, taking it without waiting for an answer. Desi proceeded to walk quickly through the house and out the front door, leaving Reverend Miller to follow behind.

Desi got in his car and sat in the driver's seat for a moment. He unlocked the passenger door and pushed it open when Emily's father arrived beside the car. Desi started to unlock the front trunk to put the blue canvas bag in the front storage area. However, on seeing Emily's blue bra on the back seat out of the corner of his eye, he quickly threw the canvas bag on the back seat to cover the item of clothing.

Reverend Miller got into the car without acknowledging what Desi used his bag to hide. "I hear that you are a gentleman, Mr. McKoy, or may I call you Desi?"

"Desi, or Specialist McKoy, whichever you are comfortable with," Desi said. "Perhaps I was not raised as, or received the training of a southern gentleman, but for what we had where I grew up, nursery school with jackets and ties, as well as music lessons starting at age six, I did suffer through that. Later, when I attended the Merchant Marine Academy, we were taught how to set a formal table and not to be the last guest remaining at a dinner party."

"Some of that has probably served you well," Reverend Miller said as they left the driveway and headed to Lexington.

"Well, as a gentleman, I have a sense that it is best to avoid talking about politics, religion and sex with someone you just met," Desi said. "And as much as I have become very fond of your daughter, within only a week's time, rest assured, I am not going to inquire as to the size of her dowry," Desi added, adopting the faux aloofness of the nouveau riche.

"If we are not going to talk about any of those subjects, it is going to be a mighty quiet ride to the airport," Reverend Miller remarked. "But I am glad to hear that you are fond of my daughter as I think she has, according to my wife and what I heard over the radio on Derby Day, fallen head over heels for you. As for a dowry, if that time ever comes around, I am not the one you need to speak with. Emily's maternal grandmother in Philadelphia is the one you have to lobby for the mansion or the *pied-à-terre*."

"Emily hasn't told me much about that grandmother," Desi replied.

"Well, both of Emma Lee's grandmothers were nurses around the time of the First World War," Reverend Miller told Desi. "My mother went up to where you are from, Long Island, to help treat soldiers going to and returning from Europe, many of whom were stricken by that virus which seemed to cause as many casualties as the fighting."

"I know that Grandma Boone was from Kentucky. Emily's other grandmother was from Virginia?" Desi asked.

"Grandma Helen was part of the Lee family of Virginia. She married into a family with a long line of distinguished medical doctors in Philadelphia going back to before the Revolutionary War. Leading up to the Civil War, they were mostly Quakers and active abolitionists. Now they are mostly FDR Democrats, but I digress."

"Yeah, I think we want to hold off on politics," Desi said.

"So, Grandma Helen, also known as Grandma Litchfield, who was studying to be a nurse in Virginia, decided she wanted to be a nurse in France. She got a job at a hospital in Paris and met a few American doctors there. She got engaged to one of the American doctors after about six months in Paris. Something happened to that doctor. He returned to the States right about the time the Allies marched into Berlin and the war was over. He didn't return to Europe. Grandma Helen met up with a group of American nurses and a female doctor who had decided to stay in France and assist French women, many of whom were widows with small children. She was part of a well-educated group of women who taught public hygiene and childcare in France. She later came back to the United States, resumed her studies and her activities as a suffragette, and went on to have a career as a public health nurse. Grandma Helen married Doctor Litchfield, one of the other doctors she met in Paris, a gentleman from Philadelphia. He got her to vow to never return to the South. Grandma Litchfield now lives in Philadelphia and is determined to see Emma Lee marry a doctor, just as she was determined to see Emma Lee's mother marry a doctor. But I came along, not an MD, only a theology student."

"I understand you have a Ph.D. in Theology, after having served as a medic in World War II, right?"

"Maybe my service as a medic helped me a little bit with Mama Litchfield," Reverend Miller suggested.

"Maybe the fact that you grew up in Kentucky didn't hurt either. I guess I might have two strikes against me if I have the opportunity to meet Grandma Litchfield."

"When we were back at Mama Boone's house earlier, Linda said something about 'when someone is really hungry for something, they don't make as much of an inquiry as they should,' " Reverend Miller said. "I hope that Emma Lee makes a serious inquiry into your true feelings about her before she gives away her heart. I feel like you aren't, at least today, going to reveal too much as to whether you can imagine Emma Lee in your future. She hasn't been very lucky in terms of the guys with whom she has had relationships. As a father, I just don't want to see her hurt or end up cynical about love."

"I am not sure that what Linda said was intended to be that deep or about love, but I don't think you need to worry about your daughter. She is beautiful in many ways and intelligent in many ways. She is high-spirited, also. As for love, she seems well grounded in knowing she is loved and that she is capable of changing other peoples' lives with the love she has to share."

"I am not sure that she loves me right now," Reverend Miller revealed.

"I know that she loves her daddy. I saw her wrestling on the ground with her cousin, Honey Boone, last weekend because her cousin made a threatening remark aimed at you."

"Now you've raised two things that I want to know more about. First is what you thought Linda was talking about when I heard her say that thing about making inquiries. Next, what could Emma Lee's cousin have said that would get them wrestling on the ground?"

"Well, I think you need to talk to your daughter about what caused the wrestling match at the distillery. And you might want to ask Linda what she had on her mind when she made that remark about making inquiries. If she doesn't remember, remind her that you were both standing near the grill."

"Oh, no, had the lamb chop fallen on the ground before I heated it up and ate it?"

"It had a more colorful history than falling on the ground, but it might be best if Linda described why it was left on the grill," Desi suggested.

"Do you think it will make me sick?" Reverend Miller asked.

"As I am not a physician, all I can give you is my personal opinion."

"So, what is your personal opinion?"

"Will you get physically sick? I don't think so," Desi concluded.

"Now I am really intrigued; maybe I'll call Linda from the airport to ask her about the lamb chop."

"Why don't you wait until after you fly home and see if you can reach Emily tomorrow, when the dust has had a chance to settle. The thing with Linda can wait."

They sat silently for the rest of the ride to the airport.

After Desi pulled up to the sidewalk outside the terminal, Reverend Miller reached back and lifted his beach bag off the back seat. "I don't know if I should ask if that is Emma Lee's or not," he said after he took a quick look at the bra and got out of the car. Adding, as he walked towards the terminal, "And you, as a gentleman, shouldn't answer in any event."

Chapter VII

NASHVILLE STORYLINE

The sound of the phone ringing in Desi's kitchen awakened him from a dream about finding Emily's blue Mustang in a parking lot at the Smith Haven Mall on Long Island. The dream had only progressed to the point of Desi walking up to her car and starting to speak to Emily; but he didn't see or hear Emily. When he got to the driver's door, the window rolled down, and it was Debi behind the wheel.

As he awakened, Desi realized he was not in bed alone, but he was sure it was not Debi. The sheets covering the figure next to him suggested someone slimmer, shaped a bit like Debi's sister Tammy. For a moment, he searched the room for anything that could belong to Tammy. The only article of clothing he saw was a pair of grey cotton briefs on the floor, which he recognized as his own. He leaned out of bed and retrieved the briefs.

Desi was still adjusting his briefs when he made it to the wall phone in the kitchen. "Yeah," he said in an indifferent tone, thinking there could be no one he knew who would be calling that early on a Sunday morning.

"Hey, baby," a voice said on the other end of the line.

"I was just dreaming about you," Desi said, still unsure as to who was calling him.

"And I was dreaming about you," the soft sultry voice of a woman replied.

"When do I get to see you again?" Desi said, now figuring that it was either Debi or Emily.

"When do you want to see me again?"

Desi had been hoping there would have been more in the way of a response, so as to aid his deductive skills, which were still in low gear given the early morning hour. He shifted up his inquiry by saying, "How long would it take for you to get here?"

"Oh, I wasn't planning to fly to Kentucky. I was thinking we would meet in Washington D.C. sometime during the second week of June. I have been assigned to help on a book tour for one of our authors who just launched his new book."

As Desi knew that Debi had landed a job as an assistant editor at a publishing house, the mystery of who was calling was solved. Next, he had to find out why she was calling. "Are you going to be in Washington on June ninth, the annual oral sex holiday of the French Virgin Islands?"

"Since we were in college, I've researched your claims about that holiday in the French West Indies. I didn't find any mention of it when I checked holidays in Guadeloupe or Martinique. I suspect that you created the holiday in that brain of yours. But I'm telling you that you have a ready and willing partner to celebrate it with. I remembered our tradition, and it looks like I will be available, if you are willing to journey to D.C.," she said in a voice both vulnerable and extremely possessive.

"Would you be a ready and willing partner for merely the purposes of resurrecting our college tradition, or would you be an enthusiastic partner like I have never encountered before?"

"I guess it depends. You know I always prefer to receive the thirty-four and one-half treatment, which I will acknowledge your special ability in providing," Debi replied. "But I am willing to let you in on one of my outdoor sex fantasies that I know you will like."

"I take it that your love life leaves something to be desired," Desi stated simply.

"Aren't I making it pretty clear that you are the one I desire?" Debi countered.

"And how is your job with the publishing company going, other than the book tour?"

"They have promised they will give me credit for the next synopsis I write. I have been mostly ghostwriting things related to books on social science topics. Today, I am working on a synopsis that I think will go to a senior editor with my name on it."

"What's the topic?"

"It's on anthropology, like that course we took together."

"I remember that professor. She seemed to hate the whole world, and me in particular."

"You got a good grade in that class," Debi said. "I think she just had a thing for me."

"You're probably right. But she would give me accusatory looks when she went on her rants about what she hated in the world. One day, she was going off on what she called the 'fake hippies.' I think she meant young people who came from middle-class families and were cruising through her class at community college on their way to universities. She ended the whole diatribe with a nasty look at the two of us, particularly me," Desi recalled.

"Maybe we were looking to happy for her liking. Could have been that she was very unhappy during that spring semester of '72."

"I am sure it wasn't just that semester," Desi replied. "I was really tempted to challenge her about that 'fake hippie' stuff, like she was the arbiter of who was or was not sincere about changing the world. At least we went to a couple of rallies to protest against what our military was doing in Southeast Asia. She didn't seem to want to make any part of the course relevant to the present or about something specific to improve the future. I thought about giving her some push back, like asking if her phrase 'fake hippie' wasn't redundant. But that wasn't going to get her to shed more light from her bleak world. Who did she think the real hippies were anyway? The people wearing military surplus clothing from the Army-Navy store while they were panhandling at the airport?"

"I guess you waited until you got to NYU to confront professors," Debi said. "Some people may have felt that you were just trying to show off your debating skills, but I always thought you were sincere with the issues you were raising. I remember that time I visited you at NYU, when your professor conceded to your arguments. He took your philosophy class to lunch at a restaurant and let me come along too. You convinced him that he really hadn't delivered much in the way of intellectual nourishment."

"He said I had effectively made the case that his presentation of the subject matter was, in his words, like providing 'a hot dog without the wiener,' so he scheduled a nice lunch at the end of the semester," Desi recalled. "I also remember that he had you seated right next to him after I introduced you. That seemed to make him happy to pick up the tab."

"I'm starting to go through a book this weekend on political philosophy," Debi said.

"Well, you took more philosophy courses than I did. It should be easy for you."

"Yeah, but you have been more involved in politics," Debi noted. "I think I might want you to use your political, as well as your philosophical insights on the book, and see if you have the same take on the book as I do," Debi proposed.

"You are going to send me the book with some lead time, right?" Desi asked. "Let me read it without your critique so I can provide you with something more than just reinforcing your view. I may come up with the same things as you, but at least that way you know I read the book without just looking for what you found."

"You don't mind doing some intellectual exercise with me before we get into the physical part?"

"If we meet in Washington in a few weeks, we can grapple with life in all its dimensions."

Suddenly, there was the sound of flute music coming from behind Desi's closed bedroom door.

"Is someone practicing a musical instrument at your place?" Debi asked.

"I better go check on that. Send me the book and I'll get back to you," Desi said before he hung up.

Desi returned to his bedroom to find Penny sitting cross-legged on his bed wearing nothing but one of his NYU T-shirts and playing the flute portion of one of Steve Winwood's songs from his time in Traffic. Desi listened to her play for a minute.

"I think I got most of the notes for the flute part of the song," Penny said. "Why don't you climb back into bed and pretend to be a saxophone so I can try to play the sax notes."

Desi smiled and climbed back into the bed. "I'm ready to be whatever instrument you want to make music with."

Concocting the Seamless Story

About an hour later, they headed to Elizabethtown to pick up I-65 to Nashville. Once on the Interstate, Penny and Desi started rehearsing answers to questions they might have to answer during the brunch.

"Since my parents have already met you, they probably aren't going to be asking you many questions. But my sister, Nicole, will have lots of questions for the two of us, and maybe a few for you that I don't even know the answers to."

Desi pulled his Super Beetle off to the side of the highway. "I thought we were just going down to a restaurant in Nashville to talk about your parents' new house and see a few pictures of the place. Now I am finding out that your twin sister is going to be there. How do you expect to put something over on her?"

"Well, I didn't know about Nikki flying in from New York until two days ago. I wasn't sure how you would react," Penny admitted. "Today is Mother's Day, and our birthday is tomorrow.

My father thought it would be a nice surprise to fly my sister in so we could all celebrate together in Nashville."

"I think I am just going to let you do all the talking," Desi said.

"I think my sister will want to talk about herself and how she is going to Europe with her group from Julliard this summer to play her violin in Germany. My parents will want to talk about the new house. And I can tell them we were out late last night in Louisville celebrating my birthday to explain why you are so quiet."

"So, I won't say that I got back to my house last evening after an out-of-control pool party at Emily's place south of Bardstown, and you called me from the A1 Garage because your car wasn't going to be ready for you to drive today."

"I'll tell my sister, not in front of my parents, that our relationship has had its challenges but that we had a great time together last night."

"Are you going to say we spent the night at my apartment in Radcliff, or that we went out to dinner up in Louisville, maybe at Shakta's restaurant?"

"Fine with me," Penny said. "And what did I have for breakfast?"

"Just say something tasty from McKoy's, or McDonald's, depending on who you are telling what."

"Don't think I am going to share everything we did last night or this morning with even my twin sister. And I expect you will keep a few things secret from my sister."

"As I have been telling people recently, I am a gentleman."

"That is important to me, given what happened to me at Michigan State. I think I have to fill you in on something that is a bit embarrassing to me, but Nikki may let it slip out in some way."

"I didn't know that you went to Michigan State. I thought you just went to the community college where your father taught English Literature. How long did you attend Michigan State?"

"Only one semester," Penny recounted. "I was in the band playing flute, saxophone, and sometimes, like for the Christmas production with the chorus, I would play the French horn."

"I love the sound of a French horn. Is this story going to explain why you never went out with anyone in the Fort Knox Army Band?"

"Sort of, but the real problem was not with anyone in the band in Michigan; it was with two guys in the chorus. We were rehearsing for this big Christmas show, and there was this good-looking junior in the chorus who took a liking to me and an even better-looking senior, who also wanted to take me out."

"So, which one did you go out with?"

"Well, my mistake was to go out with one of them after a rehearsal on a Friday night and the other one the next day after a Saturday afternoon rehearsal," Penny said.

"Resentment, I believe, is more sustainable than love or hate," Desi said. "Let me guess. You got them resenting each other and hating you."

"Yes, and suddenly rumors started flying about how I was having sex with both of them. Actually, once I got alone with either one of them, they really turned me off. Neither one of those guys were able to think or talk about anything but themselves. The band director, who was also my advisor, tried to calm things down, but then people started talking about how I was having sex with him too."

"But you weren't having sex with your advisor?" Desi inquired.

"He was a very handsome man, but he was married with a couple of kids, and I have never had a sexual relationship with a married guy."

"I think that was a wise decision," Desi opined.

"By the time of the dress rehearsal for the concert, I could hear a few guys whispering, 'Miss Choral Sex' loud, so I could hear the nickname they gave me," Penny said, with tears coming to her eyes. "So, I really had no choice. I told my parents I couldn't perform and was coming home at the end of my first semester."

"That is really unfortunate. I've always thought my months at the Merchant Marine Academy were bad; however, fortunately, I got sent out to sea and away from the chicken shit nonsense,"

Desi said. "Your situation sounds like it was so rotten it's amazing you could get any sleep."

"I wasn't getting much rest, if any. My mother was asking me about whether I thought I needed a therapist. My sister was recruited to convince me to seek some therapy, so she knows all about what happened."

"You think your sister is going to bring up something about all that today?"

"Well, Nikki may not ask directly about whether I have been getting any counseling, but my family may still be wondering if my terrible experience is still keeping me from working on a bachelor's degree."

"Sounds like both of your parents have graduate degrees, right?"

"Yes. When I received my associate's degree from the community college, they were on me as to what four-year school I was going to attend. My answer was that I wanted to be part of a military band."

"How did they react?"

"My father, very sarcastically, asked me why I didn't just go off and join the French Foreign Legion," Penny recounted. "I told him that they use a different dialect of French than what I studied."

"They probably thought you were joking and weren't tough enough to be part of the military."

"I think they wondered if I was tough enough to face going on to a university. I just felt I had to do something other than what they expected."

"Well, if your sister asks me for my opinion, I am willing to testify under oath that you don't seem to have any performance issues at my place, whether it involves the flute or anything else," Desi said as he restarted his car and pulled back on the highway.

"My sister is actually a lot more in need of a therapist than I am. She's into all sorts of things that, to me, seem very fatalistic. She's into astrology, tarot cards, fortune-telling, and palm-reading. She is musically talented, but she is certainly not a songwriter. I can't recall her ever saying anything about writing a song, or even wanting to write a song."

"Did you ever finish the song you were working on back in April?" Desi asked.

"I think I finished the melody, but you were helping me with the lyrics, and the words just didn't seem to flow once I stopped staying at your house."

"Are you saying that I was your muse?" Desi teased.

"You seemed to keep me a…mused for a couple of months. I hope I helped you with your writing in some way."

"I think that perhaps, in some ways, you did." He offered:

Your good morning kiss
was the jump start to my day,
and your goodnight kiss with a warm embrace
had me sleeping with a smile on my face.

"Yes, and you gave me the ammunition to take on the world when you loaded your sweet words into my ears." Penny took a notepad and pen out of her handbag.

"What are you writing down?" Desi asked.

"I like what you said about the 'morning kiss' and the 'nightly embrace,' and I think I could redo the song I was writing to use my 'ammunition to take on the world' line to finish my song, particularly if I title it 'Loading Up On Your Love'," Penny said as she scribbled on her pad. "Why don't you use what you said in one of your poems?"

"I'm driving right now, but if you would please make a note for me, I'll see what I can do with it this week."

"Sure," Penny said as she wrote a few key words down for Desi. Then, she folded it and tucked it into his shirt pocket over his heart. "Just don't mention anything to my sister about how I keep trying to write a decent song, that really bugs her."

"Are you going to mention any of my efforts at writing, beyond what I write for the post newspaper?" Desi asked.

"I can't because my father is like my sister. He teaches English literature, but he is very limited in his ability to write a short story or a poem. I am more like my mother who can write, within a week or two, an elementary school play with music, or at least original lyrics to classic melodies."

"Is there anything else I shouldn't mention?"

"Don't bring up golf," Penny said. "If you get him started, that is all we will hear about for the whole afternoon."

"He loves golf, I guess. Well, other than mini-golf, I don't really play."

"But don't say that either, because then we all are going to be listening to how he will teach you how to play and that you will love it more than any other sport you have ever played. Maybe you can talk about how you have played golf at Fort Knox, but you prefer tennis. That could work, so we won't be pulling our hair out with all of his golf talk."

"Well, I do play tennis," Desi said. "That's actually how I met Debi. Her sister, Tammy, always claims to have introduced us, but I had played doubles tennis at a party with Debi weeks before I ever visited their parents' house. Tammy's story is that she introduced us when she invited me over to their parent's house."

"Oh, I certainly don't want you mentioning any ex-fiancée, girlfriends, sexy acquaintances, or any female other than me this afternoon. Under no circumstances, and I really mean this, should you flirt with Nikki. Not even if she starts flirting with you."

"What do I do if she starts touching my arm when she's talking to me?" Desi asked with a smile.

"Then you are going to have to move to where she can't reach you," Penny said with exasperation in her voice. "Maybe this whole afternoon is a disaster ready to unfold."

Desi held the steering wheel with his left hand and placed his right hand on Penny's shoulder. "I don't think you have to worry so much about a couple of hours with your folks and your sister. We'll have a nice brunch, maybe walk around on that street near the Ryman auditorium and head back to my apartment for the night."

"It's not going to be that simple." Penny took a long pause. "Nikki has a ticket to fly out of the airport in Louisville, and I promised her a ride from Nashville to Louisville."

"Alright, so maybe we do have a reason to be concerned. I am still taking you back to my place tonight, if only because your car is at the service station in Radcliff."

"I have to hope that you won't be asking me to sleep on your couch by the time this day is over," Penny said with a sigh.

Nashville Skyline Revisited

Desi knew from his prior meeting with Penny's parents, Professor and Mrs. Bright, that Penny's mother loved pink roses, so when they arrived in Nashville, he drove around the downtown area looking for a flower shop. The story he heard, at a prior brunch in Nashville, was that Penny's mother's family had owned a music store in Nashville and that Penny's mother would often receive a musical instrument and pink roses on her birthday.

Desi spotted a florist a couple of blocks from the courthouse and parked nearby. Penny and Desi got out of Desi's car and walked to the store. Inside there were buckets full of cut flowers and a large open box with gladiolas waiting to be put in a bucket. They could hear someone filling a bucket in the back of the store.

"It smells great in here," Penny said. She walked to a refrigerated glass showcase to examine the roses on display. "I see red roses and white roses, but no pink ones."

"Hello," Desi called out. A dark-haired woman with grey streaks in her hair came out from the back carrying a half-filled five-gallon bucket of water.

"Can I help you?" she said. She put down the bucket near the open box of gladiolas and straightened her apron. "Is there something in particular you are looking for?"

"We are hoping that you have some pink roses," Penny requested.

The woman looked over to the showcase and shook her head. "We don't have long stem pinks."

"Would you have any pink garnets?" Desi asked.

The woman went around to the side of the refrigerated boxed area and opened a door for the rear section of the showcase. After a couple of minutes, she came back with a small container of pink garnet roses. "How many do you need?" she asked.

"We need a dozen in a vase for a table decoration," Desi said as he took out his money clip.

Stacey opened her leather-fringed handbag. "It's my mother! I'm going to pay for these."

"No," Desi said. "This is a celebration of Mother's Day and your birthday, as well as your sister's. I want the flowers to be my gift to you and your sister, as well as your mother."

Penny closed her handbag. "That is very gallant of you, Sir Desmond McKoy," she said as she gave him a brief kiss on the lips.

"These will look great on any table for any occasion," the woman said as she took them to the back of the store to arrange in a small vase with some small leafy ferns and baby's breath.

When they got to the hotel restaurant Penny's mother removed the paper covering the flowers; her mother was thrilled. Nicole wanted to know where they got the flowers. Penny told them that Desi had searched out the best florist in Nashville as he wanted to get something special for their celebration.

Desi sat at the table with Penny's family and just gave them a smile. He was hoping that he was saying everything he needed to say that afternoon with the gift of the flowers.

Such hope was not long lived as Nicole started asking him lots of questions. It seemed like she wanted to know where he grew up on Long Island, what he studied at NYU, what his favorite places to eat in Greenwich Village were, and even asked if he had seen any performances at Carnegie Hall.

"Yes, I have seen Herbie Hancock perform at Carnegie Hall," Desi answered.

"Who?" Mrs. Bright asked.

"Not the 'Who', Mom," Penny teased. "The jazz musician, Herbie Hancock."

"I don't think I ever heard of him," Penny's mom said sheepishly.

"No surprise about that," Nicole said. "You are going to have to move on from all that rockabilly music you have been listening to for the last twenty years."

"Your mother listens to lots of different types of music," Prof. Bright said defensively. "Last night, she was not only listening to her Elvis records, but she also played one of the Beatles albums."

"I am sure there is plenty of music I have played for you two over the years that you have enjoyed as well," Mrs. Bright said.

Nicole looked at Penny, asking, "I can't think of any, can you?"

Penny shook her head.

Penny's mother looked at Desi. "Young man, you see what I am up against whenever these two are together," she said, pointing at Penny and Nicole. "Is there any music you enjoy that your parents also enjoy?"

Desi looked at Penny. "There are certain operettas by Gilbert and Sullivan, like the HMS Pinafore and the Mikado that my parents enjoy, and I grew up listening to and even being part of," Desi said. "I think Penny also appreciates Gilbert and Sullivan."

Mrs. Bright began to smile. "Did your parents sing or play musical instruments?"

"My father was a singer, and my mother sang, as well as played the piano."

Penny looked at Desi and then her mother. She admitted, "I'm a fan of Gilbert and Sullivan."

Nicole's face transformed into a stern frown aimed at Penny. "Desi, you probably know that Penny got the role of 'Josephine' in junior high school."

Desi shook his head.

"Really?" Nicole said with a sense of amazement in her voice. "For years, she would tell people, within minutes of meeting them, that she knew all the songs in the HMS Pinafore and about how she got that part in the school play. I wonder about how many other things she has held back telling you."

"Please, Nicole," Mrs. Bright said, shaking her head.

"And my mother, did she tell you about the time she was in Memphis with two little girls and left them with her aunt so she could go see Elvis?" Nicole said.

Desi and Penny started to laugh. "She did tell Desi the last time we were in Nashville that she met Elvis right before he was drafted," Penny acknowledged. Professor Bright and Mrs. Bright began to laugh along with Desi and Penny.

Nicole looked around for a waiter, saying, "When is our food going to get here?"

After they finished their brunch, they walked several blocks together from the hotel to the downtown district, with numerous bars serving beer, bourbon, and whiskey. They listened to several bands playing at the bars along the main street. Mrs. Bright announced that they had tickets to a matinee music show at the Ryman Auditorium, which was only about a block or so away from the bar where they were standing. "I only got two tickets because all of these musicians are middle-aged geezers, and I didn't want to hear Nikki or Penny complain," she said.

"It's not the guys from ZZ Top, is it?" Nicole asked. "Desi probably doesn't know that the Ryman Auditorium is known as the 'Carnegie Hall of the South.'"

"If you can get tickets to see Herbie Hancock there, I am sure Desi and I would go to the Ryman for that," Penny said. "Or Dylan, neither of us has ever seen Bob Dylan in concert."

"I can't imagine Bob Dylan playing electric guitar at the Ryman Auditorium," Mrs. Bright said. "The Ryman was the home of the Grand Ole Opry for about three decades until 1974. Now the Opry is part of the new Gaylord Opryland, out by a fancy hotel they are building."

"I think I'll stick with Bluegrass music at the Ryman," Prof. Bright said. "I may have grown up in the Boston area, but I definitely have a thing for Bluegrass."

"You don't like the poetry of Dylan?" Nicole asked. "You could probably come up with a new course at the University of the South just focused on the poetry of Bob Dylan."

"I'm more likely to be asked to teach a class on Dylan Thomas," Prof. Bright responded. "They offered me a job at the university because of my Shakespearian credentials, not my passing familiarity with the beat poets of San Francisco or Bob Dylan."

"How about you, Desi? Do you have any interest in poetry?" Nicole asked.

"One of my NYU classmates helped me produce a lyric poem in a TV production class. I got to wear a Greek gown and play a Greek harp," Desi recalled.

"My father gave me a lyre, one of those U-shaped harps, for my birthday one year," Mrs. Bright said.

"Desi, the classmate who dressed you up in the little Greek skirt, was it a female student?" Nicole asked.

"I am sure it was," Penny said, answering for Desi. "But I think he would have been modest enough to either keep his legs together or wear a jock strap or something under it."

"Which was it, Desi?" Nicole inquired.

"I don't recall right now, but I think I have a video copy of all of my directing efforts and the productions in which I was asked to be an actor," Desi answered.

"Were there auditions for that part?" Nicole asked.

"Can't you just stop?" Penny requested.

"I just have one more question."

"You promise?" Penny asked.

"Yes," Nicole conceded. "I just want to know if Desi wrote the poem he recited while playing the harp."

"The answer is yes," Penny said. "He let me read that poem and then recited it to me on Valentine's Day. It is very Shakespearean."

They were all very quiet for an uncomfortable amount of time.

Desi let out a laugh. "Since my Greek is limited to only a few choice words that sailors use to express their displeasure, I wrote the poem in English. But I think that my attempt to write in non-contemporary English laced the poem with flavors harkening back to Stratford-on-Avon."

Mrs. Bright asked, "Have you ever been to the Shakespeare Theater in Connecticut?"

"We went there when I was in high school for our senior trip," Desi replied.

"I love that place," Mrs. Bright said. "Maybe more than going to a theater on Broadway."

"What production did you see?" Prof. Bright asked.

"Othello, with Moses Gunn," Desi answered.

"Who is Moses Gunn?" Nicole asked. "Would I know him from some movie or something?"

"Did you see the movie *Shaft* with Richard Roundtree?" Desi asked.

Nicole nodded.

"Well, Moses Gunn played the badass drug kingpin, whose daughter was kidnapped by the mob," Desi explained.

"Sounds like the perfect actor to portray the role of Othello," Nicole commented.

"Oh, he was perfect until some kids from the city threw apples or oranges, or both, from their lunch bags on the set," Desi said. "Moses Gunn tossed them back and stormed off the set."

"I don't blame him," Mrs. Bright said.

"We didn't either," Desi said. "It was my first experience with interactive theater. A few years later, there was a production in New York City called Liquid Theater. I think almost all of that was interactive."

"Were you down in the Village when *National Lampoon's Lemmings* was being performed at the Bitter End?" Nicole asked.

"I saw it with Garrett Morris and others who went on to perform or write for SNL."

"And the Bottom Line – who did you see perform there?" Nicole asked.

The two performances I remember were Mark Sebastian, the younger brother of John Sebastian from the Lovin' Spoonful and Tower of Power, " Desi answered. "I got in free to help the recording crew from WNEW-FM and WNYU record the performance of Tower of Power. Don't think I had to do much but enjoy the show. They blew the place apart that night."

Penny grabbed Desi by the shoulders and shouted in his face, "You got to see Tower of Power perform live, in front of a small audience? I wish I could have been with you."

Desi gave her a hug, saying quietly, "But I hadn't even met you back then."

"I'm not sure how well you know her even now," Nicole said. "Penny is crazy about Tower of Power."

Desi hugged Penny more tightly. "I guess we are still finding out more about each other every day," he said before giving Penny a kiss on the lips. Penny threw her arms around his neck.

Professor and Mrs. Bright smiled at each other when they saw the two young lovers kiss.

"Nikki, your father and I are still finding out things about each other, even though we have been married for over twenty-five years," Mrs. Bright said. "That's the way it is once you find someone you can share things with."

"There are a couple of guys in New York that I spend time with," Nicole responded. "But it's more like we are just friends."

They stopped at an ice cream parlor and had dessert before Professor and Mrs. Bright went on to the Ryman Auditorium. Desi, Penny, and Nicole crossed over to the other side of the street.

"There is a place in Nashville I have heard about that I just have to check out," Nicole said.

"I haven't seen much in the way of clothing shops that I want to go into," Penny said.

"I'm not looking for something to cover any part of my body but to uncover, maybe discover, my soul," Nicole said.

"Is this another trip to a fortune teller to get directions to your soul mate?" Penny asked.

"There is a woman on this street, Miss Diana, who reportedly has a direct line to the Goddess of Love," Nicole said.

"But it's going to be a collect call, and I'm sure she wants you to pay for it," Penny replied.

"It might be worth it," Nicole mused.

"This looks like the place," Desi said as they came upon a storefront with a sign in the window, saying, "Get connected to the Goddess of Love."

Nicole grabbed Desi by the arm, saying, "Do you believe in soul mates?"

"I thought you were coming here to ask Miss Diana about where to find your soul mate," Desi responded. "You should be addressing your questions to her."

"So, you think there may be people who have answers to questions about soul mates?" Nicole persisted in asking.

"From what I have heard, it is best not to ask a fortune teller any question that can be answered by a simple 'yes' or a 'no,' " Desi suggested.

"Okay," Nicole said. "But how do I know if she is giving me any solid information if I ask her about finding my soul mate?" Nicole asked.

"I think if you pretend to be Desi's lover and ask her if you and Desi are getting married in a few years, it may expose her for being just another phony."

"I am willing to do that," Nicole said. "You don't mind if I hold Desi's hand when we meet with the fortune teller?"

"Yeah, I would mind," Penny said. "Forget that idea."

"How about if she just puts her hand on my arm, if you can sit on the other side of Nicole without staring at her touching me?" Desi asked.

"Ok," Penny said with a resigned sigh. "But the only place you should touch is Desi's arm."

"I won't do anything under the table," Nicole said with a chuckle.

Desi sat down at a table outside the storefront. Penny went over to the front door of the fortune teller's business. When she found that the doorknob would not open the door, she knocked on the door. She heard a voice from inside. Penny went over to the round table where Desi was sitting and sat down opposite him. Nicole sat down in a chair in between them.

"Desi will not bite you," Penny said. "You better sit closer to him if you want things to look believable."

Out from the door of the storefront came a woman with long black hair streaked with grey and a turban that matched her robe. She asked them, "Would you like some tea while you wait?"

"How long do we need to wait?" Penny asked.

"It depends. Are you planning to come inside individually or as a group?" the woman replied.

"Well, how much is it per person?" Penny asked.

"The session is about 30 minutes, and it is $50 for one person, $30 each for two people, and $20 a person for three people." The woman, who seemed curiously familiar, added, "If you want a full 30 minutes each, it is $50 a person."

"How about if you bring us the tea, and we will think about what we want to do," Desi said.

The woman smiled, nodded her head, and left to go back inside the storefront.

Once she went inside, Desi said, "Penny, you know who she is, right?"

"I know she looks familiar," Penny said.

"She is the woman in the flower shop!" Desi proclaimed.

"Oh, no," Penny said. "She better not be Miss Diana."

"If she is, then it's time to hit the road," Desi suggested.

"Let's give her a chance," Nicole said.

"I agree with Desi."

They sat quietly while they awaited the return of the woman. She came back carrying a tray with a teapot and three cups; she took a long look at Desi. "You were the guy this morning wanting me to go inside the refrigerator to look for pink garnet roses," the woman said with a smile. "How did everyone like the flowers?"

"Just fine," Desi said.

"I have them here in this bag," Penny said, lifting a paper shopping bag from the cement and putting it on top of the table.

The woman looked inside the bag. "I just help part-time at the florist," the woman said. "It was the first time I arranged flowers in a vase."

"They looked lovely on the table of the restaurant," Nicole said as she took the vase out of the shopping bag and placed the vase, which was still in a cardboard stand, on the table.

"Do you mind if I take them inside to show off my work?" the woman asked.

"No, go ahead," Nicole said.

The woman took the roses inside the storefront.

"What are you doing?" Penny said to Nicole.

"I am having some tea," answered Nicole as she poured tea for the three of them.

After several minutes, the woman came back outside without the roses. "Miss Diana wants to meet this gentleman. She has about an hour before her next class. She will meet with all of you for 45 minutes for $20 each."

Nicole opened her pocketbook and pulled out two twenty-dollar bills. "This is for me and my lover, Desi," she said as she handed the woman the cash.

"This better be good," Penny said as she handed the woman two ten-dollar bills.

When they entered the building, the woman had them sit on the cushioned window seats along the front bay window, which was so heavily curtained that no light came in from the outside. There was a large silver metal table in the center of the room with a crystal ball that, with light from the inside, provided the only illumination. On the opposite side of the room, there could be seen, in the low light, a long reception counter. They could also make out, on the wall behind the reception counter, a large, framed picture of a woman with flowing curly hair, wearing what appeared to be a harem outfit.

The three of them were left alone to stare at the picture. "It looks like Jane Russell in that gypsy movie from the 1950s," Penny said. "Desi has a thing for Jane Russell, as I found out when we went to a wedding for a woman, who, like her twin sister, looks a lot like the movie star."

"All I said was that the only thing better than a woman who looks like Jane Russell is two women who look like Jane Russell," Desi admitted.

"That is enough to imply a lot," Penny said. "What about gentlemen preferring blondes?"

"The two of you are beautiful, artistic, blondish women who are each unmatched in each of your own ways," Desi answered.

Nicole, who was sitting in between Penny and Desi, smiled and put her hand on Desi's thigh. Desi took her wrist and moved her hand up to his shoulder. The woman with the grey-streaked hair and turban came back into the room. She lit some incense on the reception counter. Then, she motioned for them to move forward to the silver table. Desi put his teacup on the table and sat down.

"I think I would like some more tea," Nicole said as she sat down at the table next to Desi.

"Me too," Penny added as she sat down at the table.

"I will bring out some more tea," the woman said, disappearing behind the wall with the picture of the woman in the gypsy or harem outfit. The incense burned in such a way that the smoke seemed to encircle the woman in the picture. Then, there was the clip-clop of what sounded to Desi as being Japanese wooden sandals, along with the music of Japanese stringed instruments.

"Where is that music coming from?" Nicole asked Desi.

"Seems like it is coming out of my memories of Japan," Desi answered as a tallish woman appeared in a blue-hooded kimono with gold lining.

She looked at Desi. "Or perhaps the music is coming from your future," she said as she sat down at the table opposite Desi. "Welcome," she said as she gave a brief nod to Desi, then Penny, then Nicole. "I am Diana, thank you for visiting with me today."

The woman wearing the turban reentered the room carrying the teapot and a teacup that she placed in front of Diana. She poured the tea for Diana and then placed the teapot in front of Nicole. The woman asked Diana, "Do you want me to open the curtains yet?"

"I think we need to talk for a few minutes to clarify things before I attempt to answer your questions," Diana said. "I would appreciate you being very honest with me so I can give you the best answers I can. Can you all do that?"

They all nodded to indicate "yes." Diana smiled and pulled the hood back off of her head. "Now, Desi, how is it that you find yourself here today with two beautiful women?" Diana asked. "Most men would be ecstatic to share the company of either of these young ladies, but you seem to have both on your arm."

Desi looked at Penny, then at Nicole. "Perhaps you give me too much credit. They are twin sisters, fraternal twins."

"Please help me open these curtains so I can see them more clearly," Diana said to Desi as she stood up from the table. She walked around the table to where Desi was sitting. Desi stood up and found himself face to face with Diana. She peered into his eyes.

"Do you want me to help with the drapes as well?" the woman in the turban asked.

"No," Diana said. "Bring the vase of pink roses you put together and put it in the center of the table. Remove the crystal ball."

Diana moved Desi by the arm to where the curtains seemed to meet. "Please pull the curtains open on your side about three feet," Diana said as she pulled the curtains on the other side open. She led Desi back to his chair and he sat down. She leaned over to give him a kiss on his forehead. When she leaned over, her kimono opened enough to reveal the same sequined top of the woman in the large picture. At that moment, Desi realized that Diana was going to be nothing like the fortune teller they were expecting to meet that day.

Penny seemed uncomfortable with Diana being so close to Desi, and Diana seemed to sense her discomfort. Diana reached down and took Desi's hands. She examined his palms and shot an occasional glance at Penny to monitor Penny's expression. "My guess is that Desi has had his hands full with one of you," Diana said with a quiet laugh. "Maybe he even has a shot at getting intimately involved with both of you." Again, she looked at Penny's facial expression. "Desi, are you a Leo?" Diana asked as she continued to hold his wrists from behind him and slowly move her torso closer to the back of Desi's head.

"I am," Desi said. "My sun is in Leo, and my moon is in Leo."

"Ah, you are experienced in these matters," she said as she let go of his hands and started running her hands through his hair and massaging his scalp. She brought her chest up against the back of his head. "You have a very nicely shaped head and a great jawline."

Penny cleared her throat. "Where did you get those cool wooden sandals?" Penny asked Diana.

"I got these kimono sandals when I bought this kimono at a street festival a few weeks ago. The vendor said the Japanese call them Geta, so I told him I had to 'get a' pair of Geta to go with my new kimono."

"Desi has been to Japan, but I don't think he got the kimono sandals," Penny offered.

"But he has a kimono in his closet that you sometimes wear?" Diana asked with a smile.

"Okay, you got me," Penny responded. "Not as fancy as the one you are wearing."

Diana stopped massaging Desi's head and took off her kimono to reveal her belly-dancing outfit. She carried the kimono over to Penny. "You look like you are about my size," Diana said, handing her the garment. "Try it on and let me know if you want the business card for the vendor." Diana went back to stand behind Desi and continued the massage of Desi's head and neck.

"So, Desi," Diana said, as she moved her hands down to massage Desi's shoulders, "If you have been to Japan, you probably received a few massages while you were there."

"I did," Desi said. "I even had the opportunity to go to the famous bathhouse in Kobe."

"I bet that was great," Diana purred into his ear as she massaged his back and rubbed her sequined chest against his back.

"I was going to ask you about when I was going to find my soulmate, " Nicole said. "But I think, if I had an outfit like what you are wearing, I might find him pretty fast."

"I'm glad you don't mind me wearing my belly dancing outfit. I taught one class today, and I have another class coming into my studio in about half an hour. Desi, why don't you take off your clothes in the men's room, find a towel in the cabinet near the sink, and join us in the studio. I want to show your lady friends how to massage a man's back that gives new meaning to 'having someone's back.' "

Desi simply nodded his head though he was a bit unsure as to what would be happening next. He walked down the back hallway and found a well-appointed "Gentlemen's Lounge" with a bathroom, a few lockers, and a shower. He hung up his clothes in a locker, keeping his briefs on and wrapping a towel around his waist. He rinsed his face at the sink, and then looked in the mirror. As he dried his face, he saw another picture of Diana without the harem pants or the sequined top on the back of the door to the lounge. He went over to take a closer look at the photo. It appeared that there were only sequins covering her nipples and a bikini bottom that was underneath the belt of what appeared to be various lengths of gold coins that matched her necklace. Her hands held a very sheer see-through red fabric, which she seemed to be waving across her body.

Below the pinup style photograph was a very business-like message giving the address and telephone number of the "Studios of Diana, provider of Belly Dancing classes and entertainment."

Desi resolved to take a business card when he left.

By the time he had finished studying the photo of Diana, he could hear the voices of Penny and Nicole in the hallway outside the door of the Gentlemen's Lounge. He stuck his head outside the door and saw Diana with Penny and Nicole. "Does the ladies' lounge have a photograph like the one on the back of this door?" Desi asked Diana.

Diana laughed. "We were just having a conversation about sensual pleasures," Diana said. "I guess I was feeling very sensual that day."

"I have to take a look at the picture," Nicole said as she pushed past Desi to get into the men's room. Desi stepped out into the hallway and put his arm around Penny, who was still wearing Diana's kimono.

Penny put her arm around Desi's waist. "We are thinking about taking Diana's belly dancing class in a few minutes. It is about an hour long. Do you think you could find a place to have a drink and come back for us in an hour?"

"Yeah, I am sure I can find a place to get a drink somewhere in Nashville."

"Thanks," Penny said. "Want to see my new outfit?" she asked as she opened the kimono to expose her new belly-dancing outfit.

"Well, you certainly have gotten into the spirit of things here," Desi said as he gave her a quick kiss on the lips.

Diana asked, "Desi, don't you want to get that back massage that I promised you?"

"Penny has me doing yoga with her. She loosened up any stress in my back last night and this morning."

"Well, I told Penny that a Leo man is very sexually compatible with a passionate Taurus woman," Diana advised. "They can share unmatched levels of sensuality, as well as humor in bed, or wherever."

"Desi particularly likes outdoor sex," Penny volunteered.

"Fresh air is very healthy, as is mutually gratifying sex," Diana noted. She handed Desi a small envelope. "Here is my prediction for your future love life along with one of my business cards. Feel free to call me with any questions."

"Thank you very much," Desi said. "It was a pleasure meeting you. You brightened my day, and it seems you did so for Penny and Nikki also."

"What is keeping Nikki in the Gentleman's Lounge so long?" Penny asked.

"Penny, do you want to go in and see the picture of me that was taken a few years ago after I won a regional belly dancing contest? Most of the contestants were in their forties or older. I think I was 25 or 26 years old. I don't know that I would now do that sort of photograph."

The door opened, and out came Nicole. "Maybe I ordered the wrong belly dancing outfit. I think there is a guy in Manhattan who would absolutely love to see me in that."

Penny stuck her head inside the door to look at the photo. "You told me the guy you are going out with is almost 50-years-old and has some heart issues. That would finish him off."

"Or maybe inspire him to get all the paperwork done on his divorce," Nicole said.

"Ah, the promise of a relationship with an older gentleman and the broken promises of older men," Diana said. "Some women hope they can see a shortcut to financial contentment, but happiness usually proves to be more elusive and requires some work."

Desi stepped inside the door of the Gentlemen's Lounge to get redressed. "I will see you in about an hour. I'll wait for you outside after I get some bourbon or Tennessee whiskey."

Desi Not Fully Appreciated at the Borderline Club

Desi realized he could probably spend the free hour he had just sticking his head inside one place after another. However, he knew that attempting to find what would be the perfect atmosphere to read the message from Diana about his future love life could prove to be futile. Alternatively, he realized he might be better off just trying to discern from the outside the type of place that would fit his mood. He wanted to find a place with enough people so as not to draw attention to himself. A bar where only regulars go would not work for him; on the other hand, he didn't want a place so busy that he would have to wait for a table or fight his way to the bar. Then, he saw a sign over a place called the Borderline Club that drew his attention.

When he walked in, there was some contemporary jazz music playing in the background. It seemed like all he had to do was to figure out whether he was going with Kentucky bourbon or Tennessee whiskey. There were a few people sitting along a long bar area and a few tables. The lighting and the décor of the place were reminiscent of a place he had gone to in midtown Manhattan with Debi to see Bonnie Raitt. It was a night he would never forget because Bonnie came over during a break and talked with them. Debi was thrilled.

Since he was just having a drink, he figured he would sit at one of the several empty spots at the bar.

After he ordered Jack Daniels with ginger beer from the woman behind the bar, Desi started to open the envelope he received from Diana.

A guy who looked like he was a couple of years younger than Desi sat down two seats away. Desi tucked the envelope into the front pocket of his short-sleeve shirt.

The woman behind the bar came along and asked the young man what he wanted to drink. The guy thought about it for a few moments and then pointed to Desi. "What is he drinking?"

"Jack Daniels and ginger beer," the woman replied.

"That sounds good," the guy said as he gave a smile to Desi.

After his drink came and he tasted it, he seemed to use that as an excuse to start talking to Desi about how he liked the drink, how he doesn't usually drink Jack Daniels, and sharing a pile of opinions on about a dozen different beers. Desi said little in response. After about ten minutes of such nonsense, the guy turned to Desi saying, "This is great, that a short-haired guy like you and a long-haired guy like me can be sharing a drink together."

Desi had the impulse to question him as to whether he knew that in the early 1970s, long hair had been something more than a fashion statement. The guy looked too young to have ever received a draft card in the mail or to have stood up in some way against the Vietnam War. With his hair grown a little bit over the collar of his pressed dress shirt, the guy seemed to be just another insecure male, with maybe a few more bucks in his pocket than average, trying to feel good about himself.

Desi put a tip on the bar, downed his drink, and gave the guy (who seemed to exude a lack of any genuineness) a nod as he left. Desi thought about the encounter as he walked back to Diana's studio, and the only words he could find harkened him back to those of Holden Caulfield in *Catcher in the Rye*, as he felt he had just encountered another one of the world's many phonies.

Desi would tell Penny about the guy in the bar later that evening, after Desi, Penny, and Nicole had dinner in the Polynesian restaurant at the Louisville airport. Penny didn't seem to understand how offensive the guy's remark was to Desi. Desi found himself thinking that only Debi might be able to appreciate how he felt experiencing that level of superficial absurdity.

The next morning, Desi awakened a few minutes before seven and turned off his alarm clock so as not to disturb Penny with the unpleasant sound of the alarm. He looked at the floor alongside his bed and located his briefs. Also alongside the bed, was part of Penny's new belly dancing outfit. He swung his legs out from underneath the sheet and put on his briefs. He made his way to the living room and put on a Bonnie Raitt album. He adjusted the sound so that it would make its way into the bedroom but not startle Penny.

Suddenly, the wall phone in the kitchen rang. He quickly moved to answer it.

He was a bit surprised to hear Miss Diana's voice on the line. She apologized for possibly waking Desi up.

"No problem," Desi said as he heard Penny stirring.

"I was trying to catch Penny before you guys go off to work. Did you get a chance to read my note about the roses you brought to my studio?"

"Yes, and Penny explained that you instructed me to keep three and for Penny to keep three, and that we would both be married within three years."

"Well, Nikki asked questions as to where she had to go to find the person she would marry and how many years it would be before she got married. I decided that I would use those beautiful little roses to transmit my answers to you in a way you'll remember."

"So, I guess you are forecasting that Penny and I don't have to go anywhere to find the person we will marry, and that we will be married within three years."

"Well, Nikki seemed to interpret things as you and Penny would marry each other within three years, but all I was really expressing is, barring something very unfortunate, you and Penny would each be married within three years," Diana said. "It is not impossible for the two of you to overcome all of the challenges and obstacles you would face, but it is quite improbable that you would do that."

"I think Penny understands it that way, but she is not dissuading her sister from thinking whatever she wants to think about the two of us. Nikki, after speaking with you, thinks that she has to go up to the Berkshires in Massachusetts to meet the man she will marry within four years. But you are saying I don't have to travel to some particular place, or go out of my way to meet the woman I will marry?"

"I do not believe so," Diana answered. "I am not clear as to how or when you will meet. But your paths are already set to cross. Does Germany mean anything to you?"

"I am hoping to get orders to be stationed in Germany," Desi said.

"Then maybe that has something to do with what I am vaguely seeing for you," Diana said. "That may be an obstacle for you and Penny or may have to do with someone else. I will leave that Germany thing for you to keep to yourself or share with Penny. It's up to you."

"Thanks for your good wishes for us," Desi said as Penny entered the kitchen wearing the Japanese kimono he kept in his closet. "Penny just got out of bed. Let me put her on the phone."

Penny took the handset from Desi. "Yes, Nikki did fly back to New York from Louisville last night, and she did enjoy the class."

Desi left the kitchen to take a shower. He stopped at his bedroom door and took off his briefs. Desi tossed them into the room so that they landed on his bed. Desi made a turn in the hallway to face Penny in all his full nakedness. He pointed to the shower. He blew her a good morning kiss and headed for the bathroom.

"Is Desi doing something to make it sound like you are holding back a laugh?" Diana asked.

"He seems to be in a very uninhibited mood, and I think he wants to share his shower with me," Penny answered.

"Well, I don't want to keep you guys from anything, but can I quickly ask if you are going to be back in Tennessee on the weekend?" Diana inquired.

"My parents are hoping that I come down to Chattanooga sometime soon to see their new house in person, but I haven't given any thought as to what I am doing this weekend."

"Well, after the class on Sunday, one of the women who has been coming to the studio for several months asked if I could find a couple of belly dancers to help entertain at a house party. If you're going down to Chattanooga on Saturday and coming back through Nashville on Sunday afternoon, I could get her to pay you $100 for dancing and instructing the guests on belly dancing. It sounds like they are going to have about forty guests over to celebrate her husband's fiftieth birthday. It's too much for me to do alone, and the woman who usually helps me with the parties is going to be away."

"Can I get back to you tomorrow on this?" Penny asked.

"Sure. It sounds like they are planning to start the party around four. I think she would want us to get there by 5pm. We would dance and get them dancing before they have dinner, so I figure we will be out of there before seven. Let me know."

"Sounds like it could be fun. I'll check to see what my folks have planned for the weekend and if that works."

When Penny got into the shower, she did not tell Desi, and he did not ask about her conversation with Diana. Desi simply said, "You are wearing your birthday suit on your birthday!"

Penny moved around in the shower with abbreviated modeling poses. "What do you think about this look?"

Desi looked her up and down. "Perfect," he announced heartily as he put his wet body up against hers. "Happy twenty-first birthday," he added as he kissed her from head to toe.

Chapter VIII

A WEEK Of SURPRISES

After dropping Penny off at an auditorium on post where the Fort Knox Army Band was rehearsing that Monday morning, Desi stopped by the barracks to check his mailbox for the prior week's mail. In 1975 he lived in the barracks for several months before getting the opportunity to live off post. All he found in his mailbox were copies of the *Wall Street Journal*. His father, for a reason he did not articulate, had decided it would be good for Desi to have a subscription to the *Journal* while Desi was in the Army. Desi had read that publication, though infrequently, while studying journalism. He couldn't recall ever seeing his father reading the *Journal* or any newspaper.

Although Desi had a weekly copy of the post newspaper sent to his parents' home, he never received any feedback from them on any of the articles he wrote for *Inside the Turret*. Desi chalked it up to the "generation gap." His parents could not comprehend why he left New York to join the Army, and Desi could not comprehend why they seemed satisfied with owning a couple of hardware stores and doing the same things year after year.

Occasionally, his parents talked about someday selling their businesses, but any expression of what they would do after making such changes was vague at best.

When Desi got to his desk at the *Turret* office, he noticed a stack of various sized envelopes that had been dropped off, along with a few telephone messages. None of it looked any more demanding of his attention than what he had found in his mailbox at the barracks. He tried returning phone calls, but apparently everyone who left their phone numbers must have immediately left whatever place they were calling him from. He opened a few of the envelopes addressed to him and compiled a stack of envelopes that had been misdirected to his desk. Nothing seemed particularly interesting after the weekend he, on balance, had enjoyed.

He pulled his notepad from his desk and went through the list of writing projects he had thought about the week before. There was a possible story about a lieutenant who began a new hobby of making stained-glass lampshades. He was very willing to be the subject of an article about his hobby. But before deciding on whether to proceed with the article, Desi believed he needed to speak to his editor. While Desi felt it would be a good subject for their newspaper, the paper was only printed in black and white. Desi had seen *Soldiers* magazine, which was printed in color, but he didn't know the requirements for submitting articles with color photos.

On Desi's weekly calendar, there was also a possible after-hours assignment regarding the local chapter of the Association of the United States Army (AUSA).

More Generals for Desi's Photo Album

Desi had been recommended by the prior publicity person, who covered the Daniel Boone Chapter of the AUSA, to write articles and take photographs for the organization. The job had provided Desi with some extra monthly pocket money and the opportunity to go to Washington D.C. earlier in the year with the chapter members for the annual national AUSA Convention. By merely walking around the convention hall, Desi got to see many military leaders and public officials, including NATO Supreme Commander General Alexander Haig of Nixon White House fame (or infamy). Desi got invited to attend some of the parties in suites where the alcohol flowed so freely that at least one commanding general of a large U.S. Army base was sacked out (in civilian clothes) on a couch. Most of the general officers at the convention seemed able to maintain their composure, but in such a setting, the stars on their uniform did not seem to transform them into supreme beings, as in other settings where they were not mingling with others who also had stars on their shoulders. The exception was the somewhat frail-looking general with five stars, sitting in a wheelchair. There had been a significantly louder buzz in the AUSA convention hall when General Omar Bradley was wheeled out to meet guests. There, in front of his eyes, Desi observed the Field Commander of U.S. soldiers on D-Day graciously greeting as many people as he could. After Desi shook the General's hand and stepped back, he remembered part of Bradley's famous quote about how our world is a "world of nuclear giants and ethical infants…" When others jumped in to get pictures with the General, Desi realized he had missed his opportunity to ask the General if he was more or less optimistic about the fate of the world in 1976.

Desi may have had doubts about how well history would regard some of the generals he saw at that convention, but he firmly believed that not only did General Bradley perform his duty honorably and ably, but he also had a key role in the righteous effort to defeat the Nazi war machine before it obtained the ability to manufacture and utilize nuclear weapons.

Many of the soldiers at the convention had made sacrifices and suffered hardships to serve the United States and fulfill their oaths, but there seemed to be a sense that what Omar Bradley did, from the perspective of world history, was extraordinary. Certainly, Desi had the sense that he truly had seen someone who was able, when the world was in a precarious balance, to soldier through to the benefit of our country.

What Desi didn't know that Monday morning as he sat at his desk going through his notebook, was that come afternoon, he would be working on a story about another general facing new challenges concerning the direction of the United States Army. That Army officer would use his experiences, including his service as a commander in World War II leading troops through the hedgerows of Normandy, to, by the mid-1970s, help lead efforts to define a post-Vietnam volunteer U.S. Army. Desi would be the one in the *Turret* office assigned to cover several of the activities that General William E. DePuy, Training and Doctrine Command (TRADOC) Commander, would attend while visiting Fort Knox. With General DePuy that week was TRADOC Deputy Commander Lieutenant General Frank Camm. While that morning started off slowly, by the end of the work week Desi would have the opportunity to fly on a presidential jet when he was directed to accompany the two generals back to TRADOC headquarters at Fort Monroe, Virginia.

However, as of that morning, Desi was only semi-focused on the paperwork in front of him as he awaited a telephone call from Penny to find out whether she needed a lift to pick up her car at the A-1 Garage.

A call from Penny came in a few minutes before noon. She told Desi she would not need a ride as several of the members of the band were taking her out to dinner for her birthday, and one of them would get her to the garage. Penny said she intended to meet Desi back at his apartment later in the evening to have their own private celebration of her turning twenty-one.

Shortly after noon, Desi got the news about the TRADOC Commander and Deputy Commander visiting Fort Knox and his assignment to cover a number of activities with the TRADOC Commander. A civilian journalist in their office, Rosemary, was assigned to develop a feature story about Lieutenant General Camm's background, including the fact that he had been born on post in 1922, many years before Fort Knox had been designated as the Armor Center, or even as a Fort. Back in 1922, it was only Camp Knox.

Desi's assignment for the next day was to go out to the tank ranges and meet up with the TRADOC Commander. He figured he got the better assignment. He spent Monday afternoon trying to learn everything he could about General DePuy's background and what the General was doing to redefine the Army's mission and make sure that the Volunteer Army was going to be an effective fighting force. Desi was a bit surprised to learn that General DePuy was commissioned after ROTC and was not a West Pointer. Desi wasn't sure how his research would help him, but he didn't want to approach the assignment as merely taking a picture of General DePuy on a tank.

When Desi got home to his apartment that evening, he called his contact in the local chapter of the Association of the United States Army. The scribbled phone message left on his desk the next morning mentioned an update related to one of their events scheduled for Thursday. Desi knew from the prior week that there was an upcoming dinner. The update was that the TRADOC Commander and Deputy Commander would be coming to the Chapter dinner with the Commanding General of Fort Knox. Maybe, he thought, his research regarding General DePuy would come in handy.

Desi made himself four little pizzas out of two English muffins, some marinara sauce, some parmesan cheese, and some dried basil that his neighbor dropped off a few weeks earlier. He got a cold beer out of the refrigerator while the little pizzas were cooking in his toaster oven.

The phone rang just as he was biting into a college dorm-style pizza muffin. It was Roger, wanting to know if Desi was going to the Preakness Stakes that Saturday, May 15th.

"Not sure if I have anyone to go with," Desi answered as he chewed and talked with a mouthful of mini pizza.

"You've got Daisy and me to go with," Roger said, sounding like he was happily sharing good news about his love life.

"No kidding," Desi replied in an incredulous tone.

"Are you surprised that such a refined, attractive lady would be willing to be seen with me at another public event?"

"No, no," Desi said. "I'm just surprised that she doesn't have a husband or a long-term lover who hasn't reappeared during the last week or so."

"She's telling me that there really isn't anyone else that she is seeing," Roger advised.

"Good for you, man. I am very happy for you. I know she is a couple of years older than you, and certainly more mature," Desi said with a laugh.

"Actually, she isn't even a full two years older. But you're right about her being much more mature and refined."

"I guess I'd have to get out of work early on Friday if I'm going to drive to Baltimore. "I'll have to work on that and get back to you."

"We have four tickets, so if you would let me know if you are bringing someone by Thursday morning, that would be good."

"I should know by then," Desi said. "Thanks!"

"I should be thanking you for inviting me to the Derby. I might even be going with her to New York on June eighth for the Belmont. Her brother, the Kings Point grad, has already invited her up to see his new house on Long Island and is getting race tickets for that day."

"Wow," Desi said. "Would that be some sort of trifecta?"

"That would be my definition of the Triple Crown, " Roger answered.

"I'm betting on you to make it happen," he said, as Penny came in the side door. "I've got to run," Desi said as he hung up the phone.

"What are you betting on?" Penny asked.

"My friend Roger is getting tickets for the Preakness this weekend. Do you want to go?"

Penny hesitated for a few moments. "Can I have one of these pathetic mini pizzas?" she asked.

"Sure," Desi said, pushing the plate with the remaining pizza muffin across the table to her. "But what happened? I thought you were going out to eat with your bandmates."

"The Mexican place I wanted to go to is closed on Mondays, so we went to another Mexican place that should be closed permanently by the local authorities," Penny responded. "To call the food terrible would be kind."

"I can call that Italian place on the way to Elizabethtown and get you something decent to eat," Desi offered. "It is your birthday!"

"Maybe I want something indecent to eat on my birthday," Penny said with her eyebrows raised. "Besides, you did enough for me, and my sister, this weekend to help us celebrate our birthday. Nikki thought you were really entertaining at the Polynesian restaurant with your Dick Dead Eye song from the *HMS Pinafore*. She told me she hoped the fortune teller was right about us getting married in three years."

"I am not sure Diana actually said that."

"I know, I think I may get some further clarification from Diana this weekend if I go down to Tennessee again and spend a night or two at my parent's new house."

"So, you don't want to go with me to Baltimore this weekend?"

"Diana has offered me a hundred dollars to do some belly dancing with her at a party Sunday evening in Nashville. She is promising a hundred bucks for just a couple of hours of dancing and showing others how to belly dance."

"Is that a safe thing to do? One time in Hong Kong, two dancers at the Hong Kong Hilton bar got me to go with them to a private party at a restaurant on the Kowloon side. They felt like they should go with at least one male chaperone."

"Well, what happened?" Penny asked. "Apparently, you lived to tell about it."

"Fortunately, it was mostly older Chinese couples in Western style clothing at the restaurant. One dancer was a beautiful Californian, and another woman was part Chinese, part Filipino. Everything was cool until the end when one of the waiters said something in Chinese, implying they were hookers. The woman who was part Filipino understood what the guy said, and they had quite an argument. We managed to get out of there with the women getting paid what they were promised for dancing. But the dancer who spoke Chinese had to make it very clear they weren't providing any other services."

"So, you thought you were going to have to fight your way out?" Penny asked.

"I was only eighteen years old and didn't think much about it at the time, but there was a lot of drinking going on. Who knows what might have happened, especially if they hadn't brought me along? About a month later, I heard about some Korean dancers who went to a party for some European sailors and weren't as fortunate. One of the dancers got a knife away from a sailor and ended up stabbing the sailor in self-defense. It was the dancers who ended up in jail."

"Well, Diana seems like a smart businesswoman, and she described the party as a fiftieth birthday celebration with the family and friends of a well-off attorney who has a nice home. The wife of the attorney was in our belly dancing class on Sunday."

"That sounds pretty legit," Desi acknowledged. "So, I guess I am going to Baltimore alone."

"Don't worry, Desi. Maybe you'll run into those women from Hong Kong. The beautiful beach bunny from California might feel like she still owes you something."

"Sure you don't want something more than a little pizza?"

"I will take one of those beers, if you have another cold one," Penny answered. "I guess I want to practice some more of my belly dancing in your bedroom. That's probably how I want to remember my twenty-first birthday."

Desi got two cold beers out of the refrigerator and opened one for Penny and another for himself. They toasted by clicking their beer bottles.

"I guess I will remember being with you, here in your apartment in Radcliff, where we, on a number of occasions, sang the songs of the *HMS Pinafore* together, sometimes before and sometimes after sex."

"But what about while we are having sex? You, as Josephine, can sing about Josephine wanting to get it on with my character, Dick Dead Eye, or his alias, Dead Eye Dick."

Penny raised her bottle of beer. "My sister, Nikki wants to know if you are always going to be my Dead Eye Dick."

"I will be proud to be your Dead Eye Dick on this special birthday celebration," Desi said as he took her hand and led her off to his bedroom.

The next morning, Desi and Penny woke up a bit late. Penny scrambled to find the shorts and blouse she had been wearing the night before. The blouse was in the hallway. The shorts were in the bathroom and her panties were jumbled up with her belly dancing outfit. At some point during the night, they had gotten up from the bed and done several shots of bourbon. The birthday celebration with Desi, which Penny thought she would always remember, seemed a bit hazy only a few hours later.

Penny could not recall when they actually decided to get some sleep, but it probably was after two. She straightened her blouse and shorts in front of the large mirror in Desi's bedroom. As Desi watched from his bed, Penny pulled her hair into a ponytail and put on some lipstick. She jumped on his bed and climbed up and sat on Desi's torso so as to pin him down. She kissed him on the forehead, nose, and lips, leaving much of her lipstick on Desi.

"Will I see you tonight?" Desi called out to Penny as she hurried out of his bedroom and opened the side door to go out to her car.

The response he got sounded like, "Maybe, baby."

Desi took a quick shower and had a bowl of cereal. While he sat in the kitchen, wrapped only in his towel, he listened to the music of a Louisville radio station that provided a brief news update every hour. They started off the news with a story about the Governor of Georgia, Jimmy Carter, who seemed to be building a coalition that could earn him the Democratic Party nomination for the presidential race. Desi knew a few political operatives in New York who had told him the prior year that they thought the nomination was going to someone from the south. He wanted to listen to the whole news piece, but he realized it was already after eight. At least he didn't have to think about what uniform he would wear that day; he already knew he was wearing his olive drab fatigues to go out to the ranges.

When he arrived at the *Turret* office, there was an Army jeep waiting for him. A private first class was the driver, and a first sergeant was sitting in the back.

"You're early," Desi said to them with a smile as he passed by the jeep parked near the outside entrance to the newsroom. "I have to get the Nikon camera from the office."

"Actually, we are on time," the first sergeant responded without any smile in return.

Once Desi had the camera in hand, they drove out to the ranges with Desi in the passenger seat. Desi didn't know what range they were going to or what sort of armored vehicles they were going to see the TRADOC Commander inspecting.

From the back seat, the first sergeant told Desi that he expected the General to inspect the inside of the tanks, as well as the exteriors of all the armored vehicles. The first sergeant said there was even a chance the TRADOC Commander would fire the main gun of a tank.

"That's the photo I want to take!" Desi announced over the sound of the open jeep rumbling along the trails leading to the ranges.

"It probably isn't going to be easy to do," the first sergeant shouted from the back.

Further along the trail, as a few armored vehicles came into view, the jeep driver slowed down.

"Are you a tank commander?" Desi asked the first sergeant.

"I am the designated commander of a M48-A3 today, until the General arrives, and then, if he wants, he takes over," the first sergeant explained. "The M48 Patton medium tank was the main tank of the U.S. Army throughout most of the Vietnam War. The M551 Sheridan tanks came in towards the end, but you are going to get a chance today to see several types of the armored vehicles, from the M24 Chaffee light tank to the M60 heavy tank."

"So, which one will General DePuy likely fire from today?" Desi asked.

"I am hoping he'll fire the main gun of the M48-A3," the first sergeant said as they made their way into a clearing with about a dozen armored vehicles arranged in several groupings. "Have you ever seen so many armored vehicles in one spot?" he asked Desi.

"Only once in early 1971 on a Navy pier in Japan," Desi said.

"Were you in the Navy before joining the Army?" the First Sergeant asked.

"No, I was a Merchant Marine cadet on a cargo ship. We were docked at a pier in Japan, which had received a couple dozen armored vehicles off loaded from a ship that came in from Vietnam. I don't know if they were there to be repaired or scrapped."

"They looked pretty bad?"

"And then some," Desi said. "As the sun set on the pier, it was a ghastly scene."

"Well, all of our vehicles today are in tip-top shape and ready for inspection," the first sergeant said confidently as the jeep stopped next to an armored vehicle.

"I'm hoping General DePuy picks your tank to exercise his firepower talents," Desi said as he got out of the jeep. "Show me which one is your tank, and I will stand with my camera next to it for when the General comes by."

The first sergeant positioned Desi near the front of his tank. Sure enough, when General DePuy came by with his helmet in hand and an armor officer by his side, he turned his attention to the first sergeant's tank. The first sergeant and Desi gave the General a salute. The next thing Desi knew, he was on top of the tank and taking photographs of the TRADOC Commander climbing inside.

There was suddenly the distracting explosive noise of another armored vehicle firing nearby. Desi struggled to get his head and enough of his arms with the camera inside the tank to get a photo of the General readying to fire the 105mm main gun. Desi was oblivious to what the recoil would be like and how precarious his position was on the top of the tank.

There was another explosive noise from a second armored vehicle firing at a target down range. Desi took a couple of quick photos of General DePuy awaiting word that it would be his turn to fire. Suddenly, Desi felt a tugging on his belt. He pulled his upper torso up and out of the tank and turned to see the first sergeant with a helmet on his head holding onto the steel cargo basket attached behind the turret. "Don't you think it's time for you to hold on to something?" he asked Desi with a very concerned expression on his face.

Desi, still only wearing his regular black tanker's beret, quickly wrapped one hand around the top railing of the cargo basket and assumed the half-squat position that the first sergeant was in, just as he felt the impact of the tank firing.

"Well, with one hand you managed to stay on top," the first sergeant said while Desi's head was still ringing.

"And I didn't smash up the Army's Nikon camera either," Desi said with a forced smile as he began to realize that he had jumped into, or onto, a situation that most likely pushed the outer limits of his regular good luck.

"Have you ever considered trying out for the rodeo?" the first sergeant said with a laugh.

Desi took a couple steps over to the port side of the tank while taking the lens cap out of his pocket and putting it on the camera. He pulled the camera strap up over his head with his right hand. Desi held the camera by the strap in his left and looked over the side of the tank. "I think I got the photos we need for the post paper," Desi said as he jumped off of the tank.

He landed squarely on the soles of his black combat boots, with his right hand coming down for balance and his left arm up and out to protect the camera.

"Nice dismount," the first sergeant said, who was still standing on the top of the tank. "Too many guys just sprawl on their butts."

"Guess they never had a girlfriend with a second story bedroom," Desi said as he put the camera strap over his left shoulder. "Are you leaving the range, or can I just have your driver take me back to the office?"

"Tell him I'm going to be out here for another hour or so, and I want him to get you wherever you have to be next," the first sergeant said. "Thank you, Specialist McKoy."

"Thank you, First Sergeant," Desi said, adding, "But please, just call me Desi."

"Till we meet again, Desi," the first sergeant said, giving Desi a salute with his index finger.

Desi took the lens cap off of the camera and adjusted the zoom lens of the Nikon. He took a couple of shots of the first sergeant on top of the tank. Desi gave him a thumbs-up before turning and walking back to the jeep. The driver was reading a custom car magazine. He handed it to Desi to look at as they made their way back to the building that housed the firehouse and the offices for the military and civilian employees handling public affairs and information, as well as producing the weekly post newspaper.

Desi gave the film from the camera to his editor before driving his car to the barracks to have lunch.

News from New York

When Desi arrived at the barracks, he checked his mailbox. There was a copy of the *Wall Street Journal* and a short letter from a woman who had been in several of his journalism classes at NYU. Her name was Gail. She sent news that she was finishing her first year of law school and had gotten engaged to the son of a wealthy New York businessman. Desi knew the groom to be, as well as the wealthy businessman, as the young woman had not only introduced Desi to them but also helped Desi get a job as the political press secretary for the wealthy businessman. Desi was briefly involved in the Democratic Party Primary for an open U.S. Senate seat in 1974. Desi had just finished his independent study project on the Nation's Centennial and received the last credit he needed to complete his undergraduate studies at NYU, when a call came in from Gail about the opening that needed to be filled immediately for the campaign. Desi knew it might be only a temporary gig as there were several well-known, politically experienced Democrats running in the primary. Additionally, even if the self-described "businessman candidate" survived the Democratic primary, there would likely be an experienced Republican vying to fill the seat Senator Jacob Javits was leaving.

Given that Desi hadn't found any journalism jobs in Manhattan that summer, he was happy to come in on short notice to replace the person who had been doing the press work, but who left for some undisclosed reason.

The press secretary job only lasted four or five weeks, until Primary Day in early September, but it would allow Desi to gain some insight into New York politics, including traveling with the advance team through the hotels in the Catskills known as the Borscht Belt. He had heard from his Jewish friends at NYU about Grossinger's, Kutcher's, and other such resorts, but with the advance team he had the opportunity to actually experience a bit of it.

Gail ended her letter expressing her hope to see him back in New York for the Bicentennial celebration.

Desi stuck the letter in the back pocket of his fatigues and took the copy of the *Journal* with him to read in the mess hall, which resembled a college dorm cafeteria.

While he was eating his lunch and reading an article about the tough financial circumstances of New York City, a female soldier sat down at his table. "How is your portfolio doing today?" she asked.

Desi looked up to see a rather attractive member of the Military Police sitting across from him.

"Things seem to be improving for me," Desi said. "Is there anything you want me to check for you?"

"Maybe," she said with a very sweet laugh. "How come I haven't seen you around here before?"

"I've been living off post for several months," Desi explained. "My guess is that you only recently arrived at Fort Knox."

"Is that because I'm a PFC and most of the other people here, like you, are Specialists?"

"That's part of it," Desi said.

"And what is the other part of your deducing that I am relatively new here?"

"Perhaps we can discuss that some other time, somewhere other than here," Desi said. "I have to get back to the *Turret* office and finish writing a few things for this week's paper. Perhaps we can get together for dinner some evening and have a conversation about what I can deduce about you and what you can deduce about me. I'm thinking there are still a few restaurants up in Louisville that you haven't been to yet."

"That's amazing, you are so right," she said with another, even sweeter laugh.

"And that is just the start of my deductive powers," Desi said as he stood up from the table.

"Nice to meet you, Specialist McKoy," she said, holding out her hand. "My name is Cindy MacNamara."

"Please call me at the post newspaper office," he said as he gave her hand a squeeze instead of a shake. "Just ask for Desi." He wrote down the office number on the front page of the *Wall Street Journal* with the pen he always carried. Affecting his most debonair smile, he pushed the newspaper across the table to her and left the mess hall.

Desi wrote down Cindy MacNamara's name on a yellow message pad when he got back to his desk. He ripped that page off the pad and put the page with her name on it under his desk phone. Desi felt there was more than a 50/50 chance she would call him by the end of the week.

After handing in all the items Desi needed to get to his editor that day, the editor asked him if he could help lay out the paper at the News Enterprise offices in Elizabethtown the following afternoon. Desi was more than happy to oblige with the request, especially since it didn't sound like the editor was going to Elizabethtown that week. Desi had been told his article and photographs regarding the foresters inventorying the woodlands at Fort Knox would get a full page. Now, he would be able to guarantee that happening.

As he was getting ready to leave the office that evening, his telephone rang. He answered it with the appropriate, "Post Newspaper, Specialist McKoy speaking."

"I hear that you are back in the rack with Penny," Stacey said, trying to disguise her voice.

"Is that what the scamps in the JAG Office are talking about this afternoon?" Desi teased.

"Well, people see things, like you driving her around places and having dinner at the airport, and they figure they should give me a heads up," Stacey said in her regular voice, with a hint of her U.S. Virgin Islands background.

"I can't really say what is going on with the relationship, but she needed a lift to Nashville on Sunday and one thing led to another," Desi said. "This weekend I'm thinking of heading up to Baltimore to join Roger and Daisy for the Preakness. Penny told me she's got other plans."

"So that explains why you have Cindy MacNamara for a lunch partner today?"

"What does your surveillance team do when they aren't following me around?" Desi said with a laugh.

"Not for nothing, but I think you should be very careful before you even ask PFC MacNamara if she likes ice cream."

"I am not planning to take her to Baltimore this weekend," Desi said. "But I might take her to dinner sometime. I generally don't date women who wear side arms or have boyfriends who carry side arms, but I wouldn't totally rule it out. She seems like she could be glamorous, amorous, and still remain essentially sweet."

"Promise me, for your own good, that you will not take her to your apartment or let her even know where you live until I can give you some background," Stacey said. "It is not info that is confidential. I didn't gain it working in the JAG office, but I am not comfortable discussing her over the telephone with you. Maybe we can meet after work tomorrow?"

"How about Charlie's favorite ice cream place around six?"

"That should work for me," Stacey said. "Stay clear of that chick 'til then, okay?"

"She only has my office telephone number and, since it is now after five o'clock, I will not answer another telephone call."

"See you tomorrow," Stacey said before hanging up.

Desi hung up his phone and took his black tanker's beret off his desk. While adjusting his beret, the telephone rang. He walked quickly out of the office he shared with a master sergeant, who had some sort of administrative role with the Public Affairs office that Desi never quite understood.

No one was still working in the adjacent offices, or they didn't bother to pick up his line. He locked the office door to the parking lot behind him as he heard his telephone line keep ringing on the telephones in the various offices.

When Desi got back to his apartment, he took off his sweaty combat boots and socks right after entering the side door. By the time he got to the bathroom, he had already flung his green fatigue pants into his bedroom. Desi took his formerly pressed fatigue shirt, no longer stiff but seriously wilted from being out on the ranges and dropped it in the hallway outside his bathroom. He turned the shower on and tore off his underwear. Desi was so focused on soaking his face and body in the shower he did not hear the side door to his apartment open.

However, the sound of his bathroom door opening startled him. Desi waited for someone to say something, thinking of the people who might have a key to his place. He wondered if PFC MacNamara had tracked him down and used a special skeleton key, or if his overly friendly neighbor was bringing Desi a sample of her garden. In that brief moment, Desi even began to think about whether it might be some sort of gag by someone who worked with him in the newspaper office.

After waiting for what seemed like minutes, Desi stuck his head out from behind the dark blue shower curtain to see Emily wearing nothing but a towel around her torso.

Emily cleared her throat before she began to speak. "I was going to call you, but I was afraid that after Saturday you might not want to talk to me. You don't have anyone in there with you, do you?"

"Even if I did, I would certainly make room for you," Desi said with a smile. "Don't be shy. We may not have done the deed, but we have seen each other naked in the shower before."

"I thought that if I tried to explain things in person, we might have the opportunity to rectify that lack of consummating a physical relationship," Emily offered.

"I am willing to take corrective action if you are prepared to rectify prior omissions."

"Then let me boldly lay out everything that needs to be done," Emily said as she dropped the towel and all of her inhibitions and stepped inside the shower.

Desi ran a bar of soap across her back, lathering and massaging Emily from her shoulder blades down to her hips. Desi's hands went around to the front of Emily's body, lathering and massaging her breasts. Desi then gave her a gentle kiss on the neck, causing Emily to turn around so they could kiss each other deeply on the lips. While thrusting her tongue into Desi's mouth, she jumped up to wrap her legs around his waist. Slowly, she lowered the "Garden of Emily" onto the elongating protrusion between Desi's legs.

"Oh, Desi. Why did we wait to fit our bodies together like this?"

"I can't, in words, express much of anything right now," Desi admitted as he held Emily aloft and moved their bodies as one.

"Forget the words, you are putting things so right with your poetic movements; it's like we're in a fantasy."

"I feel like Sonny Corleone in the Godfather, with the woman suspended between his body and a door to somewhere."

"Yeah, Desi, do it Sonny Corleone-style, like you are going to put me through that door to some magical place."

Sometime later, their bodies were wrapped together in Desi's bed. Emily would gently move to keep Desi from drifting off to sleep. "I want my body to be joined to you all night," she whispered repeatedly as the sun set and the room filled with the soft afterglow.

Then, the wall phone rang in the kitchen. "I will be back in a minute," Desi said, apologetically.

Still naked, Desi answered the phone, simply saying, "Yeah."

"Is it a good time for me to stop by?" Penny asked.

"I have to cover something this evening," Desi said wryly as he walked across the kitchen and took a dish towel near the sink and attempted to fasten it around his waist.

"It sounds like you might have someone there with you."

"Well, the new tenant, the guy I told you about, might be stopping by for a key to move in this weekend," Desi said. "Can we talk tomorrow?"

"Sounds like I am already too late," Penny said, slamming the phone on her end.

Desi sat down in a chair at the kitchen table after hanging up his phone. He noticed his set of keys on the kitchen table. Holding the keys, he stood up and walked to the side door, still trying to connect the ends of the dish towel. The side door was locked.

Walking back to the bedroom, he turned on a night light and put his keys on his dresser. Desi climbed back in bed with Emily.

"Everything okay?" she asked Desi.

"I just found my keys on the kitchen table. Did you put my keys there?"

"Yeah," Emily said. "When I got here, the side door was closed, but your keys were in the doorknob."

"I guess I was focused on cooling off in the shower when I got home. Then you got me wanting to see how hot we could make the shower."

Emily sat up in Desi's bed. "Sometimes I can't tell if you are the real deal or the unreal deal."

"I was thinking that shower this evening was the surreal deal. You seemed to appear out of nowhere."

"I am hoping that you are the person of my dreams."

"I'm hoping the same about you," Desi said wistfully.

Plans for a Baltimore Weekend Take Shape

"What are you doing this weekend?" Emily asked. "I have an extra ticket for the Pimlico Racecourse in Baltimore."

"Funny you should mention that. Roger called to say he is going with Daisy to the Preakness Stakes and wanted to know if I was interested in joining them."

"Friday I'm planning to drive to Glen Burnie, Maryland, where my parents live. I will even give you a ride."

"Sounds like things are really falling into place for me to be attending the Preakness Stakes on Saturday," Desi said. "But are you seriously suggesting that you will take me to your parents' house?"

"Yeah, I already told them I was inviting you."

"And what about the sleeping arrangements?"

"I told them that I've restarted the pill and threatened to petition to have a conjugal visit at the jail with my old boyfriend if they didn't let me sleep with you," Emily said with a wink.

"And they agreed? I didn't get the sense that your father liked me, even though I did give him a ride to the airport in Lexington."

"Oh, my mother calls him 'Colonel Blimp,' after the conservative cartoon character."

"Not sure I ever heard of that character," Desi said, sounding puzzled.

"It's very out of date. My mother seems to be on my side as she made my father concede he had premarital sex and was not a virgin when he married her."

"So, your mother is cool with me shacking up with you in your childhood bedroom?"

"She understands the principle of not being hypocritical, in terms of women as well as men being sexually active at the age of twenty-one, but, then again, I am her daughter, and it is the bedroom where I still keep a couple of my favorite teddy bears."

"We could blindfold them," Desi suggested.

"My parents or the teddy bears?" Emily said with a laugh.

"So, the conversation with your parents is still evolving?"

"We all agreed to talk more about the sleeping arrangements after I found out if you were available this weekend."

"A weekend with Emma Lee Miller, Reverend Miller and Mrs. Miller, I don't think I would miss that for the world."

"My mom has a Ph.D. in Health Care Management, or something like that, so it would be best if you called her 'Doctor Miller.' "

"Have you decided whether or not you are going to law school in September?"

"That is a discussion that is also evolving," Emily said. "I did call the U of L Law School yesterday and spoke to someone about possibly deferring for a year. I want to try to get a radio or TV station job and start law school not this September but the following September. That way, I would not be totally dependent on my parents and grandmother."

"Your grandmother is willing to help you pay for law school?"

"My mother thinks my grandmother might be willing to pay for the whole thing."

"That's quite a grandmother you have."

"Oh, she is something alright," Emily said. "But there are always conditions when my grandmother gets involved in funding something. My father doesn't want me to take a nickel from her."

"How is your father doing with resolving things with his cousins and Honey Boone?"

"Things are not fully resolved and, in some ways, more complicated by the financial dealings he's kept from my mother."

"Yikes! Am I going to experience a bumpy ride when we get to the Baltimore area?"

"My parents will try to put the best face on things, but I am sure there is going to be some tension."

"Maybe I will just be adding to the tension."

"Or maybe your mere presence will make everyone more careful about what they say to one another. That could be quite good."

"I'll try to not be anything but be your suave companion for the weekend," Desi said.

"What is the phrase that your friend Stacey uses about certain guys?"

"You mean 'swave and deboner'?"

"Yeah. Try to avoid that."

Desi called a local restaurant and ordered some Italian food. Emily took another shower while he went to pick it up. She was wearing one of his short-sleeved shirts when he returned. Desi fixed their plates so as to share an order of eggplant rollatini and an order of veal parmigiana.

Emily took a couple of bites of each and then started unbuttoning the shirt she was wearing.

Desi watched Emily as, button by button, she revealed that she was wearing nothing underneath. "I forgot to dish out the side order of pasta," he said absentmindedly.

"Maybe later, after you take me back into your bedroom and tell me that you want to make love to me again," Emily said, emphasizing the word "love."

Desi took a large bite of the veal and then picked Emily up out of her chair and carried her to his bed and gently let her down onto the wrinkled sheets. He took off his shirt and his pants and lowered himself into her arms. "I want to make love to you again," he said, also emphasizing the word "love" as Emily had done.

"Actually, this seems like the first time I feel we are making love," Emily said.

Hours later, Desi awakened to a rustling sound coming from the kitchen. He wrapped a pillowcase around his waist and found Emily in the kitchen warming up some of the Italian food they had left on the table. She was wearing an apron around her neck and nothing else. Desi untied the back of the apron and dropped the pillowcase so as to press his naked body against her bare back.

"Desi, I'm afraid that I am not a woman who can go all night without eating a real dinner."

Desi kissed her neck and whispered in her ear. "I am not interested in being with a woman who doesn't have a good appetite."

"I am fixing plates for the two of us so we will have the energy to keep from collapsing and requiring medical attention."

Desi took a step back from her. "You really think we are going to be able to sleep together at your parents' house this weekend?"

"Maybe, but we aren't going to be able to have sex in their kitchen, like I might be interested in doing here, once I take in some calories to burn off later."

"Then, pile your plate high," Desi suggested. "Have I told you that I can't trust a woman who claims she doesn't enjoy Italian food?"

"I don't know why a woman would pretend to not enjoy sensual pleasures," Emily said as she took a spoon and scooped veal, eggplant, and pasta into the pan on the stove. "I like my food hot," she said as she took a taste, eating only half of the food on the large spoon. Desi moved alongside her, giving her a full-frontal view of his naked body. Emily lifted the remaining contents of the spoon to Desi's lips.

Desi emptied the spoon with one quick gulp. "I think it's ready."

Emily looked Desi up and down. "When you say, it's ready, are you talking about the food or that thing between your legs?"

"Nibble on whatever you wish."

"I don't think I have ever been so tempted to try oral sex," Emily said. "Linda was telling you the truth on Derby weekend about my limited sexual experience. Not sure why I ever revealed that to her. But I want you to know that I am willing to expand my horizons."

"Limited to just receiving or expanded all the way to giving?" Desi asked.

Emily simply nodded.

"I don't think we should wait until we are in your parents' house to find out how much you enjoy receiving such personal attention. You might wake them from a sound sleep."

"You mentioned the blindfolds. Perhaps we should supply them with ear plugs as well."

"Before we get too distracted, why don't we eat what you have prepared?" Desi asked. "I'll pour some wine to go with the food. Then we can take the bottle into the bedroom and see what occurs to those sexual limitations."

"I have always been a quick learner," Emily said with a sultry smile. "A fortune teller told me that, as someone born in mid-July, I am intuitive, intelligent, and passionate."

"My guess is that you need to be comfortable enough to let your passionate side fully express itself. We can take our time enjoying the food, and the wine. When you are ready, I am prepared to give you a massage you will never forget."

"Desi, my intuition tells me that I can trust you with sharing very intimate moments. But I should warn you that I can get very emotional. If you give me another orgasm tonight, I may start crying or say something stupid. Can you deal with my happy tears?" Emily said as her eyes seemed to moisten. "What would make you happy, Desi?

"You are aware of the zodiac sign for someone born in July under the sky of Cancer, right?"

"Linda told me that it is a sideways sixty-nine. Oh, maybe that is how I ended up telling her about my ignorance regarding oral sex."

"Well, maybe sometime soon we will trust each other enough that we will find ourselves in such an intimate position."

Emily took a couple of bites of the Italian food off her plate. "Italian food must be some sort of aphrodisiac because I am thinking about trying that position with you tonight."

"I don't know what Italians would say in response to that, but the French might say, bon appétit. "

Wednesday morning arrived with both Desi and Emily sideways across Desi's bed. Desi had little time to prepare any breakfast for Emily. He toasted some English muffins and took a few jams and jellies out of his refrigerator before hopping in the shower. When he got out, Emily was spreading beach plum jam onto one of the muffins.

"Is this beach plum jam from Long Island?" Emily asked.

"Yeah. The last time I was home, I grabbed a jar from my parents' basement. My mother makes a dozen or so jars each year."

"So, she didn't send it to you as an apartment warming gift when you moved in here earlier this year?"

"No. I don't think I have ever told them about the apartment. They don't have the telephone number, no less the address. If they send me a letter, it goes to the barracks. I think my father and mother only send correspondence every month or two. Maybe that was how much mail my father received during World War II when he served in the Pacific."

"They never expressed any interest in visiting you at Fort Knox?"

"Don't think it ever crossed their minds. I am the oldest of four. They have two hardware stores to run and three other kids to deal with. The only holiday they have time to celebrate and take vacation time for is the Fourth of July."

"I think it would be very strange for me to not see my parents for months at a time."

"I think you might get used to it. It sounds like your parents were away from home for years at a time during the War."

"I guess they were, but while I was growing up, my grandparents always seemed to stop by for the holidays and we did take vacations to see them."

"Well, we can finish this conversation over the telephone later and plan out the weekend," Desi said as he left the kitchen and went into his bedroom to put on his short-sleeved khaki uniform.

"Can I spend Thursday night here with you?" Emily asked.

Desi came back into the kitchen fully dressed. "I think that works. I guess we would have to be in West Virginia by noon Friday to get to your parent's house for dinner."

"I have enough to deal with regarding the sleeping arrangements, now you want me to get them to commit to having dinner for us?"

"It might be pushing it to think we could get to the Baltimore area by dinner time. We might have to stop and spend Friday night in a motel somewhere."

"Then you would only have to worry about spending Saturday night at my parents' house. Is that what you are thinking?"

Desi gave Emily a hug and a kiss. "Stay here as long as you like. If you are going to be around for lunch, give me a call at the office. We can have lunch somewhere between here and E'Town, where I have to go this afternoon. If you leave before, then just remember to lock up the place."

"Like you lock up with the key left in the door?" Emily teased.

"I've set the bar pretty low on locking up," Desi conceded.

"I forgot to tell you; I might have an interview at the *Louisville Courier Journal* on Thursday."

"That's great! We can talk more about that later, also," Desi said as he exited the apartment.

Emily waited a minute or so until Desi drove off in his Super Beetle before she used the wall phone in Desi's kitchen. She called Linda, who was having breakfast at Emily's late grandmother's home.

"There's no sign of him moving any of his stuff into Desi's place."

Emily could hear Linda cursing at the other end of the line before the line went dead.

Desi did not get a call at his office from Emily that morning. He stopped by his apartment to change into civilian clothes before heading down to the newspaper publisher's office in Elizabethtown. When he pulled up to the apartment, there was no sign of Emily's blue Mustang.

As he was leaving the apartment, Desi saw his neighbor coming out of her house.

"I thought your new friend was moving in this week," she said.

"Didn't he get a check to you yet?" Desi asked.

"I am going to look in my mailbox now."

Desi walked with her to the mailbox and stood by as she opened it. She then took out a copy of *Playboy* magazine with an address wrapper that also served to discreetly cover parts of that month's Playmate. "I have a subscription, just to keep things interesting with my husband."

Desi raised his eyebrows. "Most people claim they just get it for the articles."

"Do you think that the letters to the 'Playboy Advisor' are really letters from the readers?"

Desi shook his head to indicate "No."

"I don't think so either," his neighbor said as she took a second look inside the mailbox. "Well, no check yet. You can tell him that if he gets me a check this evening, I'll give him a couple of Playboys to keep him company till he finds a local honey."

"Well, I don't know if he needs an incentive to get his stuff over here. I'll try to find out if he is having any sort of problem with getting his car from California or transferring his banking to an account here. I am going away for the weekend, so I would like him all settled in by tomorrow night," Desi said.

"Do you want to take a quick look at the centerfold before you head back to work?" his neighbor asked as she took the wrapping off the magazine. Without waiting for Desi to answer, she unfolded the oversized center page with the featured Playmate of the Month. "Desi, this one has that Jane Russell look, like those twins who used to hang out at your house. What were their names?" she said as she handed Desi the opened magazine.

"Kathy and Brenda," Desi answered as he took notice of the striking resemblance.

"One of them got married, right?"

"Yes, it's been a few months, and Kathy is, reportedly, still happily married to a helicopter pilot."

"You know that movie with Jane Russell, *Gentlemen Marry Brunettes*? Do you think that is true?"

Desi handed back the magazine. "I wouldn't even venture a guess on that," he said as he walked to his car.

Desi made a quick stop for lunch at a soda fountain shop in Elizabethtown, where he devoured a burger and downed a coffee shake at the counter. When asked by the waitress if he was going to have any dessert, he replied that he would be back later. Desi arrived at the *News Enterprise* office a little before two. The ads had all been filled in and it seemed that most of the copy had been printed and was ready to be laid out.

Rosemary, the civilian journalist from the *Turret* office, who covered the Officers' Wives Club activities and wrote many of the articles for the Community Page, had already assembled her stack of copy. She was an attractive, college educated, native Kentuckian in her late twenties who had been married a couple of years. From casual comments, she seemed to be at least thinking about when she would like to have a family. She would also, on occasion, inquire of Desi as to whether he had found "any special Kentucky woman."

She smiled when she saw him, saying, "I came down early to make sure they had everything ready for us."

Desi smiled back. "It looks like you got them to focus on our stuff before their E'Town paper."

They took their respective stacks of copy and laid them out for about an hour. As usual, there were unplanned jumps of copy, as well as a few formatting issues, such as fitting in the headlines and some of the photos. He made sure that the page regarding the Fort Knox Foresters had a large type byline that read "Story and photos by Desmond E. McKoy."

While they waited for the publisher's staff to resize a few things, they discussed a story Army Community Services (ACS) at Fort Knox wanted to put together about unplanned pregnancy. At first, it seemed like Rosemary was seeking to have Desi work with her on the story, which would include information on counseling and services available on post, as well as outside organizations like Birthright and Planned Parenthood. By the end of their conversation, it seemed like Rosemary was seeking to simply introduce Desi to the Army Child Advocacy Program Officer and a Specialist 5, who was a social worker with ACS.

They would be available for Desi to interview on Monday or Tuesday of the following week if not sooner. Rosemary said she believed Desi "would be able to get enough information from interviewing them to write the article." That didn't sound to Desi as if she was intending to do any of the writing. Desi might also have to shoot an accompanying photo of a pregnant young woman if another photographer was unavailable.

"I talked it over with our editor and the people upstairs and everyone agreed that you would be the best one to do that article," Rosemary said.

Desi wasn't sure if she was complimenting him or just relieved that she didn't have to have her byline on an article that could trigger various reactions by readers. Only later, when recounting to Stacey his being drafted to do the ACS "Childhood to Motherhood" article, did he also consider that Rosemary might be very sensitive regarding the subject of pregnancy given the unknown factors regarding her own personal situation.

Desi and Rosemary were finished laying out the paper well before five. Desi called Stacey at her office and told her that he was heading to their meeting spot. Stacey said she would be getting on the road in a few minutes.

Rather than driving back to the parking lot right next to the soda fountain shop, Desi drove to a public parking lot a few blocks away and took a leisurely stroll past several of the stores in the central downtown area, which only encompassed a few blocks.

There was a storefront with a "Carter for President" sign in the window and an open front door. Desi peered inside the office and saw an older gentleman sitting at a table and going through a stack of papers. There was an FDR poster from the 1930s on the wall behind him.

"Young man," he called out to Desi, "are you registered to vote?"

Desi nodded in the affirmative.

"Are you from around here?"

"No, I'm from New York. I've been politically involved up there."

The older man stood up and walked around the table towards Desi. "My name is Henderson; Ray Henderson and I live up in Louisville." He put his hand out to Desi.

Desi shook the hand of the man, who looked a bit like Colonel Sanders, saying, "I am Desmond McKoy, but please call me Desi."

"Have you been involved in a presidential campaign?"

"I worked a little bit on the McGovern campaign when I was in college. It was fun to talk to students on campus, but it was much harder to convince older people that the Vietnam War was a lost cause and only George McGovern was determined to end it sooner rather than later."

"What are you doing now?"

"I'm an Army journalist stationed at Fort Knox."

"A journalist, eh, did you ever hear of Robert Worth Bingham, publisher of the *Louisville Courier?*"

"I've heard of the Bingham family in Louisville."

"I knew the old man. Franklin Roosevelt appointed him as Ambassador to Great Britain, and he held that job until he became ill and died at the end of 1937. Joe Kennedy was appointed by Roosevelt to succeed Bingham."

"I didn't know all that, but I did meet Robert Kennedy in 1964, when I was twelve and Bobby was running for the U.S. Senate."

"I guess there are a few decades of difference in our ages, but you seem like you might be able to help me locate a person to help me run this campaign office."

"Do you have a card, Mr. Henderson?"

"Please, just call me Ray," the gentleman said as he reached inside his suit pocket and pulled out a business card.

Desi looked at the card, which read, "Raymond W. Henderson," with "Attorney at Law" printed underneath. "Maybe I will just call you Attorney Henderson. "

"My friends call me Ray, and I hope you'll let me call you Desi."

"Did you ever get the chance to meet FDR?" Desi asked.

"How about if we save that story for another time?"

"Good idea," Desi agreed. "I have to meet a woman I know at the ice cream shop."

"Oh, don't let me keep you from that. I may be getting up in years, but I understand priorities."

"It's not that kind of a relationship. We aren't doing the two straws in the same milkshake glass thing."

"You never know where any sort of relationship with an attractive woman can lead," counselled Attorney Henderson. "She is good looking, right?"

"She is the girlfriend of one of my best friends."

"Where's your friend?"

"He's in Germany."

"Hey, isn't your generation's favorite song, "Love the One You're With"?"

"How about if we also save that for another time?" Desi suggested.

"Looking forward to it," Attorney Henderson said as walked back around the desk and sat back down in his chair.

Desi smiled at him, then walked out of the campaign office.

Stacey arrived at the ice cream parlor only a few minutes after Desi. She still was wearing her uniform with the jacket and skirt.

"I think your new housemate is moving in tomorrow," Stacey said as she sat down in the booth opposite Desi.

"Good thing, since the landlord is starting to get anxious."

"You haven't had to give her a back rub or anything to calm her down, have you?"

"No, but I had a talk with her this afternoon as she retrieved this month's *Playboy* from her mailbox. She said she gets it 'to keep things interesting' with her husband."

Stacey laughed. "Otherwise, he would have lost interest in sex a long time ago."

"Since we are talking about sex, I just found out that I have to start working on a story with Army Community Services about the possible risks for young people who approach having intercourse as simply fun, with no sense of responsibility."

Stacey laughed again. "Like getting knocked up?"

"You guessed it! I can't claim it's a breaking news story; it's more like a public awareness article about what counseling services are available on post and off."

"I think your neighbor is looking to get knocked up. Are there going to be helpful suggestions for women like her in your article, or would you have to suggest something in person?"

"She is never going to convince me to put one foot inside her house," Desi said.

"Her husband invited Charlie over to their house one evening to give his wife a massage because the husband claimed he had poison ivy and couldn't do it himself."

"Charlie never told me that story."

"Charlie claims that the husband directed him to their bedroom and then left Charlie to find the wife naked on top of the bed, with only a towel draped over her. It sounded like she was willing to do whatever Charlie wanted in exchange for an attempt by Charlie to give her a massage."

"And what was the husband doing while Charlie was in the bedroom with his wife?"

"Charlie claims that the moment his hands touched her bare shoulders and she started talking about where he could put his 'weenie' while he gave her a massage, he went totally limp. He left the bedroom, and the husband was down the hallway looking out a window and would not turn around when Charlie said was leaving. He thinks the husband may not have turned around because he was giving himself a hand job."

"Sounds crazy but believable."

"So, you're right about never accepting an invitation into their house or the hot tub. I will warn your new housemate about them after he has paid his first month's rent and moved in."

"Yeah, wait a little while to tell him, or he may bail out."

"And you need to wait a while before you do any massaging of Cindy MacNamara," Stacey said as she took a look at a menu. "Can I order dinner before I start giving you the straight business on her?"

"Sure," Desi said as he picked up a menu.

Later that evening, Desi worked on cleaning the apartment in anticipation of the new tenant appearing the next day. He even pulled the refrigerator away from the wall in the kitchen to clean behind it after vacuuming the entire apartment, paying special attention to the empty bedroom.

He called Roger and told him that he would be in Baltimore on Friday night or Saturday morning. Roger said he thought Daisy had figured out some spot for them to meet up on Saturday morning for brunch. They agreed to talk more the following night.

After not having received a call from Emily, Desi tried her at her grandmother's house around nine, but there was no answer. When he tried again around ten, Linda answered the telephone. Desi learned that Emily was scheduled to turn in a job application and take some type of test at the *Courier Journal* the next day and had gone to a shopping mall earlier in the evening to get a new outfit for the interview. Linda thought that Emily would be back at their place any minute.

Desi went to check on how clean the bathroom looked. A few minutes later, Emily called. She sounded a bit frantic and perturbed. Desi suggested that she call him at his office number the following afternoon. He explained that he might be out doing some interviews in the morning, but that he would probably be in the office writing a story most of the afternoon.

The next day, while Desi was at his desk in the afternoon, he received a call from Cindy MacNamara, who had read and apparently enjoyed the article about the foresters working in the woodlands of Fort Knox.

"You know," Cindy said, "I found that story really interesting, and I thought the photos were cool of the guys with the metal detectors on the trees."

"Most people here in the office thought the photos looked crazy until they read the article."

"I used to go out with a guy who was studying to be a park ranger."

"What happened to him?"

"He went back to being a logger in Canada after he failed the park ranger test."

"Is the park ranger test difficult?"

"Not really," Cindy said. "I took it with him, and I passed, but it was in English and he had only taken tests in French when he was in school in Quebec."

"Where did you meet him?"

"In Ithaca, when I was going to Ithaca College, majoring in biology."

"Tree biology or human biology?" Desi kidded.

"Very funny," Cindy said with a sigh.

"But you didn't become a park ranger, or a biologist, but an MP."

"I took a leave of absence from college after my sophomore year, spent a summer up in Canada walking through lots of forests with him and ended up back in Pennsylvania with my parents."

"I understand that your father is someone in law enforcement."

"Are you just using your deduction skills or your investigative reporter abilities?"

"Maybe we should just talk about how beautiful Ithaca is this time of year," Desi suggested. "I have a friend who went to the ILR School at Cornell, and I went up a couple of times to see him. He is now in law school in Washington D.C."

"That's what I want to do," Cindy revealed. "I want to go to law school so I can become an FBI agent."

"Is that your idea or your father's?"

"Pretty much my idea. My father would have been happy with me being a park ranger."

"But you want to fight the bad guys?" Desi asked.

"I want to be an FBI agent who understands enough biology so that I can do forensic work. It wouldn't just be catching the bad guys but also freeing people who were wrongly accused."

"That sounds like a good specialization as well as very noble on your part."

"I understand that you want to go to law school after you get out of the Army," Cindy replied.

"Where did you read that?" Desi asked. "I don't think I included that in any of the articles I have written."

"Maybe we should save some questions until that dinner in Louisville."

"Well, I have to take a couple of photos at a dinner tonight of the TRADOC Commander and Deputy Commander with people from Fort Knox, including the Commanding General, so tonight is out for that dinner. And it looks like I am flying to Fort Monroe tomorrow and going to Pimlico on Saturday for the Preakness Stakes. Perhaps you can give me a call next Wednesday or Thursday?"

"I was hoping to talk to you about a couple of things before then. I've heard that you have a lot of good contacts. I have to make some tough choices in the next few days."

"Well, as you know, I am not a lawyer, and if the issues you face have legal consequences, then all I am going to be able to tell you is that you need a lawyer."

"That's my first problem. I don't know any good local attorneys. I need someone who has taken on Army investigators and JAG attorneys but hasn't folded like a napkin. I don't need a lawyer who makes their client become someone who ruins other people's lives."

"I understand what you are saying," Desi said. "Can you meet me at the snack shack by the *Turret* office in ten minutes?"

"I'm calling you from the pay phone at the burger place right now."

"Then walk through the parking lot, and up the steps to our office. I will meet you inside the office door."

Desi hung up the phone. He started to write the name of an Elizabethtown attorney on a blank sheet of paper but decided to put the paper into his typewriter and typed out the name. He folded the sheet of paper and waited in the hallway outside his office for Cindy to open the outside door to the main newsroom.

That room was set up in an arrangement of desks for several reporters. When Cindy opened the door, the reporter closest to the door immediately asked her, with a sigh of exasperation, if she wanted to place a free "Bazaar" ad in the paper for the next week. Desi indicated to Cindy, by nodding his head, to say "Yes."

Cindy agreed and took a form from the reporter, who passed it over her shoulder. Desi beckoned to Cindy to walk towards him. As soon as she got close to him, Desi started walking towards the part of the building that housed the fire trucks. Cindy followed him and took the folded piece of paper that he handed off to her with a relay race type pass.

They reached a foyer with a door into the space occupied by the fire and emergency department and a staircase up to the offices of the military and civilian Public Information Officers. There was also a door leading out to the street. Desi pointed to that door to direct Cindy out of the building and went up the stairs to talk to the civilian Public Affairs Officer, Walter Freeland, about the AUSA dinner that evening.

"Is Mr. Freeland available?" Desi asked the PFC receptionist.

"I think you can just walk into his office," she replied.

"Desi are you ready for tonight?" said the retired Army officer serving as the civilian who oversaw most of the dealings with the local community surrounding Fort Knox. He was also the chief of the local chapter of the AUSA and a board member of the Fort Knox Credit Union.

"Yes, sir. My camera is all ready," Desi answered. "I've been thinking about setting up a shot of the Commanding General with the TRADOC Commander and Deputy Commander sitting at a table with you and several members of the Daniel Boone Chapter standing behind them. I think I'll need your help with coordinating and getting everyone's cooperation with that."

"I've also been thinking about the dinner tonight," Freeland said. "Why don't you shut my door and sit down for a few minutes so that we can talk about it."

Desi shut the door and sat down.

A few minutes later, a CID officer came up the staircase and asked the receptionist if she "had seen Specialist McKoy." The receptionist advised the young officer that Desi was "in with one of our public affairs officers discussing arrangements for a dinner with the Commanding General and the TRADOC Commander."

The lieutenant paused for a moment before asking the receptionist, "If I give you my card, do you think you can have him give me a call tomorrow?"

"I think Specialist McKoy will be in the office tomorrow."

The lieutenant gave her his card and left.

When Desi's meeting with Walter Freeland broke up, the receptionist asked Desi if he knew Lieutenant Rogers as she handed Desi the business card. "He asked that you give him a call tomorrow."

Desi merely nodded his head as he took the card.

Chapter IX

NEED TO KNOW BASIS

After a brief tour of Fort Monroe, Virginia, and a meeting with a staff sergeant that led to lunch at a nearby seafood restaurant, Desi found himself on Friday afternoon in the back of an Army staff car on the way to the Pentagon. Not once, either before or during the flight from Fort Knox on the blue and white jet with a presidential seal that morning, did anyone tell him that he was being sent to Fort Monroe to be interviewed for a position. The only other passengers aboard the jet, which looked like it could accommodate about twenty people, were the TRADOC Commanding General and the Deputy Commander.

Desi said "Good Morning" to each of them when they stepped inside the plane but was not going to ask them why he was on-board. During the flight, Desi revised drafts of articles he was preparing for the post newspaper. As they disembarked from the corporate jet-style aircraft and were directed to separate vehicles, Desi suddenly had the thought that perhaps the two generals had no more idea than he did as to why he had been flown to the TRADOC Headquarters.

Once on the base, Desi was driven to a long warehouse-style building with a rounded roof which he was told served as the printing plant for various Army training manuals. The only person Desi observed inside the building was Staff Sergeant Williams, who invited him into his very utilitarian office. All the furnishings, including the desk and the chairs, looked like they had been surplus items from World War II. Sergeant Williams didn't volunteer any information as to the number of staff members or any explanation as to why there was no one else in the building. He confirmed with Desi that Desi was a graduate of New York University and was the "Distinguished Honor Graduate" of his class at the Defense Information School (DINFOS). Sergeant Williams seemed to have read some of the articles Desi had written for the post newspaper at Fort Knox, particularly mentioning the one about soldiers "choking" on a new testing format that had been expected to be a "piece of cake." The new Military Occupational Specialty (MOS) testing was supposed to focus on activities the soldiers had already been trained to perform, but the results had been disappointing.

When assigned the article, Desi was given reports the Army prepared on the test results and then he interviewed a few people from advanced training units at Fort Knox. They seemed to be scratching their heads as to what happened. Desi sensed there were some career officers who were trying to seize on such results as a way to question the viability of an all-volunteer Army. Desi felt his article steered clear of delving into that issue, and he told Sergeant Williams that he personally hoped that "everyone would someday be onboard with the volunteer Army."

When they went to lunch, Sergeant Williams asked Desi about his own experiences in Basic Training and what he saw that could be improved. As for making his own adjustment from civilian life to being in the Army, Desi told his story about attending the U.S. Merchant Marine Academy right out of high school and the challenges he experienced at the Academy.

Desi shared that the Army's physical training was "tough," but the Kings Point experience more than prepared him for the psychological stress of a military environment. Desi suggested that perhaps the Army needed to provide some counseling to soldiers who, in their everyday assignments, would succeed in performing their tasks but had a "hang up" when it came to any form of testing. When further questioned about Basic Training, Desi took the opportunity to critique the three or four hours of Race Relations Training he received at Fort Dix, New Jersey. Desi even shared his conclusion that the presentation he experienced at Fort Dix was "superficial and meaningless."

Desi spoke about how he, along with a few other young men who had bachelor's degrees in the liberal arts and social sciences, tried to make the discussion more meaningful but found everything very scripted, with presenters delivering observations that did not challenge individuals or the Army to do better with recognizing and resolving matters that impeded getting beyond differences. Those presenters seemed satisfied with merely ending their lesson with "everyone has prejudgments and prejudices." Desi admitted that the seminar left him questioning whether or not the Army was merely positioning itself to claim it addressed the topic of diversity in the Armed Forces. "The time I spent in that lecture, along with the time spent by the approximately two hundred soldiers in our Basic Training Company, seemed pointless." The assembly of soldiers of various ethnic, religious, racial, and socio-economic backgrounds were left with, in Desi's view, little or nothing more than when they were marched into the event. Desi explained that the presentation "lacked any legally or philosophically sound basis and didn't provide any forward perspective."

"I would be interested in helping rewrite the syllabus for training regarding the recognition of barriers between members of the Army, in communicating and working together as team members," Desi told Sergeant Williams. "The Army needs to address concerns from members of various minority groups regarding fair and respectful treatment, concerns that I am sure you and everyone at TRADOC are aware of. In Basic Training, there should be an open discussion of when and how the Army will address such concerns. If you want me to help TRADOC with Diversity Training, I will consider moving to Fort Monroe. That could work for me, if I could be involved with a significant project like that and go to law school at night at one of the law schools in this area. I see the Army as a social experiment for our country, and I hope the Army succeeds so our country can succeed. However, if such an opportunity is not available, then I hope to get assigned overseas. One of my goals when I enlisted was to actually live in another country. Not just for the fun of new experiences, but to get a better perspective on the United States and its role in the world."

"So, I guess you would not be interested in working here to upgrade our training manuals," Sergeant Williams concluded with little hesitation.

"I'm not sure who thought it would be a good fit for me."

Desi never got an answer regarding that question. He was politely told by Sergeant Williams that he would be provided a ride to the Pentagon by the courier who delivered mail and packages between Fort Monroe and the Pentagon. Desi would get a plane ticket back to Kentucky from the travel office at the Pentagon.

As they arrived at the Pentagon, Desi asked the courier if he knew where the transportation office was located within the Pentagon. The courier responded by saying, "I have to think about whether I have ever been to that office." He got out of the vehicle, walked around the back of the car, opened Desi's door, and took the box of mail out of the front passenger seat.

"I think you are going to have to ask someone inside," the courier finally added as Desi followed him towards the huge office building, carrying his suit bag over his shoulder.

Someone at the security desk made a call for Desi to the NCO in charge of travel expenses and put Desi on the phone. Desi spent about five minutes trying to explain how, after being flown to Fort Monroe, he was told that there would be a ticket for him to get back to Fort Knox. He acknowledged that only government aircraft flew in and out of Fort Knox. He also requested that his commercial flight to the airport in Louisville be for a flight on Sunday afternoon or evening from Baltimore.

The Army Specialist on the other end of the call asked him a couple times why, if they flew him into Fort Monroe, they were not flying him out of Fort Monroe. Desi just responded by asking if she had received any messages from anyone at Fort Monroe authorizing the commercial flight back to Kentucky. The third time she asked him why he was not flying back to Fort Knox on the same Army aircraft that he came in on, he asked to speak to her supervisor. She put him on the phone with an Army Major who went through his teletype messages and found something with Desi's name on it. "I am sending Specialist Gaines out to help you," he said as he hung up the phone.

Desi waited at the security desk as a procession of colonels and a couple of generals came through the security post. Then, the tall and shapely Specialist Gaines, the acting NCO in charge of travel arrangements, appeared and beckoned Desi to follow her. They walked through several corridors, making rights and lefts, but Spec. Gaines always stayed one or two steps ahead of Desi and held her head so that no matter which way they walked, Desi did not see her full face. By the way she moved her hips, Desi surmised that she was an athlete or a dancer. It wasn't until they reached her office that he saw the purplish discoloration that covered most of her right cheek.

"So, now are you going to tell me how you flew to Fort Monroe?" she said, staring him in the face.

"I can only tell you that General DePuy was at Fort Knox with the TRADOC Deputy Commander and apparently there was room on the jet to fly me to Fort Monroe with them," Desi answered.

"I went to Fort Knox High School, my father was a helicopter pilot, and I know that there aren't many jets that fly in or out of Fort Knox," Specialist Gaines said, again turning her face so that Desi couldn't see her right cheek. "What sort of jet was it?"

"I have a top secret clearance," Desi said with a smile. "I am not sure if I can share that information with you."

"I also have a top secret clearance. Probably everyone one in this building has at least a top secret clearance."

"Ok," Desi relented. "And if I do tell you, will you make sure that I get transportation to Baltimore this evening and a commercial flight from Baltimore to Louisville Sunday evening?"

"I will make sure you get to Baltimore this evening if I have to drive you myself," Specialist Gaines said, putting a hand on Desi's shoulder. "I guess you have a hot date?"

"A woman I met right before the Kentucky Derby two weeks ago has invited me to Pimlico tomorrow and is going to show me around Baltimore."

"So, you don't actually have plans for tonight?" Specialist Gaines asked. "I might be able to change my plans for this evening so I could give you a tour of D.C. before I drive you to Baltimore tonight or tomorrow morning."

"I couldn't ask you to do that; perhaps you can give me that tour some other time."

"Well, another time my boyfriend might be back here in the States."

"He's been gone for a while?" Desi asked.

"He's one of those Special Forces guys who can be sent to places like Panama, and he can't even call for months at a time."

"And he can't even tell you, with your top secret clearance, when he is coming back?"

"Or if he is even expecting to make it back," Specialist Gaines said as she once again stared at Desi with her full face towards him. "But now you have to tell me about the jet from Fort Knox to Fort Monroe. Were Air Force pilots flying it?"

"Yes. It was blue and white, and I would estimate that it would be able to have about two dozen passengers as there was a sort of booth on the port side up front with a small table. One of the Air Force Officers told me it is where Henry Kissinger gets comfortable when he is flying on that jet with the presidential seal."

"So, Desi, did you take that booth on your flight?"

"That Air Force officer offered it to me, but I thought of the picture of Kissinger as a pinup in the *Harvard Lampoon.* I found myself wondering what Dr. K might do at that comfy table if he had a few drinks. Did he strip down to get relaxed in that booth?"

Specialist Gaines started laughing and put her hand on Desi's arm as if it would help her control her laughter. "Did you go to Harvard?"

"No. I'm a graduate of New York University."

"That's even more cosmopolitan," she said as she tightened her grip on Desi's bicep.

"Since I want to be wearing the civilian clothes in my suit bag by the time I get to Baltimore tonight, is there a place I can change around here? Do you have a key to the men's room?"

Specialist Gaines went behind the middle desk in the office and opened a door behind the desk. "You can change right here in our storage room."

Desi carried his suit bag into the storage room and closed the door. He had started taking off his short-sleeved khaki shirt when Specialist Gaines opened the door. "You have to keep the door partly open so I can ask you questions about the travel arrangements. Also, I have to be able to make sure you are not snooping into the documents that are stored there."

"Specialist Gaines, is this where they keep the 'Pentagon Papers'?" Desi sarcastically asked.

"No, but you might see the poster of me in a yellow polka dot bikini on top of a tank at Fort Knox. And please, just call me Pamela."

Desi looked around and, sure enough, there was quite a revealing photograph of Pamela's long legs and womanly torso with a side profile of her face. Long, platinum blond hair flowed over her left shoulder. "When was this picture taken?" Desi asked.

"Right after high school, during my very brief modeling career. I had a boyfriend who is now a photographer for men's magazines. He told me he could help me get some great exposure."

"I am sure you helped the Army with enlistments," Desi offered as he turned around to take off his khaki pants.

"Desi, you have to turn around so I can ask you about your travel arrangements," Pamela said with a smile. "And I need to see if, after you saw that picture of me, you might now be more interested in having dinner with me this evening."

"I know I have to get back to Kentucky by Sunday evening. I don't know if you can get me a flight or just a train ticket from D.C. to Baltimore."

"What about me having you for dinner tonight?"

"I don't know if I'd get any sleep if I stayed at your place tonight."

"I didn't say anything about sleeping."

"How do you know your warrior boyfriend won't show up, or if he has one of his buddies watching your place?"

"All right," Specialist Gaines said, taking a few moments to think about Desi's objections. "Do you have off-post housing in the Fort Knox area?"

Desi nodded in confirmation.

"I'll make you a deal. You need to find me a place near Fort Knox to store my boyfriend's motorcycle for about $25 a month instead of the $65 a month that I am paying here in D.C. In a couple of weeks, if my boyfriend hasn't resurfaced, I'm going to drive the bike to Kentucky, and we are going camping down at Dale Hollow Lake on the Tennessee border. Have you been there?"

"Yes, I've gone scuba diving in the former rock quarries. It's a beautiful area to go camping."

"Ok, so you are going to have to ditch your Kentucky Derby girl for that weekend, if you are still seeing her by then. I won't tell anyone where we are going, and I'll just fly back to D.C. from Louisville. You'll drive me to the airport after our weekend together, won't you?"

"Sure, and I will take care of getting us a tent," Desi said as he finished pulling up his blue jeans.

"Ok, maybe I can get you a flight to Baltimore or a train ticket to Baltimore."

"For this evening, right?" Desi said as he buttoned up his blue dress shirt.

"Yes, I don't want to be the cause of you disappointing the young lady who is taking you to the Preakness tomorrow. What did you say her name was?"

"Emma Lee Miller. She's graduating from the University of Kentucky sometime this month and just interviewed with the *Louisville Courier Journal.*"

"I think I've heard her on some religious radio channel. She's the daughter of the Reverend Miller, who my mother used to listen to. Not sure what happened, but I don't think she is still listening to that church radio anymore," Spec. Gaines said as she leafed through flight and train schedules. "You're having dinner with Emma Lee Miller this evening?"

"And maybe with her parents also," Desi said as he put on his blue blazer.

"You'll have some more interesting stories to tell me in a couple of weeks. No, wait a minute," she said while writing on a memo pad. "Here's my direct office number. Give me a call Tuesday or Wednesday and give me an update on what might be available for storing the motorcycle. It can't be in a horse barn. That would get it stinky."

"I'll check with my landlady, who owns a few places in Radcliff. And if I need someone to verify that I was at the Pentagon this afternoon, will you serve as my witness?"

"I'll do what I can to help you, and I hope you can help me with what I need," Pamela said, turning her head so she was facing Desi straight on.

She held up the travel information. "For what you are saving the government by flying out of Baltimore on Sunday afternoon instead of tonight, I can also print you out a train ticket so you can get to Baltimore this evening. Since I came into work early this morning, we can leave as soon as the tickets are printed. I'll change into my jeans. You are going to have to watch the printer as I change in the storeroom."

"And you are going to change with the storeroom door open, right?" Desi asked.

"Of course. How else would I know if you started peeking inside drawers and saw something you shouldn't?"

In Baltimore in Time for Dinner

Desi called Emily's parents' house from the train station in D.C. and briefly spoke to Emily's mother, who he remembered to call Dr. Miller. Desi learned that Reverend Miller had gone to the Baltimore airport to meet Emily's flight from Louisville. They were expecting Desi to have dinner with them. Emily's mother asked him if he liked tandoori chicken. Desi said that was one of his favorite Indian dishes. Apparently, Reverend Miller was picking up some Indian food after retrieving Emily from the airport. Desi advised Emily's mother of his scheduled arrival time in Baltimore. Dr. Miller said she would pass the information on to Emily and Reverend Miller.

When he got to Baltimore, Desi spotted Emily in the crowded station. She was sitting on a bench reading *Fear of Flying.* "Have you been waiting long?" he said to her.

Emily looked up and shook her head to say "No." She leaned forward to kiss him.

"Are you here with your dad?"

"He's with the car down the block," she said as she linked arms with Desi. "I had been looking forward to driving with you from Louisville, but it's a lot easier just leaving my car at the airport in Louisville."

"My mother always says that things have a way of working out,"

"Well, now that you're here, I'll call in the order to the restaurant," Emily said as she took a piece of paper out of her pocket and started pulling Desi along to a bank of payphones.

"I hear that we are going to have some tandoori chicken."

"My mother likes to have Indian food when she meets new people as it gives her the perfect excuse to talk about her time in India right after the War. There are never any awkward silences in the conversation because she always has another story to tell," Emily said with a quiet laugh.

"I am glad to hear that you don't expect any awkward silences. Give me a kick in the shins if I start telling too many of my travel stories."

"I won't hesitate to bop you in the nose if you try to take over the whole conversation," Emily said with a smile as she dialed the restaurant.

As they walked to the Reverend Miller's car, Emily asked Desi about his religious beliefs.

"Why do you want to know about my religious background? You aren't telling your parents that you are planning to have children with me, are you? I did bring condoms."

"That may be something I don't want you to share with my parents," Emily said with a sigh.

"I guess the sleeping arrangements have not been finalized."

"I don't think they want you sleeping with me upstairs because my bedroom is across the hall from their bedroom. And what used to be my late brother's bedroom hasn't been slept in for over four years. That leaves the couch downstairs, but maybe I can sneak down during the night."

"How about the treehouse in your backyard. Is that still an option?"

"Only if it isn't raining tonight. I think the roof has a couple of leaks."

"I haven't asked you about your religious beliefs," Desi acknowledged. "Can you recite the Nicene Creed?"

"I am not Roman Catholic. Maybe all your Italian and Irish girlfriends back in New York can recite the Rosary and stuff, but aren't they merely regurgitating things they were taught as children?"

"I know you studied religion in college, and you seem to be very conversant regarding Thomas Merton," Desi said.

"Don't go too crazy on all the Merton stuff you've read," Emily warned. "Tell me something about your goals in life so I will be able to sound like I really know you before I tell my mother that I may be sharing the couch with you downstairs. I have a need-to-know things about you."

"Well, I like tandoori chicken, but I love lamb saag. There is a restaurant in the East Village that makes naan bread sandwiches with lamb and spinach that seem to melt in my mouth."

"I'll call the restaurant again and will order some lamb saag for you to share with my father. He enjoys it also." Emily said as she spotted another pay phone.

"Perfect. We found something for me to agree on with your father."

In the car to Emily's parents' house, Emily's father spoke mostly to Emily. He wanted to know all about her interview at the *Courier Journal.* Emily said she was not sure if they were offering a five-days a week paid internship, but she said she felt like they would at least offer her something.

Desi mentioned the lamb saag to Emily's father to have something to contribute to the conversation.

At their dining room table, Reverend Miller said grace and Emily's mother said another blessing in Hindi. As they passed around the food, a silence fell upon the diners, which apparently made Emily uncomfortable enough to blurt out, "Desi has read the Bhagavad Gita."

"I think all soldiers should know the story of Arjuna," Emily's mother commented.

"Provided they have first educated themselves as to their own religious tradition and read the Bible," Emily's father added.

"Desi has studied Philosophy of Religion and is familiar with all the major religions."

Reverend Miller fixed his gaze on Desi. "Are you, or have you ever been, a practicing Christian?"

Desi took a look at Emily and noticed that she had scrunched her forehead into wrinkles. He then turned to Reverend Miller and simply said, "Yes."

"Good," Reverend Miller said, sounding a bit relieved. "Emma Lee seems to attract atheists and Marxists."

"I don't know if that is fair," Emily protested.

"As for where I am today in terms of religion, I now describe myself as a monotheist," Desi explained. "And with respect to philosophy, I'm in the Hegelian camp that allows for the metaphysical and isn't totally materialistic. Marx was critical of Hegel, and Hegel did have his flaws, particularly his Bonapartism, but Hegel's writings seem to have a spiritual core."

"I think that Desi gives a good account of his intellectual prowess, but I am still wondering if there is a story in the Bible that you feel resonates within your own spiritual life?" Reverend Miller asked.

"New Testament or Old?"

"Let's stick to the New Testament," Reverend Miller said as he put another helping of the lamb saag on his plate.

"I think the most cited story of the New Testament is the Road to Emmaus, but I also find the story of Jesus and the Samaritan woman by the well of Jacob to be inspiring." Desi then put some of the green and brown spice sauce on a piece of naan bread.

"Is there a particular line from that Gospel of John that inspires you?" Reverend Miller continued with what seemed to Desi to be a cross-examination.

Desi took a bite of the naan bread and thought for a moment. "Well, it definitely is a story about an encounter with Jesus, but in that story, Jesus gives insight into how we must worship God, which is in Spirit and truth."

Emily's mother looked up from her tandoori chicken. "Desi, are you going to share with us an encounter with Jesus that you have had?"

"It is not something I've talked to anyone about other than the person I experienced it with, and she's an agnostic," Desi said as he felt the stares of Emily, her mother, and her father.

After a silence of over a minute, the Reverend Miller cleared his throat. "It is understandable that something like that can be very personal, and I thank you for sharing what you are comfortable disclosing," the Reverend Miller said.

"I know I'm curious to hear more," Emily said.

Dr. Miller then turned to her daughter. "Why don't we finish our dinner and then you and Desi can take my station wagon out and get dessert?"

"Sure, we can do that," Emily said to her mother. Emily looked at Desi. "I felt you were a special guy but having a religious experience with a witness who is not religious seems beyond whatever I expected to hear from you."

"Well, I certainly wasn't planning to share that tonight," Desi said as he served himself some more basmati rice and lamb saag.

A Private World Inside a Ford Station Wagon

Desi had a feeling from the first afternoon he met Emily that he had much in common with her, but Desi was still a bit surprised when Emily took him to her parents' garage, and inside the two-car garage was a Ford station wagon. It was almost identical to the vehicle that Desi's mother drove.

"Does it have the V-8 engine?" Desi asked Emily.

"Yeah, it does eighty-five with no problem at all."

"I took my mother's up to a hundred on the Long Island Expressway a few months after they finished building the LIE out to Riverhead."

"I don't think there are any roads around here where I can find out how fast it can really go," Emily said as she got in the car.

"Why don't you drive us to the local drive-in, and we can see how fast we can get things going?" Desi suggested as he got in on the passenger side.

"Oh, you think I am the type of girl who is flexible enough to do it on the front bench seat?"

"Yes, and agile enough to climb over to the large back seat for a double feature."

"If we get a bottle of wine along with the dessert, it might be a double feature night," Emily said as she started up the car and backed out of the garage.

"We could have our ice cream during the intermission."

"I guess you already know that I like ice cream," Emily said as she reached over and put her hand on the inside of Desi's thigh and gave his leg a tug to have Desi sit closer.

Preening for the Preakness

The next morning, Emily was awakened by the sound of her mother banging around in the kitchen. She and Desi had fallen asleep in their clothes on the couch after returning from the drive-in movie theater. Emily stood up, ran her hands through her hair, straightened her skirt, buttoned up her blouse, and went into the kitchen.

"Well, look at what the cat dragged in," her mother said. "What time did you two get in last night? I thought you were bringing some dessert home for us to have together, but I gave up on you around midnight."

"I think we got home a little after that," Emily said as she took some orange juice out of the refrigerator.

"I was planning on making breakfast for us, but your father doesn't think I should bother."

Emily wiped some sleep from her eyes. "I think we are meeting a couple of Desi's friends for breakfast this morning. They were with us on Derby weekend."

"Well, can I at least fix Desi a cup of coffee for when he gets up? Do you want some?"

"We are both tea drinkers," Emily said as she looked at her watch. "I should really hop in the shower."

"Alright, I'll make some tea for the two of you. How do you like it?"

Emily started walking up the small staircase in the kitchen that led to the upstairs. "Desi knows how I like it. He should be getting up in a few minutes. Let him fix mine and bring it up to me."

Emily's mother just shook her head as she filled a tea kettle with water.

Desi started to move around on the couch about the time the teakettle started to whistle. When he wandered into the kitchen, Emily's mother was putting some English muffins into a toaster. She turned to Desi. "Emily told me you two have breakfast plans, but I thought that you might want a muffin to start off the morning."

"Yes, I would. We're meeting my buddy Roger and his friend Daisy some place downtown near the Harbor."

"Emily said she wants you to fix her tea and take it upstairs to her."

"I can do that," Desi said as he took a mug off the table and poured some tea in it. He added some milk and honey to the mug for Emily and to the mug he fixed for himself.

The toaster popped the muffins up just as Desi finished fixing the two mugs of tea.

"Do you want butter on the muffin?" Emily's mother asked.

"Yes, thank you."

Desi picked up the plate with the buttered muffin with one hand, grabbed the handles for the two mugs of tea, and then started up the staircase.

"Emily may still be in the shower," Emily's mother called out as Desi disappeared from her sight.

Emily had just turned off the shower when Desi knocked on the door. "Who's there?" she inquired.

"Tea service," Desi said in a wolfish baritone.

Emily, wearing just a towel, opened the bathroom door. "What is on the plate?" she said as she pulled him into the bathroom.

"Your mom thought I would like to start the morning off with nibbling on a muffin."

"She encouraged you to do some muffin nibbling this morning?" Emily said as she opened her towel. "It took some real scrubbing after last night to get it prepared for some more nibbling."

"I'm not sure that was what she meant to encourage but I am willing to do a taste test if you are so inclined, for hygiene purposes."

"Yes, for hygiene purposes, and in the interest of checking that I don't smell like yesterday's seafood catch when we go to Pimlico today."

Desi handed Emily her mug of hot tea and then bent over to give her a quick kiss between her legs.

"You also have to supply me with the plots of those movies last night, in case my mother asks me what they were about," Emily said.

Desi took off his clothes as he sipped his tea. When he was naked, he asked Emily, "You want to do a before and after the shower taste test on me?"

"I would, but I think we may already be running a bit late," Emily said as she watched the smile on Desi's face fade. "But I don't believe that this will be the only opportunity I'll get to give you a taste test today."

Desi's smile returned. He kissed Emily on the lips and hopped in the shower. Emily started drying her hair.

While Desi was shaving, Emily went downstairs in what she called her "aubergine interview outfit," a dark purple sundress with matching purple pumps and clutch. Desi joined her while she was showing off the outfit and talking to her mother. He was wearing just his blue jeans and a towel covering his shoulders. Emily adjusted his towel to cover his chest more as he ate another English muffin, which he found waiting for him on the kitchen table. After devouring the muffin, he went to retrieve the suit bag he left near the front door the night before. He used the half-bath in the front foyer to change into his grey dress pants and shirt. Desi inspected his blue sports jacket to see if the wrinkles had dissipated overnight. He tried smoothing a sleeve by holding the shoulder of the jacket with one hand and using the other hand to run down the sleeve.

Emily suddenly appeared in the hallway by the front door. "Do you want me to try to press that sleeve with my mom's iron?"

"No need to bother. I'm probably just going to be throwing it over a seat this afternoon."

"Well, I probably can't ask my mom for her iron right now because she just got a call from my grandmother. It sounds like my grandmother might need to go to the hospital again. But I did get a chance to show off the dress to her."

"That's your new interview dress?"

"One of them," Emily replied. "This one I wore with the white sweater I will probably take along with me today."

"The way you look, I'm sure you will be getting some sort of internship with the *Courier Journal*," Desi predicted.

"I think my mother headed to my father's office after that call," Emily said as she turned and started walking down the hallway towards her father's home office.

A couple of minutes later, Emily came walking back. "My parents want to talk to us before they head up to Philadelphia."

"I thought they were going to Pimlico today."

"My grandmother is being taken to a hospital. My mom had dinner all prepared for us to eat together tonight. She says we can have Roger and Daisy over to share it. But my father is a little concerned as he doesn't want any parties here tonight, like the pool party we had in Kentucky."

"Do we have to agree to anything in writing?" Desi asked.

"Are you going to want one call to your lawyer?"

"I hadn't quite thought of that, but it might be a good idea."

The two of them walked down the hallway and stopped outside of the office. Emily took a quick look at Desi and took a piece of lint off his lapel before straightening her dress. "How do I look?" Emily asked Desi.

"Absolutely beautiful," Desi answered as he opened the heavy oak door.

Emily's father was sitting at his desk. There were a few photographs of Emily's father with Republican members of the U.S. Senate and the House of Representatives on his wall alongside the desk. There was also one with Secretary Kissinger.

Emily's father noticed Desi looking at the photographs. "I used to have one with Richard Nixon giving me a hug, but I think you can guess what happened to that photo after what happened to him. You're the one who mentioned the 'Spirit and the Truth' last night. Guess the Truth caught up with Tricky Dicky."

Desi nodded his head. He looked at Emily's mother. "I think Hindus would say that when someone imposes a viewpoint that is not tethered to the truth, the world becomes illusory and ensnaring."

"Yes, Desi. He did ensnare himself," Dr. Miller said before a pause. "The two of you look wonderful together. I'm finding it a bit spooky." She looked at Emily, then again at Desi, and walked out of the office.

Emily sat down in one of the leather chairs in her father's office, facing her father.

"I think I just wanted the two of you to know that we had been looking forward to spending some time together today, but there is an emergency that is calling us away to Philadelphia." Emily's father got up out of his seat, walked over to the chair where Emily was sitting, and kissed her on the forehead. He gave Desi a casual salute as he left the room.

"I think they have pre-packed bags and are ready to hit the road at a time like this," Emily said.

Desi looked at his watch. "We better hit the road pretty soon also."

Emily stood up. "Wait here for a few minutes. I just want to go give my mother a kiss."

Desi nodded and took a framed photograph on Emily's father's desk and turned it around to see who was in the picture.

Basking in Baltimore

Desi and Emily met Roger and Daisy at a restaurant on Baltimore Harbor. Desi had only been to downtown Baltimore once before, during the fall of 1971. Debi had spent her first semester of college going to school in Maryland and brought him to the same place for lunch. Desi didn't mention how Daisy selected the only restaurant in Baltimore where he had already eaten.

Since Desi enjoyed seafood with any meal, he could not resist the crabmeat eggs benedict. Roger went with the eggs and kielbasa. Emily had her eggs over easy with steak. Daisy just had one poached egg with rye toast. They all opted for Bloody Marys as their beverage with their brunch choices.

Emily took Daisy's copy of *Fear of Flying* out of one of the bags she carried into the restaurant and handed it to Daisy. "Thanks for letting me borrow the book, but I did find some of it somewhat depressing."

"Well, I hope it didn't take time away from enjoying things with Desi," Daisy said with a smile.

"Maybe I felt sorry for the main character because she didn't seem to be finding life as enjoyable as I am seeing it lately," Emily said as she took Desi's hand.

"Last night, we went to a double feature at a drive-in movie near Emily's parents' house," Desi offered.

"I've asked Desi to remind me of what the plots were to the movies as all I can remember are the women wearing skimpy tops or no tops at all in a variety of scenes, mostly while in convertibles." Emily paused. "Now that I am thinking about all of those boobs on that huge screen, I'm not so sure that those movies were produced to even try to develop a storyline."

"We may have also been distracted by the wine we were drinking," Desi added.

"I flew into Baltimore on a standard commercial jet. Desi got to the east coast and to Baltimore by less conventional means," Emily said. "We had dinner with my parents. I couldn't be sure if they were honestly interested in Desi or if my father was just trying to trap him with some of his questions. We got a couple of bottles of wine on the way to the drive-in. I think I must have had half of the bottle of the Pino Noir and another half a bottle or so of the cab."

"But that was over the course of about three hours," Desi interjected.

"Yeah, but when we got back to my parents' house, I crashed on the couch in front of the TV with my clothes on."

"Probably better that they found you in the morning with your clothes on rather than the alternative," Roger suggested.

"Roger stayed at my place one night and he didn't realize I had a roommate who had to come through my bedroom to get to the bathroom," Daisy said. "They both got a surprise that morning."

"Is it difficult to make introductions after something like that?" Desi asked.

"I tried to politely introduce them, but my roommate was so flustered that all she could say was something about her family once having a dog named Roger. "

"That may have been appropriate, given the circumstances," Desi said.

"Very funny," Roger said. "I bet you don't know what Desi's middle name is."

"I think it is Edward," Emily said. "I've seen a leather portfolio in Desi's room which has the initials 'DEM.' "

"It's Ezra," Desi said defensively. "Sure, it's a biblical name, but it's also a family name that goes back to the time before the American Revolution. I don't know why Roger finds the name Ezra to be humorous."

"Well, my family had a cat named Ezra, " Roger said.

"I'm still not getting it," Desi said.

"Maybe there is nothing to get other than whatever human name is given to your family dog or cat, you are going to think of that animal whenever you meet some person with that name," Emily suggested. "A woman is not going to bring some guy home to meet her parents if the guy's name is the same name as the family's dog, cat, or hamster."

"I had a cat when I lived with my aunt Arbie, but I named her Fluffy, " Daisy noted.

"And you never invited a guy upstairs to meet Fluffy?" Emily asked.

Desi and Roger laughed.

Daisy took the copy of *Fear of Flying* off the table and put it in one of her bags. "Emily used to be so sweet. I should never have lent her this book."

Then they all laughed.

Betting Against the odds

By the time they found their seats in the grandstands, Emily and Daisy had decided they wanted to sit together. Desi and Roger each looked at the racing information and, after several attempts to talk to one another around the two women, they decided to leave their seats and take a walk to the betting area.

"Do you remember that time when we were in Monte Carlo, and we walked into the casino wearing the clothes we brought along for hitchhiking?" Roger asked.

"You mean our good set of clothes, right?" Desi responded.

"Yeah, and there were dudes in the casino who were wearing tuxedos. Well, I sort of feel like that right now. I know we are wearing blazers, but the women we're with are decked out and looking great. And there were guys eying us as we were coming into the grandstands as if to say, 'Why are those women going to the Preakness with those two?' "

"I imagine they are thinking we either have a lot of money, or are great in the sack," Desi suggested. "But, since neither of us is dressed like we have a lot of money, they must be conceding our sexual superiority. And maybe they do."

"Okay, but let's not take a lot of time in the betting area because I don't want a bunch of guys coming around to hit on our ladies."

Desi looked at Roger. "Emily is good at brushing guys off, but if you are concerned, let's place our bets, get Emily and Daisy some drinks, and quickly get back to our seats." After walking over to one of the betting lines, Desi looked at Roger again. "You're not worried about going to Belmont Racetrack next month and meeting her brother, the admiralty lawyer, are you?"

Roger shrugged. "Maybe," he admitted.

"Hey, it sounds like her brother really cares about Daisy. Remember that story she told about how he flew her to Hong Kong to help her get clothes for job interviews. And what brother doesn't want their sister to be happy? You aren't competing with him."

"I guess it's difficult for me to see it that way."

"All you need to do, if you really care about Daisy, is to be the best man you can be for her," Desi said. "Remember the words of Janice Joplin."

Roger put his arm around Desi. "I'll never forget the outdoor concert that night in the Swiss village. That band with the female lead singer. I felt like I was watching Big Brother and the Holding Company."

"Yeah, that singer seemed to be able to channel the sound and soul of Janice," Desi said, giving Roger a couple of pats on his shoulder.

When they got back to their seats, Emily and Daisy were having a very animated discussion about something having to do with Emily's decision regarding law school. Emily and Daisy stood up to receive their drinks and to allow Desi and Roger to get seated.

While they were all standing, Daisy raised her cup. "To Roger and Desi, two of the most considerate gentlemen I have ever met." After the toast, they sat down so that Roger was on the aisle, with Daisy next to him and Desi in between Daisy and Emily.

"How did the betting go?" Emily asked Desi.

"Well, there were a few guys betting hundreds on the favorites, but with my twenty bucks, I felt I had to go with the longshots."

Emily wrapped her arm inside Desi's arm. She winked at Desi, saying, "Sometimes the longshots are the best shots to take."

While the Parents are Away

After the racing was over, Emily drove Desi back to her parents' house in Glen Burnie. Daisy and Roger, in Daisy's baby blue Pinto, followed Emily's mother's station wagon.

Emily shared with Desi what she learned about the living arrangement Roger and Daisy had going. Roger would stay at Daisy's apartment two or three nights during the week, and Daisy would spend a weekend night or two on the sailboat Roger captained for a charter company that did tours of the Chesapeake. Apparently, Roger and Daisy were so interested in spending every minute they could on the water that they had split the cost of a new waterbed for Daisy's apartment.

Emily asked Desi if he had ever had sex on a waterbed. Desi simply answered, "Yes," avoiding any details.

"Do you think I would like it?"

"It depends," Desi answered. "You know the story about the princess and the pea?"

"Sure."

"Well, if you are very sensitive to the motion of the water, you probably shouldn't try sleeping on one."

"So, did you have a good experience or a bad experience?"

"The only other thing I am going to say about having sex on a waterbed is that it is like everything else - it all depends on who you are with. Someday, I hope we can try one out together."

"I'm hoping that someday we can try doing something that you never did with anyone else."

"Well, the evening is still young."

"We can't have sex on the couch. I've already promised Daisy that the two of them can sleep there tonight. We will unfold it for them, of course."

"Yeah, that will probably be more comfortable than sleeping on the couch like we did last night."

"I don't think you have a reason to complain about last night after all those hours at the drive-in. And I liked opening my eyes this morning and seeing us all cuddled up on that couch."

After Emily gave Roger and Daisy a tour of her parents' house, Daisy asked if they could eat dinner on the back patio. Emily agreed and asked Desi if he could open some wine and take some cold appetizers out to the table on the patio.

Emily, Daisy, Roger, and Desi all had a toast with their wine glasses before Emily went into the house to heat up the chicken casserole her mother had prepared and stored in the refrigerator that morning.

Desi went into the house to see if she needed any help. Emily handed him some cheese and crackers to take out to the patio.

Daisy was sipping her glass of wine and admiring the large backyard when Desi returned to the patio. Roger took the cheese tray from Desi.

"Desi, is that the treehouse where Emily played as a girl?" Daisy asked.

"Yes. And I've expressed my willingness to play with her up there sometime," Desi replied.

Roger laughed as he spread some cheese on a cracker.

"It's worked out pretty well for all of us, I guess," Daisy said. "I can have wine with dinner and not have to drive to Virginia tonight."

"And after all the craziness yesterday, Emily and I get to fly back to Louisville tomorrow afternoon on the same plane."

Daisy walked over to the bottle of Sauvignon Blanc on the patio table and poured herself another glass of wine. "Did Roger tell you that I am traveling to Louisville on business Friday morning?"

"Well, maybe we can all get together in Louisville Friday night," Desi suggested.

Roger shook his head. "I'm not going to be able to make it. I have a list of charters that start early and go well into the evening. Instead of the normal two, it is three or four."

"Roger, would you mind if I met Desi and Emily for dinner Friday night?" Daisy asked. "I have a meeting with some election lawyers around noon or so, and then I can meet up with Desi and Emily. That's if you and Emily are available Friday night in the Louisville area."

"I'll make myself available Friday," Emily said as she walked out onto the patio with a vegetable tray. "What law firm are you going to in Louisville?"

"It's a small firm, but the partner I am meeting with is a well-known election lawyer."

"What's his name?" Emily asked as she offered Daisy the vegetables that were arranged on the tray around a cup of sour cream dip.

"Raymond Henderson," Daisy answered.

"I've met him," Desi volunteered.

"Really?" Emily said with a look of amazement.

"I think he's going to share a story about FDR with me some time," Desi added.

"How do you know him?" Emily persisted.

"He asked me to do him a favor recently," Desi recounted. "But I don't know if I am free to tell you anymore."

Emily gave a frown as she put down the tray on the patio table. "You better tell me," she said as she brought her fist back and punched Desi in the arm.

Desi just smiled. "It's going to take more than that to get it out of me."

All four of them began to laugh.

Chapter X

THE BEST LAID PLANS

On the Sunday evening flight to Louisville on May 16, 1976, Desi and Emily had the opportunity to ask each other a few questions. Emily wanted to know if Desi would mind her moving in with him if she was offered a position with the *Courier Journal.* Desi said he would be very pleased if she would move in. After expressing his willingness to have Emily live with him, they each thought about the ramifications of Emily's suggestion for a few minutes. Emily found herself thinking about how bold she had been to ask the question and what her parents would think if she actually started living with Desi. The biggest question in Desi's mind was whether living with Emily would nourish a blossoming relationship or sink it.

What Desi found himself asking Emily was: "If you get a job offer from the *Courier Journal,* would that mean putting off law school, or would you try to work for the paper and go to law school at night?" To Desi, that second possibility seemed to be a scenario that would wreck things pretty fast.

Emily answered by saying, "If I was a journalist by day and a law student by night, I would never get a chance to see you."

Given the newness of their relationship, Desi had hoped for such an answer, but he still had to test her response. "We would share a bed each night," Desi replied.

Emily looked at him and smiled. "That might be nice, but it sounds like I would never get any sleep. I need my sleep. Besides, I don't know how much I actually want to be a lawyer. I know I want to try to become a real journalist." She clasped one hand around one of Desi's hands. "You get to write about and take pictures of all sorts of people, from tank soldiers to glass lamp shade designers, so you get the opportunity to meet all different types of people, not just lawyers every day. By the way, how did you happen to meet Attorney Ray Henderson?"

Desi looked around to check whether anyone seemed to be listening to their conversation. "I guess I can tell you. I was walking around Elizabethtown and he was inside a 'Carter for President' campaign headquarters. Do you know him?"

"I think I met him once, but very briefly. My former boyfriend, the one who is in jail now, had me drive him to Attorney Henderson's office in Louisville to get the name of an attorney in West Virginia who could defend him. I waited in the outer office when they went into a conference room."

"Since your old boyfriend is in jail, I guess Attorney Henderson didn't find the right attorney for him."

"At first, I think Attorney Henderson thought it was going to be easy to get Michael off. It wasn't like Michael had ever actually been in the Army. He never took an oath or did anything like his older brother, who went AWOL."

"What's the story on his older brother?"

"Michael's older brother, Oscar, got drafted in 1970 and did all his Army training. Oscar thought he was going to be assigned to a supply unit in Europe but somehow got stuck in an infantry unit in Vietnam. When Oscar figured out a way to return to the States on leave, he then decided he was never going back to Vietnam. The FBI didn't know about Michael when they came looking for his brother at their parents' house. Michael's parents thought Michael's older brother did go back to Vietnam, so when the FBI came to the door, his parents blurted out something about Michael because they knew he never responded to letters about reporting to some induction site," Emily explained.

"Did the FBI tell the parents that they were really there for the older brother?"

"Yeah, so when his parents told Michael about the visit from the FBI, Michael was pissed off at his parents for bringing up his name. Then, his parents got defensive and upset with Michael for not telling them that the older brother was in Canada, not Vietnam. His poor mother was really confused. She was feeling guilty, as well as relieved that she didn't have to worry every day about her oldest son getting killed in Vietnam. I felt like I had a good idea of what Michael's family was going through."

"And this was all happening in 1972 as the war was wrapping up?" Desi asked.

"Yeah, I went to a friend's high school graduation party and met Michael, who knew my friend's older sister. He told me that he wasn't seriously dating that girl and asked me out. We went out on a few dates before my family got the news about my brother. Michael let me cry on his shoulder for a week or two before he asked me if I wanted to go to an event sponsored by the Vietnam Veterans Against the War," Emily said, pausing to wipe tears from her eyes.

Desi put his arm up and around the back of Emily's seat, bringing his hand down on her shoulder. "You can stop if this is getting too upsetting for you."

"No. I want you to know about Michael so you will know why I really needed him at a point in my life, but, more importantly, why you can trust me when I tell you that I feel my relationship with Michael is over now that I have met you. Our conversations about law school made me realize why I let my parents talk me into applying to law schools this year. I thought I could go to law school and learn something that might help Michael get out. But I'm realizing how crazy it was to think I was going to be some sort of hero law student, trying to be Michael's Joan of Arc and be able to save him."

"Maybe your willingness to sacrifice yourself for someone else is a trait that I find attractive. When Linda first told me that you had a boyfriend who was in jail, and he might be a sort of political prisoner, that sounded rather dramatic. Now that you have told me the story, it seems very dramatic."

"Still a bit delusional on my part," Emily conceded. "But the really dramatic part is what happened after we went to a couple of weekend rallies together and my parents found out that my boyfriend was being pursued by the FBI because he failed to report to be drafted. There was an anti-war rally in West Virginia one weekend, right as I was starting college. My parents managed to end my summer of protest by threatening not to take me and my stuff to the University of Kentucky, where I desperately wanted to go." Emily paused to take a cup of tomato juice from the flight attendant before continuing. "So, Michael went alone to the rally and got arrested, along with some other protesters, for blocking access to a building. He was thrown in a jail cell with a couple of white guys and three or four black guys. While in the cell, Michael read the *Autobiography of Malcolm X,* which he brought along to the protest in his backpack. They held his backpack in a locker, but they let him take out the book. Have you read that book?"

"I have," Desi said. "It was in a stack of suggested reading material Kings Point gave the cadets going out to sea in early 1971. Did his reading the book piss someone off?"

"Sure, and what he said while he was in jail didn't help him much either. Only he didn't tell his lawyer what he said to the guards and how the interrogation seemed to focus on something one of his white cellmates claimed was discussed by Michael and the black guys in the cell."

"So, an easy case of springing Michael became something that took a sharp turn."

"Yes, a very bad turn," Emily said. "His parents posted bail and he got out after a couple of days, but the proceedings went on for years. They charged him with a couple of felonies, including inciting to riot, but he ended up having a jury finding him guilty of only a misdemeanor charge. He will be out in a couple more months, but he wants to somehow get the whole thing in the West Virginia State Court System expunged."

"So you thought that law school might help you find a way to clear him?"

"But then there is the question of what the Feds are going to do about his not reporting for military service."

"Well, you might want to speak to Attorney Henderson about what he thinks Jimmy Carter will do regarding people who avoided the draft," Desi suggested.

"Do you think you might be able to set up a meeting for me to ask him that?"

"He did give me his business card," Desi said.

Emily smiled at Desi for a few moments before her expression turned serious. "I gave you the story about my relationship with Michael. I think it's time you gave me the scoop about where things stand with you and someone who Linda refers to as 'that beautiful sister of a famous model.' I mean, I don't want to move in with you and find out that she is still expecting to spend some weekends with you."

"That would be pretty awkward, wouldn't it?" Desi teased.

Emily glared at him. "You know that I am the one with a car parked at the airport in Louisville, and you are now at risk of having to walk to your apartment in Radcliff."

"I don't know if my philosophy professor at NYU who teaches Logic would find that to be a persuasive argument or a coercive threat, but you make a good point. I do have to decide whether I need to end it with Debi if I am going to live with you."

"Well, which is it?"

"I think these issues will resolve themselves if you move in, and I tell her that I'm not able to meet her in Washington in June because I'm living with you."

"That will end it with her?"

"Maybe she'll find someone else to spend that weekend with. I don't think it will be difficult for her to do that," Desi said.

"Look, she has not told me she loves me in a couple of years. I'm only her backup plan. If I finish my time in the Army without meeting someone who will really love me and wants to have my children, then I'll probably end up living with Debi. But I don't want to be anyone's backup plan."

"But she witnessed what you consider your 'religious experience.' Doesn't that count for something?"

"At first, I thought that it did. To me, it seemed like it was not only a sign from God that I was not alone, but also that she was meant to be with me. But she did not see the experience the way I did. So, either her ability to discern God's presence was lacking, or our relationship was not special enough for her to commit herself to it. Looking back at it, the experience seemed to reveal to me that she lacked the ability to discern things in general, as she was not able to focus on us and make the necessary effort on our relationship. I think even the best relationships require conscious effort."

"Desi, do you feel able to put in some real effort to nurture our relationship?" Emily asked. "I think you're a guy who is clever enough to know how to avoid sabotaging a special relationship. Maybe it was your experience with Debi that has made you aware of what things poison the well of happiness you can feel with another person. Do you feel like you want a special relationship with me?"

Desi unlocked his seat belt and turned his body to look Emily straight in her eyes as he moved his face closer to hers. "When you say a 'special relationship,' you are referring to an intimate relationship, right?"

"Are you willing to put in the hard work to keep our 'special relationship' moving along?" Emily said with a smile.

"That's the only way to do it," Desi answered.

The Extra Vehicles in Radcliff

It was getting dark when Emily pulled her Mustang into the driveway at Desi's place, but there was still enough light to see a pickup truck and a VW van parked at the house.

"Oh shit," Desi said. "I left my VW at Godman Field when I flew out on Friday morning."

"That's nothing," Emily responded. "Don't you see the pickup truck from Mama Boone's house is here?"

"Does that mean Linda took your pickup truck and drove it up here? Why does she want to meet you here in Radcliff?"

"I'd bet it isn't me who she drove up to see in Radcliff."

"Oh really, I didn't know the two of them were in touch with each other."

"I think there may be quite a bit of touching going on."

"Maybe you should just drive me over to the airfield so I can get my car."

"I think I need to go into your house to take a pee before I do any more driving around."

"The door may be locked; I'll go with you to open it."

When they entered the side door to the house, they were surprised by how quiet it was inside. No voices, no music, and no TV.

"It's like there's no one here," Emily said as she walked past the open doors of the two bedrooms and went on to the end of the hallway and into the bathroom.

Desi went into his bedroom and threw his suit bag onto the bed. He walked down the hallway to inspect what had been Charlie's bedroom when Charlie and Stacey lived with him. The bed was all made and covered with what looked like a Mexican bedspread. The décor seemed to be very different from the decorations Charlie used in what had been Charlie's bedroom. Someone that weekend had taken down the Bob Seger poster Charlie left on one of the bedroom walls. That poster had served as a last remembrance of his former housemate and their Louisville concert scene exploits.

Among their exploits was Desi having used his press pass to get a chance to talk to Bob Seger. After they spoke for a few minutes, Seger graciously extended the VIP treatment to Desi and Charlie as "protectors of the gold at Fort Knox." They got to eat backstage with the warmup band and several groupies before the concert started. However, the best part of the evening for Desi was when Seger asked Desi to stand on the side of the stage as the Silver Bullet Band performed. Seger told Desi that he enjoyed having part of the audience up on the stage with him.

There was a new poster on the bedroom wall. It was a large picture of his new housemate Sam playing a Stratocaster somewhere with palm trees in the background. Desi was sure there was a story behind that poster also.

Emily joined him in the bedroom and started counting the unpacked boxes in the room. "Well, if Linda drove up to help him, there are still about a dozen boxes and a couple of suitcases they seemed to have ignored. Knowing Linda, she probably got him distracted, and they went off and are screwing around instead of putting the stuff away."

"As I came out of my room to check out Charlie's old bedroom, I think I noticed that someone seems to be sleeping on the couch in the living room. It's my turn to hit the bathroom. Why don't you go into the living room and see if Linda is sleeping on the couch?"

"Alright, but I'm not volunteering to help them put stuff away," Emily said as she walked down the hallway and into the kitchen. There are a couple more boxes here in the kitchen."

Emily noticed some stirring on the couch. She walked through the kitchen and stood in the living room over the couch, where she was expecting Linda's face to emerge from under the blanket. Instead of Linda's face, she found herself staring back at the face of a middle-aged Asian woman. The woman smiled at Emily and, almost in a whisper, said, "Hello."

Emily retreated to the kitchen and sat down at the kitchen table. The woman got up from the couch and walked into the kitchen. She ran her hands through her long dark hair a couple of times and then sat down at the table. "You must be Emily," she said.

Emily nodded her head. After a brief pause, Emily then asked, "And who are you?"

Desi appeared behind Emily and supplied the answer. "I think you are Sam's mother. And you drove Sam's VW bus all the way from California with Sam's stuff."

"How long did it take you?" Emily asked.

"Well, I visited a few friends along the way, so I have been on the road for almost a week."

Emily extended her hand across the table. "And no problems driving alone all that way?"

"Don't tell Sam, but I did give a couple of people a lift, so I wasn't driving alone the whole time. And like I said, I got to spend time with a few people I hadn't seen for a while."

"I've never picked up a hitchhiker," Emily said. "I don't know if I could tell who would be a lunatic and who would be so nice that you would want them as your neighbor."

Sam's mother said, "I figure that most of them are like my neighbor. Actually, I started the trip with a neighbor who doesn't drive that much but who wanted to visit a relative in Phoenix. It turned out that I had a nice place to spend the night in Phoenix."

"I think I know where your son is," Desi said. "Let me go tell him that I am thinking about getting some food from an Italian place."

"You don't have to do that. I told him I am going to make some Korean food for all of us. I found a good Asian grocery store just up the street. I was just taking a little nap while we waited for you guys to arrive."

Desi stood up. "Well, then I'll just let him know we're here."

Emily stood up also. "I'll go with you so I can catch up with Linda."

"I'll get started on dinner," Sam's mother said.

When Desi and Emily got outside, Emily grabbed Desi's arm. "I don't know if I like Korean food. Did you eat any when you were in the Far East?"

"It can be hot, but I don't think she is going to try to burn out our tongues."

"Ok, I'll let you taste it first, and you can judge whether I should try some," Emily said as she held Desi's arm more tightly in the dark. "Where do you think Linda and Sam went off to?"

Desi stopped as he walked alongside the VW bus. Desi tapped on the driver's side window.

"You think they are in there?" Emily asked.

"Yeah. I used to have a van like this. He probably has a bed in it like the one I put in mine."

"You were one of those guys with a bed in the back of their hippie mobile? My father would never let me date any guy with one of those. A guy could be in the church choir, but if he pulled up at my parent's house driving one of those beds on wheels, my parents wouldn't let me out the door."

"It probably is not the vehicle to show up with on a first date," Desi conceded. "Debi and I had known each other for quite some time, and her mother knew she was on the pill when I took her back to college in my hippie mobile. "

"There you go talking about Debi again," Emily said as she let go of Desi and started walking to her car. "I thought you wanted me to take you to get your Super Beetle, with the bed-less small rear seat."

"Actually, if you pull down on the back of the rear seat, there is enough room to stretch out a bit."

"I am not sure that I want to hear any more," Emily said as she got into her car. Desi followed and got into the passenger side of her Mustang. As they were backing out of the driveway, Linda emerged from the van. She was only wearing a men's long sleeve blue dress shirt. Without anything on her feet, she carefully walked on the gravel driveway towards Emily's side of the car.

"Where are you guys going?" Linda asked Emily.

"Desi left his car on Fort Knox, and we have to go over and get it," Emily said. "We should be back in about twenty minutes."

"Ok," Linda said as she kissed Emily on the cheek. She blew a kiss to Desi. "Thank you, Desi, for finding a great housemate."

Emily was only about a hundred yards down the street when she pulled over and stopped her car. "You drive," she said as she got out of the Mustang.

Desi got out and met Emily in the glare of the headlights as they were both rounding the front of the car. "Are you alright?" Desi asked with his arms preparing for an embrace.

Emily sped past his arms and got into the car on the passenger side. When they were both back in the car, with Desi taking the wheel, Emily let out a chain of expletives, ending with "Linda is back to being a happy slut."

"I think that might be a bit harsh," Desi responded. "You are upset about something, but I'm not sure what."

"Are you going to keep her from moving in with Sam? I'm sure that is what she is going to want to do if my father rents out my grandmother's house in June."

"Well, I guess our two-bedroom apartment is big enough; we've had that sort of living arrangement before."

"Debi never lived with you here, right?"

"No, she never did, but…"

"But, what?"

"Can't we wait to see if Linda even brings up the possibility of living with us in Radcliff?"

"I don't think I want to live there if she is going to live there," Emily said.

"At this point, I have no idea if Sam would even want to have her living with us."

"Oh, I know how crazy men get around Linda. He'll be pleading with you to let her move in."

Desi started to reduce speed as they approached the guardhouse at the Radcliff gate.

"Please let me concentrate on picking up my car," Desi said as he reached into his pocket and took out his money clip, which contained his ID. "We can discuss this more after dinner if you think Linda says something that supports your concern."

They reached the guardhouse and one of the MPs stepped out and checked Desi's identification. "Oh, you're the guy I see sometimes at the mess hall who writes for the *Turret*." He looked at the front bumper of the car. "I don't see a bumper sticker. Did you recently get a new car?"

"No, it's her car," Desi explained as he pointed to Emily. "I left my car at Godman Field to fly out Friday on an assignment. I'm just going to pick it up."

"So, she is your guest on post this evening?" the MP inquired.

"No, we are just picking up the car and going back to Radcliff," Desi responded.

"I think I need to see her driver's license and the registration for the car. I'm probably going to have to take her ID into the guardhouse and log it."

Emily handed her documents to Desi, who, in turn, handed them to the MP.

"I'm sorry for all the hassle, but I'll be right back in a few minutes," the MP said.

Desi smiled at him, saying, "No problem, I understand."

Desi and Emily watched as the MP went back into the guardhouse and started talking to the other MP stationed there. After three or four minutes, the first MP came back out and handed Desi the car registration. "I am going to hang on to her driver's license, and I also need your license to hold onto until you drive back out this way. The other MP wanted me to have you open your trunk, but I told him that I knew you."

"I appreciate that," Desi said. "See you again in a few minutes." Desi pulled forward onto the Army base and headed for Godman Field.

"What is so damn special about Godman Field that they are making it seem like they have special weapons stored there?" Emily asked.

"Well, they do have helicopters, and there might be one armed in the event there is an attack on the Gold Vault."

"Is that to impress foreign countries that might need to store gold there?"

"Maybe."

"I think the Brits stored some gold here during World War II," Emily said. "Actually, I heard that the crown jewels of several countries were kept here."

"There are also lots of rumors about all the things that might be stored in the Gold Vault, including a year's supply of morphine for a million people."

"Are you planning to unlock the secrets of the Gold Vault during your journalistic efforts here?"

"No, but it would be nice to be able to take away a souvenir," Desi mused.

"Even Auric Goldfinger didn't seem to be able to do that."

"He just wanted to spoil things for everyone else," Desi observed.

"So, did Mr. Goldfinger visit Godman Field?"

"In the movie, Goldfinger commandeers a presidential jet right before James Bond gets on board," Desi recounted.

"That's a pretty good souvenir."

"Well, I am not looking to snatch any aircraft tonight. I just want to get my car back to Radcliff."

"What if someone asks to see your identification. You left your driver's license with that MP."

"I still have my press pass, and I know some people who work at Godman."

"All women who have been to your apartment, I assume."

"A few air traffic controllers and helicopter mechanics, who have attended parties."

"But mostly women, right?"

"Probably."

"You don't have to introduce me to them if we run into them tonight. Besides, I don't know how you would introduce me."

"I think I would just say that you were my roommate."

"But I don't know if I am definitely moving in with you."

"Well, I could qualify that and say that you are my roommate for the night."

"That really sounds terrible."

"How about saying that you are going to be my roommate for the next month or so?"

"Not much better, but how many of the women at Godman Field can claim to have commanded your attention for a full month?"

"Not one. But then again, it could be said that I didn't command their attention for a month."

"It's all semantics," Emily said as they arrived at Godman Field.

There were two women in Army fatigues taking a smoke break near the hangar. Because the area around the hangar where the women were standing was in the dark, Desi could not recognize the women. Desi's Super Beetle was under a light. One of the women walked over as Desi was starting his car.

"Hey, Alice," Desi said after he recognized one of the air traffic controllers and rolled down his window.

"We were wondering earlier why your car was parked here," Alice said. "When we were grabbing a smoke, we noticed your car again. Then I saw someone getting into it. I was concerned about whether somebody was ripping off your wheels."

"Thanks for walking over to check on things."

"Who brought you over here?"

"Let me introduce you to Emily, she is a good Samaritan who gave me a lift from the airport in Louisville. The Army flew me to Virginia but did not arrange transportation all the way back to Fort Knox," Desi said as he pointed to Emily sitting in her Mustang with the engine and lights off.

"The Army must have known that you would get some woman to come to your assistance," Alice said as she gave a wave of her hand to Emily.

Emily gave a wave back and started up her car.

"Did you get a new roommate yet?" Alice asked.

Desi thought for a moment before he replied. "Yeah, you'll have to stop by some night and meet Sam. He just moved in this weekend. Sam works at the JAG Office as a paralegal."

"Sounds like you didn't have to cast a big net to find a replacement for Charlie, although I can't believe anyone could truly replace Charlie."

"It's a tough act to follow," Desi said.

"I'll give you a call, and we'll come over to meet the new guy," Alice said as she turned and walked back towards the hangar and the tower.

Wanting More History at Dinner

When Desi and Emily returned to the house in Radcliff, Emily wanted to know all about Alice.

Sam's mother was putting the finishing touches on dinner when they arrived. Emily didn't even want to enjoy a glass of wine before dragging Desi into his bedroom to find out if Alice had lived in the house or spent a few nights there. Desi gave Emily a couple of kisses on her neck to distract her, but she insisted on an answer.

"Before I give any more thought to living in this house, I want to know about who has lived here during the past year and what the sleeping arrangements were."

Desi explained that Charlie and Alice had an on again, off again relationship before Charlie started dating Stacey.

"I think it would be terrible if your friend Charlie was cheating on Stacey, who is so nice," Emily said.

Desi looked at Emily, "Do I need to tell you that, if you move in with me, I would not be having sex with anyone else?"

"You know what, I guess I need to hear you say that."

"Okay, if you care enough about me to move in with me, I will do everything in my power to make sure that you don't regret your decision, even if it means distancing myself from women who might want to go for a ride on my joystick."

"I would say that was the sweetest thing a guy has ever said to me, but it only conjured up images that I find disturbing."

"Sorry, I wasn't trying to trigger your imagination in that direction."

"Maybe you are just showing off how imaginative you are with different names for your penis. Frankly, I'm fine with you just calling it a penis or cock."

"I'll try to keep that in mind and not get too clever."

"It seems to undermine your sincerity," Emily said as she pulled away from him and opened the bedroom door. She stepped out into the hallway, awaiting Desi's lead back to the kitchen.

Sam came in the side door.

Desi met him in the hallway. "It's great of your mom to fix dinner for us," Desi said. Emily nodded in agreement.

"She told me she was napping when you arrived earlier, and she felt a bit silly meeting you when she had just gotten up from the couch," Sam disclosed.

"We have had people on that couch sleeping through a party, with the music blasting. Your mom taking a nap doesn't seem strange at all."

"I also took the liberty of telling her that she could spend the night on the couch so she will be well-rested for her flight back to Cali tomorrow."

"Are you going to sleep in your bed tonight?" Desi asked.

"Maybe," Sam replied. "Linda keeps saying how much she enjoys the bed in the van."

"Do you think your mom would like a glass of wine or something else to drink with the dinner she's prepared?"

Sam's mother turned around and said to Desi and Emily, "You guys can call me Arlene, and I would like some Kentucky bourbon now that I have made it to Kentucky."

"I'll pour some bourbon for all of us, and we can have a toast," Desi said.

"Sounds good to me," Sam said. "Let me go get Linda."

Desi poured a generous amount of bourbon into five glasses.

"That is a lot of bourbon, isn't it?" Emily asked.

"I didn't think that anyone was going to be driving tonight," Desi responded.

"If I drink all that bourbon," Emily said, as she picked up one of the glasses on the kitchen table, "I know I won't be able to drive."

"Then we will just celebrate. I think there is a lot to celebrate."

"Okay," was all Emily found herself saying.

Linda came bounding into the house wearing just the blue men's dress shirt that she had on earlier.

Emily looked at her intently. "Is that my father's blue dress shirt?"

"I found it in one of the closets at the house this morning. It's very comfortable," Linda pleaded.

"Take it off right now," Emily said.

"Alright," Linda said as she started to unbutton the three buttons that were holding the shirt together. "But I don't have anything on underneath it."

Emily grabbed her just as Linda was undoing the last button and dragged Linda off to Desi's room to find a pair of gym shorts and a T-shirt for Linda to wear to dinner. "I can't believe you took the pickup truck and my dad's shirt. You act as if you are entitled to everything you can get your hands on."

"Don't you always get whatever you want?" Linda responded.

"The pickup truck was my grandmother's; now it belongs to my father, and that blue dress shirt is probably his most expensive shirt. The problem is that you don't see any need to ask before you just take stuff."

"Well, if I don't ask, then nobody can tell me 'No.' "

"So, you think that is less disrespectful?"

"Well, I found some papers in the same closet that the shirt came from that make it difficult for me to respect your father anymore," Linda said. "Your father was soliciting for Pastor Rick's mega church, and he helped take money from a lot of people who are never going to be repaid."

"Well, perhaps my father sinned by getting too close to Pastor Rick and the Pastor's destructive money grabs, but why are you trying to ride on some high horse when you got even closer to 'Pastor Disaster' and broke up his marriage and his family. Are you ever going to his ex-wife and kids and apologizing for what you grabbed from their lives?"

Linda started crying. "I probably will never apologize to them. I don't even want to apologize to you for looking at those documents."

"You don't? Why not?"

"Because what I saw explains why your father wants to rent out your grandmother's house for the summer and why he is fighting with his cousins and nieces for every dollar he can get for that piece of land."

"And why is that?"

"He signed some personal guarantees to people who gave money for the construction of the church. I don't know if your father is going to have that much money, but your father is going to be on the hook."

Emily sat down on Desi's bed and buried her face in her hands. She let out a whimpering sound as she cried. "My father will somehow make good on his guarantees, but my mother is going to be furious with him. She warned him about what a pig Pastor Rick was."

Linda sat down beside Emily and put her arm around Emily. They cried together for a moment.

Emily stood up. "Did I ever tell you about how my parents hosted a fundraiser a couple of years ago for Pastor Rick? That piece of crap got to our house an hour late and drunk as a skunk. When my mother answered the door and made the mistake of asking him if he felt alright, he smiled, grabbed my mom by the boobs, and squeezed them like he was honking a couple of horns. Then, he said something like, 'never felt better,' and laughed before going in to collect the checks."

"Well, your mom does have a great set for a woman her age."

Emily just shook her head. "She was wearing one of my new turtlenecks that night and made me throw it out." Emily saw a tissue box on Desi's nightstand. She pulled out a couple of tissues for herself and a couple to hand to Linda.

Linda dried her eyes with the tissue and put on the gym shorts and T-shirt that Emily found in Desi's dresser.

"Should we ask Desi about me wearing his clothes?" Linda asked.

"I think that is the same outfit he gave you the last time you needed something to wear," Emily observed.

"I hope that things work out between the two of you. I think he deserves someone like you, and you deserve someone like him. You deserve each other."

"Not sure how you mean that, but the next time I get upset with him I'll remember that line."

"Sorry, I guess that can cut both ways," Linda said.

"We better go before the food Sam's mother made gets cold," Emily said.

When Emily and Linda got to the table, Desi and Sam were passing around a plate with strips of beef and vegetables for putting on the pasta bowls filled with rice.

"May I say grace?" Sam's mother asked. "I've belonged to a Christian church outside of LA for many years now, and whenever our members gather for a meal, we always reflect upon how fortunate we are, not only having the physical sustenance of the food, but the sustenance we gain from those around us."

"Well, we are especially fortunate tonight to have new members of our sanctuary," Desi observed.

"Very nice of you, Desi," Arlene said. "Let me just add my thanks for the opportunity to meet the three of you and my observation that the Lord blesses us in many ways, sometimes in obvious ways, and other times in ways that we only come to understand later. God, please give us the physical and spiritual strength, the wisdom, and the material resources to help us keep moving towards your light, as well as the love to encourage others to do the same. In that spirit, we say, Amen."

Desi, Emily, Linda, and Sam all joined with a collective "Amen."

Sam's mother looked at Linda. "I understand from Linda that Emily is graduating from college in a couple weeks and that Linda will be earning her degree by the end of the summer. And Desi, I understand you have a journalism degree from NYU."

"I have a Bachelor of Arts degree from NYU," Desi clarified. "I majored in journalism."

"And he minored in philosophy," Emily added.

"Well, I am hoping that you inspire Sam to get working on his B.A. With all the touring and music stuff, it took him quite a while to get his associate degree."

Sam frowned at his mom. "And you got your Bachelor of Arts degree last week, the day before you started driving here."

Desi held up his almost empty glass of bourbon, saying, "Congratulations, Arlene!"

Emily and Linda joined in holding up their glasses.

"Well, every mother wishes for better things for their child," Sam's mother said.

"I may never be a financially successful musician, but I am hoping to learn enough about the law, especially contract law, that I can keep playing music and be part of the music business," Sam said.

Desi smiled at Sam. "You may know that Gottfried Leibnitz, the famous German philosopher and mathematician, said that 'Music is a hidden arithmetic exercise of the soul, which does not know that it is counting.' "

Sam smiled back at Desi. "I have not heard that before, but it makes a lot of sense to me."

"I wasn't meaning to say anything that sounded like I wasn't very proud of Sam," his mom said defensively. "It's just that with all the traveling and the grungy places where he had to work well into the night, I felt that the music scene was terrible for Sam, particularly with his asthma. I was afraid that he wouldn't be able to breathe in some of those smoke-filled nightclubs."

Linda put her hand on Sam's shoulder. "Desi, Sam's mother brought his Stratocaster, and he played a few things for me this afternoon. He's amazing!"

Emily looked at Sam's mother. "We are sure you are very proud of your son. But I think every parent remembers an embarrassing moment for their kids. Do you have any good ones for us?"

"The only one I know is the one Sam's late father used to tell at family events."

"I think you should spare Linda, Emily, and Desi, especially since you weren't actually a witness," Sam protested.

"A witness to what," Linda asked.

"It had to do with the high board at a public pool in California," Sam acknowledged.

"Right, so Sam's father and his brother, your uncle Al, were there with Sam at this public pool that had three diving boards of different heights off the water," Sam's mother said.

Desi looked at Sam and his mother a bit skeptically. He asked, "Is this going to be the old joke about the high board?"

"No," Sam's mother submitted. "This really happened, right Sam?"

"It depends on how you tell it," Sam contended.

"Okay, the way I heard the story, multiple times from your father and your Uncle Al, is that Sam was playing with some kids, and they were using the average two-foot diving board. Then, a couple of the girls about Sam's age challenged the boys to go off the four-foot diving board. The kids were all around eleven or twelve. The boys go off the four-foot board first, and then the girls follow along. Then, one of the girls challenges the boys to go off the high board, which is ten or twelve-feet high. They aren't so keen to try that, but she tells them that if she is brave enough to do it, then they should all try. She climbs up the ladder to the top and does some fancy dive right into the pool. The boys all line up to go up the high board ladder and, one by one, they say to one another something like 'You go first.' Sam ends up at the front of the line, and all the girls are encouraging him on. He goes up to the top and just stands at the end of the diving board. The lifeguard blows his whistle finally and tells Sam he has to dive or climb back down. One of the girls yells something like 'Indians aren't supposed to be afraid of heights.' Sam's Uncle motions for Sam to leap off, and he does. Somehow, he manages to avoid hitting the bottom of the pool. But Sam gets to the shallow end and realizes that his bathing suit was pulled off by the impact of hitting the water. One of the girls asks Sam if he wants her help to get the bathing suit back from the other end of the pool. Sam was very shy back then and just kept shaking his head 'no,' he didn't want her to bring him the bathing suit."

"So, he had to find his own bathing suit?" Linda asked.

"He yelled to his Uncle Al. And his uncle, despite his rolling in laughter, did dive in and got it from the deep end of the pool for Sam."

"That sounds believable," Emily said. "What was your high board joke, Desi?"

"It's actually a very old joke, but if you insist that I tell it..."

Yes!" Sam's mother and Linda both exclaimed.

"Alright," Desi said, feigning his reluctance to tell the story, which was his favorite pool joke. "There was this junior high school kid in town, named Johnny, who was at the community pool almost every day in July. Then, none of the other junior high school kids saw him for a week or two. Some of the kids ran into him coming out of the movie theater on a Saturday night. They all wanted to know why they weren't seeing him at the pool anymore. Johnny explained that he lost his pool privileges for peeing in the pool. The kids all laughed and admitted they had all peed in the pool on occasion. Johnny took a cigarette out of his pocket, lit it up, and after taking a long drag, blew smoke in their faces. 'Yeah, maybe you have, but not off the high board.' "

Sam and his mother laughed. Emily chuckled.

Linda just shook her head. "That joke would be much funnier if we had been smoking a joint while Desi was telling it."

Sam took out a chewing tobacco tin from his pocket and handed it to Linda. "Maybe this will help you?"

Linda protested, "I don't do chewing tobacco. I like an evening joint or a couple of drinks of bourbon but chewing tobacco won't do it for me."

"Look inside the tin," Sam said. "I had that stashed under the bed in the van. My Uncle Al was smoking some really good stuff and gave me a tin of it before I went into the Army."

Sam's mother explained, "Sam's uncle was going through cancer treatments, and he was smoking it for medicinal purposes."

Sam looked at his mother. "Oh, I forgot to ask you, how is Uncle Al doing?"

His mother put her head down on the table. She did not look at Sam. "The cancer spread through most of his body, and he died while you were in basic training. I thought I should tell you in person, but now I'm feeling like I should have called you on the way here and told you over the phone. I think his wife is suing the company in Arizona, but they may already be out of business."

"I think I need a couple of minutes alone," Sam said as he got up from the table. He went out the side door of the house.

Linda started to go after Sam, but Emily grabbed her by the arm.

Sam's mother picked her head up from the table. "There was a uranium mining company in Arizona that managed to destroy many Navajo lives. We never lived there, but what I learned from Sam's father and news reports is, the Navajo people didn't just suffer in the 19th century but were made to suffer through the 20th century right up to today. The Navajo in the early 20th century lived in their traditional matriarchal society. The women passed the wealth on to their daughters. But in the 1930s, the government claimed the Navajo were overgrazing their animals. Federal agents rounded up cows, horses, sheep, and goats on the reservation, and with the livestock gone, the Navajo were no longer self-sufficient. Navajo men had to leave Arizona to find work. Then, in the early 1950s, uranium mining in Arizona went into full swing, so the Navajo had work close by. The miners had minimal protective equipment. They were not aware of the dangers from the uranium ore that caked onto their clothes and skin. The government very likely knew that the uranium miners were going to have a high risk of lung disease and cancer. Sam's uncle, like many of the other Navajo miners, died from what began as lung cancer."

"That is absolutely terrible," Linda said with a horrified expression on her face.

"They could not even live peaceably on their reservation," Emily added.

"I was not there to see how feeble Al became at the end, but I understand from his wife that Al suffered quite a lot." Sam's mother put her head back down on the table.

Linda reached over and put a hand on her shoulder. "Do you want me to go outside and look for Sam?"

Emily looked at Linda. "I don't think you should be going outside in just what you are wearing, with no bra or panties underneath."

Sam's mother picked her head up and smiled at Linda. "Thanks for offering, but I should really be the one going out to Sam. I don't think I picked the best time or place to break the news to him."

"I don't know that there would ever be a good way to share such news about a loved one. Maybe I should pour Sam another glass of bourbon that you can take to him," Desi offered."

"If one of you could roll some of the stuff in that tin, maybe we can smoke it in Sam's uncle's memory when I bring Sam back here."

Linda nodded her head. "I'll take care of that, no problem."

After Sam's mother left, Linda went into the living room and retrieved her pocketbook, which she had wedged between the couch and the curtains.

Linda came back to the table with a packet of rolling papers in her hand. "I was going to suggest that we all listen to Sam play his guitar this evening, but I don't think I can ask him to do that now."

"I'm sure I'll get the chance to hear him play another time," Desi replied.

Chapter XI

RACING TOWARD UNCERTAINTY

Desi is a Scratch at Belmont Racetrack

On the morning of the Belmont Stakes, Emily's alarm clock went off like a coastal foghorn in the dark. The clock was on the side of the bed that Desi found himself. His eyes still closed, he fumbled with the alarm buttons as it went off a second time. Emily climbed over him to silence the device and prevent a third blast.

Before she could get off of Desi, he embraced her, kissing her neck and behind her ear. Emily then turned her head to kiss him on the lips when she suddenly seemed to realize why she had set the alarm clock. "I have to get up and showered if I am going to get to my meeting by eight o'clock," she said as she rolled away from Desi and out of bed. Emily stood briefly at the foot of the bed in one of Desi's NYU T-shirts and blew him a kiss before she headed to the bathroom to shower.

Linda came out of the bathroom wearing just a towel. "What are you doing up so early on a Saturday morning?" Linda asked.

"I guess the same as you, trying to get somewhere," Emily answered abruptly.

"Well, aren't you tart this morning," Linda said with a chuckle.

"We probably look like a couple of tarts, if my parents saw us now."

"You haven't told them where we are staying, have you?"

"My mother doesn't even know we moved out of Grandma Boone's house. All my father apparently cares about is that we cleared out in time for the renters to move in by the first of the month."

"What about Fred, the handyman?"

"He knows that I have a part-time job with Attorney Henderson in Elizabethtown," Emily said. "But I only gave him the number for the campaign office in Elizabethtown, not the number here."

"I only gave Sam my number here," Linda said with a laugh. "I wrote it on pink paper."

"How convenient; that way, if he forgets the phone number for his apartment, all he has to do is check the pink paper," Emily said with a smirk.

"But I feel like it's my apartment too so that's why I used the pink paper. And now that I have the job at the Education Center on post, I'm thinking about giving some money to Sam and Desi towards the rent and stuff," Linda said proudly.

"You're working at the Education Center this morning?" Emily asked.

"Yeah, they want me to come in for a couple of hours this morning to meet with a counselor who works on Saturdays in case she ever needs help or a Saturday off. But I'll be back in plenty of time to get ready for Stacey's party."

"I have to go up towards Louisville for a campaign meeting with Attorney Henderson, some Carter Campaign staffers from Washington and someone from the National Headquarters in Plains," Emily revealed. "I can't imagine that it will take more than a couple of hours."

"I am looking forward to the party out at that farm this afternoon. I hear Stacey's mother is going to be there."

"And Desdemona's mother also," Emily said. She paused and looked at Linda. "I hear what you are saying about making some sort of financial contribution to where we are living right now. I know you want to be a responsible adult, but before you mention a specific amount to Sam or Desi, please speak to me first. I'm afraid that if you are too generous, it's going to make me look like a freeloader. I'm only working part-time at the *Courier Journal* as an intern, and I think if it wasn't for the influence of Attorney Henderson, I wouldn't be getting any money from that internship. Besides, I'm not getting much from working three or four days a week at the campaign headquarters in Elizabethtown."

Linda put her right hand out to touch Emily's forearm and, in doing so, had to quickly snatch her towel with her left hand to keep the towel from coming loose. "I won't say anything about money until I speak to you."

"Thanks," Emily said, folding her hand over Linda's. "I'll see you back here around eleven or so."

Emily went into the bathroom. Linda headed into the kitchen to get a glass of orange juice.

The telephone on the kitchen wall started ringing as Linda was pouring the juice. She answered it.

A female voice simply said, "I need to speak to Desi."

Linda hung the phone cord over a chair and walked into Desi's bedroom through the half-open door. "There's a woman on the phone who says she needs to speak to you," Linda reported.

Desi got out of the bed, wearing just a pair of briefs. As he stepped into the hallway, Linda was walking towards the door of the second bedroom. Desi called out to Linda, "Did she say what she wanted?"

Without turning around, Linda reached back with one hand, and with a laugh, lifted the towel to reveal her derriere. Desi, still a bit groggy, just shook his head.

He grabbed the telephone and tentatively said, "Good morning, can I help you?"

"You've got orders to go overseas. They're being sent from the Pentagon."

"Specialist Gaines?" Desi asked. "Are you in Kentucky?'

"I'll be at your house around 11, after we check out of the Gold Vault and borrow a car."

After he hung up the phone, Desi poured himself a glass of orange juice from the container Linda left out on the table. He sat at the kitchen table, thumbing through a copy of *Cosmopolitan*, as he waited for Emily to come out of the bathroom.

When Emily joined Desi in the kitchen, she asked him, "Are you actually reading an article in *Cosmo*?"

"I think Linda left the magazine open to this article so the guys here would read it," Desi responded.

"Is it about making sure to put the toilet seat down after you're finished?" Emily said with a laugh.

"It's a bit more complex than that. It talks about how people form long-term relationships based on compatible needs for sex, sensual activity, and intimacy."

Emily got a glass out of a cabinet over the sink and put the glass on the table for Desi to pour her some juice. "Are you learning anything?"

"I think the conclusion is that you have to be your 'authentic self' in a relationship in order for it to work out, but I'll leave it out for you to read this evening."

"Maybe I'll read it after Stacey's party and after we watch the Belmont Stakes back here," Emily said as she closed the magazine. "There seems to be a lot to do today, so you better hop in the shower and start getting ready in case Linda needs a ride to the Education Center. I can't give her a ride today."

"Yeah, I think I'm going to have to take her because Sam has to get the oil changed in his van before we head over to that farm with the guru."

"Meeting that guy seems to intrigue you," Emily said. "You think you can get him to tell you what your 'authentic self' needs in terms of sex, intimacy, and more sex?"

"You sound very skeptical."

"I have to get dressed and on the road," Emily said. "You need to hop in the shower - a cold shower."

"That doesn't sound very sensual," Desi said as he stood up and started heading to the bathroom.

"You could come into the bedroom for a minute or two and watch me powder myself," Emily suggested.

Desi turned and followed her into their bedroom.

Daisy Swings by Louisville

Emily was quite surprised to see Daisy standing alongside Attorney Henderson when she arrived at the Carter Campaign meeting at a hotel near the airport in Louisville.

Daisy and Emily embraced each other and had to give Attorney Henderson a quick explanation as to how they already knew each other. Daisy told Emily that she was flying to New York right after the meeting to join Roger for an afternoon at Belmont Park. Emily handed Daisy ten dollars to place a bet for her.

The meeting started a few minutes late as the slate of attendees wandered in. Daisy and a couple of people from the Washington D.C. office sat up front at a table with Attorney Henderson. It appeared to Emily that Daisy was looking stressed as the discussions went on for over an hour. The organizer from the National Headquarters in Georgia never arrived. Daisy started whispering to Attorney Henderson as the attendees offered what seemed to be an endless number of statements and opinions as purported questions to the panel.

Daisy, after whispering something to Attorney Henderson, then pointed to Emily. Attorney Henderson nodded. Daisy stood up and walked to one side of the ballroom. She motioned to Emily to join her. When Emily met Daisy at the wall near a long hallway, Emily could tell that Daisy was upset.

"The Carter staffers want me to take a bunch of campaign lit to Lexington this morning because the guy from the University hasn't shown up here today and the Lexington office needs to have people out walking this afternoon. We have a bunch of lit for the E'Town campaign office to give to you, and I am hoping you can also take the stuff for Lexington. We can have someone from that office come by and meet you in Elizabethtown. You just need to give them the lit."

"Will someone here help me load up my car with all the stuff for E'Town and Lexington?" Emily asked.

"I would do it myself if I didn't have to get going to the airport," Daisy said. "Thank you so much for appreciating my predicament. I think we have someone who'll help you. That guy wearing the tie sitting up at the table."

Daisy gave Emily another hug and a kiss on the cheek.

"Say hello to Roger for me," Emily called out to Daisy, who was practically running to the hotel exit.

Unfortunately, the guy with the tie had little experience with distributing campaign literature in bulk, no knowledge of the whereabouts of the hotel's loading docks and was even unwilling to take off his tie or lift anything over twenty pounds. He said he was limited by his doctor after suffering a sports-related injury. It took over an hour for Emily to get her car to the right loading dock and get all of the campaign literature for the two offices loaded into her car. She had to supply her phone number to a guy on the loading dock to get any help lifting the boxes. However, she only gave the telephone number of the campaign office in Elizabethtown.

All the warnings she had received from people, including Desi, as to how political campaigns can often be very discouraging, seemed to be more meaningful after that morning. The weight of the campaign material, filling the trunk and the seats of her Mustang made it feel like her car was in low gear all the way to Elizabethtown. By the time Emily got to E'Town, she was hoping that someone from the Lexington campaign office would already be waiting for her; that didn't happen either. It was almost eleven o'clock before she received a call from anyone at the Lexington office, and all they were able to report was that someone was on their way.

If there had been more than just one other person present in the Elizabethtown campaign office, Emily might have just unloaded her car and headed up to Radcliff, but she wasn't sure if someone from Lexington would really show up.

Emily is a Scratch for Stacey's Party at the Kentucky Vedic farm

Emily called the house in Radcliff from the campaign office in E'Town, and Linda answered.

"You guys are going to need to leave without me. I know Sam has to play his guitar at the party, and I am stuck here."

"Are you sure?" Linda asked.

Emily saw a taxi pulling up in front of the campaign office. "I see that somebody is getting out of a taxi."

"You want me to hold on in case you are going to be able to leave in a couple of minutes?"

A woman came up to the door of the campaign office and opened the door.

Emily fell back in her chair. She put a hand over the lower part of her face and whispered into the mouthpiece, "Linda, it's my mother!" Then, she hung up.

Desi came out of his bedroom and saw Linda with a blank expression on her face with the telephone cord hanging in her hand. "Is everything alright?" he asked.

"Emily is not going to be able to go with us to the farm today."

"Did she say why?'

"It sounded like there was something about to happen at the campaign office."

"Campaigns are unpredictable," Desi commented.

"Life is unpredictable," Linda said as she hung the phone back on the wall.

Suddenly, there was the roar of a large motorcycle, which got louder and louder until it pulled up on the front lawn of the house, within a few feet of the front door of Desi's apartment. About a minute later, there was the sound of a fist pounding on the front door.

"I don't know who that could be, but it sounds like they're pissed off about something," Linda said.

"We've only been back here a few minutes. Did someone follow us here after I picked you up at the Education Center?" Desi and Linda stared at each other for a minute. "Sam should be getting back here from the service station any minute. Maybe he knows why we have some character banging on the door."

Another minute or so went by, and then there was the sound of Sam's VW van pulling onto the gravel driveway. Desi and Linda waited and listened.

They could hear a gruff male voice say, "Are you Desi?"

"What's it to you?" Sam answered.

"Now I know who it must be," Desi said as he headed for the side door.

"I was going to ask you something about parking my bike, but, since my girlfriend is a couple streets away, maybe I should start with asking if you have been screwing around with my girlfriend?" the gruff guy could be heard to say. From the kitchen window, Desi and Linda could see Sam outside of his van, standing within three feet of a bearded, long-haired guy in a black, fringed motorcycle jacket.

Desi came out of the house and stood by the side door, keeping his distance. "I'm Desi, and you look like Che Guevara, so you must be Specialist Gaines' boyfriend, Rinaldo."

Rinaldo glared at Desi. "Well, what's your answer to my question about anybody screwing around with my girlfriend?" he said as he took a step towards Desi.

Sam also took a step forward, keeping the guy from advancing further towards Desi.

"Hey, I know you are a Special Forces operative and, chances are, have plenty of opportunities to get tough with people down in Panama or wherever. But we are in the same Army," Desi said as he stepped towards his antagonist. "I am sure Pamela Gaines has already told you that we haven't even kissed, so why don't we just deal with finding a storage space for your motorcycle."

"Miss Gaines is over at the house where she had been told we can store the bike. The problem is, the people living there don't seem to know anything about it," Rinaldo replied.

Desi looked over at the house next door. "My landlady doesn't seem to be around this morning. Their cars aren't in this driveway we share with them. I'll check the garage and see if their garage door is locked. If we can't get your motorcycle in on their side of the garage, I'll unlock my garage door and pull my car out. You can park your bike on our side of the garage until they get back." Desi started walking towards the two-car garage.

After watching Desi approach the garage, Rinaldo then turned to Sam. "I'm sorry for accusing you of doing something when I didn't even know your name."

Sam assessed Rinaldo's expression and concluded it would be alright to reach out to shake Rinaldo's hand. "I'm Sam."

Rinaldo shook Sam's hand, saying, "You can call me Rinaldo or Che."

"Is that the same type of motorcycle that Che Guevara drove all around South America?" Sam asked.

"She is pretty close to being the same bad girl that Che bonded with," Rinaldo answered.

Sam pointed to Linda. "That's my bad girl, Linda. She's told me that she has never bonded with Desi, even though she and Desi have had a couple of opportunities. With respect to your lady friend, I can't be 100 percent sure, but I can tell you that in the time I've lived here with Desi, I've never seen or heard about anyone named Specialist Gaines."

"So, you think I should refrain from beating a confession out of Desi," Rinaldo said dryly.

"I am sure you would gain nothing from clobbering Desi or your girlfriend, that's all."

Rinaldo shook Sam's hand again and put his hand on Sam's bicep. "I'll keep that in mind and think about it while I answer nature's call," Rinaldo said. "Can I use the bathroom in your house?"

"Sure, use the side door to go in the house, over by Linda."

Rinaldo smiled at Linda as he passed by her.

Desi managed to open the garage door on his landlord's side of the two-car garage. He saw Edna's car inside in that bay, so he reclosed it. As he turned and walked towards Sam, a red Mercury sedan pulled into the driveway. Out jumped Pamela Gaines in a white sleeveless T-shirt and short shorts. She ran towards Desi and gave him a warm embrace and a kiss on the cheek. She put a folded piece of paper into his shirt pocket.

"Desi, it's so great to see you," she said.

"Pamela, it's great to see you again also, but I thought you were going to be here a few days ago. And I am even more confused by you saying something about being at the 'Gold Vault.' "

Specialist Gaines put one arm around his shoulder and leaned her body on Desi. "Well, Rinaldo showed up, without much notice, right about the time that I began thinking I would never see him again. He said he wanted to ride his motorcycle for a few days but would need a cheap place to store it before he went on his next assignment to South America. We took turns driving the bike from D.C., along the Pennsylvania Turnpike, to Columbus, Ohio, and hung out with a few people there. Yesterday, we made our way down here and spent the night at the Gold Vault Motor Inn. We borrowed the sedan from a friend so we can get some camping equipment and go down to Dale Hollow to camp for a couple of days. Then, if Rinaldo reenlists, he has to report somewhere, and I have to get back to the Pentagon."

"So, for how much of that ride did Rinaldo trust you to drive his motorcycle?" Desi asked.

"He doesn't mind sitting on the back for an hour or so. I am not sure I would have been able to drive it the whole way here. It probably wouldn't have been safe driving it that far all alone."

Linda approached Desi and Pamela Gaines and pulled Desi away from her. "I am sure it wouldn't be safe for you in that outfit," Linda said. "You know that your boyfriend is in our bathroom and might be walking out here any minute."

Desi put his arm around Linda's waist. "I'm sorry, Pamela, I should have introduced you to Linda and Sam. They live here also."

"So, is it share and share alike?" Pamela asked. "Rinaldo is so jealous; he would never want me to live somewhere with two guys while he goes off to who knows where. But, maybe someday, I might try that."

Desi shook his head. "I didn't give you the whole picture. Our apartment is a two-bedroom with Sam and Linda living in one of the two bedrooms. Emily, who is not here right now, lives in the second bedroom with me. We have to leave for a party in a little while, but why don't you come inside for a few minutes and have something to drink?"

"Well, since Rinaldo hasn't emerged from your apartment, why not?" Pamela Gaines said as she made her way to the side door of the house. "My only question about the set up here is whether or not the girls pay rent?"

"We do contribute in our own way," Linda responded.

"I don't doubt that. I'm just still thinking about what it would be like if I was living with two men," Pamela said. "I don't think I would have to ask one of the guys twice for anything."

On the Road to the Farm

Sam wanted Desi to drive his van as he hadn't attempted to learn the roadways outside of the Fort Knox area, and he wanted to sit on the bed in the back of his vehicle to put new strings on his guitar. Linda sat up front in the passenger seat to talk to Desi.

"I think that chick back at the house was either trying to get a fight going between you and her boyfriend or just has a screw loose in her head," Linda said.

"Thanks for pulling her off of me," Desi said. "I temporarily forgot her warrior prince was nearby."

"What did you do with her to have her kissing and hugging on you like that?" Linda asked.

"Maybe it's because she is still a bit curious as to why I didn't jump at the opportunity to go home with her and spend the night on the first afternoon we met."

"I think she is more than a bit curious," Sam said from the back. "I think she wants a second chance."

"Was it because of the birthmark, or whatever that is on her face?" Linda asked.

"I think most men would be able to overlook that, especially in the outfit she was wearing today," Sam said.

"Hey, Sam," Linda said. "Desi and I are having a conversation, and you don't need to be talking around me about some other structurally impressive woman."

"Sorry, babe."

That's right. I am all the babe you need."

Desi attempted to explain. "I wanted to get up to Baltimore to see Emily and needed to get on the next train. Specialist Gaines offered to drive me from the Pentagon to the train station. Stopping at her place was just not in the cards."

"She took you to the station on the motorcycle?" Linda asked. "If you were holding onto her jugs, she might have gotten the idea that you wanted to spend the night."

"No, no," Desi said. "We were in her car, not on the motorcycle."

"But what happened in the car?" asked Linda. "Did she reach over and drop her hand in your lap?"

"Yeah," Sam said. "It's not always the guy who cops a feel."

"No one got handsy in the car," Desi insisted.

"Okay, so why did you invite her and her commando boyfriend back to the house to watch the Belmont Stake with us this evening?" Linda asked. "You want to see if you can scare him off with your Kendo stick?"

"He's probably not as tough as he talks," Sam volunteered.

"I think it might get very interesting at the house when Emily gets back," Linda said.

"Why do you think that?" Desi asked.

"I think there is a chance she might be bringing one or two other people along," Linda said. "I know her mother is in Kentucky, and her father might be around also."

Perspective From the Farm

Desi helped Sam by carrying Sam's small amplifier and a microphone stand from the farm's parking area to a large barn. Sam carried his twelve-string guitar and a metal stool that had a woven, multi-colored burlap seat. Linda hung a few yards of microphone cable over one of her shoulders to wear as a bandolier and carried a tambourine.

As they entered the barn, Stacey called out to Desi. "Do you know how to drive a tractor?"

"Yeah, my uncle has a farm out on eastern Long Island. I think I can drive most tractors."

"Most of the farm equipment is out of the barn, but they left a tractor in here," Stacey said.

"Where do you want me to set up?" Sam asked Stacey as they walked towards her.

"I think you can set up, along with Randy and his equipment, right here in this corner of the barn where the tractor is now parked."

"Nothing like putting pressure on me to get the tractor moved out," Desi said. "I hope it will start without too much trouble."

"I guess I can go find one of the men if you can't get it started," Stacey said.

"Thanks for your confidence in me."

Stacey laughed. "Maybe it's a female tractor, and all you need to do is massage it a couple of times."

Desi moved the throttle back and forth a few times in an attempt to start it. The tractor started to sputter. Desi kept adjusting the throttle until it made almost a purring sound. He put it into gear and slowly drove it out the barn doors.

"I hear that Desi prefers to do his plowing outdoors," Linda said to Stacey.

"Can't say I'm surprised to hear that, but where is Emily to confirm that preference?"

Linda rattled the tambourine as if she was doing a drum roll, and then smacked the head of the percussion instrument. "I think she is stuck explaining to her mother, who showed up in Kentucky today, why she hasn't been living where her mother thought she was living for the past couple of weeks."

"Hmm," Stacey said. "Do you want to meet my mom? She might be willing to share her perspective on what she needs to hear from her daughters regarding situations like that."

"Sure," Linda said, slapping the tambourine against her thigh. "Though it might make me feel like I should give a call to update my mom as to where I am these days."

Sam walked over to Linda and motioned to have her turn over the tambourine.

Linda handed it over to Sam and walked out of the barn with Stacey. "Guess I will not be performing today."

"And we won't be smoking any weed today because the guru doesn't like people getting high on anything other than Transcendental Meditation," Stacey said.

"So, they aren't growing any pot on this farm?"

"Only vegetables. The hippies have all gone. Most of the people here now are vegetarians. There are several families, some with kids. Even most of the kids are vegetarians."

Stacey pointed to one of the seven buildings facing east along the western boundary of the property. "My mother, Kadiatu, is in that building, talking with one of the teachers about meditation. They have forty-seven acres here and, basically, they just farm and teach people how to meditate. My mom was very excited to meet their spiritual leader. The farm's guru was at Rishikesh when the Beatles went to India to meditate with Maharishi Mahesh Yogi. The guru here loves Beatles music, but he doesn't think they behaved well at Rishikesh."

"I heard a story from some woman, I think she was someone I met at Woodstock, that one of the Beatles took LSD in India when they were supposed to be learning how to get off of drugs," Linda said.

"Well, it seems that most of the hippies who were here in the late sixties and early seventies learned how to meditate, and either cut back or stopped doing drugs. Then, they decided to go live where they could make some real money and live in their own houses, not these farmhouses," Stacey said. "But my mom is really digging this place. I think she wants to move here. She and Desdemona's mother, Isata, only got in from South Carolina yesterday afternoon, but they seem to be feeling right at home."

"So, does the guru work in the fields or in the restaurant?" Linda asked.

"No, he might go to the TM office downtown once in a while, but he mostly instructs the TM teachers here and translates books written in Sanskrit to English."

"Desi wants to meet the guru," Linda said. "He spent a day or two with a group of meditators in Barcelona during the summer of '72. They had been with Maharishi at some event on an island off the coast of Spain. They convinced Desi that he had to learn to meditate someday. Maybe today is the day."

"I think my mother is watching a video of Maharishi talking about the effects of meditation right now," Stacey said. "But from what I've heard, it takes more than a day to learn how to meditate."

"Desi may be disappointed," Linda said as they reached the house where Stacey's mother and Desdemona's mother were meeting with a TM teacher. "But maybe we can arrange a meeting between Desi and the guru, and maybe the guru can teach Desi how to meditate in one afternoon."

"I think the guru is going to stop by my party," Stacey said as she opened the door to the house for Linda.

There was the aroma of sandalwood incense that greeted them when Stacey opened the door. They stepped into a foyer.

A young man in his twenties appeared and led them to a room where Desdemona sat in front of a video screen. On the screen was a man, wearing a shirt and tie, talking about his own personal experiences with practicing Transcendental Meditation. When Desdemona saw them, she motioned for Stacey and Linda to sit in the two folding chairs on either side of her. The video ended a couple of minutes later with the man in the shirt and tie being asked if he felt "it was easy" to learn how to meditate. He smiled and nodded affirmatively.

The young man who had met them in the foyer asked Stacey and Linda if they wanted him to restart the video.

Stacey stood up from her chair, "No, thanks. We have a party that is starting over at the barn in a few minutes."

"Perhaps some other time," the young man said.

Desdemona also stood up. "I think our mothers are in another room here, learning what they have to do to get their mantras tomorrow. Maybe Stacey can watch the video when we come back with our moms tomorrow."

The young man put his palms together and gave a little bow. "Jai Guru Dev," he said before turning to walk away.

Stacey waited a few moments after he left. "What does that mean?" she asked.

"I think it is sort of like Aloha," Linda offered. "It's like, 'Hello and Goodbye.' "

Desdemona shook her head. "No, I think it has something to do with Maharishi's teacher."

"Perhaps you are both sort of correct," Stacey suggested.

A door down the hall opened. A woman in a traditional Hindu sari stepped into the hallway and directed Kadiatu and Isata towards the foyer, saying, "I will see you again tomorrow. Don't forget that each of you has to bring a piece of fruit, some flowers, and a handkerchief."

Kadiatu and Isata nodded their heads in agreement.

Stacey gave them each a hug. "I can't believe that you guys are going to learn how to meditate before me. I'm going to have to wait until I get to Germany."

"I'm going to come back next weekend and get initiated," Desdemona said.

"I wonder if I would have to stop smoking weed in order to learn TM?" Linda said.

"I don't think so, but from what I hear, you would probably phase out wanting to smoke pot every night," Desdemona surmised.

"That might be good if I don't end up having a hard time getting to sleep," Linda questioned.

"Maybe Sam can also help you find ways to relax and get more rest without the weed," Stacey offered with a laugh.

Desdemona put an arm around her mother. "Linda's friend, Sam, is here to serenade Stacey and all of us with his twelve-string guitar. I think he is going to do a bunch of Beatles tunes. And when Sam is on break, Stacey has lined up a DJ with a collection of Bob Marley records."

"Bob Marley is my man," Desdemona's mother said with a smile. "And everyone enjoys the Beatles."

As they approached the barn, they could hear Sam tuning up. A few minutes later, the party was on with a barn full of people. The buffet tables held numerous trays of special vegetarian appetizers and entrees.

As promised, the spiritual leader appeared after a few songs and made his way through the sixty or seventy people in the barn, talking to visitors and members of the farm. Stacey introduced the guru to Desi. "What is your practice?" he asked Desi.

"I do yoga, sometimes," Desi said.

"That is your discipline?" the spiritual leader asked. "Did I hear you say, sometimes?"

Stacey looked at Desi, who seemed to be at a loss regarding his spiritual accomplishments with his answer. Stacey responded for him, "Desi minored in philosophy while in college and studied a number of religions in connection with those classes."

The guru stepped in closer to Desi and smiled as he looked into Desi's eyes. "Have you ever heard the story about Maharishi and the philosopher?" he asked.

Desi shrugged.

"The philosopher, who identified himself as an 'existentialist,' was in a garden with Maharishi, where they were examining how some of the flowers and trees in the garden were in bloom, some were getting ready to bloom, and some were already having their blossoms fall off. The 'existentialist' sat down on a bench in the garden and bemoaned the fact that the garden and the world was 'ever changing,' and that the garden did not seem to be as pleasing as it had been a week before."

"I've been to places like that garden," Desi said.

"But what is he missing when he is focusing on the change?" the guru asked. "Obviously there is the change, what about the 'ever,' the constant derivative element which we can also allow ourselves to experience."

"I get what you are saying," Desi responded. "It is similar to derivatives in calculus. But are you being fair to philosophers who consider themselves to be existentialists? Instead of simply despairing 'change,' some existentialists, like Jean-Paul Sartre, would say that we have to take responsibility for our existence." Desi paused for a moment before adding, "I think Sartre would say if someone believed in free choice, then they have the burden of creating meaning in their life."

"And what about consciousness?" inquired the guru.

"Sartre seems to also believe an individual has to make their individual consciousness in some way concrete, like drawing their own spiritual or intellectual portrait. But that seems like it would be a bit too much for me, at least at this point in my life."

"So, what do you believe?" the guru persisted.

"I think it is important to live as if we can make a difference in the world," Desi said. "But the consciousness thing, I am still trying to puzzle that out."

"Are you open to the possibility of experiencing pure being in terms of your consciousness?"

Desi nodded his head.

"Then let your intellectual interests lead you to what Maharishi calls 'Transcendental Consciousness.' "

Desi looked into the guru's eyes. "I am heading overseas in a few weeks. Maybe after I make that move, I'll be ready to begin the TM practice."

"It seems like you are ready now, but you are the one who has to commit." The guru reached inside his robe and gave Desi a business card that had something written on it in characters that Desi could not read.

"You know I can't read this," Desi said.

"Someday, you will have someone translate it for you, and you will understand." The guru smiled at Desi again and turned to greet other guests in the barn.

Stacey and her mother huddled around Desi to find out what the guru said to him. Desi showed them the card. Neither of them had any idea what it meant.

Desi put the card inside his money clip and turned to Stacey. "I was a bit surprised to find out that you invited Randy here today. I thought he got you pretty upset on Derby Day."

"We are cool now. I ran into him two weeks ago, and he must have known that he ticked me off. He apologized for the way he behaved and explained that he was going through some stuff with his wife and their trouble with getting housing on post. But Randy kept pushing, and they got offered a pretty nice place. His wife is no longer threatening to take their two young kids back to New Orleans and live with her parents."

"I'm glad to hear that," Desi said. "And he is going to be playing some reggae music later."

"Yeah, mon," Stacey said with a smile.

"Do I get a last dance with you before you leave for Germany?" Desi asked.

"I think it would actually be our first dance together."

"Better late than never," Desi quipped.

"There is a doctor from Louisville here who has a niece visiting from India this summer. He is trying to find her a college-educated American boyfriend. Would you be interested in dancing with her since you came stag today?"

"I'll give her a dance, but I am not into being the 'American boyfriend,' or any preconceived type of guy."

"I know, and I get what you are saying."

"Also, I am not getting involved with any other women while Emily is living with me."

"Really, did that ever stop you before?"

"Maybe Emily has changed my perspective on things."

"And here I was, thinking we might go off and have that dance in some private place and have another first-time experience with one another."

"That is very tempting, Stacey, but I am going to take a pass on that. I think you want to be able to look Charlie straight in the eyes and tell him that you never went to that place with me."

"Does that mean that we will or won't write to one another?"

Desi then embraced her, saying, "I promise to send a letter to your new address before the end of this month. I'll let you know whether I'll be joining you guys in Germany."

"I think I will be having dreams about the three of us partying in Munich, Paris, and Rome."

"I am going to call Washington on Monday and find out where they are sending me. Don't tell anyone, but I have a source within the Pentagon who knows the guy who prepares orders for Army journalists. I now have his name and telephone number."

"Really, how did you get a source within the Pentagon?"

"I'm a journalist, remember?"

"This wouldn't be someone of the female sex, would it?"

"Well, I guess I don't even need to answer that."

"What are you going to owe her? I'm sure it's going to be more than a dance."

"She has a boyfriend, a tough-looking Special Forces type."

"How do you know what he looks like?"

"He was at the apartment this morning knocking on the door. I think he is coming back this evening with Pamela."

"So, your source is Pamela in the Pentagon? You could probably come up with an interesting alliterative poem about her. What does she look like?"

"Sam and Linda met her. Linda described her as 'structurally impressive.' "

"Linda should know," Stacey said with raised eyebrows. "Hey, did Linda get a job at the Education Center? Sam told me she was going for an interview, but I never heard what happened."

"She got the job, and she got Sam enrolled for some summer classes."

"Sam's mother must be happy that he's back working on his college credits," Stacey said. "And did Linda get the final credit she needed to get her bachelor's degree from UK?"

"I am trying to help her with that," Desi said. "I was pretty much in the same situation when I was trying to finish up at NYU. I was able to do an independent study on centennial celebrations. Debi and I were in a bookstore in the East Village, and we found a book that really helped me get what I needed."

"You got lucky, like doing it in a bookstore with her?"

"She helped me find a book published in 1879 about the various centennial celebrations in New York State with respect to the State Constitution, which was adopted in 1777. The centennial celebration for the United States in 1876 was centralized in Philadelphia. There's a federal committee as well as 50 state committees organizing things for this year's celebration. I think my journalism professor who helped me set up an independent study researching centennial celebrations in the 1800s was in some way connected to the new group designated by Congress in 1974 to work on the bicentennial celebration. "

"I thought Linda was going to do something about Kentucky and the bicentennial," Stacey said.

"What she may do is figure out where in Kentucky the bicentennial celebrations are going to be held this year and then go back to old newspapers from 1876 in those communities and see what kind of celebrations, if any, they had ten years after the Civil War ended, " Desi said. "I was able to find some of the old newspapers that were published in New York City in 1876."

"And if she can't find that for Kentucky?"

"Then, I guess she is just going to have to do something on the celebrations this year and what organizations in Kentucky are participating in those celebrations. I'll get her some pictures of the celebrations in Washington D.C., Philadelphia, and New York because I am planning to be in the three Capitals of the United States on July Fourth. She may or may not need them if she finds enough in the way of events in Kentucky, but she'll have my photos just in case."

"Can you be in all three cities on the same day?"

"I'm an Army journalist. I'm sure I can figure out how to be in Washington bright and early that morning."

"Maybe your 'structurally impressive' source in the Pentagon can help you arrange accommodations in D.C. the night before. She may even have an apartment as a fallback opportunity."

"Didn't I mention that her boyfriend is a Special Forces dude?"

"You told me that you were a Defense Information School trained killer," Stacey said with a laugh.

"I think Emily would say that I am more of a lover than a fighter."

"Am I going to get a chance to see Emily before I take off this week?"

"She is usually home in our apartment by six during the week, except Mondays and Fridays. She's at the campaign office in Elizabethtown until about nine those nights."

"I'll bring over those sweet grass baskets I promised you this week before I leave on Friday," Stacey said. "But I will give you a call before I come over."

"You're not telling your mother and Desdemona's mother that you are giving away the baskets they made for you, are you?" Desi asked. "If you are going to tell them, I want the chance to thank them."

"Maybe I'll bring my mother over when I stop by, and she can check out how cozy things are in that apartment."

"Hopefully, Emily's mother is still not around by then because we only have that one couch."

"Is that where Sam's mother spent a night or two, or did she sleep in the love mobile?"

"Who knows. I've made sure that my mother is never going to stop by the apartment. My parents don't even have the phone number, no less the address."

"Guess you really need your space," Stacey said.

"My parents live over 800 miles away and are very busy with their two hardware stores. The only vacation they take is around the Fourth of July, and they usually take their boat out to eastern Long Island for a few days, along with a few other families who also have boats. They are quite unlikely to visit me here in Kentucky, and even less likely to visit me if I go overseas."

"I wonder if my mother will want to visit me in Germany," Stacey mused.

"Well, hopefully you will have a cozy place, either with Charlie or on your own, and you will have at least one extra couch."

"Having my mom around at a place where Charlie and I are living together would be really weird."

"Maybe you should bring her over to the apartment this week. She can see where you lived with Charlie without seeing your panties and his Jockey shorts on the floor next to what used to be your bed."

"Maybe she can just take a quick look at the living room and the kitchen, with no time on the couch."

"Yeah, that couch has seen some wild stuff."

"Charlie claims he caught you with two chicks on that nice big couch. He said he never thought a guy could ever get that to really happen. Charlie admitted he's had that fantasy, but I guess most guys have. Charlie wouldn't tell me if it was the twins or not."

"Well, I am not going to kiss and tell."

"I know that the three of you used to sit on the couch listening to music together, and sometimes you had a blanket over your laps. And I did find Brenda's copy of *Cosmo* in the couch." Stacey looked at Desi as if she expected him to communicate agreement, either verbally or otherwise; Desi remained quiet and poker-faced, but Stacey persisted, nonetheless. "I'll bet you were reading some of those articles to one another. Like that article about not limiting sex to just the bedroom. Maybe you all just got carried away."

"I think your imagination is carrying you away."

"Maybe you were all drinking or so stoned that none of you even had to admit what happened. Like on the night before the Derby, you were giving shotguns to Linda, Desdemona, and me. It was like you were kissing all three of us. Tell me that didn't happen."

"I will acknowledge that something like that happened, but we were pretty wasted. I'm not sure if a night like that really counts."

"I hope it counts for something, even if it wasn't something that carried over into the next day."

"Maybe the best way to look at a crazy night like that is simply: a good rush is a good rush," Desi said.

"Lots of adrenaline and hormones pumping, right?"

"Sometimes it can lead to something beyond one moment, even if it is just a second or third moment."

"So have you had a woman or women just appear at your door and gone 'all in' with them and not be sure if you would see them again?"

"Only one woman in particular at NYU. She would show up, usually with a joint already rolled, and we'd roll around in my bed, but there was never anything said about getting together again. She did show up again a couple of times, weeks, sometimes months later. And it was the same surprisingly intense thing each time. In most cases, the women who just showed up at my door would start talking about their boyfriends or other problems. I would be patient and listen to them. We might smoke a joint together, but I would just talk with them. I usually appreciate talking with women more than men because women tend to be more honest and interesting. But with most of them, I knew there was not going to be a real rush of excitement, at least on my part."

"So, you might, on some cold lonely night, think of that party the four of us had in Desdemona's apartment?" Stacey asked.

Desi took Stacey's hand and led her out of the barn. As soon as they got outside, he pulled her alongside the barn and gave Stacey a kiss on the lips. Desi looked her straight in the eyes. "I don't think I am ever going to forget you."

They were half-standing, part-leaning against the barn when Linda came out of the barn and joined them. "Is everything alright?" Linda asked them. "Sam is finishing his set, and Randy is ready to do his thing. I'm thinking that Emily might be stuck at the apartment with her mother. Maybe we should go?"

"Don't go without taking some food," Stacey said.

"Thanks, I'll go inside and fix some plates," Linda said. "Sorry if I interrupted anything."

"No, you're right," Desi answered. "Emily may be in the apartment trying to entertain. Who knows?"

"I think we have an extra tray or two you can take," Stacey called to Linda. Stacey looked at Desi. "I'm going to help Linda put some food together for your people at the apartment. How many could you have over to watch the race at Belmont?"

"Maybe seven, or even eight," Desi calculated.

When Desi, Linda, and Sam got back to the apartment, Rinaldo was sitting on the couch with Emily's mother while Emily and Pamela from the Pentagon prepared a pitcher of margaritas and a pitcher of Sangria. Desi carried in a tray of mushrooms stuffed with various vegetables. Linda carried in a tray of vegetable lasagna. Sam brought in his guitar and a container of desserts popular in India.

Desi put down the tray he was carrying on the sink counter in-between Emily and Pamela. He gave Emily a kiss.

"What?" Pamela said. "Aren't you happy to see me? Where is my kiss?"

Desi looked over at Rinaldo and Emily's mother for their reaction.

"Go ahead and kiss her," Rinaldo said while holding up an opened bottle of beer. "We didn't wait for you guys to come back to start celebrating race day!"

"Ok," Desi said as he kissed Pamela on the cheek.

Emily's mother stood up from the couch. "And where is my kiss?"

Desi, dutifully walked into the living room and gave Emily's mother a kiss on the cheek. Rinaldo stood up, ready to plant a kiss on Emily's mother's other cheek.

Emily's mother backed up. "I appreciate your thoughtfulness, but we have been sitting here talking, and I don't think we have been formally introduced.

Desi made the introduction. "Dr. Miller, allow me to introduce you to Staff Sergeant Rinaldo Ricardo. I believe you may call him Rinaldo or Che."

"Anything but Ricky," Rinaldo said as he took Emily's mother's hand and formally kissed it. "I hope to also be a doctor someday."

"I am a registered nurse who holds a doctoral degree in public health care, not a medical doctor," Emily's mother clarified.

"I could see myself working in a field like that in San Juan, for my people in Puerto Rico," Rinaldo replied.

"Are people in Puerto Rico now formally U.S. citizens?" Emily's mother asked.

"Yes, since 1941. That issue has been resolved."

"Well, then, I think I may be able to help you understand all the opportunities in public health care, and perhaps, sometime in the future, assist you with getting grant money for the health care system in Puerto Rico."

Rinaldo smiled. "You've got me thinking that I might be able to use my medic experience with Special Forces on the outside."

Pamela walked over to Rinaldo and put her arm around him. "You have to think some more about whether you really want to reenlist. We could live together in Louisville. They have plenty of medical facilities where you could get a job. I can get out of the Army in a couple of months and get a job too."

"What would you do?" Rinaldo asked.

"I would use my experience to become a travel agent. Maybe specialize in vacation planning. How about if I became an expert on trips to Puerto Rico?"

"I think we have a lot to talk about."

Emily took Desi by the hand and led him to his bedroom. "I think we have lots to talk about also."

"Your mom wants to spend the night here?" Desi asked. "She seems to be getting pretty comfortable."

"Very funny," Emily said as she closed the bedroom room and pushed Desi onto the bed. She climbed on top of Desi. "I really need your help because I have no idea what to do."

"Do about what? Babysitting your mother? Doesn't she have a plane ticket back to Baltimore?"

"No! She's not leaving Kentucky unless she locates my father and finds out what he's up to."

Desi looked at Emily and pulled her closer to him.

"What are you doing? Trying to get it on with me while my mom is in the same apartment?"

"You don't think that would make her want to leave?"

Emily climbed off the bed and stood with her back to the bedroom door. "Look, you aren't leaving this room until you help me."

"Well, if it's not sex that you want, I don't see how I'm going to provide you with anything to get your mother to leave. You brought her here for some reason, so why don't you start off by telling me why in the world did you want to share our current location with her?"

"When she got to Mama Boone's house, she saw other people living there. No Emily, no Linda, and no idea of where my father was. She was freaking out by the time she got to me at the campaign office in E'Town. She didn't know what to think or who to trust. My mom was even wondering whether my dad had run off with Linda. I had to bring her here to show her that Linda was living with Sam, and you were providing me with a place to stay until..."

Desi raised his eyebrows. "Yeah?"

"Actually, she called Linda and me 'a couple of stray kittens.' She wants me to drive her home and move back into my old bedroom. But my mom is not sure if she likes the idea of you visiting regularly and sleeping with me in my room."

"I hope you told her that I prefer our sex in the treehouse."

"I didn't mention it because she probably doesn't want to think about us doing it every time she looks into the backyard. It might be easier for her to just close my bedroom door and not look at my bed."

Desi looked at Emily. "So, she's offering to provide you with your bedroom, if you drive her home."

"I told her to forget it. I need to finish my internship at the *Courier Journal* in order to put it on my resume or expect any sort of recommendation. Then there is the campaign job; I have no idea what to do about that. The internship at the *Courier Journal* only runs to the end of this month."

"So, you're thinking of moving back home at the end of the month?"

"Not really. My mom is also willing to pay for me to have an apartment in the D.C. area. Maybe you could see if that job is still open at Fort Monroe and, if it is, get a transfer."

Desi looked at Emily and shook his head. "I told you that I have no interest in writing training manuals. Besides, I may be getting orders this week to go overseas. I've been thinking we might live together in Louisville after I get back. We could both go to the law school at U of L, but that's more than a year away."

"So, what is it that you want to do right now?"

"Right now, I want to go into the kitchen and have some food with a couple of margaritas."

"That's it? How is your having margaritas going to be helpful to me?

Desi stood up and gently moved her out of the way of the door. "We need more time to figure out how we get your mom and dad together so he can drive her back to Maryland. I know I sure don't want her spending the night here in the apartment."

"Would it be better if Sam would lend out the love mobile so my mom can crash on the bed in there?"

"Here's an idea. We'll find your dad and then lock your parents in there together, and maybe they can work things out."

"You're going to have to bring me several margaritas to get me to stop worrying about my parents."

"Wait, how did your mother find you in Elizabethtown?

"She found out from the handyman, Fred, that I have a job at the campaign office in E'Town. I told him when Linda and I were moving out."

"Then let's use Fred as the go-between again. But I don't want your father coming over here to pick up your mother. You are going to have to drive your mother back to E'Town or some meeting place that Fred helps you set up."

"And what about the files with the documents Linda brought here? Should I tell my mother about those loan guarantees?"

"I think you should give your father a chance to come clean about whatever financial problems he's having. You can spill the beans later if you think he isn't going to be honest with your mother."

"How will I know that?"

"They are your parents. That is something you are going to have to figure out yourself," Desi said as he opened the bedroom door and put his shoulder against it so Emily couldn't close it before he was out of the bedroom.

Emily collapsed on the bed. She put a pillow over her head and pressed her face into the bedspread.

Linda came into the room and shut the door. Emily pulled off the pillow and turned around.

Linda sat on the bed and reached out a hand to her. "You better get out there before that crazy Pamela chick gets any more time with your mother. She's talking about how much you and Desi look like you could be brother and sister. It's getting your mom into talking about how much she needs to get you back home."

"My mom does think it's creepy for her to be around Desi. It's like she is expecting Desi to say something, as if he can channel a message from the Great Beyond."

"Well, other than your light brown hair and greenish eyes, there isn't that much of a resemblance, but Pamela is up to something by keeping that whole conversation going. She is talking like she still has the hots for Desi, even though Rinaldo took her to a nice jewelry store in Louisville today and bought her a very nice gold necklace with her initials on the pendant. Her cleavage now is labeled 'PG.' "

Emily sat up on the bed. "You realize that Desi is doing it again, don't you? He's found another vulnerable woman to cavort with so that her boyfriend gets crazy jealous. He can flirt with an attractive woman and win the hearts of everyone around him, except the jealous boyfriend, who ends up making a trip to a jewelry store. This time it's a necklace; next time they'll be shopping for an engagement ring."

"You think the jewelry stores will compensate Desi?" Linda said with a laugh.

"I am sure he expects to get something out of it. And he might get a night or two in the sack that won't interfere with his just moving on."

"What are you saying about Desi? You think he's going to try and fool around with Pamela while the two of you are living here together?"

"What's to stop him once I leave?"

"Are you really thinking about going back to live in Glen Burnie?"

"No way in hell am I going to do that now, but I'm feeling like I have to move somewhere by the end of the month."

"Wow! Are you evicting yourself, or is Desi telling you that you have to go?"

Emily started crying. "I know I love him, and I believe that he is starting to love being with me every night. But it is only a matter of when he gets orders to be stationed somewhere else and knowing he'll find some other stray kitten to spend his nights with."

"Stray kittens aren't sexually mature, so I think you have to refer to yourself as a stray cat."

"Well, I may be sexually mature now, but I think that when I first moved in with Desi, I was still like a kitten."

"So, whatever you did, or learned to do, Desi is crazy about you. It's not just my opinion either. Ask his friend Stacey. She told me this afternoon that she hasn't heard Desi talk about anyone the way he talks about you. I don't think there is anything wrong with the two of you looking alike…"

Emily scrunched up her face so that Linda stopped talking for a moment. Linda continued, "… just in some ways, not that you two look too much alike, because Desi is a guy, and you are a beautiful young woman…"

Emily smiled, "I don't really care much about all that. It might make my mom uncomfortable because Desi is about the age my brother was when he went off to Vietnam in '72. My father believes my brother 'died heroically.' I think his loss was a needless tragedy for my family, especially since the government knew the whole thing was a lost cause by then. My mother won't talk about it."

Linda started to cry. Then, they both cried and held each other for over a minute.

Linda stood up first. "We better go out to the living room and check on the Belmont race."

Emily stood up also. "I shared the Derby and the Preakness with Desi. This may be the only chance I ever get to share all three in a year with the same guy."

"What are you saying?" Linda said.

"Guess I'm just expressing the uncertainty I've been feeling today."

Chapter XII

THE PURSUIT OF HAPPINESS TOUR OF DUTY LEAVES FORT KNOX

On July 1, 1976, the weekly edition of Fort Knox's weekly newspaper featured an article on the "People Page" about Henry Knox. Desi figured there were still tens of thousands of people who lived and worked in the Fort Knox community who knew little or nothing about the young bookseller, who witnessed the Boston Massacre and would go on to not only be a 26-year-old general leading troops in the Revolutionary War, but also one of George Washington's most trusted advisors. With the bicentennial celebrations in Washington D.C., Philadelphia, New York City, and throughout the nation just days away, it seemed to Desi to be the perfect time to share his research on our country's first Secretary of War.

Desi was sitting in his office, reviewing a freshly printed copy of *Inside the Turret,* which included spending a substantial amount of time admiring the layout of the article on Knox, when Penny appeared in her dress uniform. She stood in front of his desk in a relaxed "parade rest" stance for a few moments before clearing her throat.

"I was over at the snack shack having a cup of coffee and looking at the paper when I saw the General Henry Knox article. I remembered I have something in my car that I have been meaning to give you."

Desi looked up from the newspaper. "It's nothing that will explode, is it?"

Penny shook her head. "Maybe a musician could create a blast with it, but, for you, it is probably just another toy."

"I guess that's a good thing," Desi said as he stood up.

"I would have come by your apartment, but I'm not sure of your current circumstances. I heard that your friend Emily has moved out."

"She's in the process of resettling in the Washington D.C. area for her new job with the Carter campaign," Desi said as he stood up from his chair, walked around the desk, and handed her the newspaper he had been holding. "Here's an extra copy of the paper for you, but you already seem to be more than reasonably informed. Have you been meeting with Linda over at the Education Center this week?"

"I signed up for a summer class that Sam and Linda are also taking. I know it's not my business, and you always told me that you wanted an overseas assignment, but I was a bit surprised to hear that you're going to Japan."

"I'll be there in less than two weeks," Desi said as he touched her arm. "How about if we walk out to your car for a minute and I can get a look at what, I guess, is a going away gift?"

"Perhaps we can meet for lunch a little later?"

"That would be nice, but I have been scheduled to meet with eight or nine former Fort Knox High School students who are back from college and want to share what it's like to be out in the world with college people who did not grow up in military settings. I think this may be the last article I write here at Fort Knox. Do you want to stop by the apartment this evening?" Desi said as he walked Penny through the office and out the back door that opened onto a brick staircase leading down to the parking lot.

"I think I may have to come by your place because you still have something I left there," Penny said as they stood outdoors on the top of the staircase. "I'd let you keep it but…"

"Oh, yeah. I started packing last night and was wondering how I was going to get your flute back to you. I am going out to dinner with a couple of people, but I should be home by eight. Does that work for you?"

"Eight, it is," Penny said as she turned and walked down the half-dozen steps to the parking lot.

Desi stood at the top of the staircase and watched her walk to her car as if he was expecting Penny to turn and wave. She didn't.

Desi went back to his office and located his notepad and a camera. There was a note on his desk about the Lieutenant from CID calling to confirm a meeting with him. The meeting had been scheduled and rescheduled multiple times since mid-May, but each time Desi had found an excuse to move the date. Fortunately, the interview with the college students, which was to take place at a Colonel's house, had also been scheduled for noon. He ran the note upstairs to the Public Affairs Officer's secretary and asked her to reschedule his meeting with the Lieutenant.

Desi expected to have dinner in Elizabethtown that evening with PFC MacNamara and her father. Apparently, her police official father from Pennsylvania wanted to personally thank Desi for helping them get a good local criminal attorney. Desi expected to get some update on her case from them. He was hoping that PFC MacNamara's problems regarding her receipt of marijuana-laced brownies in the mail had been resolved. But, if it had been resolved, it was unclear to him why he was still getting messages from the CID Lieutenant. Desi had been avoiding any direct contact with PFC MacNamara, but a nice dinner might be worth being seen with her. Without hearing that the matter was closed, he wasn't planning to speak to the folks at CID without the assistance of legal counsel.

His former roommate and friend Charlie had guided him through helping another soldier get an effective attorney. That attorney, who successfully defended someone who Desi felt was being singled out and treated unfairly, was now working on clearing PFC MacNamara. Desi's goal was to keep enough distance from her to avoid being pulled into an investigation himself.

In the prior case, the criminal attorney went on the offense and made it very clear there would be a suit against the Army for picking on a guy who merely received male bodybuilding magazines. However, that soldier ended up leaving active duty even after the charges of allegedly possessing "gay pornography" got dropped. Desi saw how someone who won a case could still be made to feel very uncomfortable. He hoped that things would go better for Cindy MacNamara.

He was thinking about PFC MacNamara and the dinner they were going to have at a restaurant her father let Desi pick out when he got to the house where the college students were meeting. Although Desi was a few minutes late, the "Army brats," as they called themselves, didn't seem to notice. They were munching on chips and pretzels as they talked among themselves. Desi had not stopped for lunch and was hoping for a sandwich or something more than snacks. They offered him various brands of soda, but Desi hadn't had a soft drink since he attended Kings Point. A gym coach at the Academy read the contents of a diet carbonated beverage and warned Desi's class about the long-term effects of sugary soft drinks and the mysterious contents of diet drinks.

Desi opted for some fresh lemonade, which he sipped as he started talking to the students, both individually and as a group.

They told him about the schools they attended, which were mostly in Kentucky and nearby states. Only one of the young men seemed content with getting back to Ft. Knox for the summer. He said he had been "anxious" to get back after a year of being "confined" at West Point. A couple of the college women mentioned that they had a friend who would soon be off to West Point to be in the first class at the U.S. Military Academy including women.

Desi did not mention that he had attended a federal academy out of high school but merely commented to them that "there is a big difference between going off to college and going off to an academy."

They talked about their summer jobs, as well as growing up in families regularly reassigned to various parts of the United States, as well as overseas. They seemed to agree that there were advantages to having seen more of the world than most people their age, even if it only meant having a broader perspective. They all seemed to have encountered people who had much more in the way of financial resources than the average military family.

A young woman noted that people at her college thought it was odd when she told them she was born in Germany but that she and her parents were not German. A young man, who had also spent almost two decades moving from Army base to Army base, said he thought it strange when people at college told him they had lived in one place their whole lives.

Desi found them all to be refreshingly worldly and more interesting than most of the young people he knew on Long Island. He took a few pictures of the students and promised them that the article would be in the weekly paper in two weeks. He noted that he wasn't going to be around to see it. They asked him for his address in Japan so they could send him a copy of the finished article. He wrote out his new APO address on a page of his notepad and handed it to one of the young men before wishing the students "good luck," and left the house.

A long-legged brunette in shorts followed him out of the house with the page from his notepad in her hand. "I'm the one with your new address, so you don't have to worry about getting a copy of your article. One of my younger brothers has a delivery route for the paper."

Desi knew he had seen those perfect legs before. "You look familiar, but I don't think you said anything today, and you were seated behind a few people."

"My name is Mellissa," the tall young woman said as she walked up closer to Desi. "We sort of met in a parking lot a couple of weeks ago when I was with a friend."

"Oh yeah, you were driving a station wagon and your friend had a pronounced Southern accent."

"She's an Army brat too, but she has spent a lot of time in Alabama."

"I don't see your car today," Desi said. "Do you need a ride somewhere?"

"You wouldn't be going past the Education Center, would you?"

Desi reached out and opened the passenger door of his car for her. "It's on the way back to my office."

While Desi drove to the Education Center, neither of them said a word. Mellissa's long, light brown hair was tossed around in the wind coming through the open passenger window. She was smiling and appeared to be content, enjoying the sunshine on her lovely face.

As Desi pulled his car into the Education Center, he spotted Mellissa's family's station wagon with the bumper sticker indicating that it was owned by an officer assigned to Fort Knox.

"We found your car," Desi said as he pulled his Super Beetle alongside the station wagon.

"It's the car my mother usually drives. She works here part-time. Her name is Betty. You may have met her, or my father who works over at the Armor School."

"I've written a few articles about tank training and efforts to develop a new tank, as well as about armor officers from other countries visiting or training at the Armor School. I've probably run into your father before."

"Both of my parents seem to know you. My father was telling my mother the other night about a reporter from the *Turret* who was leaving Fort Knox and was getting an Honorary Member of the Armor School certificate, signed by the Commanding General of Fort Knox and his Deputy. That had to be you."

"I guess it is because I received that at an office party yesterday evening. I think it is on the back seat, along with some other things I received." Desi reached back and pulled out a framed certificate. He showed it to Mellissa. "I also was presented with an Army Commendation Medal. It would all be a bit surprising for my friends back in New York."

Mellissa leaned over and gave him a kiss on the cheek. "Congratulations," she said before hopping out of the car. Then, just as she started to walk away, she turned and walked back. She stuck her head through the passenger window of the car. Desi and Mellissa stared at each other for a moment before she said, "Thanks for the ride."

"Thank you," Desi said, without trying to express why he was thanking her.

When Desi got back to the *Turret* office, he turned in the roll of film he had used to take shots of the students. He found himself hoping that he had Mellissa in one of the photos of the college students. He started typing up his notes of the interviews, but he still didn't have what he thought would be a good lead-in to the article. He'd have to write it the next day - his last day in the office. Clearly, he was going to be feeling the energy of deadline pressure when wrapping things up that week.

He thought about how Mellissa introduced herself and found himself typing out their conversation. Desi realized he totally forgot to ask her about what school she went to, what her major was, or any of the other things that college students talk about all the time. Worst of all, he hadn't even gotten her last name.

He consoled himself with the fact that he hadn't even gotten her first name in their encounter a couple of weeks earlier in a parking lot on Gold Vault Road. She was wearing short shorts that day, which must have totally distracted him.

He tossed his notepad into a desk draw and took the notes he typed out; in case he got a chance that evening to think about how he was going to tie all the quotes together. He walked out into the main office and found that everyone had already left. He looked at his watch. He had just enough time to get to his apartment in Radcliff, change from his khaki uniform into his civilian clothes, and then get to the restaurant where he was meeting the MacNamaras.

Strangely, the minute he got back into his car he could visualize Mellissa being in the passenger seat next to him again. And then there was a replay of her leaning over to plant a kiss swirling around in his head.

At dinner with PFC MacNamara and her father, where Desi more than made up for not having lunch, there was no talk of her case. They talked about the area in Pennsylvania, due south of Ithaca, where Cynthia grew up. Desi told them about how he was planning to take the LSAT in Tokyo and apply to a couple of law schools in New York, as well as to the law school at U of L. Desi gave Cindy MacNamara an index card with his new APO address at the headquarters of the Army Communications Command in Japan. She gave Desi a hug.

When he drove back towards his apartment, his thoughts drifted off to when Mellissa walked back to thank him for the ride. In his re-imagination of that pause, with Mellissa's head inside the passenger window and staring at one another, there would have been time for another kiss. Not a kiss on the cheek, but a profoundly deep kiss on the lips that expressed a longing for many more.

But without knowing her last name, he wondered if he would ever experience that sensation. Desi struggled to come up with a way to determine her last name without asking Linda if she knew Mellissa's mother. Maybe he could just ask Linda a general question about the people she worked with and not mention Mellissa. Once he had Mellissa's last name, he could figure out a way to get her telephone number, and then he would call her parents' house in hopes that she would be home. But what would be the chances of that?

Reality started to settle in for Desi. Clearly, there was no reasonable purpose for him calling her house that night. It was just that he wanted to have her back in the empty passenger seat of his car.

Desi tried to focus on what he had to pack when he got back to his place. He had to decide what he needed for the next week or so and pack up whatever he was sending to Japan through the transportation office. His thoughts, instead, shifted to Penny and what she might be bringing over as a parting gift of some sort.

Penny was at the apartment when he arrived. She was sitting at the kitchen table with Linda, sharing a bottle of wine. Desi could hear Penny telling Linda about her weekend belly dancing in Tennessee as he came into the house. As Desi entered the kitchen, Penny pointed to Desi saying, "And this guy thinks I am crazy to go down to the Nashville area and dance on the weekends."

Desi shook his head. "I think you are crazy to be wearing those outfits to entertain drunk guys at private houses. I just hope that you are being very careful about the clientele. Linda knows what I am talking about."

Linda nodded. "There were a couple times in the Far East when things got dicey. The problems begin when some guys just want to believe that all exotic dancers are prostitutes. There was a particularly bad experience in Macau, with none other than Tammy Tompkins. We had a close call in getting out alive from a place that, at first, seemed like a quiet catering hall. And Tammy wasn't even a dancer. We just talked Tammy into going with us to Macau. I think we met at that bar in the Hong Kong Hilton. We had several drinks and were pretty wasted by the time we hopped on the ferry to Macau. Fortunately, I had some big surfer dude along as a chaperone."

Desi looked at Linda. "I don't think I've ever heard that story. But I know of at least one instance where Penny and her belly dancing mentor went to a place without any chaperones."

Linda looked at Penny. "Well, if I join you as a back-up belly dancer, I think I am bringing Sam."

"That would be fine," Penny said as if to settle the issue.

Desi looked around. "Where is Sam?"

"He took his guitar over to the Heritage House Theater for a rehearsal with Randy," Linda said.

"But his van is in the driveway," Desi responded.

Linda handed Desi a glass of wine. "The gate guards are not going to let him on post until he gets his van registered in Kentucky. The love mobile with California plates is generating questions around the headquarters area."

Desi stared at the glass of wine for a moment. "Maybe it's time for me to put my Kentucky plates on my car. If I have to show my registration to some trooper on the Jersey Turnpike on my way to New York, I am going to have to take out my Kentucky registration. My New York registration expired months ago."

"Won't that make you someone you are not?" Penny asked.

"I'll still have the NYU bumper sticker on my car. I don't think I'll be breaking our pledge to Stacey or succumbing to the Confederacy by using my Kentucky plate."

Linda looked at Desi who was still standing alongside the kitchen table. "Can you sit down for a minute and fill me in about what sort of pledge you made to Stacey?"

Desi nodded his head and sat down at the table. "The way the pledge started was that Penny and I were driving up to Louisville on Dixie Highway with Stacey and Charlie in the back seat. Several miles up the road from Fort Knox were about a dozen Klansmen in their white robes gathered around the flames in a metal oil drum. I made a mistake by stopping at the red light at the corner where they were congregating. One of the guys came over to my car with a leaflet in his hand and his Ku Klux Klan hood over his face."

"Was this in broad daylight or at night?" Linda asked.

"It was dark out, but it was not in the middle of the night. I think it was an hour or two after sunset during the last week of February; I'd guess around seven o'clock. The guy came over and was motioning for Penny to roll down her window," Desi said.

"I didn't roll down the window," Penny added. "I told Desi to go through the red light to get us the hell out of there."

"Charlie was the only one of us who wasn't freaked out by seeing a KKK guy walking up to our car," Desi said. "Stacey was shaking. She wanted to know why Charlie was so calm about what we saw. That's when we found out that Charlie had an uncle who was a 'Freedom Rider' in the 1960s. His uncle was a Korean War Veteran who went down South to join in with the mostly black civil rights marchers."

Penny nodded. "I knew I was never going to risk my neck like Charlie's uncle, but I also knew I had always wanted to be someone who takes a stand for social justice," Penny said. "I have friends who are doing social work and are part of social justice groups in Michigan. After actually seeing the Klan trying to intimidate people on a very public road, we came up with the pledge."

"It's pretty basic," Desi said. "If someone tries out a joke or story demeaning a minority group, you just don't laugh or encourage them."

"That's it?" Linda asked.

"Well, it also incorporates the Golden Rule, but that's not that much for people to remember; it's the Golden rule, plus not letting others get away with hateful remarks aimed against racial or ethnic groups."

"So, you do take a stand," Linda observed. "It is sort of like the 'Freedom Riders.' "

"It was enough for Stacey to call it the 'Freedom Riders Pledge,' " Penny said.

"Oh, did Linda show you the baskets that Stacey dropped off for me?" Desi said as he got up from the table and headed to his bedroom. He returned with two beautiful, sweet grass baskets. Desi sat them on the kitchen table.

"Is that some sort of metaphor?" Penny asked.

"A metaphor for what?" Desi said, a bit puzzled.

"Perhaps a message for you not to put all your stuff in one basket," Linda said. "Stacey clearly has strong feelings for you and is likely saying that you are her backup plan if she gets to Europe and Charlie is being the typical twenty-something male."

"Either that or she is sending the message to Desi to go ahead and be the typical young guy," Penny said as she extended her arm to gently punch Desi in his stomach.

"I am not looking to be the typical anything," Desi responded.

"Keep telling yourself that," Linda said with a laugh. "I know I wouldn't blame you if Penny spent the night here."

"That's not why I came over tonight," Penny protested.

"I know, I know," Linda said. "You're here to get your flute out of Desi's bedroom closet."

"And to give Desi this," Penny said as she took a large bag out from under the table. Inside the large cloth bag was something wrapped in tissue paper.

"For me?" Desi said with a tone of mock surprise. "What did I do to deserve this?"

"It's not so much what you have done, but what I hope you will do when you are in Japan."

"You want me to send you some postcards?"

"I expect that you will send me and my sister Nikki some postcards. I want some letters regarding your travels around the cities and seaside villages, as well as an account of hiking through the mountains. I want your insights into Japanese culture and what you are discovering about yourself."

"You're asking for quite a lot."

"I believe that I still hold the record for living with you longer than any other woman, don't I?"

"That is true," Desi admitted. "Stacey thought Emily might break your record of almost two months, but Emily bailed out in less than a month."

"I don't know that Desi was the cause of Emily leaving," Linda said. "Her parents seemed to have a lot to do with it."

"May I open this now?" Desi asked as he started ripping the tissue paper off a musical instrument case.

"Go ahead and open the case," Penny said. "I think you are going to like it."

"It looks like a Japanese wood flute," Desi said as he took a flute out of the case.

"My mother ordered it for me, but I think it would be best if you took it. You just have to promise to let me know if you get a chance to take it to the top of Mount Fuji."

"If you give me your parents' address, I will send your mom a thank you note."

"Actually, it was more Nikki's idea for me to give you the wood flute. You can send Nikki a note or give us a call at her apartment this weekend when my family is meeting in Manhattan to see the ships of Operation Sail."

"I am planning to be in Manhattan Sunday evening for the fireworks," Desi said. "It's a small world."

"And it's going to be a crowded apartment. My parents are going to sleep in Nikki's bedroom. Nikki's roommate is letting my uncle and aunt sleep in her room as she is planning to spend a few days out in the Hamptons with her family. Nikki and I are sharing the couch in the small living room. If you need a place to crash after the fireworks, you could share the couch with us. But I don't know if you would be comfortable with that arrangement."

Linda laughed. "Desi, in bed with two women… I'm confident he could make that work."

"Give me Nikki's telephone number and the address for her apartment. I'll give you a call Sunday afternoon."

"Sounds like Nikki's apartment might be great for some fireworks - after the chaperones fall asleep," Linda said with another laugh. "I have to drive over to pick up Sam. I'll see you or both of you in the morning."

Penny spent a couple of hours helping Desi pack two duffle bags and a suitcase to drop off at the transportation office. Desi packed his dress green uniform into a suit bag and another suitcase to travel with for the following week or so. Penny left in the morning wearing one of Desi's NYU T-shirts. Desi walked her out to her car wearing her Michigan souvenir T-shirt. They gave one another a brief kiss in the driveway. She pointed to his car. "Don't forget to put your Hardin County Kentucky plates on your VW."

Walking Alongside the Memorials and Monuments in Washington

On Saturday morning, Desi loaded his car and was heading to Washington by the time the sun was rising. It wasn't as long a drive as trying to make it all the way to Long Island in one day, but it was dinner time before he arrived at the Soldiers and Sailors Club in D.C. Desi remembered what Pamela Gaines told him on the phone call earlier that week. After she confirmed to Desi that she made his reservation at the Club, she recommended, before he checked in with the desk clerk, to take his dress greens into the men's room in the Club's lobby and change into his uniform. Whether or not he would get a better room based upon wearing his uniform, Desi knew he would never really be able to tell. But he took her advice and it seemed like he ended up with a decent-sized room.

Desi noticed that the message light was blinking on the phone when he got to his room. The message was from Pamela. She was looking to come over to the Club and take a walk around the monuments with Desi. The message sounded like she was not planning to come over with Rinaldo or anyone else.

Desi changed back into civilian clothes and walked downstairs to call her from the payphone in the lobby. As he arrived in the lobby, the clerk called out to him. "Hey, I've got a call for you. Do you want to take it on the house phone?" the desk clerk said as he pointed to a phone on an antique table.

"Sure," Desi replied.

Desi picked up the phone. It was Linda. She had just spoken to Emily and learned that Emily was back at her apartment in Virginia after spending a couple of days in Atlanta. Linda asked Desi if he would be interested in joining Emily for breakfast the next day. Desi responded with a "Maybe." Linda gave Desi the telephone number where he could reach Emily.

Desi decided to call Pamela first. After inviting Pamela to meet him at the Club for a walk, he waited a few minutes before he tried to call Emily. When he eventually brought himself to call Emily from the payphone, he hesitated with each coin as he added the required additional amount. The phone rang several times before Emily answered.

"Hey, it's your old roommate from Hardin County," he said before Emily could say hello.

"Yeah, I remember you. And I also remember you telling me that I shouldn't hesitate to call you if I ever needed anything."

"What do you need?" Desi asked.

"I need a date for a multi-faith breakfast my father is co-hosting tomorrow morning."

"Can you meet me here at the Soldiers and Sailors Club so we can walk in together?"

"Yeah, that's really close to where they're having their breakfast. I'll be in the lobby by eight."

"Anything else?"

"Well, it might soften up my father if you wore your Army uniform. We usually have one or two people at the table who are in the military. This year, I don't think we will have a full table, and probably no one else will be there in uniform. I'm trying to take your advice and give him a chance, so I' m being very nice to him, whether or not he deserves it at this point. He still hasn't leveled with my mother. "

"Are you planning to lower the boom on him tomorrow morning?"

"I don't know yet. It depends. My mother is in Philadelphia, at my grandmother's house. I could give her a copy of all the papers. I might tell my father to either fill her in on what is going on or get ready for her to hit the ceiling after I give her a copy of the papers."

"I'm heading up to Philadelphia for the parade tomorrow. I'll have breakfast with you and then probably get right on the highway heading north. You are invited to ride along."

"I'll think about it. I left my car at the airport in Atlanta, otherwise I would be thinking about driving up to see my mother and Grandmother. We've celebrated the Fourth of July in Philadelphia before. I think they might try to ring the Liberty Bell."

"But there is that crack."

Emily found herself indulging in a laugh. "You realize that you just made a crack about a crack."

"Maybe it's not the appropriate time to point out the imperfections of that symbol of our republic. But can't we admit that nothing is perfect?"

"Least of all my current relationship with my father. Sorry to drag you to this breakfast but I have to talk to him, and I think I need your support. I don't need you there when I confront him about not making my mother aware of the promissory notes, but I will probably need to take you up on your offer to get me to Philadelphia tomorrow. I can't see myself going up to Philadelphia with my father. I certainly don't want to hear all his opinions on politics."

"If you mention a need for some Carter campaign buttons, that will be the signal for me to leave the table so you can speak privately with your father. By the way, don't let your father bully you with any nonsense about Carter losing. I think a majority of Americans want more than just confirmation that Nixon and Agnew were crooks. People are bothered by politicians who think they are above legal accountability and consequences. Gerald Ford hasn't made much of an argument as to why Nixon got a pardon. "

"Okay, I'll say: Desi, please bring in my 'Carter for President' buttons that I left in the cloakroom so I can put them on all of the tables."

Desi could hear Emily laughing on the telephone line.

He could also see Pamela entering the lobby. "I better let you go. I'll see you in the morning."

"Sleep tight," Emily said before they both hung up.

Even though Desi was rather tired from his drive to Washington, once Pamela linked arms with him and they hit the outside air, his senses came alive. The lights on the Washington Monument and Lincoln Memorial highlighted their majestic size. The sound of a military helicopter reverberated from one of the buildings surrounding the mall to the next, and then the next. There was also the sensation of Pamela's body pressed against him for the hour or so they walked around together.

There were no huge crowds that evening, but there were plenty of people, mostly clustered in groups. The clusters of people seemed to move in a deliberate, reverent manner as they paid their respects to the symbols of American Democracy.

After they got back to the Soldiers' and Sailors' Club, they sat and talked in the lobby for another hour. Pamela told him about Rinaldo cutting off his long hair and beard and telling his commander he wanted to get out of the Army, go back to Puerto Rico and be a healthcare worker. He had decided he never again wanted to get assigned to Panama or any other part of Central or South America.

Despite giving her an index card with his new APO address, Desi had the good sense not to talk about ever seeing her again.

Desi later learned that Rinaldo negotiated an assignment as a recruiter in San Juan. Pamela, in a birthday card she sent Desi later that summer, also advised him that she would join Rinaldo in Puerto Rico after her enlistment was up. Pamela's plan was to get a job in the travel industry in San Juan. She might give modeling another shot as she could see herself posing in a bikini to promote the beaches of Puerto Rico. Pamela, in that correspondence, also mentioned being engaged to Rinaldo.

After Desi walked Pamela to a taxi stand and went back to his room, he dug out the last sandwich he had made for his trip to Washington. He ate it, along with an apple, and went to sleep without watching the news on television.

Giving Almost Everyone a Chance on the National Holiday

Desi was up at dawn and walking around the National Mall with his camera. He remembered the first time he took pictures of the iconic structures, then with a very simple plastic camera, on a sixth-grade field trip. Desi figured Linda might be able to use shots of the Lincoln Memorial and the Washington Monument in her project. He also got what he thought was a great shot of the Capitol in the early morning light. Then, he raced back to the Club so as to be ready when Emily arrived.

Emily had overslept, so they ended up walking into the breakfast a little late. Some preacher with a southern drawl was finishing the Benediction and was ending it with a couple of "Lord Jesus" references. Desi looked at Emily. "Isn't this supposedly a multi-faith event?"

"Some of these guys never seem to be able to understand how to address an audience other than their own choir. My father tells them that even the apostles were considerate of the customs and beliefs of the Greeks and the Jews, but they seem to think they are too important to extend such courtesy."

"I do see rabbis in the audience," Desi observed.

"Let's get over to my father's table. He's sitting there all alone."

Desi let Emily take the lead as they made their way through the dozens of tables in the ballroom.

Emily's father smiled at them as they walked in his direction. The preacher who had done the Benediction was also walking towards the same table. Emily's father stood up and kissed Emily on the cheek. The southern preacher then shook Emily's father's hand and wanted to take him aside for a private conversation. Emily and Desi decided to hit the buffet line for some eggs, bacon, and biscuits.

When they got back to the table, Emily's father was still having a conversation with the same preacher. They stopped talking when Desi and Emily sat down. Emily's father reached his hand over Emily to shake Desi's hand. "Thanks for stopping by for breakfast" is all he said. Then, he stood up and announced to the preacher that he would be back in a few minutes, after he checked on something.

"So, Emily," the preacher said. "I hear from your father that you've graduated from college and are working here in Washington with some lawyers."

"That's pretty much the story," Emily replied before taking another bite of her biscuit.

"And you, young man?" the preacher asked.

"I'm an Army journalist and I'm on my way to Japan for a year or so," Desi answered.

"Then Desi is planning on going to law school," Emily added.

"And then you'll be getting your Jewish Doctor's degree," the preacher said with a snicker. There was an awkward pause as neither Desi nor Emily gave him the laugh he expected.

"You're Christian, aren't you?" the preacher said finally.

"I consider myself a monotheist at this point in my life," Desi answered.

"So you don't go to church anymore?" the preacher asked.

Desi shook his head. "No, but I am hoping to stop by the National Cathedral this morning to get a picture before we head up to Philadelphia, and then, hopefully, New York."

"I'm not sure I am going all the way with you," Emily blurted out.

There was another awkward minute or so when no one at the table spoke.

Emily cleared her throat and looked at Desi. "Desi had a religious experience a couple of years ago and saw an image of Jesus. And what is especially amazing is that he had an agnostic as a witness."

"And did the agnostic see and believe in Jesus?" the preacher asked.

"No. She is still struggling with whether there is any purpose to her life," Desi said.

"So, she is still a sinner," the preacher announced.

"Perhaps, but she is not hypocritical," Desi responded.

"What is he saying, Emily?" the preacher asked.

"It's one of Desi's philosophical observations," Emily said quietly with her head down.

"I'm not sure I get it," the preacher said.

Emily raised her head and stared him in the eyes. "Perhaps you don't, but it is quite simple. If you say you believe that God gave you a purpose to be on this earth, then you have to behave in a manner, in thought, word, and deed, as if you are fulfilling God's purpose. You can't make hateful comments about Jews or black people or do hurtful things to those who are already hurting."

The preacher looked at Desi. "You know we just met, but I'm getting the sense that you are very unkind." He stood up and started walking away quickly, practically bumping into Emily's father, who was trying to get back to the table.

The preacher then looked at Emily's father. "Where did Emily find that guy?" he snarled.

When Emily's father got to the table, he asked Emily what happened with the preacher.

"We didn't seem to be agreeing on much, nor very agreeable to one another," Emily replied.

"He's a bit insensitive at times, but you have to give him a chance," implored Emily's father.

Emily looked at Desi. "Go get the car and meet me out front."

Then she turned to her father. "I am sick of giving your friends extra chances. Where did it get us with Pastor Rick?"

Emily's father sat down at the table. "Can we smooth things out?"

Emily merely shrugged.

When Emily came out to Desi's car ten minutes later, she was still bristling with a combination of frustration, anger, and indignation. "He talks like he is the only righteous person alive. Well, I told him that I'm not giving him any more chances to be honest with me, or, more importantly, with my mother. He knows I have documents that will drive my mother up the wall."

"I'm sorry that things came to this."

"It was only a matter of time, and the time probably had to be today. I don't expect to be able to speak to him one on one like that again for at least a few months. And I also knew you would have the getaway vehicle ready," Emily said as she locked the passenger door.

"Just like a movie about getting out of an Iron Curtain country with the microfilm?" Desi asked.

Emily leaned over and gave Desi a quick kiss on the lips as Desi put the VW into gear. "Do we get to do a love scene today?" she asked.

"First, we have to decide where we want to do it," Desi said with a smile. "The National Cathedral is not an appropriate spot, but maybe when we stop there, we'll get some divine guidance."

"Maybe we will see a 'quick time motel' where I can change out of this dress, and you can get out of that uniform. I'm sorry I put you to the trouble of wearing it today."

"Save all your apologies for the motel," Desi said.

"You could just give me one of your incredible hand jobs," Emily said as she hiked her pink chiffon dress up her thighs. "I've been pretty tense lately, and that confrontation at breakfast hasn't helped."

"Well, I can't guarantee anything with all the shifting I am going to have to do between here and the cathedral."

Emily adjusted the back of her seat into a more reclined position. "Tell me about when we made that stop at my old make out spot near Mama Boone's house. Remember when we went down the road that led to the river. I knew it was going to be exciting with you, but I wasn't expecting the excitement to overwhelm me like it did." Emily took Desi's right hand off the steering wheel and placed it on the inside of her thigh.

"I think we talked about outdoor sex, didn't we?" Desi asked as he brought his hand up her thigh and between her legs. Her panties already felt moist.

"I think that was when I told you that I had a treehouse in my parents' backyard."

"Maybe we should stop there today on the way to Philly?"

"Don't stop. This sounds crazy, but I am almost there just thinking about what we did in that tree house."

Every time Desi had to shift, in his most seductive voice, he would ask Emily to tell him what she remembered about their tree house experiences.

About a block from the cathedral, he felt her whole body tighten. Emily moaned as her thighs squeezed Desi's hand and fingers. Then, she leaned her head against the passenger window and closed her eyes. Desi let her rest in his car as he got out with his camera in hand and headed to the front of the cathedral.

A couple of young women, one with an acoustic guitar and the other with a flute, were performing what sounded like a Bob Dylan song on the sidewalk for the people who were leaving after a Sunday morning service. Their instrument cases were strategically placed on the sidewalk to receive donations without impeding anyone passing by.

Desi took a few photos of the exterior of the cathedral and then walked inside. He took a couple of photos of the interior and then walked outside to put a dollar into the guitar case of the woman who had given him a smile as he was taking the exterior photos.

After thanking Desi, she took another look at Desi. "You were out by the Washington Monument this morning taking pictures, weren't you? You weren't in your uniform then, but I knew I recognized you."

"Yeah," Desi said. "You were out early too?"

"We tried to set up on the National Mall, but the police kept telling us to move. They said they were getting ready for what could be over one hundred thousand protesters on the mall. Someone from this church saw the hassle we were getting from the cops and gave us a ride here. The people at this church don't seem to mind our playing here." The young woman held out her hand to Desi. "My name is Leah. My friend's name is Esther. We are known as the Connecticut Communists."

"And I'm Desi," he said as he shook Leah's hand. "Is your band from the State of Connecticut or Connecticut Avenue?"

"We are from the State of Connecticut, near Danbury. We are students at the University of Bridgeport."

"Bridgeport is pretty much across the Long Island Sound from where I was born."

"What's a dude from Long Island doing in the Army?"

"Well, this morning I'm checking out the cathedral. I think I just got a good photo of the stained-glass Space Window that contains a moon rock."

"That's really in there?"

"The lighting was tricky, but I think I got a shot that will show it . And there are rocks and cut stones from historic sites in Israel."

"Do you think it would be alright if I went in to take a look?" Leah asked.

"I think there is still some time until the next service for you and your friend Esther to go in and look."

"Esther is a bit concerned about being recruited if she steps foot inside a church. She had a bad experience with the Jews for Jesus movement a couple of years ago. But I might go inside."

"I'm going out to my car for a couple of minutes to get my civilian clothes and tell my roommate from Kentucky that I found a place to change in the basement."

"It's not one of those churches I've read about where they keep corpses in the basement, is it?"

"It's a nice clean basement. I've read that during the Cuban missile crisis, the basement was filled with water. They were going to use it as drinking water in the event of nuclear war."

"Sounds like people could come and pray for the best but stay for the worst."

Desi nodded his head in agreement. Out of the corner of his eye he could see Emily in her pink dress, walking in his direction. "Let me introduce my friend Emily to you and Esther."

"Esther is definitely going to be asking Emily about where she got that dress. Esther and I may be in our hitchhiking clothes, but we both appreciate a great outfit. We're trying to get some money together so we can get to Philadelphia. We think that's where the big protest is really going to happen."

"Well, let me talk to Emily about whether we're making a stop in Maryland or if we're heading straight up to Philadelphia."

The Pursuit of Happiness Tour Heads North

Fifteen minutes later, Desi and Emily had changed their clothes in the bathrooms of the cathedral's basement and figured out how to not only arrange their passengers, but also Leah's and Esther's musical instruments and backpacks in Desi's car. As they left the parking lot of the Washington National Cathedral, Leah said, "We are off to the City of Brotherly Love." She gave Esther's leg a squeeze.

Esther replied, "I'm not sure how Philadelphia got that name, but I don't think it had to do with gay rights. It might have had something to do with religious freedom."

Leah laughed. "I thought you were a history major."

"Art history. And I'm still an undergraduate," Esther responded.

Emily turned around in her seat. "The name of the city comes from one of the Greek words for love and the word for brother to mean love for one's fellowman. I know a lot about the history because my mother's father's family has lived in the Philly area for several generations. You probably heard about William Penn, who was persecuted in England for his Quaker faith but managed to convince an English king that there should be a refuge for Quakers and other religious minorities of Europe in what is now Pennsylvania."

Esther nodded her head, "Yeah, I remembered something about Pennsylvania and religious freedom, or freedom from having to obey the restrictions imposed by someone else's religious beliefs."

"Different strokes for different folks," Leah said.

When they got to the interstate, Leah lit up a joint and passed it to Emily, who had one of their backpacks between her feet. Emily took a full deep hit and offered it to Desi, who declined. She then turned to Leah and asked, "Do you mind if I take Desi's turn for myself?"

"No problem," Leah said. "We have plenty. But let me warn you that this shit can sneak up on you so that one minute you are thinking it isn't very strong and then you're taking your bra off and throwing it out the window."

"What do you think about that, Desi?" Emily asked.

"I guess, because I am already braless, there's no point in me smoking it."

Leah and Ester laughed.

"Don't encourage him by laughing at his jokes," Emily warned. "Or with giving him thoughts about us all going braless," she added. Emily handed the joint back to Leah.

"Is he your guy?" Leah asked. "You do make a good-looking couple, especially when you are wearing that gorgeous dress." Leah took a hit and handed the reefer stick to Esther.

"You don't like my Kentucky Wildcats T-shirt?" Emily asked.

Esther took a hit before making a handoff back to Emily. Esther asked, "Did it come with the bare midriff and no sleeves look, or did you customize it?"

"I did make some alterations while I lived at Desi's apartment for about a month." Emily took another deep draw of the pot smoke. "But I don't think he belongs to me anymore, if he ever did."

"I did invite Emily to ride to New York with me today. But I think she is bailing out on me again."

"It's a lot more complicated than that, and Desi knows it. It was complicated right from the start because he always had a beautiful girlfriend from his college days one telephone call away."

"I think Emily is very beautiful, don't you Esther?" Leah said. "She looks like she could have been a real wildcat in Desi's apartment."

Without comment, Desi kept on driving as the three women finished the joint.

When they were about halfway to Philadelphia, there was a sudden change in the noise from the rear engine compartment. Desi pulled the car over to the side of the road. As Leah and Esther continued to doze in the back seat, Desi looked over at Emily. "I think a belt snapped."

"Are you going to be able to fix it?" Emily asked.

"I think we're going to have to ask the ladies to get out so I can get my tools out from behind the back seat," Desi said as he got out of the VW to check the engine. He opened the engine compartment and looked inside. The fan belt appeared to be severely frayed. After Leah and Esther were out of the car, along with their instrument cases, Desi pulled the back of the rear seat forward. He saw his tool kit, but not the spare belt he usually kept in the car. Desi looked under the seats, opened the front hood, and looked under his suit bag and Emily's small suitcase.

Emily, Leah, and Esther stood in their shorts and tight t-shirts nearby as a few eighteen wheelers rolled by, with the truckers honking their horns. A guy in a pickup truck pulled over in front of Desi's car and got out.

"Is Desi good with his hands?" Esther asked Emily.

"I can testify to the fact that he can do more for a woman with one hand while driving a stick shift than most men can do in a bed," Emily said, sounding more than a little bit stoned.

"Good to know," Leah said.

Desi emerged from his car with a new fan belt in hand after checking behind the backseat again and looking under his suitcase. "I got it," he said triumphantly.

The guy in the pickup truck joined him by the back of the Super Beetle.

"Hey, man," the pickup truck driver said. "You look like you are hauling some sweet cargo. Do you need any help with anything?"

Desi looked up from under the hood. "I think I can handle everything."

"Yeah, who wouldn't want to?" The pickup truck driver said as he looked again at the three young women. "Hey ladies, if any of you need some transportation sooner, rather than later, I have some room in my cab."

Leah and Esther looked at the mud flaps covering a portion of his rear tires. The mud flap design was an outline of a very busty woman. There were many sexually suggestive bumper stickers on the pickup truck. Leah and Esther, with a chorus of "No thanks" shook their heads.

Emily came over to the back of the car to be closer to Desi and took a heavy wrench from his toolbox. She nonchalantly swung it a few times as Desi worked on his car.

The guy walked back to his pickup truck and drove away.

Leah started laughing. "Did he really think any of us would get in the cab with him? The guy had a bumper sticker that read: 'Gas, Grass, or Ass – No one rides for free'."

"That's not brotherly love in my book," Emily said.

"Time to get back on the road," Desi said as he finished adjusting the new fan belt. "I'll stop at the next rest stop and check it again."

At the rest stop, about ten miles later, he did check the tension on the belt and the fan wheel he had disassembled and reassembled to install the new belt. Emily, Leah, and Ester went into a visitors' center. Desi followed a few minutes later and went into the men's room. When he came out, he saw Emily on a pay phone. He walked around the building to another pay phone. He dialed the number for Debi's apartment, but the line was busy. When he walked back around the building, he caught Emily hanging up the phone with a slam. She spotted him.

"My mother is blaming me for my father not wanting to drive to Philadelphia today," Emily said as she looked through her purse for more change. "I started to ask her if I could just have lunch with them and then leave. I'd rather go to New York with you instead of staying for dinner and watching the fireworks in Philadelphia with my grandmother."

"So you're going to call your mother back?" Desi asked.

"Yeah, why? You still want me to come to New York with you, don't you?"

Desi nodded his head.

"It's Debi, isn't it? You have plans to share the fireworks in New York with her, right?"

"I don't know. I never know with her."

"Forget it. Just drop me off at my grandmother's house in Philadelphia. Better yet just drop me off near where the parade is going to be, and I'll have my mother pick me up downtown. That way I can talk to my mother without my grandmother being around."

"I'm sorry that the day is going to end that way."

"You know that Daisy is probably getting ready to get on her brother's boat with Roger and sail down the East River to New York Harbor. Daisy and Roger will be, along with Daisy's brother and sister-in-law, checking out all the tall ships and finding a good spot to watch the fireworks later," Emily said.

"I'm sure Daisy told you that we were invited to join them. I heard through Roger that you were convinced you couldn't get to New York in time. I think we could have had them pick us up in the sailboat somewhere around Hoboken. "

"That was before I decided to leave my car in Atlanta and was able to get to D.C. by last night," Emily said sternly. "You're trying to blame this on me."

"Not really. Maybe we just have to acknowledge that it's Daisy's and Roger's time to be together as everything seems to be clicking along smoothly for them."

"I still plan to write to you in Japan, no matter how disappointing today gets," Emily said with her wonderful smile.

"Let me try calling Debi's apartment one more time before we get back in the car."

"Do what you think you have to do. I'm going to hang out with the other stray cats; maybe they have another joint to share."

"It would probably be better to smoke it outside rather than in my car."

"Now who's getting uptight? Once Debi's name is mentioned you start transforming into Mr. Uncool."

"Maybe she's not even in the city this weekend but out in the Hamptons or at Fire Island with her sister. It's probably her damn roommate tying up the phone."

"You're not going to be able to relax until you find out," Emily said as she walked away.

"See you back at the car in ten minutes," Desi said as he again fed coins into the phone.

Desi was slumped over his steering wheel when the three women came strutting towards his car, each spinning their bra on a finger. He started to smile. Emily, Leah, and Esther were all laughing and bouncing their braless breasts in their T-shirts.

"I knew we could get Desi smiling," Emily said as she opened the passenger door and pulled the passenger seat forward to allow Leah and Esther to climb into the rear seat. "Is Debi going to make you smile today?"

Desi shook his head from side to side. "No. She told the roommate she had to go to the airport. Something happened to her mother. The roommate said Debi left me a letter on her bed that I can pick up later today, but the roommate doesn't seem to know any more. All she really knew was that Debi appeared to be very upset and she was meeting Tammy at the airport."

Emily looked at the women in the back seat. "Tammy, Debi's sister, is Tammy Tompkins."

"The model?" Leah asked.

Desi looked back over his right shoulder. "Yes, the cocaine-crazed model. Unfortunately, Debi's mother has, lately, also been acting quite crazy."

"Maybe I should call my crazy mother and tell her I am going with you to New York," Emily said.

"Well, you can call her now or wait until we get to Philadelphia," Desi opined.

Emily sat quietly for a minute. "I am so wasted right now. I don't want to take the chance of her getting me into a conversation where she takes advantage of me being stoned. She will be able to hear it in my voice and start asking me stuff. Then I will really come off as being all fucked up."

"So, don't let her get you upset. Just wait until we get to Philadelphia," Desi suggested.

Emily, a Captive

When they arrived in Philadelphia, Emily still didn't sound like she was going to be able to convince her mother that the fireworks in New York with Desi would be a better plan for a young woman than hanging out with a grandmother. "Having to call my mother for permission to go to New York is ridiculous," Emily said as they parked Desi's VW a few blocks away from Independence Hall. After getting out of his car, she headed for a phone booth on a street corner.

The phone booth had most of the glass knocked out of it. The remaining pieces of glass were either scratched with names and obscene remarks or bore various forms of painted graffiti art. Emily stood inside the booth in her open-toed sandals, trying not to get any of the broken glass in between her toes. Her mother answered when she dialed the number for her grandmother's house.

Desi could see her nodding her head and hear Emily saying "Yeah" several times. Then, she turned her head the other direction and Desi couldn't hear what Emily was saying to her mother. Leah and Ester got out of the car to stretch their legs. Desi got out and stood with the driver's door open against his back and one hand on the roof of his VW. Leah walked around the car to stand next to Desi. "I think we want to ride with you to Manhattan. Esther has an old boyfriend whose mother just remarried. She has a three-bedroom place on Fifth Avenue between Eighth and Ninth. Can we leave our backpacks in your car and meet you at this phone booth around three?"

"You're going to meet up with your friends here?" Desi asked.

"If that's alright with you? We'll take our instruments with us in case we find a place to serenade an audience."

"It's alright with me. But don't be back later than three. I'm trying to be in Washington Square Park before six and I don't know if there will be traffic."

"That's where we want to be also," Leah said as she motioned for Esther to get her flute case from Desi's car. Desi pulled the driver's seat forward so Leah could get her guitar case out of the back seat.

"So, we're leaving our backpacks and our bras in your hands, ... or your car's backseat," Leah quickly added.

Leah and Esther walked towards Chestnut Street, turning a couple of times to wave to Emily, who remained on the payphone. Desi closed the driver's door and walked over to the phone booth.

He could again hear what Emily was saying. "No, I don't see any rioting here. I don't think grandma knows what she is talking about. There weren't 200,000 protesters in Washington either. I will stay safe for another fifteen or twenty minutes, or however long it takes for you to get here. Desi is not going to let me out of his sight."

Desi walked back to his car and opened the front hood. He took out Emily's small suitcase. Desi took two envelopes out of the large, zippered pocket in the front of his suit bag. He handed the two envelopes to Emily as she walked up to the car. "What's this?" she asked.

"They are the things you asked me to hang onto for safekeeping."

Emily held one of them in her right hand as if she could guess the contents by feeling its weight. "These are the loan guarantee documents?"

Desi nodded his head. "And the other contains the remaining prints of the photos from the night in the hotel in Louisville, plus all of the negatives. Your father burned a lot of the prints at your Grandma Boone's house already. Please assure your parents that I am not keeping any of them."

"But I want you to have at least one photo of the two of us. I know I may need to keep a couple for a cold and lonely night."

"Let's sit in the car while we wait for your mother, and you can decide which one I get to keep. There's also the matter of the bra you took off earlier today. I guess that's somewhere in the car."

"I think I tucked it into the glove compartment."

When they got to the car, Emily went through all of the photos and offered two to Desi. "I think I'll take the one of me covering your nipples with my hands and kissing your neck."

"Yeah, that was a special one. It captures the feeling I had at that moment. It was a sensation that we were meant to be lovers," Emily said while leaning over to kiss Desi on the lips.

"Maybe we both had a sense of that possibility from the first afternoon we met," Desi said before returning the kiss.

For the next ten or fifteen minutes, they hugged and kissed as if they were trying to store the embraces for the next year of separation. Suddenly, there was a knocking on the hood of the car. Emily's mother was standing by the passenger door. Emily gathered the two envelopes that had slipped onto the floor and got out of the car. Her mother scolded her. "If those bras in the back seat are yours, then put one of them on. You can't bounce your way into your grandmother's house."

Emily looked at the bras in the backseat. "Those belong to two college girls we met today. My bra is in the glove compartment."

"Good place for it," Emily's mother said as she steamed off to her car. "Get your stuff and let's go."

Emily remained in the passenger seat for a minute or so longer. "You know I am crazy about you. Not sure if I can provide you with any more proof given my current circumstances." Emily took her blue bra out of the glove compartment and put the photo Desi selected on his back seat on top of the two bras the young women left.

"Make time to write me, Emma Lee Miller," Desi called out as Emily clutched her bra and the two envelopes to her chest and carried her small suitcase towards her mother's station wagon.

Chapter XIII

RENDEZVOUS WITH A LADY CARRYING A TORCH

Desi reached to retrieve the photo from the back seat and looked at it for a few moments before trying to fit it into the glove compartment. He popped the front hatch of the Super Beetle again and got out of the car. He took out his suit bag and put the photo in one of the zippered pockets in the front. Desi rearranged things in the car so that the backpacks of the hitchhikers went into the front compartment and his suit bag got wedged in with his suitcase and sleeping bag that was stored behind the back seat. He took his black tankers beret, which had been on the ledge behind the back seat and facing the back window and dropped it on the two bras. Satisfied with his organizing efforts, he grabbed a map out of a door pocket and went over his planned route to New York City.

Desi took out his money clip with his list of telephone numbers. He walked over to the damaged telephone booth. Desi counted out the change he had left in his pocket before he dialed Nicole's apartment.

Not knowing if he would be able to distinguish Nicole's voice from Penny's, he listened very carefully to detect any distinguishing intonation in the "Hello" he heard after someone picked up. A voice said, "Hello, Desi?"

"Penny?" he said.

"Desi, where are you? We are ready to go out and get some lunch. Are you in Manhattan?"

"I just got to Philadelphia a little while ago. I'm planning to be in the Village by six. Are you free to catch the fireworks with me?"

"My aunt and uncle, along with my parents, have arranged for us to be on a boat this evening so we can watch the fireworks from the water. I told them that you love boats and have been to sea. There is room for you. My uncle, the history teacher from the Boston area, is interested in meeting you. I showed him a copy of the article you wrote about Henry Knox. I also told him about your relative, the member of the Continental Congress, who helped organize a relief effort on Long Island to get supplies to the people of Boston during the British occupation."

"Please tell them I will be very happy to pay for my own ticket. It's amazing that you were able to get seats on a boat. Can I meet you somewhere near Washington Square Park between six and six thirty?"

"Is there a place where we can have dinner around then?"

"Well, it is not an inexpensive place, but the restaurant at the Fifth Avenue Hotel on the corner of Ninth Street would be my choice."

"Is that the hotel NYU placed you and other students in during your senior year?"

"You got it. The name of the restaurant is 'Feathers'."

"That sounds perfect. But you have to tell my family the story about how Stevie Wonder and his band were also staying at that hotel and would sometimes practice in one of the ballrooms. And you have to tell them about how Stevie Wonder would sometimes come down to the restaurant and just start playing in the piano bar."

"I'll leave out the part about how some young lady, who I had invited over to the hotel for a drink, practically fainted when she realized who was sitting at the piano."

"That would be good," Penny said. "Otherwise, it might raise questions as to whether that young lady was so impressed that she insisted on seeing your living quarters upstairs."

"I'll only provide the PG version of that story. Actually, I've never told that story with the name of the freshman girl who seemed totally infatuated with me after that evening."

"For how long was she mesmerized?"

"I think it was two or three weeks. Not any record."

"Alright, we're going to head out and have some lunch. We'll walk around after that for a while and then meet you at the restaurant around six fifteen. I think they want us on the boat by eight."

"I think that may give us enough time to have something to eat and walk over to the piers," Desi said.

Desi Salutes from the Rooftops

Desi moved his car to a parking garage after taking his camera from his camera bag. He stowed the camera bag which contained a second camera body and a few lenses in the front compartment.

He walked down Chestnut Street until he heard some guitar and flute music on a side street, which prompted him to go looking for Leah and Esther. The street he went down was filled with people, and it took him a few minutes to find the members of the Connecticut Communists band. There were a few young people around them wearing University of Bridgeport T-shirts. Desi took the lens cap off his camera and clicked off a couple shots of Leah and Esther performing in an alleyway. Some guy in a Thus Spoke Zarathustra T-shirt called out from the alley that they were "going to party up on the roof." He called out to Leah and Esther by name and told them they could "give a concert on the roof, just like the Beatles."

They stopped playing their instruments and joined a group going up a fire escape. Leah motioned to Desi to come along with them. The new performance area was a flat roof atop a second story building. There was a utility shed in the center of the roof and the guy with the Zarathustra T-shirt spotted a couple of loose shingles on the shed that he immediately started using as Frisbees to toss to members of his entourage. What seemed harmless at first soon turned into a contest to inflict pain when the shingles started getting tossed at peoples' legs. A couple of girls in shorts complained when the rough side of the shingles scraped their bare skin. The guy in the Zarathustra T-shirt merely laughed. Leah, who had put her guitar in its case before climbing the fire escape, walked over to him and confronted him by tapping him in the back with her guitar case. "Cut the shit with the shingles, Cliff!" Leah said. He turned around and glaring at her. "I mean it, or we are going back down to the street."

There was the sound of a marching band coming up the street. On the corners of the building facing the street were American flags on ten-foot poles. Cliff went over to one of the flags and lifted it loose from its mooring. He waved it around and yelled at the marching band before sarcastically shouting out a request that they "play some Led Zeppelin."

An attractive young woman went over to him and put her arm around him, as if she was trying to calm him down. He started to hand the flag to her and then noticed that the ten-foot flagpole was actually two five-foot wooden poles screwed together. Cliff unscrewed the poles and handed the five-foot section with the flag to the woman beside him. He then found one of the shingles from the shed and held it like a shield. He approached Leah with the pole in one hand, as if it were a lance, and the shingle in the other. Esther moved alongside Leah, as if she was ready to wield her flute case in Leah's defense. Desi joined them and held the strap of his camera so as to make enlarging circles with the dangling camera.

"This does not seem very fair," Cliff surmised. "Three against one, and that dude has a metal camera to swing at my head."

Desi hung his camera strap on Esther's shoulder and went over to the flag on the other corner of the building. He unscrewed the poles and handed the pole with the flag to Leah. "Does this make things fair?" Desi asked.

Then, there was the sound of marching Army combat boots on the street. A company of what appeared to be recent recruits were moving up the street in formation. Most of the people on the sides of the street were clapping and waving small American flags, but there was a significant sound of booing also coming up from the street. An honor guard carrying several flags, including a large Stars and Stripes, was at the lead of the marching soldiers. As they came alongside the building, Desi put his hand over his heart. Several of the other young people on the roof followed with Desi's salute.

After the first few rows of troops marched by, Cliff went to the edge of the building and held out a shingle as if in preparation to throw it at the soldiers. "Baby killers," he shouted, and extended his arm back to throw the shingle. Desi grabbed his wrist before Cliff could release the shingle.

Cliff wrestled his wrist away from Desi's grip, dropping the shingle. Desi put his foot on the shingle. "The Vietnam War is over," Desi said. There aren't any more American planes bombing villages there."

Cliff raised his wooden pole and took a swing at Desi. "I came to Philadelphia to protest and say, no more Vietnams. "

"Okay, you have the right to say that, but not to hurt those young guys down there who have nothing to do with Vietnam," Desi said as he raised his pole. "You remember what The Beatles said about 'revolution' when it comes to 'destruction'?"

"I am not really sure I agree with them, so you better get ready for some destruction right now," Cliff said as he took another swing at Desi.

"Are you determined to fight me until I knock you off this roof or are you willing to stop when I force you to drop the pole you are holding?"

"I'm not dropping this pole," Cliff said as he repeatedly swung at Desi's body only to hammer the wood of his pole against the resistance provided by Desi's fluid moves of his pole. Out of frustration, Cliff brought his weapon back even further to get a bigger swing. Desi used the opening to put the end of his stick into Cliff's abdomen, bending Cliff over in pain. Desi then quickly raised and brought down his pole to smack Cliff's hand hard enough to knock the pole out of Cliff's grip and bring him to his knees. Desi stepped behind him and put his feet on Cliff's calves so Cliff could not stand back up. Cliff put his injured hand to his lips. Desi put his stick against the back of Cliff's head.

"Do I have to give you a shot to the head to end this?" Desi asked.

Cliff shook his head from side to side.

"I want to hear you say that you are not going to throw anything more at anyone this afternoon, and that you will behave as a gentleman."

Cliff took his injured hand out of his mouth. "I will not throw things and will behave like a gentleman until sunrise tomorrow."

Desi stepped off of Cliff's legs and kicked Cliff's pole along the roof towards the woman who was holding one of the flags. "Please put the poles back together for that flag," Desi said to her. Desi went over to Leah and took the flag she was holding. He screwed the pole he was using as a weapon into the pole with that flag and took it to the corner of the building where he first got it. He managed to return the flag back to its original position.

Desi went over to where Leah and Esther were standing. "How about meeting me at that urban phone booth in about twenty minutes? I know it's only a little before two, but if I can get a quick photo of Independence Hall, I am ready to head to New York. Are you guys ready to go?" Leah and Esther nodded their heads in agreement.

When Desi arrived at Independence Hall and was adjusting his camera to get a good photograph, the bells in the city began to peal. He remembered that bells were scheduled to ring at 2 p.m. on the East Coast and throughout the United States as a communal commemoration of the signing of the Declaration of Independence. Desi waited until the call of the bells ended to take his pictures.

Even with Desi having to retrieve his car from the parking garage, Desi, Leah, and Esther were on their way to Washington Square Park by two thirty.

How Leah and Esther Became Known as the 'Connecticut Communists'

On the drive up to Manhattan, Leah and Esther were asking about why Emily was not part of their jaunt.

Desi's initial response was that Emily's parents were going through some problems, and Emily thought she needed to be with her mother. That seemed to be sufficient for the first part of the approximately 100-mile ride between Philadelphia and New York City.

Leah was riding in the passenger seat and seemed happy to talk about her parents. She revealed how they had a tough time getting along with one another after she went away to college. "I think they did try some counseling because they were going through some other changes. My father, who had been a firefighter alongside Esther's father, was starting a business supplying volunteer fire departments in the tri-state area with equipment. He was very busy getting orders for the equipment and recruiting some of the other Jewish firefighters, who either lived or had summer places in the Danbury area, to help with the new business."

"My dad is now his partner in the business," Esther volunteered from the back seat.

"Anyway, my mom started feeling like she had less and less time with my father. But she is now his bookkeeper. Things did work out."

"Well, Emily's father doesn't seem like the type of guy who would even consider going for counseling as he is not going to reveal very much in terms of how he feels or what is going on in his professional life," Desi commented.

"He's not cheating on Emily's mom, is he?" Leah asked.

"No, but he got financially involved with another guy who was a liar and a cheat. That guy is now gone, and Emily's father has been left to hold the bag, an empty bag."

Leah looked over at Desi. "So, this other guy, what kind of business was he in?"

"He was selling religion. 'Old Time', every word in the Bible had to be accepted as literal truth type of religion. He claimed to be raising money for spreading the wisdom of God through radio and television. "

Ester tapped Leah on the shoulder. "What was the name of that character that Burt Lancaster played in the movie we saw in film class? That guy sounds like the character in that movie."

"Elmer Gantry. I think Burt Lancaster got an Oscar for that role," Leah said.

"The two of you took a film class together?" Desi asked.

"It was a class that only dealt with movies made after World War II that won Oscars. My favorite was the one with Sophia Loren playing a widow who leaves Rome to go back to her home village. Her family argues about whether Mussolini should have teamed up with Hitler," Esther said.

"I think she got an Oscar for that movie," Desi said. "The name of the movie was *Two Women* because her character had her daughter with her."

"Did you take any film classes in college?" Leah asked.

"I majored in journalism at NYU, but I had the chance to take a documentary film class as an elective. During my senior year, I was also able to spend most of my Fridays in a television production class. The people in that class were majoring in various subjects, from computer science to acting, and, of course, there were some from the film school."

"Our friend, the one whose mother has the apartment near Washington Square Park, is transferring from Bridgeport to the NYU Film School. You are going to have to come over with us to his apartment and meet him," Esther suggested.

Desi turned his head briefly to Leah. "So, I know that Esther is an art history major, but what are you majoring in?"

"I am hoping to be a public-school reading teacher. I took the film class as an elective, but I now believe that some films can subtly convey meaning and wisdom, like with poetry, in a deeper way than the average book. Plus, it was one of the few electives that I could take with Esther."

"So, were there any films from Soviet Russia or about Marx?" Desi asked.

"I don't remember any. I really don't know much about Marx or the Soviet Union," Leah said.

"So why are the two of you called the Connecticut Communists?"

"My uncle, my father's brother, started calling us that when we didn't have a name for our band. He's a musician and has been down South, the Deep South, like Alabama and Mississippi. He hangs out with black musicians and walks in civil rights marches. He even rode on the interstate buses with the Freedom Riders, checking on how the local police did not enforce the law against discrimination. He told us that white people who hang out with black people are called 'Communists' by the segregationists in the South. When my uncle Saul saw us play at a club in Bridgeport with an audience of white and black college students, he said he came up with the idea for the name of our band. Since many of the Freedom Riders were Jewish, we felt comfortable with his idea, and it does have the right amount of ironic twist," Leah added.

"Connecticut, which probably has the country's largest number of decoy duck displays at home decorating stores and is known for its exclusive neighborhoods like Cos Cob and the rest of the Greenwich area, is not usually linked to communists," Esther said with a laugh.

"Well, your band's name is certainly alliterative," Desi added.

Desi, Leah, and Esther arrived at Washington Square Park around four thirty. Desi found an empty parking space on the north side of the park. He helped Leah and Esther with getting their backpacks on their backs and their musical instruments in hand for their trek up Fifth Avenue a couple of blocks. "You are coming with us to meet our friend Siggy, aren't you?" Esther asked.

"Actually, he's Esther's old boyfriend," Leah revealed. "But he's now with a rich, attractive NYU student who he met right after he moved in with his mom on Fifth Avenue. I think they are both taking a summer film class. Siggy has always had a roving eye. I've known him longer than Esther, but I was never stupid enough to date him," Leah added.

"But you were stupid enough to go out with that jerk Cliff for almost a year. How did that play out?" Esther countered. "Desi, did you know that guy Cliff, who you had to teach a lesson to on that rooftop, is someone who Leah practically lived with?"

"I am not going to criticize anyone for making an occasional mistake when it comes to romantic partners. I just find it sad when a woman keeps making the same mistake."

"Such as?" Leah asked.

"Mistakes like getting into relationships with married men," Desi said bluntly. "You two haven't fallen into that trap, have you?"

"No," Leah said adamantly. "Has that happened to Emily?"

"Emily's friend, we'll call her 'Linda,' suffered through a time when she was so vulnerable, she would go out with men who took advantage to only hurt her more. They would get her hopes up for a more stable life and then she would find out that she was only one of the fillies in their stable. One guy Linda met up with had all sorts of responsibilities, including a wife and kids."

Esther asked Desi, "So you don't want to be one of those sought-after guys who has a wife, but also a couple of girlfriends on the side? I thought that was the dream of most guys."

Leah looked at Desi. "You mean to say that if Siggy invites us to spend the night at his mother's apartment, you wouldn't be tempted to have sex with the two of us?"

"Let me be clear, I was talking about what a married man should not do. Did Emily say that I was married to her or anyone else?"

Leah and Esther laughed.

Desi walked towards his car. "I'm going to park my car in a nearby garage. What's the room number of Siggy's apartment?"

"It's six twelve," Leah answered.

Desi Has Three Options on Where to Spend the Night

When Desi walked over to Siggy's apartment building, he found Leah and Esther standing outside the entrance.

"What's up?" Desi asked.

"We checked our stuff with the doorman. Siggy went out for a walk with his girlfriend," Leah answered.

"I have to meet some people for dinner at six thirty, but it's only about five now. Would you like to walk with me over to St. Marks Place to get a letter?"

"Will there be any pictures of Tammy Tompkins and her sister at the apartment?" Esther asked.

"I'm sure there are. What is probably more entertaining is the window of the adult store that is located on the ground floor of the building where Debi lives."

"And Debi was your college girlfriend?" Leah asked.

"My junior and senior prom date in high school and my on again, off again lover all through college."

"Did you ever live together?" Esther asked.

"We talked about finding an apartment in the city and living together one summer, but it didn't happen."

"And you talked about the possibility of getting married someday?" Leah asked.

"But you chickened out and joined the Army instead?" Esther asked.

"From time to time, we talked about getting married, but I couldn't visualize that lasting very long. And Debi seemed to be thinking about it in the future but wasn't very clear on how we would get to a point where it would be more than just an expected thing to do."

"Why don't we walk over to Debi's apartment, and I'll see if her note even hints that she might still love me. I have to go to the St. Mark's Adult Store anyway to get a few things for a cousin of mine who's getting ready to go off to college around Labor Day."

"I'm up for a visit to the adult store," Esther said.

"I'll go with you to see what photos she left out in her room. If there is one of the two of you, she is feeling that she still wants or needs you in her life," Leah offered.

"I would also appreciate your take on the roommate, who mentioned more than once on the phone that I can stay in Debi's room tonight. She seems to have more than a casual interest in me crashing there."

"Why don't you suggest that I'll be helping you keep Debi's bed warm. I'll see how she reacts."

"I really don't think Debi is thinking that I would mess up the sheets of her bed with anyone else."

"It was just an idea as to how to get the roommate to reveal what she is planning for when you turn out the lights in Debi's bedroom tonight," Leah replied.

"We may need to think of another way to test what the roommate may be up to, but let's get going," Desi said. "I only have about an hour to get over there and back."

When Desi, Leah, and Esther got to Astor Place, Esther started tugging on Leah's arm. "Look across the street - I think it's Siggy and that girl he's been telling you about."

"I guess she really does exist," Leah responded.

"I want to go over there and give him a piece of my mind," Esther said.

"What good is that going to do when he has a new piece of you know what for tonight," Leah said. "What are you going to offer him, a pastrami sandwich between your legs? Besides, he is cool with us staying in his mother's apartment, so let's not mess that up."

"You told me that he's letting us stay in the apartment with him and his girlfriend tonight because he's told the girlfriend that we are gay. That pisses me off! I mean we have gay friends and I'm cool with people loving whoever they want but why should

I have to pretend something. I don't want to live with Siggy's rule about nobody mentioning that I was the one sleeping with him just a couple of months ago. "

"You told me that he was terrible in bed, so why do you care?"

"Maybe I'll tell her that Siggy was so bad in bed that I'm trying some girl-on-girl action now!"

"No, just don't mention that you ever slept with him," Leah cautioned.

"I still want to go over there and kick him in the nuts. Maybe Desi can find a stick and do to Siggy what he did to Cliff."

"That was a different kind of situation," Desi said. "That guy Cliff was looking like he was preparing to hit Leah."

"Desi, if I go over there and he starts menacing me, will you get a big stick and defend me?" Esther asked.

"If Desi pulls out his big stick, that sexy chick with Siggy may step forward and offer up her own body," Leah said.

Desi stopped walking. "I think I know that woman. She was in a couple of my classes. She's a tough one."

Esther started crossing the street, indifferent to the traffic. Leah called out to her, "You're going to get a ticket for jaywalking."

"I'm just going across the street to give Siggy a joint to smoke. It will probably put him to sleep and solve everything for me."

Desi and Leah walked to a crosswalk and waited for the light to change before following Esther to the other side of the street.

Desi and Leah watched Esther confront and engage Siggy and the woman he was with. "Is Siggy's female friend called Loretta?" Desi asked Leah.

"Yeah. How well do you know her?"

"She was in one of my journalism classes and one of my philosophy classes," Desi answered in a very matter of fact tone. "I remember that in the journalism class, when we had a guest lecturer who specialized in covering environmental matters, Loretta somehow managed to get everyone sidetracked onto an issue about whether it was acceptable to leave air conditioners on all day during an energy crisis. She made it sound like she wanted everyone's opinion, when she, in fact, acknowledged at the end that she had been running her air conditioner continuously and intended to keep doing so for as long as it took to keep herself comfortable."

"And were you guilty of contributing to the heat in her apartment?"

"I was brought up to believe that a gentleman does not reveal such personal matters, even when it pertains to one of the strangest women I ever met at NYU."

"Strange, because she refused to be environmentally considerate, or because she had a kinky side to her."

"Did Siggy tell you that she has a kinky side to her?"

"Not in so many words, but that is something that he sort of conveyed to me when I spoke to him about his new girlfriend."

"Then, maybe I can just flat out tell you. I did not feel comfortable with what she seemed to be into."

"Can you give me an example?"

"Well, I hadn't really talked to her in our classes. We would just smile at one another and maybe say hello. Then, one day at the student union, where I volunteered at the student radio station, she asked if I wanted to go to a movie series with her."

"She worked at the radio station also?"

"No, I'd been at the radio station, taking stuff from the wire services and rewriting it for the on-air people. I went downstairs to the cafeteria on a break, and she was sitting all alone, so I went over and sat with her. She told me there was a film series she wanted to go to but did not feel comfortable going alone. She offered to pay for my ticket if I went along with her."

"That doesn't sound all that strange," Leah said.

"Well, it turned out that the NYU Student Union was hosting the Greenwich Village Erotic Film Festival that year, and that is what she dragged me along to. The movies were so trashy and depressing that I told her that I couldn't sit through all of the films. The sex and dialogue in the movies was robotic, without any human warmth or emotion. She thought she would be able to make it more enjoyable for me by rubbing my crotch. But when she started to unzip my pants, I knew it was time to leave."

"So, you just left her there?" Leah asked.

"She followed me out and we went to an Italian restaurant in Little Italy. She told me she thought I would enjoy the movie more if I 'wasn't just a spectator to the sex scenes.' Loretta also claimed that there was a guy at the end of our aisle 'who was doing himself,' and that was how she got the idea to unzip my pants. I told her that I was not looking around at the other members of the audience to see what they were doing."

"Did she pay for your dinner and invite you back to her place?"

"She did, but at that point, I really did not believe it would be more than some sort of sex scene she wanted to reenact from the movies. I had a feeling that if I had sex with Loretta, I was going to love myself less."

"Maybe you felt that way because you had a real lover, Debi?"

"Perhaps, but I think it was also the feeling that Loretta had no real love to give, at least to me."

"She might have done better with the guy down the aisle who had to give himself a hand job," Leah said with a laugh.

Desi pointed to the green 'Walk' sign. They crossed the street and met up with Esther, Loretta, and Siggy.

Esther then pointed to Desi. "This is our new friend, Desi, who gave us a ride from D.C."

"Your new friend is one of my old classmates at NYU," Loretta said as she stepped closer to Desi and gave him a hug. "Desi, your hair is quite a bit shorter, but you look great. What have you been up to?"

"I've been serving in the Army as a journalist and photographer."

"That seems strange. I don't think I would have imagined you in the Army."

"Well, if you think my being in the Army is strange, I guess you don't know about Professor Gurland taking a position teaching philosophy up at West Point. And I hear that he did really well on the physical training test."

"That's crazy," Loretta said as she put a hand on Desi's upper arm. "I guess you did well on the physical training test also."

"I even learned to run a mile in combat boots, and then two miles."

Siggy was having a private conversation with Leah while Loretta was seemingly interested in getting updates from Desi. While Desi was talking to Loretta, he kept an eye on Leah and Siggy. It appeared to Desi that Siggy asked Leah a question, but Leah only shrugged her shoulders in response. Siggy then walked over to Desi. "I hear you might need a place to crash tonight. You are welcome to join us. I think we'll have some extra room at my mother's apartment."

Desi just smiled and thanked him for the invitation.

When Desi, Leah, and Esther got to the apartment building where Debi lived, they were a bit taken back by the display in the window of the adult store located on the street level. There were three female mannequins in the window: one with brownish skin tone and a red, white, and blue headband around an Afro, with the inscription, 'Patriot for the Inclusion Evolution'; the second with a summer tan and a patriotic-colored headband tied around long blonde hair with the inscription 'Patriot for the Sexual Revolution'; and the third, with a pale white skin tone and a patriotic-colored headband with the inscription 'Patriot for the American Evolution' around dark black hair, mostly pulled up to the top of the head and decorated with ornate chopsticks. The mannequin in the middle had a very skimpy red, white, and blue bikini on display. The other two featured some gauze-like lingerie.

"Desi, you were right about this store having interesting windows," Leah said. "I'm thinking about getting one of those red, white, and blue headbands, but I don't know what kind of a patriot I want to be.

"I think I am ready to get my head into the 'Sexual Revolution'," Esther said as she walked into the store.

Once inside, they examined a pile of headbands. Leah looked at Desi. "Here is one for a guy in the Army - the one that says, 'Patriot of the American Revolution'," Leah said as she held a headband up and put her hands on Desi's temples. She tied it together at the back of his head. Desi went over to a mirror and looked at it before taking it off and handing it back to her.

"I had ancestors who had to leave Long Island during the occupation by the British. This seems to commercialize what they went through," Desi explained.

Leah selected a headband for herself and walked over to the mirror where Desi was standing. Leah explained her selection, "Because all my grandparents were immigrants and I consider myself a feminist, I'm going with the 'Patriot for the American Evolution'."

"I'm thinking of buying a couple of those," Desi said. "I can probably use them as gifts."

"Hey, look at that sign," Esther said. "They do custom engraving for whatever message you want on any of their headbands. I see a few customized headbands along the wall that are more than a little bit obscene. Probably not something for the front window, even on St. Marks Place," Esther said.

"It looks like there is plenty in this store that they can't put in the front window," Leah said as she picked up a large, silver, cylindrical vibrator from a shelf. "This one must be the industrial strength model."

"I didn't know there were so many you could choose from," Esther said as she walked along the display of vibrators. She picked up a book regarding the treatment of women for hysteria in 19th Century London. After a quick scan of the cover flap, Esther advised, "This is some wild stuff about doctors who seemed crazier than their female patients."

"Desi has to get some condoms for his cousin, who is going off to college and has a birthday this week," Leah said to Esther. "Enjoy that book. I'm going to help Desi pick some out for the birthday boy."

Before Leah could join Desi, a female employee of the store started assisting Desi. The lingerie-attired employee had selected several of her "favorites" before Leah stepped alongside Desi. "Like I said, these are some of my favorites, but it would probably be best to let your girlfriend make the final choices," the employee said as she took one of Desi's hands and deposited several individually wrapped prophylactics into his cupped hand.

"Is there a fitting room for him to try one or two on for me?" Leah said with a sardonic smile to Desi.

The adult store employee seemed to entertain Leah's question.

"She's just kidding," Desi said to the young female employee.

"Oh, I couldn't tell," the employee said. "We did have a couple come in here last weekend. They went into our bathroom together and hadn't paid for the condom first. But they did buy a lot of stuff before they left."

"So, I guess you had to come up with a new rule," Leah said with a laugh.

"Yeah, if you go into the bathroom together, don't make so much noise that everyone knows what you are doing," the employee said with a smile. She then went over to help Esther.

"Sounds like this can be a very exciting place for someone to work," Leah said.

"I think I'm set with these specialty condoms she picked out. I think I'm also going to grab a box of Trojans," Desi said.

Leah took a look at the specialty condoms that Desi had in his hand. "Those look interesting," she said. "I have a niece that is going off to college. Perhaps I should buy some for her."

"This might be your best opportunity," Desi said.

After paying for their items, Desi and Leah left Esther to talk to the female store employee about Esther's newly found book concerning how female sexual needs were diagnosed by male doctors in prior centuries. Desi led the way up the stairs to the entrance of Debi's apartment building. He pushed the intercom button and Debi's roommate buzzed them in.

Debi's roommate, Sarah, was surprisingly different looking from Desi's expectations from talking to her on the phone. Although she had a tiny, childlike voice, Sarah looked to be about six feet tall in bare feet. She had large, sturdy hands and wrists, and gave Desi and Leah firm handshakes, but the rest of her body seemed quite thin. Her baggy pants and cotton blouse, which clung to an almost totally flat chest, seemed to accentuate her lack of body fat.

"I'm sorry I don't have much more to tell you about Debi and Tammy flying out to Las Vegas," Sarah said. "I think something happened to their mother, but I don't know how serious it is. Debi didn't say when they would be back, but I know she was supposed to start a new job this week."

"Debi's not going to be working at the publishing company anymore?" Desi asked.

"No. There was a problem at the office because one of the authors had a drink or two at the Algonquin Hotel with Debi. The author's wife came into the office, ranting and raving about Debi meeting him there, and it seemed that the wife knew someone on the Board of Directors. She wanted Debi fired. Debi found a job at a big law firm and quit her assistant editing position at the publishing company a few days ago." Sarah saw the look of surprise on Desi's face. "Debi's going to be alright. She'll be making more money as one of the paralegals on an antitrust case than she would have made if she had gotten a promotion with the publisher."

"I guess I should get the letter from her room so you can go out and enjoy the holiday with your friends and family," Desi said.

Sarah shook her head. "My family lives in Ohio, and my only friends here are Tammy and Debi. I've done a couple of modeling assignments with Tammy, and I was working at the publishing company with Debi. You are welcome to spend the night here. Tammy told me that Debi wouldn't mind."

"It's nice that you are comfortable with the idea of me sleeping here tonight, but I might be out really late, and I don't want to disturb you later."

Leah looked at Sarah, "Can I check out Debi's room to see if there are any pictures of Tammy?"

"Sure, you can also check out my room and see my photo with Tammy," Sarah offered.

Desi and Leah went into Debi's room. Desi picked up the envelope on Debi's bed with his name on it. He put it in his back pocket. Desi pointed to a framed picture on Debi's night table. "There is Debi with Tammy sitting on the edge of their parents' pool, splashing the water with their toes."

"I guess that was at a happier time," Leah said.

"I took that photo a couple of years ago. It was a week or two after we picked out an engagement ring, and we were getting ready to go away for a long weekend together to a hotel where we registered as a married couple."

Leah nodded her head. "That explains the smile on Debi's face."

"But a week or two after that, we agreed that we weren't ready to pick up the ring. We both seemed to realize it would probably take another couple of years for us to be ready."

"Is the store still holding it for you?" Leah asked.

"I haven't really checked with them lately. I think I would get a store credit for the deposit I left if somebody else took the ring."

"I guess nobody loses that way," Leah mused.

Sarah stuck her head inside the bedroom door. "Are you ready to see my picture with Tammy?"

"Sure," Leah said, as she and Desi followed Sarah to her bedroom.

"This was taken at the Waldorf-Astoria," Sarah said as she pointed to a large, framed photograph of herself with Tammy standing in front of a six-foot tall cardboard cutout of a bottle of ginger beer. "Debi thinks this picture is very funny as Tammy has spent her whole life telling people not to call her Ginger."

"She does get very angry with anyone who assumes they can call her that," Desi confirmed.

When Desi and Leah met up with Esther outside the St. Mark's Adult Store, Esther wanted to know if Leah saw "anything of interest" in the apartment.

"There aren't any pictures of Desi, but there is a photo of Tammy and her beautiful sister that was taken by Desi. So there is an element of Desi's artistic creativity in the apartment. As an art historian, do you take that to mean something?" Leah asked Esther.

"Most definitely," Esther said. "They must have dozens, if not hundreds of pictures together. Was it on her night table next to her bed?"

"It certainly was," Leah replied.

"So, it represents a moment they had; not just with each other, but also with Desi," Esther surmised. "Anything else that was interesting?"

"I don't think Desi is willing to share with us the letter Debi left for him - on her bed!" Leah noted.

"My guess is that Desi is going to pick his own place and time to read the letter."

"I guess we won't find out anything, unless he tells us he is intending to hit the jewelry store before heading off to Japan. He's had an engagement ring on layaway," Leah recounted.

"He's got an engagement ring on a layaway plan? When did you hear about that?"

"Desi told me when we were upstairs in the apartment. But I am wondering if Emily knows about the ring that Desi put a deposit on. She might like having it if Debi's still not ready to commit."

"Emily isn't in a place where she can make any commitments either. Maybe things will be different for me in a year or so," Desi said.

"It sounds like you're not ready, and neither are your two most likely candidates." Leah said.

"I know I'm not ready for the commitment that comes with an engagement ring on someone's finger," Desi said. "Besides,

I don't have the money to pick up that ring at the store. I pretty much put myself through undergraduate school, and I am going to have to work to get through law school. Emily has a grandmother who is willing to put her through law school."

"So, you are choosing your own layaway plan that has nothing to do with that jewelry store right now?" Esther said with a laugh.

"That may not be a not very flattering way to put it, but it could be accurate," Desi conceded.

"You know that many women are looking for a guy who'll accept an accurate assessment of where they are at," Leah offered. "I know guys who get so into selling themselves that they would rather wrap themselves in circles rather than be honest. If guys would skip the BS, that would be refreshing for women who wouldn't later be disappointed."

"Let's not be too harsh on the fellas. I've met women who have told me that the most important thing in a relationship is finding a guy who isn't exaggerating and lying all the time."

"And what happened to them?"

"I found out that they were projecting their own thoughtless behavior. It's bad when, on the third date, they have to change their story about their job title and go into how they really need to borrow some money from someone to pay the rent."

"So not all the women you have gone out with are sisters of famous models or have rich grandmothers?" Leah asked.

"I've had a wide range of female friends and lovers," Desi replied. "I have plans to have dinner with a woman who plays the saxophone and flute. Her twin sister attends Juilliard."

"That sounds like Desi will go out with musicians," Esther said.

"I guess there is hope of not having to sleep alone tonight after all," Leah said with a laugh.

Back in His Old Haunts

Desi was sitting at the piano bar, drinking a beer, and reading a copy of the *Village Voice* when Penny and Nicole arrived at the restaurant inside the Fifth Avenue Hotel. They sat down on either side of him.

"So, you aren't reading the *Wall Street Journal* today?" Penny asked, putting an arm around him.

"My father has it sent to me in hopes I don't become a lifelong Democrat. The only papers I buy in New York are the *New York Times* and the *Voice*."

"McGovern won Massachusetts in '72 because people, like our family, which includes a lot of Republicans, acknowledged that Agnew and Nixon were crooks," Nicole said proudly. "Even our uncle's in-laws, who own a big garment business in New England, accepted the fact that "Tricky Dick" was a power-hungry 'co-conspirator' and voted for George."

Desi looked at Penny. "You told me about your uncle, and you made him sound like a humble history teacher. But his wife's family is very well off?"

"I don't know how the business is doing now in the recession, but a few years ago they bought a yacht. We are going to be on it to watch the fireworks. And our parents are going to be sleeping on the boat tonight and heading up to Boston on it sometime tomorrow. They are over at Nikki's apartment right now getting their luggage."

"So, we're not having dinner together?" Desi asked.

"We had a big lunch at an Italian place over on Ninth Avenue. There will be some appetizers with our drinks on the yacht. Maybe you should have a sandwich or something here at the bar, but we did some serious eating at that family style Italian restaurant," Nicole explained.

"We had to warn my parents and uncle not to take a nap in Nikki's apartment because they might end up missing the boat," Penny said.

"How about if I just finish my beer and then I'll pick up a sandwich on the way to the boat, yacht, or whatever you call it," Desi suggested.

"It's called the 'New England Pinafore'," Nicole said.

Penny put her hand on Desi's arm. "It's not the 'HMS Pinafore', but they will play some of the Gilbert and Sullivan songs when we are out there this evening."

"Well then, maybe I should have another beer before we leave this place so I will be in good voice later."

"You will have everything you need to keep your good singing voice. Drinks are free on the boat," Penny added.

"There is a great falafel place on the south side of Washington Square Park. I'll grab something there before we walk over to the 'Pinafore'," Desi said.

Penny noticed the bag on the bar in front of Desi that had the St. Marks Adult Store logo on it. "What's in the bag?" she asked.

"Oh, I forgot to tell you. I have headbands you might consider wearing today." Desi reached inside the bag and pulled out the two headbands he purchased and a bonus free headband. Penny took one of the 'Patriot for the American Evolution' headbands. Nikki grabbed the free 'Patriot of the Sexual Revolution' headband the adult store cashier put in Desi's bag.

"Are you going to wear one, Desi?" Nicole asked.

Desi unfolded the remaining 'Patriot for the American Evolution' headband and wrapped it around his head.

"Isn't that more appropriate for women and immigrants?" Nicole asked.

"Desi does have one grandparent, his father's mother, who came from Ireland as a teenager," Penny noted.

"Let's hear it for the Irish," Nicole said as she grabbed Desi's glass of Guinness and held it up towards the bartender.

"Actually, both of my grandmothers have Irish roots. One was a Roman Catholic, born in County Monaghan, and the other a Protestant, born in Massachusetts."

"Let's hear it for those born in Massachusetts," Nicole added, holding Desi's glass up again before taking a drink.

The bartender came over to them. "Are all your families from Massachusetts?" the bartender asked. "If they are, you all get a drink on me!"

"I'll take bourbon," Desi said.

"Me too," Penny said with a nod.

"And I'd like Kahlua and cream," Nicole chimed in.

The bartender looked at Nicole. "I'm only going to serve you Kahlua and cream if you can tell me about the day people in Boston celebrate as 'Evacuation Day'."

"In March of 1776, the British troops were forced to end their occupation of Boston," Nicole answered.

"Yeah, but what day in March?" the bartender pressed on.

"I think it is the same day as St. Patrick's Day, March seventeenth," Nicole answered.

"Okay, you know your stuff," the bartender conceded.

After they finished their drinks, Penny, Nicole, and Desi headed over to Washington Square Park. The park was filled with people skateboarding, dancing, singing, and simply strolling around the fountain. As they walked through the archway with the two statutes of George Washington, a disheveled man was ranting about something that Desi could not, at first, understand.

The man, through a very long scraggly beard, was chanting: "It's a motherfucker," over and over again. The more Desi looked at him, the closer the man came to them. "The government is a motherfucker," he said to Desi when he got into close range.

"It sounds like he's trying to provide us with a personal critique of our state of affairs. Not so much a persuasive argument, but an articulation of his sense of hopelessness," Desi said to Penny and Nicole. "I gave him two dollars and it seemed to brighten his day."

As they walked towards the fountain in the park there seemed to be increasing numbers of jugglers and other street entertainers. A woman stepped in front of them and handed Nicole a flyer. "I am dressed as a Quaker," she said, explaining her garb. "The Quakers were vocal abolitionists in the decades leading up to the Civil War. If every state did what New York did and phased out slavery, then perhaps there wouldn't have been a Civil War. I am commemorating July 4, 1827, when ownership of other human beings ended for New Yorkers."

"Is that true, Desi?" Nicole asked.

"Slavery was legislatively phased out in New York, starting in 1799," Desi answered. "That was long before the Emancipation Proclamation and the Thirteenth Amendment. But efforts to legislatively end slavery in other states, such as Kentucky, were not met with success."

"Somehow, I knew you would know the history," Nicole said.

"As a novelist, Harriet Beecher Stowe did what she could to give Northerners a perspective of what happens to slaves who get sold from a farm in Kentucky to work in the Deep South. Her character 'Uncle Tom' didn't want to fight, but her book, *Uncle Tom's Cabin,* may have helped spark the Civil War. Lincoln even suggested that it could have."

Penny turned to Nicole. "I am back to wondering whether Desi is a fighter or a lover."

"Maybe he loves a righteous fight," Nicole wondered out loud. "That could be good if he is going to law school."

"I have been around a few lawyers in Tennessee, and they're not all idealistic or righteous," Penny said.

Desi looked at Penny. "So, you haven't found one at your belly-dancing parties who shares your progressive spirit?"

"Well, there is a guy who, when he is alone with me, is cool, but when he's with the 'good ole boys,' he laughs at all of their jokes and becomes almost another person," Penny reported.

"Is that his fault?" Nicole asked. "You showed me his picture. He is very good-looking, and you said he is probably going to make partner in his father's firm in a couple of years. So, what's the problem?"

Penny looked at her sister. "It's a big problem for me. He has to decide who he is and stick to it."

"Nikki, I agree with your sister," Desi said. "Penny not only knows all the notes but wants to put her heart and soul into her music and her life."

Penny looked at Desi. "That is the nicest thing you ever said about me, and probably the nicest thing that anyone could say about me. I am definitely going to write to you in Japan." Penny put her arms around Desi and gave him a kiss on his lips.

"Hey, what about my heart and soul?" Nicole protested. "Desi, make sure you give me your address in Japan so I can write to you. My talented sister may find some young lawyer, or even a doctor in Nashville during the next year who doesn't hang out with red necks."

Desi and Penny ended their embrace and looked at Nikki. Desi said, "I just gave out my last two index cards with my new address, but if you have something I can write on, I'll jot it down for you."

Nikki grabbed a dry-cleaning receipt from her purse and handed it to Desi. "I don't mind being your backup plan. Most people can't tell us apart."

"I'm sure Desi could tell, even in the dark," Penny replied.

"What if we test that later tonight?" Nicole asked. "Are you game for that, Desi?"

Desi hesitated in giving any response. After a significant pause, he answered, "You both know that I have been driving most of today. I started off this morning in Washington. I took a break in Philadelphia and headed here. I might have to get to bed early."

"Don't worry, even if they take the boat around the Statue of Liberty after the fireworks, we'll probably be back at the dock before eleven," Nicole said. "My apartment is not that far away."

"Desi, you see how Nikki is less than subtle with what she expects from you when she gets you in her apartment. I think she is going to pull your headband over your eyes, spin you around, and have you decide which of us gives you one for the road."

"Maybe Desi might need or want more than 'one for the road'," Nicole suggested.

"And if your roommate gets back early from the Hamptons tonight, who knows what kind of send-off Desi will be getting," Penny said.

"We might have to carry him to his car in the morning," Nicole said with a laugh.

"I better get a couple of falafel sandwiches to keep my strength up," Desi said as he headed to the south end of Washington Square Park. "I should also stop at the parking garage and get my camera bag out of my car, so I'll be ready if we're going to be near the Goddess of Liberty. I promised Linda some Bicentennial photos."

As Desi, Penny, and Nicole crossed over Sixth Avenue at West Fourth Street, Nicole pointed to a drugstore. "I better get some motion sickness medicine before we go out on the boat," she said.

Desi waited outside the pharmacy as Nicole and Penny went in. Someone tapped him on the shoulder. It was Daisy.

"Desi, what are you doing here?" she asked. Before Desi could answer, Daisy inquired, "Is Emily with you?"

Desi shook his head. "No, Emily only made it as far as Philadelphia. She rode with me from Washington this morning but had to spend some time with her mother and grandmother."

"Yeah, she seems to have a very close family. She's very lucky."

"Sometimes, I guess," Desi replied. "Where's Roger?"

"He's over at one of the piers with my brother helping to fix some problems on a boat owned by one of my brother's lawyer friends. The guy got a good deal on a sailboat but doesn't know anything about what to do when something goes wrong. He can't get any boat mechanics on the phone today either."

"Which is all part of what we affectionately call the 'boating experience'," Desi said as he eyed the package in Daisy's arms which had the logo of a marine supply store. "Did they send you out to get repair supplies?"

"It was my suggestion, and we got there right as they were starting to close. My brother got a call on his ship to shore radio this morning from his friend and we towed him to the pier around noon. It was crazy with all of the ships in the Harbor. They have been working on his auxiliary engine for a while so my sister-in-law, Joanne and I volunteered to take a walk to the marine supply store for the things they need. Joanne just went inside the drugstore to get something for the motion sickness she has been feeling out on the boat. She hasn't told my brother that she isn't feeling well, only me."

"Sounds like she is more than just a good sport with boating."

Daisy's sister-in-law emerged from the drugstore and gave Daisy and Desi a quizzical look.

"This is Desi, one of Roger's best friends!"

"He's on the invite list, right?" Joanne asked.

Desi looked at Daisy. "The invite list?"

Daisy shifted the package in her arms so she could hold up her left hand. A diamond ring brightly shining in the summer evening sun served as her response.

"Wow," was all Desi could muster as racked his brain as to whether Roger, in any of their telephone conversations, had given him any hint of his intentions.

"Roger got my brother's blessing yesterday and he proposed to me last night. I haven't had a chance to let Emily know."

"I'm sure she will be very happy for you two. I know I am."

"The wedding is going to be the day after Derby Day next year. Make plans to be in Louisville that weekend. The reception is going to be at my Aunt Arbie's home. She's been the only one I've had a chance to tell. I think it's great that she wants the reception to be at her place. I don't think we are inviting many people anyway so that will be fine. It's going to be a traditional small Kentucky wedding, not like those events you guys have in New York."

"I haven't been to many weddings. I guess you guys are the first of my friends to be comfortable doing something really traditional. I take it that the ceremony will be in a church?"

Daisy nodded her head.

"Does Desi know the story about how your Aunt Arbie got engaged as her fiancé was heading off to World War II?"

Daisy nodded her head again."Do you think there is a chance you and Emily will both be at our wedding?"

"I can't speak for her but I did ask her to write to me in Japan. If we regularly write to one another, I'm sure that is something we will be writing about."

"I hope you will try to be there. I realize that it might involve flying from the other side of the world to join us. I think Roger is planning to ask you to be his best man." Daisy paused, "Maybe I shouldn't have mentioned that. Guess I am just getting too excited about things."

Joanne put her arm around Daisy. "It's good that you're excited." She then turned to Desi. "I've heard a little bit about you Desi. Daisy and Roger both say that you helped bring them together. You should be there, whether you are still an eligible bachelor or engaged yourself by then."

"I don't know what role I had in their meeting and getting to know one another. But I have felt since Derby Day that Daisy and Roger are people who deserve to be happy as they aren't selfish. They regularly look for things to do for other people. I am very glad they found each other."

Daisy, still with her marine supply store bag tucked into her right arm, put her hand with the engagement ring on Desi's right shoulder and brought her left hand down his arm to the hand that held the Adult Store bag. Desi noticed her gaze at what he was holding.

"I just got a few things for my cousin. He's going off to college in a few weeks."

"Guess he will be prepared for an onslaught of female friends. But I'm not sure that freshman guys need that much preparation," Daisy mused.

"Do you want to walk over to the piers with us and see Roger?" Joannne asked. "You can also meet my husband. I think you guys have some things in common," she added.

"I'm waiting for a couple of friends who are inside, also buying something to head off seasickness. We are going over to the piers after I get my camera bag out of my car. The garage is a ways down the street. Maybe we will see you later."

"Alright, enjoy your boys night out. Guess we ought to be heading back," Daisy said.

Daisy and Joanne started walking west towards the piers. Daisy was about half a block away when she turned and was in the process of blowing Desi a kiss when Penny and Nicole exited the drugstore and huddled with Desi.

"Did that woman up the street just blow you a kiss?" Penny asked.

"Maybe. Guess she is in a very good mood today."

"Why do you think that?"

"It's sort of a long story, but she is wearing a new engagement ring."

Nicole looked down the street. Daisy had already turned and was again walking away. "Desi must have very good eyesight."

"He does," Penny said with a sigh. "Especially when it comes to spotting attractive women."

Around eight o'clock, Desi, Penny, and Nicole arrived at the boarding ramp for the 'New England Pinafore'. They could tell from the pitch of the voices on board that the 'happy hour' was well underway.

Penny and Nicole gave their Uncle Pete and Aunt Nicole hugs and kisses as they came aboard. They introduced Desi, who shook hands with each of them. Uncle Pete, who seemed as if he had already been drinking for a couple of hours, wrapped an arm around Desi and asked him, "Desi, I still can't tell them apart. How do you know who your date is this evening?"

Aunt Nicole slapped her husband on the back of his head.

"He's here with both of us tonight," Nicole announced. "Desi's already told us that the woman who writes the most to him while he is in Japan for the next year will be the one he takes out on his family's boat on Labor Day 1977."

"Is your family out here in their boat tonight?" Uncle Pete asked.

"No, I think they spent most of the weekend out at Block Island and are probably now at the marina in Greenport. They planned to watch the fireworks out there."

"We've spent some time around Eastern Long Island on the 'Pinafore'," Aunt Nicole said. "But we hear that the fireworks show here in New York Harbor is going to be the best."

"Well, I think that Desi is already planning his cruise with me next Labor Day with some extraordinary fireworks," Penny said.

"You have always told me that you don't like the smell of fireworks," Nicole protested.

"That was before I joined the Army," Penny said. "Now I understand that the smell is an important part of the aesthetics of the Fourth of July. America the Beautiful would not be what it is today without the smell of gunpowder."

"Here, here," Uncle Pete said as he raised his highball glass. "We are very proud to have a niece in uniform, protecting our Country. A country our Irish ancestors have fought for since the Revolutionary War. And I understand that Desi had a relative or two who were early Patriots."

"Should we put on our headbands?" Nicole asked.

"Why not," Penny said as she put on hers.

"I'll put on my tanker's beret from Fort Knox," Desi said as he unzipped his camera bag and pulled out his black beret.

Nicole put on her 'Patriot of the Sexual Revolution' headband.

"I don't think my brother-in-law is going to appreciate one of his daughters wearing that headband," Aunt Nicole said.

Penny looked at Desi. "Give her your headband."

Desi reached back into his camera bag and pulled out the 'Patriot for the American Evolution' headband.

Nicole switched headbands just as her parents were coming up from the lower deck.

Penny and Nicole hugged and kissed their parents. Desi shook hands with their father and gave their mother a brief hug. "Desi, I heard that you were in Washington this morning. Who was the Grand Marshal of the parade there? Was it Vice President Nelson Rockefeller or was it Johnny Cash?" Penny's mother asked.

"I didn't stick around for the parade, but my understanding is that Johnny Cash was the Grand Marshal, and the Vice President and Mrs. Rockefeller were going to walk alongside him."

"Good for Johnny Cash!" Penny's mother said.

Aunt Nicole rang a bell and announced, "I have to ask you all to give your attention to the captain for a couple of moments before we leave the dock."

The captain, who wore a formal jacket with gold braid, took center stage. "We are going out tonight with half of the regular crew. Our Chief Steward has given passes to all of the kitchen crew and a couple of the deck hands. They will rejoin us in Boston in a couple of days. We are going to need a couple of you men to help with the lines. The First Mate will give you instructions."

Aunt Nicole again rang the bell after the captain stepped back. "We have, in the past, teased the Chief Steward about being the only Englishman aboard. But today, he confided in me that he recently became a citizen of the United States. So, obviously, we can no longer sing to him as if he were still an Englishman. But I think we can sing the same melody and just modify the words. He'll be coming up from the galley with some appetizers from a local caterer in a few minutes," Aunt Nicole said as she handed glasses of rum punch to Desi, Penny, and Nicole. She filled Uncle Pete's glass from a pitcher.

Within two minutes, the Chief Steward came up the stairs with a large platter of appetizers and was greeted by a chorus of "For He Was an Englishman."

His only response was, "Perhaps, on a day like today, Gilbert and Sullivan would not be the only ones enjoying the ironic twist."

The appetizers were devoured within a few minutes.

Aunt Nicole looked at her watch and rang the bell once again. "It looks like it is time to cast off and head out towards Lady Liberty."

Desi put down his drink and handed his camera bag to Penny. "Guess it is time for me to be a deckhand."

"But later you should be able to get a good photo of the Goddess of New York Harbor holding her torch at night." Penny said as she put her right arm up as if imitating the famous Statue. "What do the French call the torch?" Penny asked.

"The Torch of Enlightenment," Desi said before giving her a quick kiss on her lips and heading off to the forward deck.

ABOUT THE AUTHOR

Bill was born in Port Jefferson, New York, in 1952 and grew up in Smithtown, NY, where he was actively involved in student government starting in seventh grade. Interested in politics, he seized an opportunity to speak to Robert F. Kennedy in 1964 at a campaign stop in Smithtown.

In 1970, Bill received a Congressional Recommendation to attend the United States Merchant Marine Academy at Kings Point. He was sent out to sea in 1971, sailing to various ports in the Far East, including Yokohama, Kobe, Inchon, Pusan, and Hong Kong. Although he found his months at sea exciting, Bill resigned to pursue another academic path. He received a Bachelor of Arts degree from New York University in 1974, where he majored in journalism and minored in philosophy. Bill went on to graduate from St. John's University School of Law in 1982.

From 1975 to 1978, Bill was an active duty member of the United States Army and served as a reporter and photojournalist. At Fort Knox, Kentucky, he was part of a post newspaper staff that won the Thomas Jefferson Award from the Department of Defense. At Camp Zama, Bill was awarded an Army Commendation Medal for his reporting on the activities of members of the United States Army Communications Command - Japan.

After his service in the Army and graduation from law school, he was employed for several years by CBS in Manhattan as a litigator and broadcast counsel. During his career, Bill was appointed to several governmental positions on Long Island and was twice elected to the Suffolk County Legislature.

Bill and Laura, his wife of forty-two years, have lived in Queens County, Manhattan, and Long Island. They have a daughter and son, as well as three grandsons.

Where to Next?

Whether you have your own memories of the Bicentennial or not, I hope you enjoyed the ride with Desi. In my upcoming book, Desi will be in Japan. I encourage you to visit my website and subscribe to the newsletter to receive information about launch dates, book signing events, and more.

Bill@*BicentennialTrifecta*

Made in United States
North Haven, CT
30 January 2022